The
FALLEN

ERIC VAN
LUSTBADER

HEAD
of ZEUS

First published in the UK by Head of Zeus in 2017
This paperback edition published by Head of Zeus in 2017

9 7 5 3 1 2 4 6 8

A catalogue record for this book is available
from the British Library

ISBN (PB): 9781784973070
ISBN (E): 9781784973049

Typeset by Adrian McLaughlin

Printed and bound in Great Britain by
CPI Group (UK) Ltd, Croydon CRO 4YY

Head of Zeus Ltd
First Floor East
5–8 Hardwick Street
London ECIR 4RG

WWW.HEADOFZEUS.COM

For Victoria,
with a full heart,
as always

THE HISTORY
BEHIND THE FICTION

The Franciscan Observatines, here known as the Gnostic Observatines, are recorded in history, as are the Knights of Saint John of Jerusalem, who inspired the story's Knights of Saint Clement of the Holy Land. In those early days, the pope was the most powerful monarch in Europe. Like all monarchs, he was obliged to maintain his power in the face of rivals and enemies. Thus were the Knights formed, as a form of papal army, who fought in the pope's name both at home and in the Levant.

From as far back as the early 1300s, there was a deep division within the Franciscans regarding the strict vow of poverty demanded by Saint Francis upon the founding of the Order in the beginning of the thirteenth century. The Observatines believed in it; the Conventuals did not. The dispute came to a head in 1322 when Pope John XXII sided with the Conventuals and their allies, the more established Dominican Order.

The papal bull *Cum inter nonmullos,* which stated, among other things, that the rule of poverty was "erroneous and heretical," was likely a subterfuge. It seems far more plausible that the pope wanted to stamp out a faction of the Franciscans bent on roaming the world, spreading their gospel and, in the process, their power and influence, rather than staying put intra muros, within the walls of their monasteries, as the Conventuals were bound to do.

However, the papal bull was hardly the end of the Observatines. Quite the opposite, in fact. In the latter part of the fifteenth century and the first two decades of the sixteenth century, a good number of Observatines who had accepted the pope's ruling were settled in the Middle East, especially the area in and around Trebizond and Istanbul, serving as emissaries of Christ, proselytizers of Catholicism. It is here that I have imagined my Gnostic Observatines discovering many of their secrets, including the Quintessence, which is recorded in history as the so-called fifth element, sought after by every alchemist on earth, but perhaps created by the cadre of alchemists employed by King Solomon.

Gnosticism is, in and of itself, anathema to the Vatican and its staunchly traditionalist orders. Its name derives from the Greek word for knowledge. Gnostics, to put it simply, believe that the physical world is corrupt, evil, and that the true path to salvation lies in adhering to spiritual truth and goodness. Some Gnostics pursue study in the so-called esoteric mysteries, which lie beyond normal human comprehension. The Church, in its infinite wisdom, has, sight unseen, always judged these mysteries to be magic and, so, heretical.

The Knights, champions of both Christ and the pope, would naturally be predisposed to despise and fear the Order as much as the Holy See. It's entirely logical that the Knights would be only too happy to do the pope's bidding in dismantling the Order's power.

The
FALLEN

PROLOGUE

BAATARA GORGE WATERFALL, TANNOURINE, LEBANON

"Is it time yet?"

The shadows surrounding the four men were angular, formal, and, therefore, mysterious, beyond Val's ken. They contained the muscular quality of the stone itself, ancient and inscrutable.

Michel shook his head, his thick lips pouty. "Val, you listening to me?"

They were the exact opposite of the shadows found in twilit cities, which were constantly in motion like fish around a sunken ship. These shadows were unmoving, impenetrable, and hid the cleft in the mountainside from which, at their backs, the Baatara cataract shot like ten-thousand cannons. The roar was visceral, the air shivering and shuddering from the spill's kinetic energy. On either side, beyond veils of spray, stone blocks, square and rectangular, rose up at the vertical, as if stacked by some child-giant.

Michel's Charles de Gaulle nose lifted in the air like that of a hound scenting prey. "Do you smell that?"

Michel's two men were clad in military camo fatigues and blouses, and high hiking boots with thick rubber soles. They had been smoking incessantly since they made the last leg of their climb up onto this lip of rock hidden behind the waterfall. Now they paused in their puffing and joke telling, sniffing the heavy air themselves. Finding nothing, they returned to the butts of their cigarettes and their obscene jokes. They needed to get as much nicotine into their systems as they could now. Val had given strict orders that there would be no smoking once they entered the cave, which opened before them like the immense jaws of a prehistoric creature.

Val, his back to the cataract, made no reply. He was sitting so far back on the stone lip his clothes were soaked through and clung to the sunburned skin of his neck and arms like a second skin. He liked the feeling of being submerged and yet not, as if he were occupying two realities at once, the one overlapping the other.

He stared intently at the blackness that filled the cave mouth. Except for the area just inside the lip, the blackness was utterly impenetrable, like a night without either moon or stars, a night close with a lowering cloud ceiling so thick it appeared solid as stone.

Michel opened his mouth, closed it again out of deference to his client, the man paying him and his men a small fortune to make this trek, which, so far as Michel could tell, was a wild-goose chase. Apart from the scat and, occasionally, the bones of small mammals, they had found no artifacts in any of the caves they had been exploring for the past eight days. Used to the action of regional and sectarian wars, his men were restless. He could sense their discontent. They wanted something to shoot dead, or, failing that, a target to shoot at. They wanted to smell blood. That's what mercenaries were all about. Michel was a bit different; moving up the food chain into management would do that to you, he supposed. He had learned the value of patience. Still, he glanced back at Val and wondered when he would give the signal, when they would enter the cave that had never been mapped, the very presence of which had surprised even Michel, who knew this part of Lebanon like the spread thighs of Chloe, his current girl of choice. Val was smart as well as clever—so smart he had hired Michel and his cadre for a spelunking mission because in this day and age, with Lebanon a hotbed of religious intolerance and murderous violence, heavily armed mercs were far more valuable than a handful of professors and archeologists or whomever his client normally hung out with.

For Val, the incessant roar of the cataract was acting on him like a temporal trampoline, flinging him backward and forward in time. First, he was a child, entering the cave he had been literally dreaming of since he was a boy of five. So young, he hadn't understood its significance, nor had he when he reached his adolescence. And yet the dream had continued to stalk his sleep, the precise configuration of the cave mouth becoming as familiar to him as the rhythm of his own breath just before he fell asleep.

Now the trampoline returned him to last night and his over-heated hotel room with its wartime blackout curtains drawn securely across the smoke- and ash-streaked windows, as he talked to Maura on the cusp of his thirtieth birthday, telling her that this was it, that tomorrow he would summit the area of the cave, explore it, and at last find King Solomon's mine.

"And all because of your dream?" Maura knew enough not to laugh. She never laughed at his bouts of near clairvoyance; why should she? They all became realities, from her car being stolen to the offer of a plum job as an animator that she never saw coming, being certain she had not survived the interview. At the callback she became a believer in Val's gift.

"Yes," Val breathed into the phone in the shallows of last night. "That cave has been calling to me ever since I was a child."

"What do you think it wants with you?" Maura's voice was soft, blurry, sensual. They had just finished making love over the intercontinental connection.

An insane question only Maura would ask. "It wants me to find the true secret of King Solomon. You know that's why I took this assignment in the first place. The Knights of Saint Clement want the king's hoard of gold. But I'm convinced Solomon had a secret more vital, more valuable, than mere gold."

"You're talking about the shadow figure you saw in your room when you were five."

"It told me it was my fate to find the Testament of Lucifer."

"The Book of Deathly Things."

"Yes. The first of the Unholy Trinity. I was meant to bring the Testament of Lucifer back from the darkness into which it had been cast so long ago."

Maura had shivered. "But really, Val, Lucifer? Even if it were real—"

"It is real!"

"Even more reason not to go into this cave. I mean, what if you do find the book? It's the Devil's property. We're Catholic. We believe in the Resurrection and the Light. This is a darkness you shouldn't touch."

"What would you have me do if I find it?"

"Destroy it. Val, please. You must, at all costs. If it really is the Testament of Lucifer it's a dreadful thing. It mustn't be brought into the light."

The cataract's trampoline launched him forward to the present. He glanced at his chronometer: almost time. He needed to clear his mind of his hotel room, of the long-range sex he'd experienced with Maura, of Maura herself—the scent of her, a mix of lime, hibiscus, and plumeria so powerful he was once again engulfed by it.

His nostrils flared in order to rid himself of her, and he smelled it—whatever scent Michel's truffle-hunting nose had picked up. Without rising, Val frog-hopped a pace closer to the cave mouth. His sopping clothes now felt cold and clammy. He sniffed again, inhaling more of the humid atmosphere this time. There was no doubt about it. No doubt. The odor was emanating from the cave.

"There's definitely someone in there," Michel whispered as he hunkered down next to Val.

"Or some*thing*," Val said, eyes not moving from the cave mouth. "Recent reports have put a leopard in the vicinity."

"Worse for us, it could be a wild boar," Michel said. "I myself have seen three in this region over the years."

Without turning, Michel gave a hand signal, and his two mercs brought their AK-47s into the fire-ready position. One of them licked his lips. There were no more jokes or smokes, no talk at all. These men were hardened professionals. Whoever was in there wasn't going to get the best of them. They'd be bullet-flayed to kingdom come. The men were looking forward to beginning what to them had become an assault. Action, at last!

The light was failing, burnished gold into inky indigo, as if the sky itself were falling. For Val, who had dreamed of this moment virtually all of his life, there was no need to check his chronometer again. His inner clock, by which he had set sail into the sometimes frightening and not altogether wholesome world of adults, told him it was time to move. He rose off his haunches, having seen this moment play out in his dreams since time immemorial, at least as he sensed it. Before the age of five he had no memories at all. Every once in a while he harbored the absurd notion that he had been born that age.

Michel followed him. His two men, with no palpable signal from their leader, flanked out on either side. At the edge of the darkness, they turned on their headlamps, adjusting the beams. Michel did the same, but Val, rejecting the technology, fired up the first of a half-dozen phosphorus torches he had brought and was carrying in a rubber gasket-sealed quiver at his left hip.

Together, the four men were swallowed by the cave mouth.

The blackness outside the narrow beams of light and the phosphorus glow closed around them so heavily it was as if they had immediately sunk to the bottom of the sea. A dozen paces in, Val realized that the air was different. The cataract's humidity had died away behind them, supplanted by a desert-like aridity. The soft tissues lining their nostrils were sucked dry so quickly and completely the men were instantly assaulted by sinus headaches.

The torch illuminated the cave walls, the limestone more or less identical to that of the caves they had explored previously. The ceiling here was not nearly as low, however, and the men were able to walk upright, rather than crouched over, "like beetles," as one of the men had said with an unmistakable quaver.

"The smell," Michel said in Val's ear, and Val nodded, the odor unmistakable now, stronger. An element within it tickled a vague memory as it worked its way from Val's nose into his brain. Something familiar. Had he been somewhere he had smelled it before? It seemed that way to him, the notion more firmly embedding itself in his consciousness the deeper they penetrated into the cave.

There was no animal scat here, no piles of tiny bones, white as the face of the moon. Only darkness, desolation, and an unspeakable loneliness. The way now slanted down, and with their descent came a stirring in the air that brought the odor to them at what surely must have been full strength.

"Animal, vegetable, or mineral?" Michel whispered beside him, nearly choking on his words. "What the hell is it?"

Again Val shook his head. He gave no answer to Michel, just as he had provided no answer when, on the third day, after visiting eight caves, Michel had said to him, *What are you looking for?*

The Testament of Lucifer. Those were the words that had formed in Val's mind, but he didn't voice it. Why would he? It would only confuse Michel, and the last thing Val wanted was for Michel to lose confidence in him, for Michel to think his mission was one driven by idiocy or vanity. Val, an excellent judge of character from the time he had been a child, knew that Michel wouldn't tolerate either, and who could blame him? Not Val. He wouldn't have tolerated them, either.

Once again he was hurtled back in time, to the day before he left for Lebanon.

"You can't go," Maura was saying, gesturing to a suitcase on the bed in their Paris flat in the Marais. "What you're looking for—"

Val, smiling and shaking his head simultaneously, said, "I have to go, Maura. I have to find it. Don't you see? It's my life's purpose."

He could feel the edge of her anger protruding from her like a blade and behind it, propelling it, her anxiety for him. So he took her in his arms, kissed her tenderly, as he would a child awakened by a nightmare, which was a mistake; Maura hated being treated like a child.

She pulled away from him, and he said, "No. Not like this. We can't part on a sour note."

She tossed her head, impatient, angrier than ever. "You say that it was promised to you, Val, but the Devil's promise . . . do you know how insane that sounds?"

"Have my visions ever been wrong?"

"And that's what terrifies me the most: that it's all true, that Lucifer somehow chose you, whispered in your ear." She shuddered.

"The Testament of Lucifer does exist: I was never more sure of anything in my life." But now he experienced a sudden stab, not of doubt about his mission, but of the nature of its purpose. For a moment he was surrounded by a bubble of clarity. Maura was smart—more, she was far shrewder than he was. Could she be right about this? Was he really in danger, or would the shadow figure protect him from all harm, as it had promised?

"Val," Maura said, her arms around him. "Think for a moment. What is the Devil's promise worth? The Church teaches us that Lucifer is a seducer and a liar. Nothing he says can be trusted."

And just like that, the bubble of clarity burst, and once again Val's mission was all. "The promise of power beyond mortal ken," he whispered into her ear, in the honeyed tones of Lucifer himself.

"'Beyond mortal ken,'" she repeated. "You see? This promise you say . . . it's not . . . it's false, Val. It has to be. This Book is not for mortal eyes, yours or anyone else's." Her gaze had locked with his. "I'm begging you not to go. I'm so afraid it won't end well." A silence as profound as that he had experienced in his childhood room closed its fist around them.

There was silence now, as he was hurled back into the present, but it was of an altogether different kind. It was the silence of something alien, unknowable, holding its breath.

The Book of Deathly Things, purportedly conjured for King Solomon, through the arcane work of his cabal of alchemists.

Michel looked around, the beam of his light swinging from left to right. "Val, now you must tell me why we really have come here. It has to do with King Solomon, yes?"

"I'm looking for signs that these caves were inhabited by a sect of Canaanites," which was a truth his guide could accept.

Michel pursed his lips. The tip of his nose was almost touching the limestone wall, as if he felt it was the source of the strange odor. "Wasn't it the Phoenicians?"

"*Phoinikies* is Greek for purple." Val stood farther back, the better to gain perspective. "The Greeks, who were everywhere three thousand years ago, called the Canaanites Phoenicians because of the purple dye they manufactured from murex sea-shells." Michel's men remained at the center of the cave floor, peering into the emptiness beyond the light of their headlamps. "It was the Phoenicians who gave the Greeks twenty-two magic signs called the alphabet that the Greeks codified into a written language. Eventually, it became the Latinized alphabet."

Did the Canaanites know of the Book of Deathly Things? Was it three thousand years old, like the twenty-two magic symbols that formed the alphabet? Where had those symbols come from? Were they part of the Testament of Lucifer, the language it was written in in fiery cuneiform? Val stirred, as if these thoughts caused a restlessness, driven by a sense of his long journey's end at last close at hand. Was it Lucifer he had heard when he was five? Was it Lucifer he had smelled? Was *this* the same smell? How could it be? Val asked himself as he led the way down, ever down, the floor of the cave steepening. At the same time, the ceiling rose so high that finally it was beyond the reach of even the torch's blue-white fluorescence.

After a few moments, he paused, sensing some unfathomable

change in the deeply shadowed surroundings. He shone the torchlight on the left-hand wall and something like a galvanic shock passed through him. He moved the torch nearer so that he could better distinguish the images painted on the limestone: armed horsemen, warriors in chariots of gold, a procession leading to a seated dark-bearded personage of obvious great rank, a circlet of gold around his head. Behind him rose a shadow, taller, thinner, but somehow more majestic, even, than the king.

Knowledge, long buried in his psyche, burst forth, staggering Val. *The Book of Deathly Things.*

"How old d'you think these are?" Michel said. "And who the hell are they kowtowing to?"

"Impossible to say for certain," Val said as he played the torchlight over the paintings. "The pigments are rich; it's as if they were painted yesterday."

"But they weren't?" Michel was asking a question.

"No." Val peered more closely. "No sunlight to fade the pigments, and the style is unquestionably Phoenician." The phosphorescence flickered, and he pulled a second torch from his quiver, lit it as the first guttered out. He squinted. "The king could be David or Solomon. The Phoenicians built temples out of their fragrant cedar for both of them." He leaned closer. "But see here, this seal. Solomon's seal."

Michel's eyes opened wide. "King Solomon's mine. Rivers of gold! So that's what you're after!"

"Don't be foolish. King Solomon's mine is a thing of fiction."

Nevertheless, Michel's two mercs abandoned their posts, moving nearer, lest they be left out of the action. Their faces projected their greed as if it were a moving image thrown on to a theater screen.

Val snorted. "Solomon's rivers of gold occupy the same fantasy space as El Dorado." But now he knew that to be a lie, for he suspected that here lay the portal to Solomon's mine. The wall painting was far more fascinating and frightening than he let on, for the thin, shadowy figure behind the king was holding out an object. Apart from its seeming to be round, Val could not make out what the object might be: a ceremonial platter, a royal disc, something other? On it was incised a golden square. Within the square was a white-and-black triangle with bloodred trim. The oddest feature was that this sigil appeared to be depicted three-dimensionally, like an M. C. Escher drawing: a single uninterrupted surface over all three dimensions. Val squinted, his nose only millimeters from the painting. It seemed impossible; he had never encountered any Phoenician paintings—or from any ancient civilization, for that matter—that depicted three dimensions, let alone in this meta-geometrical fashion. Something primitive deep in his lower belly contracted, and the odor from his childhood bedroom came to him again more assertively. This so exhilarated him that he could scarcely draw a breath.

"Look at this, Michel. Have you ever seen an object like this?"

His guide frowned. "I couldn't say."

"The one the shadow figure behind the king's chair is handing to King Solomon."

Michel turned from the painting to stare at Val. "What shadow? There's nothing behind the king, except this weird circular writing that looks like a combination of Greek, sort of, and mathematical symbols." He peered a bit closer. "It looks like a language older than the human race."

Val and Michel kept descending, the way steepening even more. The mercs followed, somewhat reluctantly, throwing covetous glances over their shoulders, as if they thought Solomon's gold lay behind his image.

For his part, Val was deeply disturbed. It seemed impossible that Michel hadn't seen the shadow standing behind King Solomon on the wall painting. Had Val imagined it? Was it just a smudge or the shadow of one of the mercs behind them that had been there for a moment, then, as the merc moved, was gone? Both of these explanations were, of course, possible, but deep in Val's gut he knew the truth. The shadow was there; it had been handing King Solomon a disc or a sphere covered with writing so bizarre that—Michel was right—it looked older than the human race. That shadow threw Val back in time to his childhood bedroom. He shivered, both in fear and in anticipation.

A thousand yards farther the ground abruptly leveled out.

"What the hell is going on?" A degree of awe had entered Michel's voice, turning it wavering, fluty, as if he were speaking underwater. "This isn't like any cave I've ever been in."

"No," Val said. "This part is man-made." *Three thousand years ago,* something buried deep in his mind told him, but, again, he did not give voice to the thought.

Michel squatted down, his hand running across the limestone surface. "It's smooth," he said, almost overcome. "Like the floor of a room."

And instantly Val was hurtled back to his childhood bedroom. It was the night of his fifth birthday. He had gotten a tricycle, a plush Babar, a huge LEGO set, from which he'd already constructed alien spaceships more than once, having destroyed them with LEGO star fighters.

Apart from the dim multi-colored glow of Val's slowly revolving flying-saucer night-light, all was dark as he lay in his bed, far too excited to sleep. He cradled Babar, whispering to the elephant-king, whose storybooks his father read to him nightly in their original French.

A breeze crossed his face, like a distant challenge. He turned his head, saw a stirring of the Star Wars curtains, heard the chirruping song of the cicadas through the now open window. He had seen his mom close it just before turning off the light, under the mistaken notion he might catch a cold, as if the night wind, mild as it was in April, in some way had sinister designs on him. Outside, a pockmarked full moon rode on a sea of clouds like a ship, an unearthly transport, spilling its light across his bedroom floor. And then the odor came to him—animal, vegetable, mineral? None of those. Something other, and he looked to the moon, the unearthly transport, and wondered what it had brought him.

That odor. Forward again, slingshot through time, into the present, standing on the verge of the cavern's vault, at the sill of his childhood bedroom, the two overlapping until they became one and the same.

"What are you doing?" Michel tried to grasp Val's arm, to pull him back, but Val shook him off, ran toward the heart of the cavern.

Michel was stymied. He was alarmed by Val's action, yet reluctant to physically restrain his client. He turned to his mercs. "How big is this thing?"

"Fucking huge," one said.

"Impossible to see the far end of it," the second one said.

"Christ." Michel ran a hand through his hair, was appalled to find it wet with sweat. "Go after him," he ordered. "Keep the fucker from harming himself."

He drew his 9mm Glock, placed his forefinger alongside the trigger guard, followed in his men's wake. His nose twitched, and he began to feel an itching in his brain from the odor, which was now so strong it overpowered even the extreme dryness of the cavern that had produced the headache that was making his vision pulse and his inhalations painful.

Before he had gone a half-dozen paces, he saw the violent bursts from an AK-47, heard the deafening thunder-like detonations, echoed over and over again. He sprinted forward, calling to his men, then shouting Val's name.

Another burst of fire, this time so close it nearly blinded him. He almost stumbled over one of his men who lay twisted and motionless. Michel knelt down, reached out, and almost immediately flinched away. It seemed to him as if every bone in the man's body had been broken.

Michel quickly made a visual survey of the immediate area but saw no one, nothing moving. Everything still as death. He gingerly reached for the corpse with his free hand and turned the body so the head was facing him. He sprang to his feet, cursing and starting to cry all at once. The man's face was gone, as if eaten away by acid. But there was no acid on earth that could eat through skin, viscera, muscle, and cartilage so quickly, leaving just the bare skull. Had his face been ripped off? But there was no blood, no ribbons of skin and muscle at the edges. It was as if the face had just melted away.

Michel stood and backed away, pressed his throbbing temples with fingers and thumb. He wiped his eyes on his sleeve, hoping what he had seen was a hallucination, possibly brought on by inhaling that terrible odor. But even as he turned back, he felt his gorge rise at the sight of the impossible carnage.

Whirling, he pressed deeper into the cavern, his Glock pointed ahead of him, his forefinger itching to pull the trigger the moment he came upon whatever it was that had massacred his man in such a way.

Val turned his head toward the shadow, or what he thought was a shadow but might only have been movement within shadows—a deeper black in the darkness beyond the aurora of his torch.

And again he was swept back in time to his childhood bedroom on the night of his fifth birthday, the cicadas' tuneless song, the full moon, and the shadow within the shadows of his room. The curtains flickering and twisting. The floor from window to bed barred with shadow and moonlight turning the bedroom into a kind of cell from which there was no escape.

In his bedroom the shadow within the shadows moved; in the cavern the shadow within the shadows moved, their movements seemingly synchronized, overlapping, becoming one, annihilating time and space. At once, Val felt immensely heavy, as if gravity, having been summoned, was streaming into the cavern, pooling at his feet, immobilizing them. He tried to move but could not.

As if intuiting his distress, one of Michel's mercs appeared at his side.

"Do you see it?" Val whispered. "There, in the shadows, moving from right to left."

The merc squeezed the trigger on his AK-47, sending a spray of bullets in the direction of the movement. At almost the same instant Val yelled, "No! Don't shoot!" but his voice was drowned out by the rapid gunfire.

"Stay here," the merc growled, and sprinted toward the shadow.

Michel advanced into the cavern and came up beside Val. He seemed oddly out of breath, as if he had run up the mountain path they had taken to get to the cave. When Val shone the phosphorus torchlight on him, he saw that Michel was sweating profusely.

"What's going on?" Val said. "What's happened?"

At that moment, they both started as the merc a dozen paces ahead of them burst into flame. It wasn't that he was on fire so much as that he had, in the space of a heartbeat, turned into a pillar of flame, the heat so intense his body's galvanic system had been short-circuited. The merc didn't writhe, didn't so much as flinch, but stood straight as a sentinel while the flames consumed him utterly, and his charred bones collapsed in a heap.

"Jesus God! Whatever's in here, you want no part of it!" Michel cried, but when he grabbed Val's arm to pull him into a retreat back up to the cave mouth, which seemed as far away as Beirut, Val shook him off.

"Go if you want to," he said in a steely voice, "but I'm staying."

"How can you . . . ?" Michel was fairly goggle-eyed. "Pym was killed, too. You'll end up like both my men."

Val shook his head, his gaze never leaving the patch of blackness where the shadow now existed, for the moment unmoving.

He was close to the Testament. This was the childhood promise fulfilled. "Whatever is here, whatever this is, won't harm me."

"How can you say that?" It was clear Michel was losing his composure. The two deaths—the *manner* of those deaths—had come close to unhinging him. He was a professional soldier of fortune, and it was true that he had seen many deaths, as well as caused more than a few. But this—this was something completely beyond his experience. His brain worked on pure rationalism. He didn't believe in ESP or telekinesis, UFOs or aliens, past lives, reincarnation, or power spots. What, then, was he to make of the manner of his men's deaths deep inside this godforsaken cave? He didn't know. He had no answer, but fear and greed were at war inside himself, and it was suddenly clear to him that greed was winning.

"Fair warning." He licked his lips, which were as dry as the Gobi. "We're on the edge of King Solomon's mine. I don't know how much gold is in the cavern beyond our sight, but I'm not leaving without my share."

He started forward, and Val called out to him to stop, to stay where he was. But Michel had caught the fever; greed suffused him; he was deaf and blind to anything else. *You are meant to be here,* Val heard inside his head, *but he isn't.*

Val made a lunge for Michel, one last attempt to forestall him, but the guide shook him roughly off, kept going deeper and deeper into the blackness, his Glock trained at something in the shadows beyond his own dazzling beam and the sputtering torchlight.

Val opened his mouth to make one last attempt to save Michel. But then the shadow within the shadows stirred and it was as if it spoke to him, and he was struck dumb.

The shadow within the shadows barely moved, but the air around Michel seemed to rip apart, as if shredded by the hand of God. And as if Michel had ventured too close to the Burning Bush he too burst into flame, an incandescent candle flaring in the cavern. And by that flare, for just the flicker of an eye, the shadow within the shadows revealed its shape, just as it had so many years ago in Val's bedroom in the fifth year of his existence.

Val, heart beating like a trip-hammer, stood his ground. He knew as sure as he knew humans inhaled oxygen that he would not be harmed. Abruptly freed from the lock of gravity, he advanced into the darkness. He was taking the small detour around Michel's remains, a pile of charred bones still smoking like the dregs of a pyre, when his torch guttered and extinguished.

Dropping it, he reached in the darkness for his quiver, fumbled out another torch. He was about to ignite it when the cavern suddenly blazed with light. It wasn't like any light he had seen before—and yet he had. Once.

In his childhood bedroom the window was wide open; his bedroom was filled with the cicadas' shrill song and the moonlight, striped by the moving curtains caught by a strange wind. Then his revolving night-light winked out, so that only the moonlight illuminated his room. And then, a breath or two later, the blaze of light . . .

Just the same as this light now that filled the cavern and chased skittering shadows across the floor, along the curved walls. He was in a kind of cathedral, hewn out of the naked rock, and as he blinked, trying to take it all in, and failing, the shadow within the shadows stepped out into the unearthly light, and Val saw it. *At last,* he thought. *It has come to me at last.*

PART ONE

THE BLOOD-DIMMED TIDE IS LOOSED

MALTA / ISTANBUL

ONE

"What has happened?"

In a red-velvet-draped castle room on a granite bluff overlooking the Mediterranean, seven robed men sat around a circular table of polished pearwood. On the table were silver pitchers of ice water and individual chalices in front of each man. The walls between the curtains were hung with a pair of tapestries so old and valuable they rightfully belonged in a major museum. One depicted the Ascension of Christ, still bleeding from being crucified; the other was a hunting scene of a stag at bay, bleeding from the bites of a pack of slavering hounds.

Seven men, and Cardinal Duchamp makes eight. An unfortunate number, thought Aldus Reichmann. *Inauspicious.* As *Nauarchus* of the Knights of Saint Clement of the Holy Land he was not supposed to believe in numerology, banned like other esoteric disciplines by the Vatican. But what he studied on his own time, what he believed in . . . well, whatever helped him gain power would help him retain it. Eight was the number of death. But it could not be helped. The Vatican, in the person of Cardinal Duchamp, had come to Malta on urgent business.

The cardinal cleared his throat. He was a tall, imposing individual with a ruddy complexion that belied his soft, rather feminine Irish-French skin and the lax muscles beneath. He gave the appearance of being powdered all over, as if being nearer to God had sucked all the juice out of him. Proof that he wasn't even interested in altar boys, Reichmann thought wryly. He was as dry as a date, only it was his insides that were shriveled.

"Again we ask: What happened?"

On the other hand, Reichmann thought as he aligned the manila envelope in front of him with the arc of the table, *one mustn't forget that being the pope's personal emissary, Duchamp wields untold power, even within the College of Cardinals in Vatican City.*

"Where is Valentin Kite?"

Like crickets in a field, there was a rustling around the table as the members of the Circle Council, the ruling body of the Knights, shifted uncomfortably from one buttock to the other, as if on cue.

"The truth—"

The cardinal's cold, clear eyes settled on Reichmann like ravens on a carcass. "We wish *only* the truth, *Nauarchus*. Always and forever."

"This is of course understood."

"We would pray so, *Nauarchus*." Cardinal Duchamp's ruddy lips compressed, further showing his extreme displeasure. "Now. What happened?"

"Evidently, Valentin found the entrance to King Solomon's mine," Reichmann began.

"Evidently?"

The cardinal put such a sarcastic spin on the word that six of the seven Knights all but cringed. Not so Reichmann, who had risen within the ranks to become *Nauarchus* by employing a great deal of cunning, knowing how and when to apply stressors, and dispensing highly effective measures of intimidation. He was damned if he was going to let Felix Duchamp intimidate *him*. Nevertheless, before he delivered his answer, he buried the fingers of his right hand in the thick black ruff of Maximilian, his Caucasian shepherd, a massive guard dog with the size and aspect of a small bear. The dog, with good reason, terrified the castle's staff, along with a good number of the Circle Council, though they would rather be strung up by their thumbs than admit it out loud.

Reichmann nodded, as if deaf to the cardinal's tone. "That was the last communiqué we received from him."

"And then?"

"Then, presumably, he entered the cave with his guide and guards."

"Who are now . . . ?"

"Dead, Your Eminence. Unfortunately."

"Unfortunate for all of us who sent Kite on this mission."

Reichmann said nothing; there was nothing to add. The Knights, ancient and irretrievably linked to the pope, who originally granted them their charter in return for their undying fealty, were a religious and military order. Though founded around 1023, they didn't come to prominence until the First Crusade in 1099, when the pope moved them into the military sphere as soldiers of Christ.

"Who killed them?" the cardinal asked now with the tone of one who already knew the answer.

"Where they set up outside the cave mouth was in complete shambles. The working hypothesis is they were set upon by one of the cadres of local rebel jihadists that infest the area."

"Isn't that what the guards were there to protect against?"

"Of course," Reichmann said. "We don't know how large the jihadist cadre was, but from the damage inflicted we can glean that Val's group was heavily outnumbered."

"Evidence."

Reichmann drew several photographs from the manila folder, spread them out for the cardinal to look at. Duchamp leaned forward but would not touch the photos, as if they had been contaminated by the abominable methods of the deaths they had recorded.

"What . . . ?" He could not go on. His lower lip trembled minutely.

"We simply don't know, Your Eminence."

"Am I seeing right?" The cardinal peered from the in situ photo to the close-ups. "Is every bone in this man's body broken?"

"That's what my people tell me."

"And two were burned to death," Duchamp said. "That's clear enough."

"Val's group was attacked while they were inside the cavern, which would have made defense exceedingly difficult."

"What of the mine itself?" Duchamp said abruptly.

"Unknown. Our people found nothing to indicate a shaft or a gold hoard. Perhaps it had already been looted. But they had little time for exploration; the jihadists who attacked Val and his team were still in the area. They had to fight their way out."

"I'm beginning to think Valentin didn't find the mine at all." Duchamp's hands were working on the table, as if, deep down, he was harboring violent impulses. "I'm of a mind to believe that this was all a folly, that you have ill-used Vatican funds."

"I can assure Your Eminence—"

"Your assurances are unacceptable, *Nauarchus*." Cardinal Duchamp's head wagged from side to side. "What evidence have you that Valentin did, in fact, discover King Solomon's mine?"

Reichmann handed over another set of photos, these fairly blurry, obviously taken in haste. "Wall paintings inside the cave depict King Solomon. His seal is quite evident, Your Eminence. There can be no doubt."

Cardinal Duchamp's fist rose and fell onto the table with a crash that caused Maximilian to raise his regal head. "Then where is the mine itself? Where is the hoard of gold Solomon secreted away?" He leaned forward. "You understand the special nature of this gold, *Nauarchus*."

"I do, Your Eminence."

Nevertheless, out of either spite or pedantry, Duchamp felt obliged to explain. "Solomon's gold is unlike any other ever produced. It is said to have been created by his cabal of alchemists by an arcane method known only to them. There is an added element to the gold—perhaps, as it is rumored in certain historical texts—"

"I believe you mean banned religious texts, Your Eminence."

This not very subtle reminder that the cardinal himself was dabbling in a subject heretical to canonical law clearly did not sit well with Duchamp, who revealed his intense displeasure through a scowl.

"These *texts,*" he emphasized, "posit the theory that what made the gold in Solomon's mine so intensely valuable was that it had been infused with the Quintessence, the so-called life force of the universe. Anyone who came into possession of the gold would have their life extended far beyond normal human parameters." He lifted a finger, wagging it in warning. "Let me remind you, *Nauarchus,* that your predecessor promised, and failed, to unequivocally ascertain whether Braverman Shaw's father had indeed unearthed the Quintessence." He glared at Reichmann with open hostility. "Now you too have failed at *your* mission. I can only guess at His Holiness's reaction when I report back to him."

Abruptly Reichmann was fed up with this pompous creature. He resented in extremis that Duchamp had been dispatched to reprimand him and demand answers he could not, as yet, provide. It seemed to him now the last straw in the increasingly adversarial relationship with the Vatican. Ever since his predecessor's death, the Holy See had turned its eye on the Knights as never before. No one knew better than he did the rampant political infighting that led to the corruption within Vatican City. The new pope was trying his best to eradicate all corruption, but over the centuries it had become so institutionalized that nothing short of replacing the entire College of Cardinals would suffice. That, Reichmann knew for a certainty, would never happen. The Church was too addicted to money, to filling its coffers, to catering to those wealthy individuals who gave most generously.

The cardinal had sat back, crossing his arms over his chest.

Not only his body language but also his expression told Reichmann a storm was fast rushing toward him. But rather than intimidate him, the darkening horizon only fueled his anger. Normally, he kept it on a tight leash, but there were triggers that set it free, snarling like Max with strangers.

"What of Valentin Kite?" Duchamp said, his voice tight and coiled like a deadly thing. "Where is he? What happened to him?"

Reichmann was again being humiliated in front of the Order's ruling body. "The *extramuros* team found no trace of him, either in the cave or in the immediate vicinity."

"You told me they were being hounded by the local jihadists."

"We know for certain that no one made it out of the area." The two men were now making a habit of not answering each other directly. "The photos prove that Valentin's entire team perished."

"But what about Valentin himself?"

The cardinal repeated his question in a pro forma voice, while he studied his perfectly manicured nails. Reichmann wondered whether he even cared what happened to the explorer.

"Valentin is either dead or, worse, captured by local jihadists. He's a good Catholic. What do you imagine they'd do to him?"

Breaking the ensuing silence, Reichmann continued. "And as for the Quintessence, Your Eminence, my spies report that no one has it. Not us, not the Gnostic Observatines. Braverman Shaw led my predecessor on one nasty wild-goose chase that cost him his life."

"And elevated you to his exalted position," Cardinal Duchamp said with evident distaste. "The Gnostic Observatines—even speaking their name makes me sick to my stomach. They have been a thorn in the pontiffs' side since the fourteenth century. We can never forget how their rise after the split in the Franciscan Order in the early 1300s caused both chaos and consternation in the Holy See. Pope John the Twenty-Second quite rightly sided with the Franciscan Conventuals.

But instead of complying with his order to stay inside their monasteries and obey the pontiff's will, the Observatines chose to rebel, and dispersed into what we now know as the Middle East. They won't fight the Islamics as good Catholics should, although everyone knows that there are Islamic practitioners of heretical magic, Sufi mysticism, what have you. No, the Observatines believe in the rights of all men, a secular notion that has no place in the Church." The derision in Duchamp's voice was unmistakable. "It is whispered by some that they have completely forsaken the dictates of Christ, that they even help the Islamics. What can you do with people like that but exterminate them?"

Duchamp curled his hand into a fist, slammed it down onto the table so hard the chalices rocked on their bases. It was good that Reichmann had hold of Maximilian, else the dog would have leapt to his feet. As it was, Reichmann could feel the quiver of the beast's powerful haunches.

Oblivious to this potentially lethal byplay, the cardinal continued. "Then why hasn't the Order been eradicated?"

Reichmann kept his voice mild, as much to reassure Maximilian that he wasn't in danger as to keep up his front with the cardinal. "May I be frank, Your Eminence?"

Cardinal Duchamp waved his hand. "The day you are not will be your last as *Nauarchus.*"

"Then allow me to say that we have never had to deal with an individual like Braverman Shaw. We believed that when we killed his father, Dexter Shaw, the man who sought to be *Magister Regens,* we had broken the back of the Gnostic Observatines." Now he did take a drink of water. *To hell with Felix Duchamp,* he thought. After he had swallowed the long draught, he continued. "However, they're like cockroaches— hiding everywhere, impossibly difficult to exterminate. In addition, we did not reckon with the fact that Dexter Shaw had trained his son in secret, had left secret instructions for Braverman. When we did find out, we moved heaven and earth to stop Braverman from finding and acting on his father's instructions."

"Yet you failed," Cardinal Duchamp said heavily. "You failed to prevent the Haute Cour from voting Braverman Shaw as the first *Magister Regens* in centuries, and now he has become more powerful than his father. He has extended the Order's businesses more deeply into the lay world than we have. Under Bravo Shaw's direction, they have further infiltrated into every area of business and politics. They have, in effect, become as much religious warriors as your people are."

Reichmann resisted the urge to glance at Collum, who, as usual, was sitting directly across from him, his eyes cast down as he took copious notes. "The people who preceded me failed to eradicate the Gnostic Observatines, Your Eminence. With respect, I have been trying to clean up their mess."

The cardinal seemed not to have heard, or, possibly, he didn't care. "Why have you not attempted an all-out assault on the Haute Cour? A mailed fist, wiping them out once and for all. We believe that is what's needed."

Reichmann marshaled his resources. *This is what comes of men of God thinking themselves warriors,* he thought drily. "That direct tactic has been tried, several times, without success," he said. "In fact, it appears that the failed attempts are what has caused Shaw to ensure that his Order is stronger and more determined than ever. A remarkable example of cause and effect gone wrong."

The cardinal shook his head. "Need we remind you, *Nauarchus,* that the pontiff agreed to your elevation so that you could fulfill your promise to put an end to all incompetence?"

"Not at all, Your Eminence," Reichmann said with far more equanimity than he felt. "But I feel I must reiterate that Bravo Shaw has instituted policies that make our mission exponentially more difficult."

"For instance."

Reichmann could not filter out the cardinal's condescension.

"He has dispersed the Haute Cour, for one thing. The heart of the Gnostic Observatines no longer gather in one place. He has scattered them across the globe."

"The answer to that is simple, *Nauarchus*. Dispatch your men to eradicate them."

"I have." Reichmann took a breath. "None return."

"We would offer the observation that they are not sufficiently trained."

Not wanting to get into the whys of his men's failures, Reichmann moved on. "Over the centuries, the Observatines have made powerful allies who go to great lengths to protect them. An all-out assault is now out of the question."

"And Shaw himself?"

"He employs multiple layers of protection." Reichmann raised a finger. He was determined to end what had turned into an interrogation, but before he could continue the cardinal broke in.

"You have failed and now you must pay the price. There must be changes made to our partnership. As of today we will now be taking fifty percent of the profits from the three financial and transnational shipping companies you have established with our money."

Reichmann was reeling. These three companies were his idea. He had founded them, it was true, on the back of Duchamp's private fortune floating somewhere between the Vatican Bank and a bevy of offshore accounts. But it was Reichmann's vision as well as his expertise that made them both money out of the probing eye of Vatican City or any other authority. Was he not entitled to the lion's share of the proceeds? What did Duchamp do but sit on his butt and collect the fat rolls of cash every month? What Reichmann really wanted to do was to let Maximilian rip out the cardinal's tender throat. Instead, he said, "Our verbal contract is for a seventy-thirty split."

The cardinal leaned forward. "'Verbal' is the operative word, Reichmann. You operate at our command; the contract is at our discretion. It is fungible."

"Indeed, Your Eminence." Reichmann smiled winningly, all too aware that Duchamp had dropped his official title. "I understand." Inside, he was seething. Inside, this outrageous penance had finally tipped the scales. The situation had become intolerable. He knew he needed to do something drastic to get out from under Duchamp's thumb. It was time to sever ties with the Vatican entirely. But how? As Duchamp had needlessly pointed out, the Knights had been chartered by the Holy Father centuries ago. The Order had been his strong right hand ever since. But times change. Living in the past was no longer a viable option.

Change, Reichmann thought as he continued to smile with perfect calm, *must come.*

TWO

The old building stood shoulder to shoulder with its elderly brethren overlooking the cerulean blue of the Bosporus, at the confluence of Europe and Asia. At her desk in her third-floor office, Emma Shaw looked up from her Braille keyboard and said, "Good afternoon. How may we be of service?"

The sign outside the offices' front door declared this to be THE HALLBROOKE INSTITUTE FOR ARCHIVAL STUDIES, which, if you stopped to think about it, revealed nothing at all about the business of those inside. That was, more or less, the point.

"Madam?"

As a sighted person would use a visual once-over, Emma drew in the new scent of perfume. Having identified the citrus, green, and tropical notes of Hermès's Un Jardin sur le Nil, she began to extrapolate the following: The person standing just inside the door was relatively young and definitely not someone wandering in off the street. It was a woman who had come here with a purpose. "Perhaps you have the wrong office?" Emma queried gently, and waited as she sensed the woman marshaling her thoughts.

"No," the woman said at last. "No, I . . ." She cleared her throat and came across the carpet to stand in front of Emma Shaw's desk. "I've come to see . . ." Again she paused, uncertain how or perhaps if to continue.

The hesitancy in her voice was ripe with anxiety, fear, perhaps even a touch of panic. Emma heard it clearly and she smiled her thousand-watt smile, known to defrost the iciest personality. "Be at ease," she said, and, as if by an almost telepathic intuition that had been hers since birth but had been honed to the sharpest edge since she had lost her sight, added, "You're among friends here; on this you can rely."

"The fundamental things apply," the woman replied, voicing the next line in "As Time Goes By."

The two young women had completed what was known in clandestine circles as a parole: a call-and-response known only by a few, a form of identification for the newcomer.

At once, Emma's neck tautened, her heightened senses questing. "And you are?"

"Maura." Again the clearing of the throat, more nervous this time. "Maura Kite."

Oh, my God, Emma thought, her heart abruptly thrust into the deepfreeze.

Bravo Shaw was ensconced behind a massive crescent of ash wood, which presented a sleek, featureless front to anyone entering his office. Built into his side of the curved halfwall, however, were shelves, filled with ancient books, manuscripts, letters, drawings, and multitudinous ephemera his father had unearthed, collected, and hidden over his abbreviated lifetime. Since Bravo had moved his headquarters from New York to Istanbul, he had been engrossed in the information contained in the documents, which were slowly but surely reshaping his conception of the past. Astonishments at every turn.

He looked up as Emma knocked on the door, opened it, and came in.

"Hey, Em, what's up?"

"Something urgent." Closing the door softly behind her, she picked her way to the chair that was always in the same place and sat down. "Maura Kite is here to see you. She said her husband instructed her to come."

Bravo frowned. "You remember Valentin Kite," he said. "He's the freelance hunter after antiquities—the odder and more arcane the better. The three of us met in Cairo."

"Six or seven years ago, I remember."

"I'll bet you do."

"What does that mean?" Emma held her breath.

"I remember how well the two of you got along."

"That was a long time ago."

"For all of us."

"Why is his wife here now?"

"Val had been on an assignment given to him by Aldus Reichmann."

"An assignment for the Knights of Saint Clement?"

"And, as it happens, also for me."

Used to his secrets, she seemed to accept this on face value. "Now that Maura's here . . ." She took a breath, let it out. "It can't be good news."

"I'm afraid it isn't."

Emma, heart pounding in her chest, sat forward, perched on the edge of the chair. "This would be a good time to spill it."

"Frankly, at this point, I'd rather not. The danger has clearly escalated. But I can tell you that Val has been reporting back to me on where he is and what he's been doing." Bravo's frown deepened. "But without warning he stopped sending updates. Now his wife arrives on our doorstep."

Emma bit her lip, her eyes overbright.

"I had Val give her instructions to come here if he didn't come back."

"Can you at least tell me where he was sent?"

"Lebanon. The Tannourine area, more specifically."

Emma stood up. "I suppose I'd better bring her in." Retracing her steps, she put her hand on the doorknob, then, hesitating, said, "I'd like to sit in."

"Out of the question."

She turned to him so he could see the implacable expression on her face.

"Damn it, Em. Okay. Do as you wish."

Opening the door, she called out Maura's name, then stood aside for the very pretty dark-haired, pale-complected woman.

"Maura Kite," Emma said succinctly. She seemed to give the other woman a tiny shove in the small of her back, impelling her into Bravo's office; then she stood still as a statue.

"You're Bravo?"

He nodded.

Maura stood immobile with her hands clasped in front of her like a choir girl. In her polka-dot dress and Mary Janes she could have passed for twenty, though Bravo judged her to be perhaps five or six years older.

He stood up. "Val spoke about you often." Coming around from behind the halfwall, he gestured at an upholstered love seat. "You're his wife."

Maura sat at one end of the love seat. "His widow."

Sapphire light filtered in from windows treated with chemicals to block the sun's UV rays. The office was high ceilinged and spacious, even judged by American standards. It was oddly shaped, not a rectangle at all, but more of a lozenge-shaped space, for no reason that was readily apparent. It was furnished more as a library or a study than an office, with comfortable seating, bordering on the informal. There were no lamps or direct lights of any kind—because of the delicate nature of the documents stored—but where the walls met the ceiling, where moldings and cornices might have been, was a continuous band of cove lighting, indirect, discreet, also of the curious sapphire hue.

"This is dreadful news you bring with you, Maura," Bravo said. His eyes closed for a moment. With enormous inner effort, he slowed his breath enough to feel the loss welling inside him. He had warned Val off, but the man had been implacable in his

34

desire to take the assignment—eager, even. Now he was dead. "I think we both could use a drink."

He crossed to a sideboard on which stood a tray with a trio of bottles, along with several glasses and a metallic ice bucket.

"Emma?"

His sister shook her head.

Carrying the entire tray, he sat down next to Maura, placed the tray on a mosaic coffee table. When Maura pointed to the rum, he plucked ice cubes out of the bucket, sloshed the liquor into two glasses, handed one to her.

"To Val," he said, lifting his glass. And when the glasses touched rims with a bell-like note, he added, "I'm most sorry for your loss."

"Yours too," she said in a very small voice. "I know how close you two were."

Bravo halted his glass on the way to his lips. "Nobody was supposed to know. Nobody *should* have known. Not even you. It isn't safe."

"I know." Maura downed her rum in two long gulps, refilled her glass herself. "Val knew how to keep secrets."

"Nevertheless . . ."

There was a small silence. "Concerning safety," she said. "May I ask a question?"

"Please."

"Considering the level of peril you're—we're—in, why do you have your sister as your first line of defense?"

"Who said Emma is my first line of defense?"

Maura's brows drew together. "But I didn't see anyone else. . . ."

"I think," Bravo said, "you've answered your own question."

"Huh." She glanced down into the depths of her drink. By her body language, Bravo deduced that she was preparing herself to resume the main topic of their conversation. "'Nevertheless,' you said." She glanced up, watching him from beneath long lashes. "Nevertheless, when Val accepted this latest . . ."

She paused again, swallowed more rum. "When he accepted this *last* assignment, he told me about you." She looked away for a moment, then back at Bravo. "I think he must have suspected . . . had an intimation, anyway . . . that something like this might happen."

Bravo set down his glass. "Something like what, Maura? That he might die?"

Maura's eyes were moist, magnified and quivering with her incipient tears. "That's why I'm here. He instructed me to come if . . ." Once again her voice trailed off. She was breathing hard and fast as if she were running away from something, or toward it. "If he died."

Bravo leaned toward her, took her glass away, and took her hands in his. They were cold as ice. "I'm so sorry, Maura."

Maura looked at him with a stricken expression, tears sliding slowly down her cheeks. "Words," she said. "What use are words to me now?"

THREE

"Do you think he knew you were lying?" Collum Fireside said.

"Not divulging the truth—the whole truth—" Reichmann said, "isn't the same as lying."

Gulls swooped and dove, straining, riding the tricky eddies, just to keep their places. The southern horizon was clogged with gunmetal clouds, and a bitter wind had swept in off the Mediterranean. With a storm coming across from North Africa, Reichmann had taken to the paddocks near the cliffs behind the castle, to get the horses back in their stalls. There were grooms for this, of course, but he liked to be near the horses, even Fireside's, to gentle them when they became agitated. Collum had invested in Arabians—idiotic, so far as Reichmann was concerned. Arabians were undeniably beautiful, but they were delicate and high-strung, not at all useful for real racing.

His long dark cloak was buttoned to the neck against the chill. It flared out from the waist and the wide bottom whipped about his ankles. Beside him, Maximilian crouched, staring at the oncoming storm with the baleful, ashen eyes of a demon, as if by will alone he could alter its course. The dog disliked storms, thunder even more. The charged air lifted his thick coat, made him twitch as if insects were crawling over his skin.

Collum Fireside, on Reichmann's other hand, began to lead his horses back into their stalls. As expected, they were in a near panic as the bottom dropped out of the barometric pressure and the air filled with electricity. He was stocky and as muscular

37

as a British footballer. When he wasn't using them, as now, his hands, large as meat hooks, were jammed into the pockets of his heavy wool trousers. Collum always wore wool, even on the hottest days, a holdover from the donnish life he'd led in Cambridge before being inducted into the Knights of Saint Clement. He had been personally recruited by Reichmann, who had been raking through the colleges and Catholic churches outside London in search of the perfect adjutant and the perfect enforcer. In Collum Fireside he had found both in one package.

"Nevertheless," Collum said as he gentled his steeds, "you wouldn't hesitate lying to Felix." Between themselves, they referred to Cardinal Duchamp by his Christian name, as a sign of their contempt.

"The trick to lying," Reichmann said mildly, gaining a grip on his horse's bit, "is in not getting caught."

Reichmann knew whereof he spoke. He had been a foundling, a ward of the state, then, after escaping like a convict, a street urchin in the filthy back alleys of East London. But he was as free as a bird. He had made his way by lying, cheating, pilfering, and, best of all, learning the con from the best of the grubby best. But, presently, he became lonely for the company of women, as well as of men who weren't as broken as he was.

He came to the Church in this way—in disarray, suffering bouts of despair. The C of E was no place for him. He found it cold and forbidding, but the Catholic Church was another matter altogether. Within its fold he discovered warmth from a parish priest who was less interested in saving his soul than in him finding a way to save the parish itself. When Reichmann did so, the priest never asked how and Reichmann, who, when needed, knew how to keep his mouth shut, moved up in the theological world when the bishop learned what he had done. He stayed three years with the bishop, during which time he made his benefactor—as well as the Church—a great deal of money. At the end of this time, Reichmann was visited by a cardinal from Rome, who took him to lunch in the back room of a restaurant that clearly the cardinal frequented with great regularity. The restaurant was part of something called the Canonic Club. It was housed in one of those magnificent limestone town houses adorned with balustrades, bow windows, and faux columns on Charles II Street, near St. James's Square in Belgravia, a posh neighborhood that Reichmann had previously visited, but only in the dead of night on little cat feet for sleek, discreet break-ins.

It was in the hushed, pious atmosphere of the restaurant, over a sumptuous meal that successfully dazzled Reichmann, that the Knights of Saint Clement of the Holy Land were first brought to his attention. By the time the rich puddings were set before them Reichmann had been recruited. And that was before the coffee, petit fours, Napoleon brandy, and Cuban cigars as they sat in oversized chairs on either side of the magnificent roaring fireplace. Outside, in the misty-laden night, the Canonic Club was guarded by a toothy wrought-iron fence and horned lamps reminiscent of dragons' eyes.

The cardinal was a keen judge of character. Reichmann took to the Knights like a swan to water. He was immediately in his element, and in no time he found himself rising in ruthless fashion through the ranks, impressing his patron cardinal no end. This unprecedented run culminated in an invitation to Vatican City, a visit both sacred and profane. In one day, Reichmann's cardinal ushered him into an audience with His Holiness, where he was complimented on his skills, introduced to the College of Cardinals, their moist handshakes and insincere smiles, sat with the officious head of the Vatican Bank to open an account into which the cardinal immediately transferred a sizable sum, and, finally, after a gut-stretching dinner in Nino's back room, had the pleasure of choosing one of three stunning Roman women, bedding her through the night, while his cardinal vanished with the remaining two. That's when Reichmann knew he was home.

Now he fluttered a hand into the wind, and as if by magic Maximilian took off along the rocks, apparently unfazed by how high up they were. "But what we are currently confronted with is an altogether different kettle of crows."

"How so?"

"Felix is out of control. He wants to punish us—all of us—and he's hell-bent on doing it."

Closing the last of the stall doors, Collum turned to him, caterpillar eyebrows raised. "What d'you propose?"

"One step at a time," Reichmann said. "For the moment, let's keep our eye on the prize, which is Solomon's gold."

Fireside's eyes gleamed. "Then you don't propose to hand it over. Assuming, that is, we ever find it."

The dog leapt high in the air—higher than it would seem his bulk could manage—and he caught a seagull unlucky enough to be swooping down to investigate what looked like a piece of food trapped between the blue-gray jaws of a rock.

"I'm convinced Valentin found what we set him to look for."

"But Val is dead."

"Of that I'm not convinced." Reichmann's horses were calmer, but the Arabians' agitation disturbed them. "Which means you need to take your best cadre and return to Tannourine, follow in Val's last footsteps."

Fireside glowered into the storm, as if he were personally ready to fight it off. "Less than half my *extramuros* team returned alive, following the lethal firefight with the local rebel forces." *Extramuros* meant, literally, "outside the walls." In other words, the world beyond the realm of the Knights: the outsider world.

"Are you telling me you're too frightened to do this work anymore?"

Fireside bristled. "Certainly not. But I can't sustain another loss of that magnitude."

"I'm counting on you to make sure it doesn't happen again." Reichmann patted the arched neck of one of his horses. "I want that gold, Collum, and you're going to get it for me."

The men left the care of the horses to the grooms. As they

stood just outside the horse barn, the first raindrops struck their faces with a wildness all their own. Neither man flinched or even batted an eye. Maximilian came trotting back, a ragged strip of the gull dangling from his muzzle. Reichmann buried his fingers in the beast's ruff, bloodying them.

"Mrs. Kite, you told us that you believe your husband may have had an intimation of his death," Fra Leoni said. "Would you be kind enough to be more specific?"

Maura regarded the old man with his thick shock of white hair, aggressive nose, and blazing blue eyes that belied his age. In fact, she thought, everything about this man belied his age: his crow-like expression, his strongman-like body, his furnace-like energy. And yet the deep creases in his face surely marked his advanced years.

"Call me Maura, please," she said now, as much to be generous as to give her space to collect her thoughts.

"Fra Leoni," Bravo said with a reassuring smile, "is a gentle-man of the old school. Formality is bred in the bone."

Maura nodded. "I see," she said, though in truth she didn't see at all. These two men were the strangest people she had ever come across, though if she had been quizzed she'd be hard-pressed to say precisely why. By contrast, Emma was a pleasant surprise. She was open and friendly. Above all, as a woman who had been traumatized she was receptive to Maura's shaky emotional state.

She licked her lips. "Well, there's really no answer to your question. Val often had what you might call visions." Her brief laugh turned into a choke of emotion. "I don't mean to say he was another Joan of Arc. Nevertheless, every once in a while he would get—maybe a 'feeling' is a better word for it. Yes. A feeling that something was about to happen."

"And you think one of these incidents happened just before he left for Tannourine."

"I'm speculating. I mean why else would he have told me about you, left your address with instructions to come in the event of his death?" she said, looking at Bravo.

"On the other hand, you may be reading too much into instructions I had given him before he left. It was a matter of routine, nothing more. He wanted to make sure you'd be well taken care of."

Maura nodded. "You may be right. In the shock of his death . . . I think we all look for reasons, for justification, for events to make sense when, really, they don't. They can't, right?"

"When it comes to death," Fra Leoni said, "we humans can't help but try to understand the unfathomable."

"That's it," Maura said. "Thank you, Father."

Bravo rose. "Will you excuse me for a moment?" He left, hearing Emma empathetically consoling Maura, while Fra Leoni listened with eyes closed, as he often did while concentrating deeply.

A half hour later, Bravo returned and led Maura through a hidden door in the back wall of his office suite, down a dimly lit corridor. Fra Leoni followed them.

"Watch your step," he said as they passed over what appeared to be a structural I-beam. The floor ahead of them was different —carpeted, instead of bare wood slats—and the corridor was better lit. They had, it seemed, crossed into the adjacent building.

Bravo fell back, guiding Fra Leoni over the rough landings. He had first crossed paths with the old priest in Venice several years ago, during his intercontinental search for his father's hidden legacy. He had been crossing the crowded piazza in front of the Church at l'Angelo Nicolò, had taken the priest for a mendicant, and had given him a coin. It was only much later that he had discovered this encounter somehow had been arranged by Fra Leoni, by way of an introduction into Bravo's life. He had been Bravo's constant companion, advisor, and historian ever since. The monk was uniquely suited for this task; he had been born in 1421. The living testament of history.

Now they were seated with Maura Kite at a mosaic-topped table on the terrace of a private café. The tables surrounding them were bare, their chairs empty. No other customers were in sight, and after taking their order the server had discreetly vanished into the café's darkened interior.

Below them, cries and shouts from the ceaseless bustle of Istanbul rose into the air like steam, collecting on the underside of the striped awning above their heads before evaporating into the afternoon, creamy as the yoghurt that was now set before them, along with a bowl of fresh and stewed yellow figs. A long-necked green glass carafe filled with steaming mint tea was set down beside the dishes. While they fell silent, the server poured their tea into tall, narrow glasses encased in worked-silver holders, then left them alone again with their words and their thoughts.

"Maura," Bravo said as he spooned both kinds of figs atop her mound of yellow yoghurt, "we have been questioning you since you arrived, which is of course natural. Do you have questions for us?"

She picked up her spoon, made a weak attempt at digging into her figs and yoghurt, then reversed course, put the spoon down. "Do you know—I mean, do you have any idea . . . ?" She grabbed her glass, gulped down some tea, wincing as she burned the tip of her tongue in the process. "What happened to the people with him? The guide and—?"

"Dead, so I've been told by the people I called," Bravo said. "Of the team, only Val's body hasn't been accounted for."

Maura pressed fingers to her mouth. "Oh, my God. How could such a dreadful thing happen?"

No one said a word.

Maura's knit brows had not relaxed. "Perhaps . . . ," her voice trailed off. Taking a breath, she began again. "Is it possible that Val slipped off the ledge at the cave mouth and fell into the cataract? The, um, what is it called?"

"Baatara Gorge waterfall."

She nodded at Bravo, the ghost of a smile flickering across

her lips, gone almost before it had begun. "Yes. Thank you. The Baatara Gorge waterfall."

"Anything's possible, Maura."

Her eyes were beseeching. "Then it's possible he's still alive."

But none of them really believed that to be true.

FOUR

The sun, on its weary way to its resting place, was a fiery red oval slowly sinking into the city's haze. Through the open windows in Bravo's office, boat horns could be heard, along with the ululating wails of the Muslim call to prayer from the spire of a nearby mosque.

"I don't know what to believe," Bravo said. Maura had left them, escorted by Antonio Bazan to the guest room Bravo had assigned to her. "Emma?"

"There's more to her. . . ." Emma shook her head. "I don't know."

"Time is of the essence. I need more than that. I need to know what she knows."

Emma rose, bent to brush her lips against her brother's cheek. "I'll see to it, then."

As she turned to go, Bravo stayed her with the tone of his voice. "Em, what also must be determined is if Reichmann got to her before she arrived here. Reichmann has become increasingly aggressive toward us. Over the last year, a dozen of our men have died because of his initiatives."

Emma nodded.

"Em, you're sure you're up to this?"

"Why shouldn't I be?" Emma said somewhat too defensively.

Turning on her heels, she made her way out, navigating as if she were still sighted.

When she was gone, Fra Leoni said, "There was no reason to be short with her, Bravo."

"Was I?" Bravo looked away. "I didn't notice."

"That's part of the problem. The root of your anger . . ." He allowed his voice to trail off into silence. When Bravo refused to speak, he sighed deeply. "Val was a friend; I know that. But it's not him you were thinking about when his widow was here, was it?"

"I should have been. After what she told us—"

"No, in this moment, we are not dealing with *shoulds,* only with what *is.* We'll get to Val soon enough. What we need to speak of now—what we have all been guilty of avoiding—is Jenny."

"This is not the right time," Bravo snapped.

"It's never the right time," Fra Leoni said softly.

A long, uncomfortable silence ensued, punctuated only by the sounds of the city around them.

"For months, we all have been grieving, each in our own way," Fra Leoni went on. "But silently, saying nothing to each other. And what has happened? We have created closed loops that exist side by side, but never intermingle."

"It hasn't yet been a year. The pain of her dying is still too fresh," Bravo said, after a time.

"To deny yourself comfort and solace is a form of punishment." Fra Leoni tilted his head. "Why do you blame yourself for what is clearly the will of God?"

"Why would God take her life?"

"Because it was her time." Fra Leoni laced his fingers as he leaned forward. "Here we have a perfect example of what has happened to the members of the Order following your father's decision. In turning your attention outward to the world at large you have turned your backs on God and the Word of Christ." He reached out, touched Bravo's arm. "Solace only comes from forgiveness, my son. You must forgive yourself for Jenny's death."

"But I can't." It was almost a cry.

"It may not be what you want," Fra Leoni said, "but it's what you need. It's what we all need. We're all grieving, Bravo."

"But surely not in the same way! I loved her." And then in the charged silence that followed, "That was unfair."

"No apology necessary," Fra Leoni said as lightly as he could.

"So." Bravo let out a long-held breath. "Jenny."

"You had the chance to save her with the Quintessence," Fra Leoni said.

Bravo spread his fingers, as if to see if the grief he'd been holding on to so tightly might slip through the spaces he had made. "But it seemed she was getting better—she *was* getting better—until she wasn't." He took a deep breath. "I ran as fast as I could to get it, but by the time I got back she was already gone."

"It was too late," Fra Leoni said. "It was always too late."

Bravo's head came up. "What does that mean?"

"I've told you before. The Quintessence is not to be used lightly. There are effects beyond immortality." He smiled sadly. "There's always a price to pay, Bravo. Action and reaction. Even in such arcane matters."

Bravo's glare was a form of indictment. "What would have happened to her if I'd used it?"

Fra Leoni pressed against his closed eyelids with his fingers. "You know very well what would have happened to Jenny. She would have become immortal."

"Like you."

Fra Leoni nodded. "She would have watched helplessly as you grew old, sickened, and died. And then she would have been without anyone. Utterly alone. And in the unlikely event she fell in love again, what immortal wants to relive losing a cherished loved one again and again? The emotional toll is simply too much. You would have been condemning her to an isolation the depths of which you could never fully comprehend."

Bravo stared at the old man. He had never really considered all the ramifications of immortality, being alone among ripe fruit you could not pick.

There was more than a touch of ruefulness in Fra Leoni's

smile. "Immortality was thrust upon me; I never sought it out. I have repeatedly outlived my time. Contrary to popular belief, it's a terrifying experience. All the changes coming at you from all sides, in ceaseless waves." He took a breath. "It is why, sooner or later, the majority of immortals go insane.

"Grief comes to all of us. You're not alone, Bravo," Fra Leoni said. Those simple words were loaded with both compassion and irony.

Bravo lowered his head, deeply grateful. "Thank you."

"To return to Val," Fra Leoni said. "It seems Emma is under the impression that Maura Kite has something more to say to us."

"I want you to be clear," Bravo said. "Do you believe Maura has been lying to us about Val?"

"What I *suspect*," Fra Leoni said, "is that she's so traumatized she's lying to herself. Whether she's deliberately lying to us is a matter for Emma's further investigation."

"I need to know," Bravo said with no little intensity. "Did he find King Solomon's mine or not?"

"Perhaps the mine found him," Fra Leoni said gravely. "This is, legends say, part of its insidious power."

"Yes," Bravo acknowledged. "I've read that it's supposed to be akin to a living entity, but I can't quite make out why."

"It's because of the Book of Deathly Things. It's said that the king's alchemists infused his gold with the Quintessence, but that's not the true story. Rather, they used formulae in this unholiest of books to create Solomon's gold hoard."

"If that's true then getting to the truth Maura may be withholding is more vital than ever," Bravo said. "We both know who the purported author of this so-called Book of Deathly Things is."

Fra Leoni nodded bleakly. "Lucifer himself."

"But really," Bravo said, "that sounds just plain . . ."

"Insane?" Fra Leoni said. "More insane than the concept of the Quintessence, which your father found and you now possess? And consider this. From the era I was born into, notions of airplanes, the motorcar, telephones, not to mention mobiles, television, the Internet, ad infinitum, would be considered at best black magic, at worst the ravings of a lunatic." He shrugged. "Besides, the Church believes fervently in Lucifer; he's an integral part of the Bible."

"I take your point."

Fra Leoni's expression darkened considerably. "There's more to this, Bravo. The Book of Deathly Things, also known as the Testament of Lucifer, is one of three relics known as the Unholy Trinity. Three possessions were ripped from Lucifer and cast out, at the same time he was. In fact, he fell from God's grace because in his overweening arrogance he created the Unholy Trinity. The Unholy Trinity, font of much of Lucifer's knowledge and power, was hidden from him, and it was decreed by God Himself that Lucifer could never again lay a hand on them." Fra Leoni lifted a crooked forefinger, as if testing the air for evil signs. "But Lucifer's evil is clever and ever changing. He is always scheming to find the Trinity and make himself whole again."

"What, precisely, does the Unholy Trinity consist of?" Bravo asked. "Assuming, of course, that it exists at all."

Fra Leoni apparently chose to ignore Bravo's last remark. "The first—the sigil's square—is a manuscript: the Book of Deathly Things, also known as the Testament of Lucifer. It is whispered that King Solomon's alchemists found it, used it, tried to destroy it, but could not. So, through a series of complex incantations, they hid it again. And it's just as well. The words of Lucifer have a way of working even on the strongest of minds. The siren song of the Fallen Archangel will, it is told, seduce all who hear him or read his Testament."

He shrugged. "As for the other two—the circle and the triangle—what they depict remains a mystery. But together they encompass all the forbidden knowledge left by God in the Garden of Eden. Don't forget that Eve, tempted by the Devil, took only one bite of the fruit—a pomegranate, by the way, not an apple—before God intervened. All the rest of that forbidden knowledge was gathered up by Lucifer and codified into the Unholy Trinity."

"A fine story." Bravo shook his head. "Nevertheless, I trust you won't be disappointed if I place myself on the side of the skeptics."

"Your grandfather Conrad believed fervently in the existence of the Unholy Trinity. With good reason. It is said that should Lucifer manage to obtain all three, it will trigger a return to his full power. His reascendancy would be assured. For this very reason, Conrad spent much of his life in search of the Unholy Trinity. In fact, he claimed there was another manuscript, *Nihilus Inusitatus,* written in part by each of King Solomon's alchemists, which described what they had found and why knowledge contained in the Unholy Trinity would lead to the destruction of mankind."

"Really? My father never breathed a word of this."

"You know perfectly well why."

Bravo was silent for a moment. "I can believe in many things, Fra Leoni. But not this . . . not this."

"You must suit yourself. Skepticism is normally a healthy attitude to take. But I must warn you in this instance continued skepticism is the work of the Devil. It will surely get you killed."

Emma Shaw made her way to Maura's room, which was in the same building as the terraced café. She greeted Antonio Bazan with a warm smile and said quietly, "Tell me, how does Mrs. Kite seem to you?"

Bazan was a dark-skinned Andalusian with a good deal of Berber blood in him. His shiny black eyes looked out of deep sockets with an uncanny inquisitiveness, undeterred by his hawk's nose. His fleshy lips turned down slightly at her question. "Still in shock. Unquestionably depressed. In mourning. Semi-unresponsive. Has she said anything at all?"

"What *can* she say?" Emma told him. "Her husband is dead.

Even worse, there is no body to mourn or to bury. For Mrs. Kite there will be no closure."

"Sad."

"Terribly."

Emma listened to Bazan's gait as he sloped off down the corridor. She waited until she was alone before she rapped her knuckles on the door once and, without waiting for a response, pushed it open and entered.

Emma was familiar with the room, which was spacious, with a high ceiling, ochre-painted walls, comfortable furniture in the exotic, florid Ottoman style, including a pasha's low bed strewn with brightly colored pillows. A window with oxblood curtains on either side overlooked the Marmara, black and indigo, streaked with flat metallic silver where lights on the shore struck it.

She smelled Maura, sitting at a delicate writing table. Pen in hand, she had taken a blank sheet of paper on which she had begun to write.

"Maura, I just wanted to make sure you are comfortable and have everything you want."

"What I want is my husband returned to me."

"We all understand that."

"Indeed." Maura was in the process of gesturing when she caught herself. "Please sit down. There's a chair—"

Emma smiled. "I know where everything is in the room, even you."

Maura arranged her mouth in a bleak smile that was just shy of a rictus. Again she caught herself, and, chagrined, watched as Emma sat on the chair opposite her. "I'm sorry I spoke about you that way before."

"Don't give it a second thought. You're overwrought, grieving. Plus, you have every right to question our security."

Maura dropped her head. "You're very kind."

Emma felt the flush in her neck and cheeks and turned her mind to the matter at hand.

"It seems you've been writing," she said, starting a different tack.

Maura was startled. "How did you . . . ?" She cleared her throat. "I was just writing him a letter."

"Is it helping?" Emma asked. "The letter."

The pitiable rictus relaxed its grip somewhat. "It is. For the moment at least I can pretend he's still out there somewhere, that he'll get my letter someday." She laid down the pen. "But I know that won't last. It's a fantasy, isn't it?"

Emma had settled her hands in her lap like birds returning to their nest. "Bravo has told me that your husband was an expert climber. Do you really think he could have fallen into the gorge and is still alive?"

"I . . ." Maura's gaze flicked aside to the window, where the evening's glow pulsed like a buried heart. She licked her lips before her eyes returned to Emma's face. "It was—I mean, it's still hard to say that: Val is dead. I couldn't face it back there."

"But you can now."

Maura nodded. "Yes. With you, I feel I can be myself."

"Maura, please forgive me when I say that I don't feel as if you're being yourself."

Maura's brows gathered. "But . . . I don't understand."

"And yet, I believe you do."

Something hard and close flitted across Maura's face before vanishing into the night like a bat. The smile she presented now was thin and brittle. "I don't want to take offense, but—"

"Then don't."

This was said so sharply Emma could sense the other woman flinch.

"Relax, Maura," Emma said with a winning smile.

"I thought—"

"There are many layers to all of us. You agree, yes?"

Maura hesitated, then nodded tentatively. "Simple human nature, I suppose."

"Except there's nothing simple about human nature." Emma's

hands smoothed out the skirt of her cream-colored dress. "And more often than we'd care to admit we're strangers even to ourselves." Silence. Maura's breathing turned ragged. "I believe shock has caused your estrangement from yourself. It's nothing to be ashamed of, but it must be addressed, and quickly, for the sake of your mental health."

Emma shifted on the chair, her torso leaning slightly forward. "Maura, will you read me the letter you have begun to your husband?"

The younger woman flinched again. "No, I . . ."

Emma's smile widened, softened. "For your own good. And for Valentin's."

Her husband's name engendered a direct response in Maura. With a jerky, almost robotic series of movements she clutched the sheet of paper to her breast, fell to her knees before Emma.

"Forgive me, Emma, for I have sinned."

Emma gave no hint of her surprise. She rested her hand on Maura's bowed head, thinking, *It should be me asking forgiveness*. "How have you sinned, Maura?"

"I've lied."

"How so?"

"I've withheld the truth." She glanced up. "That's the same as lying, isn't it?"

Emma's hand touched the sheet of paper Maura still held close to her breast. In a shaky voice Maura read the few lines she had written: "'Dear Val, I wonder in these dark days whether you are lost, or lost to me forever. I remember with fearful clarity our last moment together, what you told me I must do if you didn't return. I never believed I would have to come to Istanbul, but here I am. I've done what you asked, but please tell me what to do next. Are you alive or are you dead? There—'" And here Maura stopped, as if unable to continue.

Emma, one hand on the point of Maura's chin, felt the tremble in her lower lip, her rush of scalding tears. "What is it?" Emma said softly. "You must go on."

Maura, weeping, said, "That's all I wrote."

"But that's not all you were going to write."

"No. There was a . . . Someone came to my door. I think he was a rebel. He looked like one, acted like one, so I had to assume . . ." Her voice trailed off.

"This is my shame, Emma, that I should live a life in which such dreadful souls were the last to see my husband." She shuddered. "That they touched him, looted his person . . ."

Emma knew she had to keep this woman talking or else she would sink back mutely into her grief and shame. "This group has Val's body, is that correct?"

Maura caught herself nodding. "Yes. They . . . A man showed up at my front door. That's how I know Val actually did go over the waterfall. They found him, drowned, pulled him out of a side eddy in the rapids. They said they think he must have hit his head on a rock or a fallen tree."

Emma's muscles had contracted, but she was careful not to let her tension show. "About the man who contacted you . . ."

Maura shivered. "I'm scared. I'm so scared."

Scared enough to have immediately contacted Reichmann? Emma asked herself. *You couldn't have been thinking clearly. Well,* she reassured herself, *you are now. I've seen to it.*

"What has frightened you so?"

"The man . . ." Maura choked on her words or her feelings, most likely both. She swallowed convulsively, seemed incapable of continuing on her own.

"This man," Emma prompted softly, gently, "was he a foot soldier, do you think?"

Maura shook her head. "He had the look—" Her shoulders quivered as she sobbed.

Emma rose and, moving her chair, sat down beside Maura. She handed her a handkerchief. Maura blew her nose.

"Courage, Maura." She put her arm about Maura's shoulders and smiled the smile that could light a room. "Remember that you're protected here. You're among family."

Emma's warm arm around her, as well as the reassuring words, calmed her enough for her to go on. "No, not a foot soldier. I've seen enough of those on TV. This man radiated power. He must have been a leader of some kind."

"Can you describe him for me?"

Maura stared at Emma, an expression of dread pinching her face. "I can't. . . ." She shook her head. "You wouldn't believe me anyway."

Emma's smile broadened further but thinned as it did. Something inside her curled in on itself, as if waiting for a physical blow. "My dear Maura . . . well, let me just say that nothing will surprise me."

"Really?" Maura seemed to have shrunk down, taking on the aspect of a little girl.

Emma, aware of the change in her demeanor, nodded reassuringly. "Really."

Maura studied Emma for a moment. "He . . . Now you won't laugh."

"You have my word."

"He looked like a cadaver—no, that's not quite right, like a death's-head. He was tall and thin—beyond thin, I remember thinking, as if he hadn't eaten in weeks. But that's impossible, isn't it?" She shuddered again.

After allowing Maura a moment to recapture her composure, Emma said, "Please go on. This is helpful."

"It is?"

"Extremely. What can you remember about his face?"

"Everything!" Maura exclaimed. "I'm not about to forget a face I see in my dreams every night." She took a breath. "His skull—and I use that word deliberately—his skull was long and narrow, like a . . . like a tombstone. His skin had a grayish tinge, his thin lips bloodless. His eyes were pure black, and glossy, like pieces of jet had been inlaid where his eyeballs should have been." She took another ragged breath. "And then there were his hands. They were curious."

"Curious in what way?"

"Though he was clearly a youngish man, his fingers seemed stiff, like my father's, as if he was suffering from rheumatoid arthritis."

"You're doing so well, Maura. Now who else did you tell about this strange man's visit." It was not phrased as a question.

Maura's eyes opened wide. "Why, no one."

"Surely in your distress, fear, and grief you thought to reach out to someone."

"Yes, I did. I followed Val's instructions to the letter. I came here at once."

Emma placed a hand over Maura's. "I can sense you're growing weary."

"I *am* rather tired."

"Just one more question, and then you can lie down. Did this man say anything else that I might find useful?"

"He only said what was necessary. And I didn't believe a word of it. I was convinced Val was still alive." She unfastened the first three buttons of her blouse. Taking Emma's hand in hers, she placed it on a small, exquisitely carved gold crucifix hanging on a chain around her neck. "But then, as proof, he returned this to me." Unclasping the chain, she slid the crucifix off, placed it in the center of Emma's palm. A small red blotch inflamed her skin where the back of the crucifix had lain against her chest. Emma couldn't see this, of course, but she was aware of a certain heat, concentrated as a laser beam. "It's Val's."

"Are you certain?"

"Yes." Maura's eyes were enlarged by tears. "I gave it to him. I'd know it anywhere."

Emma rubbed the surface of the crucifix with her thumb. When she got to the center of the underside, she said, "What did you have engraved here?"

"What?" Val's widow bent forward, her brows knit together. "I never ordered anything engraved on it." She took the crucifix, looked closely at its underside.

"It . . . it's a symbol."

The incisions against the pad of Emma's thumb had formed it in her mind: an upside-down triangle inside a circle inside a square. "Do you recognize it?" she asked.

"It's . . ." Maura turned the object so more light shone on it. "No, not at all."

The question that arose in Emma's mind was: Was it the triangle that was upside-down, or the crucifix?

Maura looked up, her expression puzzled. "How did it get there?"

"That is a legitimate question," Emma told her. "One for which I, at the moment, have no answer."

FIVE

When Antonio Bazan left Emma, he went along the corridor, turned left, and opened the door to the stairwell. The street was, as usual, boiling with merchants, tourists, messengers, the prayerful and the profane, petty criminals, and deliverymen. An old man sucking on a cigarette in the shadow of an open doorway to a carpet shop watched him with eagle eyes. A harried woman, loaded with net bags, herded three laughing children ahead of her. Bazan's eye was caught by a beautiful young girl as he crossed to the old man's side of the street. Several blocks farther on Bazan plucked a mobile phone from his pocket.

Picking his way toward the water, he punched a speed-dial number. The phone had hardly rung before Reichmann answered.

"Good evening, Tony. What news?"

"Maura Kite showed up."

"When?"

"A couple of hours ago. You know what that means."

"The wife wouldn't even know about the Gnostic Observatines if her husband hadn't been secretly working for them. What is she saying?"

"She's been in with the bigwigs, but I've seen her. She's obviously in shock."

"Did she have anything of interest to tell them?"

"It would appear she believes her husband's dead."

There was a moment's pause when Bazan heard nothing at all.

"How can she be certain he's dead and not missing?"

"A wife's intuition. She said she just knows he's gone."

"Do you believe her?"

"You didn't look into her eyes. I did. The woman's dead inside."

"Fair enough," Reichmann said. "Keep me informed."

"Always."

As Bazan disconnected, he continued along the street, then abruptly turned left, down a street packed with shoppers, copper and silver merchants, made a right after at the end of the block. He was in one of the older quarters, where fishermen still bought their handmade nets, floats, and hooks as their fathers and grandfathers had before them. The Marmara was only a block or two away, and the air was thick with salt and phosphorus.

Midway down the block, he slipped into a tiny café, open to the street. He made his way through the packed interior to a corner table shrouded in shadow and acrid cigarette smoke.

"How did it go?" Bravo said after ordering Bazan a Turkish coffee.

"No problems," Bazan said. He handed the mobile over to Bravo, took possession of the coffee, spooning sugar into the thick, dark brew. He took an appreciative sip. "Reichmann believes that Valentin is dead."

"He *is* dead, until proved otherwise," Bravo said. "The regional extremists found his body. One of them paid Maura a visit with proof."

"That's a pity."

The waiter came with more coffee for them both without being asked. Bravo came here often; the owner, Omar Tusik, was a close friend and informant. Omar would not allow Bravo to pay; rather than argue, Bravo made a monthly donation to the secular school where Tusik's daughter, Ayla, had gone. Such schools were becoming more and more endangered here, where conservative Islam was on the rise.

Bazan spooned sugar into his second cup, sipped it experimentally, added more. "Why d'you think they came to her?"

"They wanted money for a trinket of his," Bravo said. He looked beyond Bazan for a moment, at the parade of passing strangers. They all looked strange to him. His eyes went out of focus as a memory surfaced. Then it was gone, and when he looked again at Bazan his eyes were clear. "I promised Maura that I would find Val and bring his body back."

"Those rebels probably stripped him bare and buried him somewhere."

Bravo stared at him until Bazan was forced to look down. "Apologies. I shouldn't have said that."

"One of the things I like about you," Bravo said, "is that you doubt everything. I find that refreshing. It's good to have you around."

Bazan dipped his head, acknowledging in his own way Bravo's compliment. "You're heading over there."

"*We* are," Bravo said. "I need both your brains and your brawn. Besides, you spent ten years in Lebanon. You know it better than I do."

Bazan nodded. "When do we start?"

"We leave tomorrow," Bravo said.

Bazan was silent for a moment, brooding.

Bravo hunched forward. "What is it, my friend?"

"When I was in Lebanon, I worked for a short time in a shop selling grains. The owner was often absent. He was a randy fellow—though he was married and had four children he had liaisons with at least three women I knew about. Anyway, that left me alone in the busy shop for long hours. One morning when I opened up I was met with a horrific smell. I searched high and low but could find nothing that would even remotely give off such an odor."

Bazan drained his coffee cup, licked his lips to savor every drop of sweetness. "The stench got so bad it gave me a headache. When it began to drive even our best customers away I phoned the owner. He was, quite naturally, angry at being interrupted. But when he calmed down enough to hear my story, he came right over."

Bazan twirled the cup between his fingertips. "To get at the stench, the owner and I had to break open one of the walls. It turned out a rat had died inside. It had gorged itself on so much grain its stomach had burst."

As if abruptly disgusted, he pushed his cup away. "Bravo, it is my contention that there's a real rat inside the Gnostic Observatines," he said. "Quite possibly inside the Haute Cour itself. Someone, in any event, close to you, privy to your decisions."

"And this person is passing on information to Aldus Reichmann."

Bazan nodded. "He's far too clever to rely only on me."

"Have you any proof?"

"I do not."

"Any suspicions as to the identity of this so-called genuine rat?"

"I have some." Bazan shrugged his meaty shoulders. "But nothing yet I'd want to pass on, let alone act on." His shoulders twitched again. "Anyway, as our *Magister Regens* that's your bailiwick."

Bravo nodded and stood. Bazan followed suit. "Get your gear together, Antonio. Emma is procuring the tickets as we speak."

Bravo waited outside the restaurant until Bazan was lost to view, then pushed through the crowds, circling the block until he reached the rear of the café. There he found Omar standing in the open doorway. He was smoking one of his vile cigars, but he dropped it, ground it beneath his heel the moment Bravo appeared.

"You are about to leave," Omar said. "I can see it in your eyes."

"What?" Bravo said. "What is it you think you see?"

"Not what I *think* I see, but what I *do* see." Omar laughed good-naturedly. He was a slender man with a head like a basketball and the face of a bulldog. He wore a luxuriant handlebar mustache, which was his personal pride and joy. It also happened to hide a harelip. He was not so much ugly as plain looking. A bald pate, with its deep longitudinal creases, was reminiscent of an old-fashioned globe.

"Bravo, my good friend, you have no secrets from me." He held up one slim forefinger as if testing the direction of the wind. "You get a certain faraway look in your eyes that for me, at least, is unmistakable. Where are you off to this time?"

"You're better off not knowing," Bravo said, meaning it.

Omar waved a hand. "That's what you always say. And I know you have your reasons. It's not in my nature to pry."

"Oh, I don't know," Bravo said lightly. "It seems to me that all Turks love their secrets."

"Who doesn't?" Omar replied, laughing. "So tell me, how is the beautiful Emma?"

"Still too young for you, Omar. Besides, you're married; you have a lovely daughter."

Omar chuckled. "Such a wag you are! I have no perfidious designs on your sister. I simply find her charming. What a mind she has!"

"So you have a crush on her mind, is that it?"

Omar raised both hands, palms outward. "Is that such a terrible thing?"

Bravo could not help being put in mind of Bazan's story of the man he had worked for in the grain shop. He could not, however, imagine Omar cheating on his wife. For one thing, Dilara would cut his twig from his body if she found out. And knowing Dilara as Bravo did, he knew she *would* find out, by hook or by crook. She was embedded in a vast network of women throughout the city in all walks of life.

"You know," Omar said, switching topics, which he was wont to do at the drop of a hat, "I was thinking of taking a hammam. So you'll join me, yes?"

"Very kind of you, Omar. Any other time I would be delighted, but I'm leaving tomorrow. I have too much to do this afternoon."

"My friend, nothing is more important than taking a hammam with a friend. Now, I insist."

"But—"

"Call the darling Emma. She'll be only too happy to make all your arrangements. These things make her happy, yes?"

Bravo had to admit it. "Yes."

"So. It is done!"

SIX

And so it was.

After they had been soaped down, brushed free of dead skin cells, oiled, massaged, and, finally, sprayed with jets of hot water, they met in the steaming pool. It sprawled in all directions, like a shoreline, rife with many nooks and crannies in which to sit in private and talk or simply relax and let one's mind drift away in the fragrant heat. Enormous skylights towered over them, revealing a sky gradually transitioning from sunlight to city light.

"And then," Omar said just as if their conversation had never ended, "you must come to dinner. And you mustn't say no. I told Dilara you were leaving tomorrow. She will be angry with both of us if you don't come to say farewell."

Bravo nodded. "As you wish." When Omar was in this sort of mood there was no point in arguing with him.

"No," Omar laughed, "as *she* wishes." Throwing his arm across Bravo's shoulders, he said, "And you know, the best part is Ayla has returned home for a visit from working abroad in London. She's a lawyer. Have I mentioned that?"

"A thousand times," Bravo said. "At least."

He snapped his fingers. "What is it the British call her profession?"

"Barrister."

"Precisely! Ayla's a barrister! And, by all reports, a very fine one indeed. Finally you'll get to meet her."

They soaked in silence for some time, but Bravo could see Omar shooting him clandestine glances out of the corner of his eye from time to time. In another culture, Bravo might have asked his friend what was up, but this was Turkey. Patience was called for.

And, finally, Bravo's patience was rewarded. "You have been brooding ever since Jenny died." When Bravo looked away, he said in his gentlest voice, "You can't save everyone, Bravo."

"She was doing better," he said. "All her doctors said as much. And then . . ."

"And then, even with all their knowledge and expertise, they couldn't save her." He turned to Bravo. "This is life, my friend. Death is a part of it."

"Too large a part, in my case," Bravo said.

"We all have a time," Omar said, "as well as a purpose. Jenny was important to you; this is understood. But she's gone now and you're still here. Think of her, if you wish, mourn her passing, of course, but do not brood on what might have been. It's unhealthy." He grunted. "Besides, Jenny wouldn't have wanted that."

Bravo nodded as he managed a smile. "You're right, of course." He grasped Omar's hand. "Thank you, my friend."

When he was almost back at the office complex, Antonio Bazan came in sight of the carpet shop. Inside, it smelled of hemp, wool, silk, and tobacco. Dust motes quivered through the cones of lamplight. The old man who had been smoking in the doorway still had a lit cigarette dangling from the corner of his mouth while he cleaned up for the evening. He looked up when Bazan entered but did not bother to bring out the tea service as he would for any normal customer. Bazan was not a normal customer.

There was no need to exchange a word. The moment Bazan placed money on the countertop, the old man reached beneath the countertop, produced the mobile phone he kept for Bazan. Bazan picked his way around the counter and into the rear of the shop. No word of thanks was needed; his money had done the talking for him.

In the semi-darkness, he punched in a local number that changed every three days. One ring and he heard the switching, the hollowness on the line as his call was redirected overseas. Ringing again.

It was only after the ringing ceased that he began to talk to Aldus Reichmann.

SEVEN

Dilara's beauty, fine and crystalline, appeared to flower open the older she got. Time, it seemed, was her servant, not her master. This, at least, was Bravo's first thought when she opened the door to her husband's bellowing call: "Wife, your men are home!"

"Hello, lover," Dilara said as she kissed her husband. Then she was in Bravo's arms as he kissed her on both cheeks. She held him for what seemed an unnaturally long time before abruptly breaking away. She stood back, admiring them. "It's always good to see you both together." Nevertheless, there was something in her face Bravo could not account for.

The men followed her into the apartment, which was spacious and, considering Istanbul's crowded infrastructure, light. It was in a spectacular location, on the Moda seaside, in the Kadikoy district. Dilara had left the windows open. The sea breeze ruffled the lace curtains, bringing with it the smells of grilling fish, strong coffee, and anise. Out on the strand, the old men who played backgammon all day while they drank endless glasses of tea had packed up for the night, but the cafés were teeming with diners eating fresh seafood and drinking beer.

With a wide smile, Dilara poured the three of them cups of Turkish coffee, rather than raki. This was, after all, a Muslim household. As they toasted to the success of his upcoming trip, Bravo noticed that Dilara did not touch her coffee.

"Ayla will be here any moment," Dilara said. Her beauty was

burnished by the soft lamplight. By some mysterious alchemical process, she still possessed the angelic aspect of a virgin girl. Dark of hair and eye, her feline face with its wide, straight brows and sharp chin was the epitome of Ottoman beauty. She wore a two-piece abaya of a soft pink cotton. Her hair, thick, lustrous, and unbound by the hijab she wore out on the streets, cascaded around her slim shoulders. "I sent her round the corner. Our baker makes the best *pudingli* pasta and I know it's your favorite." She rose and said hurriedly, "Omar, keep Bravo entertained while I see to dinner."

The two men took their coffee to an overstuffed sofa. The view through the French doors to the narrow terrace and beyond was magnificent. Lights winked and twinkled on the water. A ship's horn sounded. Sails could be seen, scudding like clouds across the star-strewn sky, carrying their passengers from West to East and back again.

Omar set his coffee down on a side table. "Bravo, I have some sense of your real work, and I want you to know that you can count on me. I am Muslim and you are Catholic. If it seems on the surface odd that I should want to help, I can assure you that it is not. Allah wishes only peace. These animals— these conservatives and extremists—have the dubious gift of misinterpreting the words of Allah to fit their own bloody ends. Their perverted idea that the West—the soldiers of Iblis the devil—wishes only to bury their men and keep their women from paradise by luring them with the baubles of Western culture consumes them. It will be the death of them, surely. But this is not the Muslim way; this is not the path of Allah, the font of all wisdom. I assure you that the vast majority of Muslims want only to live peacefully in the world."

Bravo was both deeply touched and faintly amused by Omar's oration. "Is that what you want, my friend? To be left alone and live peaceably here in Istanbul?"

"It might have been my ambition five years ago, but now with the rise of the conservative element telling me what I can and cannot do, what I can and cannot think, living the life I want has become increasingly complicated. This is why we want to help you. I sense that you seek to restore a more peaceable order. This is what we want, too."

"What I do, Omar, is dangerous—and increasingly so. It's true that I'm ceaselessly working to keep the uneasy equilibrium in the world through the unified policies of the like-minded businessmen, lobbyists, American Super PACs, and politicians. But as you yourself have so eloquently pointed out, inch by inch we're losing the battle."

"All the more reason, Bravo. Dilara and I can no longer sit idly by and do nothing while our world changes for the worse. And there's something else."

Bravo could sense it in his friend's abruptly tense demeanor.

"I hesitate to say this, though in truth it's what spurred me to talk to you now, while we're alone, safe inside my home, where no big ears can . . ." He cleared his throat. "Dilara had a vision." Omar's wife was famous for her visions, which, so it was said, always predicted disruptive events. "She believes— and, it must be admitted, so do I—that you are in grave danger."

Visions were nothing new to Bravo; he took them with the utmost seriousness. "Did her vision say from what?"

"Just a . . . blackness, like a hole or an abyss."

"Or a cave?"

Omar nodded. "Possibly, yes."

"I'd very much like to speak with her about this."

"No, my friend, she won't speak of it again—ever. It scared her nearly out of her wits. This is why you must let us help. If anything happened to you she would never forgive me."

He considered Omar's request. While he had asked Omar— and once or twice Dilara—for help, he had been scrupulous in keeping them far out of harm's way. He had come to cherish the friendship he had developed with the Tusiks in the deep and abiding way of people who live in the shadows at the margins of society, who—because of either the inherent danger or the transient nature of their own lives—enter into such liaisons infrequently, and then only with extreme caution and no little misgivings.

Nothing could ever be traced back to them, and, if he agreed to Omar's request he would make sure they were protected in every way he knew how. For that he would, of course, require Fra Leoni's help. The old monk had just begun to teach him the esoteric secrets he had learned over the centuries. Bravo did not yet have a fifth of the knowledge Fra Leoni possessed.

Accordingly, Bravo took a deep breath before he said, "Are you absolutely sure this is what you and Dilara want?"

"She insists that one of us goes with you."

Before Bravo could say that it was out of the question, the front door swung open and Ayla strode in, set down the package of the cake Bravo was so fond of, and entered the living room, where Bravo and her father rose to greet her.

EIGHT

Ayla was Omar Tusik's only child. Not surprisingly for a barrister in London, she was in Western dress—high heels, jeans, a long-sleeved silk shirt of Mediterranean blue, and a stylishly cut jacket of umber leather.

As Omar kissed his daughter on both cheeks and made the necessary introductions Bravo had a chance to take her in. She was, first and foremost, her mother's daughter. The shape of their faces was virtually identical, but whereas Dilara's beauty was delicate, almost ethereal, Ayla's was rich and earthy. Her deep coffee eyes were larger and longer, her nose more aggressive, her lips more sculpted. It was as if Dilara's beauty had been distilled down, concreted, made more of the physical world. Drinking Ayla in was like taking a double shot of liquor: the shift that occurred was both physical and emotional.

Bravo kept all of these thoughts out of his expression as he kissed Ayla on both cheeks in the traditional greeting. Her scent was heady, as well, redolent of licorice, cinnamon, and clove, with a hint of aromatic tobacco. It was a combination that for him would come to embody her, that he would take with him when he left later that night. But for now, as her mother bustled in with the first course, there was no time for such matters.

They sat around the oval dining room table, which had been set as if for a feast or a festival with fine silverware, sparkling crystal, and Dilara's best china. Through the lavish five-course meal not a word was said regarding Bravo's trip, Dilara's vision, or Omar's offer. Instead, Dilara directed the conversation, which centered on relocation: Ayla's new life in London and Bravo's move from Manhattan to Istanbul. It was hardly lost on Bravo that Dilara was making parallels between his recent life and that of her daughter. Again he felt that intermingling of gratitude for being cared for and amusement at Dilara's attempt to get him to move on from Jenny's death.

Through it all, Ayla spoke and acted in what seemed to Bravo to be a tone-deaf manner. Possibly she was used to her mother's powerful ways, had developed effective defense mechanisms to protect herself from being manipulated with silk gloves. She sat across from Bravo but scarcely looked at him. Rather, her gaze was directed at some unknown point above his right shoulder. This afforded her the illusion of looking at him without actually having to do it. Bravo knew that ignoring him would have angered her mother, something Ayla clearly did not want to do. And yet she just as clearly was resisting her mother's attempt to use her to take his mind off his brooding for a lost love. Bravo did not quite know whether to embrace Dilara for her thoughtfulness on his behalf or to be angry with her for forcing her daughter into this uncomfortable position.

At length, just as the dessert she had been ordered to bring was being served, Ayla excused herself, pushed her chair back from the table, and left the dining room. Bravo watched her leave the apartment.

"I feel I must apologize for my daughter's rudeness," Dilara said as she set a slice of the cake in front of Bravo. "Clearly, life in the Western world has affected her judgment when it comes to social situations."

"You have nothing to apologize for, Dilara *teyze*," Bravo said, using the word for aunt, which was a sign both of affection and of respect. "Ayla is her own person. I respect that." He grinned at Dilara as he rose. "I'll just take this downstairs."

Dilara smiled back at him—the shy smile of a little girl anticipating a birthday gift or a holiday treat. "Here. You'll want these." She handed him two forks.

He found Ayla on the strand, her back to the boulevard and the lively cafés that lined it. It seemed to Bravo, dodging the slow-moving traffic, cake in one hand, forks in the other, that she was turning her back on all of Istanbul, her old life, and was looking out across the strait, dreaming of her new life in the Western hurly-burly of London.

She was leaning on a railing, smoke trailing out of the corner of her partly open lips. Between two fingers was a cigarette, hand-rolled in black licorice paper. In a revelatory moment he understood the complexity of her scents and, thus, a layer of her personality.

She made no move, voiced no indignation, when he came up beside her, as if her indifference to him was complete. Nevertheless, she took the fork he offered her. When he set the plate on the railing, balancing it with one hand, she dropped the remains of her cigarette, ground it out beneath the pointed toe of her expensive shoe. He allowed her the first bite, then dug the tines of his own fork into the cake.

"What is it about *pudingli* pasta you like so much?" she asked. "The cream biscuits or the filling?"

"What I like most about it is that, unlike most Turkish desserts, it's not so achingly sweet."

"I have a terrific sweet tooth. The sweeter the better," Ayla said, dipping her fork in for another bite, a larger one this time.

"Another one like that," Bravo observed, "and there won't be much left for me."

Ayla grunted, stared out across the water at the lights sema-phoring their mysterious messages. She chewed meditatively, then swallowed. "Mom doesn't like me to smoke in the flat. In fact, she doesn't like that I smoke, period."

"Do you like it?" Bravo asked. "Or do you do it to piss her off?"

A mischievous smile lifted a corner of Ayla's mouth.

Bravo was aware of an almost magnetic component to her extraordinary beauty. What uncanny intuition had led Dilara to invite him tonight when her daughter was visiting?

But that smile proved fugitive, vanishing into the glittering city-dark like a twist of candy wrapper.

"Don't let me infringe on your enjoyment."

"Too late."

She dug another black-wrapped cigarette from a gold case, snapped it shut, and was about to light it when Bravo took the lighter from her and flicked on the flame. Their eyes met in the instant before she took her first inhalation.

"I dislike people taking things from me."

She held out her hand, but he held on to the lighter. Their gazes locked, and he said, "Is there anything about me you do like?"

"Off the top of my head, I can't think of anything." She took the lighter from him, stowed it away in a pocket of her leather jacket.

"It seems we've had enough of each other."

When she made no reply, he took the forks and the now empty plate and turned to go.

"Wait," she said.

He turned back, his expression neutral. He found he was fiercely interested in what was going on beneath her skin. He had not taken anything personally—neither her icy demeanor nor her inflammatory words—and he could not quite make out why. Was it simply because she was Omar and Dilara's daughter? Was that enough?

She smoked some, the aromatic smoke drifting out of her flared nostrils. She looked conflicted, as if she had been holding at bay two or three mutually exclusive thoughts and was now unsure which to voice. "I came all the way from London," she said at length.

"Not such a great distance, these days."

"The distance I'm referring to can't be measured in miles or kilometers."

"Back to the homeland."

"But not for long." She turned away from him, put her elbows on the railing as she leaned in, almost as if she might take a perfect dive into the water. Bravo imagined everything she did would be perfect—or nearly so. This much he had gleaned from her. It was all or nothing. Ayla's world had no room in it for shades of gray, which was a shame, he thought, because sooner or later she was due for a very rude awakening.

"What is it you want from me?" he said to her back.

She turned around, her elbows on the railing still. "You've got it back asswards," she said.

He shook his head.

"About what my father said to you."

"Your father has said many things to me."

"Not tonight, he hasn't," Ayla said, taking another long drag, hissing the smoke out through her nostrils. Now she just looked angry. Oddly, this only increased her beauty, a diamond blazing in an onyx setting. "There was only one topic of importance. Your trip."

Bravo frowned. "How on earth would you know about that? It was never mentioned in your presence."

"Yesterday I was happily going about my life in Saint John's Wood. Then I got the call on my mobile."

"Come on. How would your mother know yesterday what was going to happen tomorrow?"

"Have you met my mother?" Ayla eyed him. "My father told you about her vision."

Bravo felt blindsided. "She had her vision yesterday?"

"She called me straightaway."

Bravo shook his head. "But why would she call you? I assumed you were here on a family visit."

Ayla took another deep drag. "You're still not getting it."

"Enlighten me then, by all means."

"My mother summoned me." Smoke swirling around her head made her look otherworldly. "I'm the one who's going to accompany you tomorrow."

NINE

"Recalled home?" Reichmann said. "Whatever for?"

"As yet we have no idea," Fireside said, stretching like a cat. "The Tusiks, as you well know, are masters at keeping secrets."

Reichmann stood, hands clasped behind his back, staring out the window. "Braverman Shaw has been using them for some time now. I need to know what he's up to."

"Frankly, I'm surprised Antonio hasn't found out."

Outside the castle perched on Maltese rock, the restless sea, blacker than the night, pulled and sucked against the massive rocks at the cliff's base. Far out, a string of fairy lights moved left to right, signaling the passage of a cruise ship.

"About Ayla," Reichmann murmured.

"We have a confirmed sighting. She's in Istanbul, on leave from the firm."

"For how long?"

"Only her mother knows."

Reichmann gave an involuntary shudder at the thought of Dilara Tusik. He'd had his eye on the Tusiks from the moment he had ascended to the Circle Council, another of his predecessor's oversights. As Muslims the Tusiks were, of course, enemies of the Holy See, but over and above such a mundane matter, the Tusiks were a special case. Omar was as dangerous a busybody as Reichmann had come across. He was always sniffing around the dark corners of Istanbul where Reichmann's agents lurked. If anything, Dilara was more dangerous. She had traveled to

Lebanon, had ties there among the rising tide of jihadist rebels who were giving the entire Western world nightmares.

"But why are you asking me when you have a perfectly fine agent embedded in Braverman's inner circle?" Fireside said.

"Bazan is working on the disquieting occurrence of Maura Kite showing up on Shaw's doorstep."

"Disquieting?"

Reichmann's left hand twitched. "You never liked Bazan."

Fireside shrugged. "He's not one of my people. I didn't recruit him; I don't control him; I don't trust him."

"You question my trust in him?"

"Not at all," Fireside said, eyes wide open. "I simply question his efficacy, since my people are providing more intel on the Istanbul situation than he is."

Reichmann thought about this for some time. "Valentin was working for us, Collum. What is his wife doing in the enemy camp?" He faced his lieutenant directly. "On your way to Tannourine I want you to make a stop in Istanbul. Take a larger than normal cadre. I want a full assessment of the current state of affairs, and I want you to take action."

"What form of action?"

"I want Maura Kite rescued from the Gnostic Observatines and brought back here."

"Done. And?"

"The situation has become unexpectedly fluid. There may be more for you to do in Istanbul. That done, you will continue on to Lebanon as discussed."

As he walked away, Fireside allowed himself a small, grim smile of satisfaction.

TEN

Now Bravo understood Ayla's iciness, her contempt, her barely suppressed anger. She had allowed herself to be drawn back to the East, to Istanbul, from a job and a city she clearly loved, from the freedom she cherished. Bravo could not work out why Dilara had interfered in her daughter's life, and so felt compelled to ask her, knowing full well that the chances were high that she would simply sneer at him.

Ayla surprised him, however, as she seemed to do at every turn.

As they had spoken—though "sparred" seemed more like it —the sky had turned overcast, lowering and thickening. Now it started to rain, and by unspoken mutual consent they left the strand, recrossing the boulevard, walking three blocks, though they might have taken shelter beneath any one of the gaily striped awnings of the cafés lining the sidewalk.

"We'll take our coffee here," Ayla said in a tone of voice Bravo imagined her using on some poor bastard trying and failing to make her happy on a first date.

"Sure, why not?" Bravo said, and then because he couldn't help himself, "Gives you more time to smoke."

Sure enough, she had a cigarette out by the time they were seated at a small, round table with side-by-side chairs facing the now wet strand. The water had grown choppy with the wind accompanying the incoming rain squall. Boats rocked in their slips: rigging slapped rhythmically against masts. The awnings had been hastily extended. At their edge, pedestrians clustered, huddling, their massed bodies obscuring the view but providing a windbreak.

While Bravo ordered, Ayla put her cigarette between her lips, took out her lighter. But then a curious thing happened. She did not fire it, instead putting it and the cigarette away. "You know, my dad used to take me here when I was little. He loved to let me sip his coffee, and I loved it, too. We never told Mama; it was our little secret."

Bravo, interpreting this as the first sign of a thaw, no matter how temporary, chose this moment to ask her why she had heeded her mother's call. "It seems your family is full of secrets."

She shrugged. "Whose isn't?"

"I just want to reassure you." The coffees were set before them, steaming and headily fragrant. "You've made it abundantly clear to me that you don't want to be here and that you resent her wanting you to come with me tomorrow. Well, you can relax; it's not happening."

Her mouth twitched fetchingly, and he felt again that magnetism, disconcerting and also dislocating. "You'll take that up with my mother," she said, stirring the tiniest bit of sugar into her coffee. "I don't envy you that."

"Ah, I see," he said. "You can't give Dilara a hard time so you're taking it out on me."

She held her spoon suspended, and for the briefest moment he wondered whether she was going to hurl it at him. Her face certainly had that look. Instead, she put the spoon down and, surprising him once again, said, "Perhaps you're right." Then, more introspectively: "Probably you are."

He felt the ground slipping away under him, as if the cement beneath him had turned to mud. In trying to right himself, he made a mistake. He misinterpreted her admission as a further thawing and jumped at it. "I can't understand why you would drop everything the instant your mother called."

"Before the dawn arrives you'll be taking that up with my mother."

"It won't matter," Bravo said. "First, where I'm going is too dangerous for you."

"Because I'm a woman."

"Because you have no experience with jihadists, with whom I most certainly will have to deal."

"And because you know me so well." Her contempt was again palpable. "I'll bet you think I'm a pampered brat who always got what she wanted, was sent to the best schools money can buy, and now makes a fortune in London."

Bravo was appalled that she so accurately summed up precisely what he had been thinking. Ashamed, as well, that he had so pigeonholed her. But still he had to press on. "Second, I can't imagine why your mother would put you in harm's way."

"First," Ayla said, "I know more about the Lebanese jihadists than you do."

Shock was inadequate for what Bravo felt. "How did you know—?"

"And, second," she pressed on, "without me beside you, you're never coming back."

ELEVEN

"In the years before I had Ayla and for the first eleven years afterward, I was devout, my faith unshaken." Dilara poured arak into a *barik* half-filled with water. From the wicker basket she had brought up to the roof she withdrew an ice-filled glass. When she poured the liquid into the glass it turned milky, causing the oil of anise to form an emulsion that gave arak its distinctive flavor. She pushed the glass across the small folding table to Bravo.

When he and Ayla had returned to the apartment he had noted the barely perceptible nod daughter had given mother. Dilara, already prepared, had taken up the wicker basket. He saw now how all of the interactions, from Omar's hammam invitation to his discussion at their apartment, had been planned in the most meticulous fashion. The one thing he couldn't quite make out was whether Ayla's anger had been an act, as well. If so, he thought, she was in the wrong profession. She should be in Hollywood or on Broadway. In any event, as he accepted Dilara's invitation to join her on the building's roof it became clear to him that she was the mastermind of this trap he now found himself in.

In a corner of the roof, what appeared to be a Bedouin tent had been set up. Picking their way through the rain, they entered the shelter of the tent, where a table and two chairs had been placed in the center. A hanging incised brass lamp threw light across the table like a scattering of gold stars.

"Then I took Ayla on a trip to Lebanon," Dilara said now. "There were things we witnessed there I prayed would never come to light again."

Now she did the most astonishing thing. From the wicker basket, she drew out a second ice-filled glass, poured in the arak, and fixed the drink. Then she lifted the glass and, as Bravo did the same, she clinked the rim against his. "To the success of your trip to Tannourine," she said. "And we shall never speak of this to Omar."

They drank, the sharp anise scent rushing up Bravo's nostrils as well as over the back of his throat. Dilara was staring into the depths of her arak. Deep booms of thunder echoed off the water. "The moment you and Omar became friends I had an intimation this day would come." Her gaze shifted to Bravo. "Oh, I don't blame you, not in the least. What you have been doing . . . what you plan to do now . . . Well, no one else has a prayer of surviving."

Bravo felt a cold chill run down his spine, invading the very marrow of his bones. The rain battered the tent as if giant fists were trying to whip it away, but it was firmly anchored, the sides lashed down tight. A tent like this was meant to withstand desert sandstorms; this downpour was as nothing.

"You have every right to look at me that way, Bravo." As thunder rolled again like an instrument in an atonal orchestra, Dilara pushed her glass away. It was clear that she did not care for arak—probably any liquor—that her pour-and-sip ceremony, though important, was wholly symbolic. And she was correct. What she had done had far more impact than anything she could have said. "I have not been truthful with you. I make no excuse; I've learned never to do that. But I will say that I thought it necessary—I still do."

"Now I have to interrupt you to ask why."

"Enemies, Bravo. Specifically, the Knights of Saint Clement."

Bravo turned his glass around and around on the table but didn't drink the arak. The first sip was ceremonial for him, as well. "I have to say that I'm surprised at how much you know about me, what I do, and who my enemies are. Omar doesn't know any of this, or, at least, only in the vaguest of terms."

"That must never change," Dilara said with finality. "What Omar doesn't know can't hurt him."

"I understand perfectly. Still, I can't help but say I wish the same for you—and Ayla."

Dilara waved a hand. "Oh, I chose a different path a long time ago. When I was in Lebanon. As for Ayla—well, she and I were both witnesses. Our fates are now bound inextricably to what we saw years ago in Tannourine."

"So this is why you drew me up here, inside this tent, in the storm."

"Your enemies—even if they should know you're here—will not be able to overhear what will now be said."

"About what happened in Tannourine?"

Dilara nodded. "In Tannourine," she said now, "Ayla and I were witness."

Bravo hunched his shoulders forward as he leaned onto the table. "Witness to what?"

"Not to what." Dilara's dark eyes glittered in the propane glow. "Now listen closely, Bravo. It was raining that night, too. Ayla loves rain, thunder even more. In those days, nearly twenty years ago, Lebanon was an entirely different country; the dogs of war had not yet picked it apart, feasting on its bones."

In the next instant, the world was turned upside down.

TWELVE

The entire building shook, trembling like a leaf in the wind, throwing them off their chairs. Entangled in the tent's material, they heard the barely muffled percussion, a pressure in their heads, straining their eardrums.

Gaining the rain-swept rooftop, they saw flames gouting out of blown-out windows.

"Our apartment!" Dilara screamed.

Down below, the patrons of the cafés were on their feet, scrambling, screaming, frantically running, a few shouting into mobile phones as they dodged flaming debris that would doubtless have set the line of awnings on fire had it not been for the storm.

Bravo and Dilara raced down the fire stairs. The stairwell had already turned hazy with drifting smoke. The heat from their floor made it impossible to get much past the landing. Still, Bravo was obliged to prevent Dilara from running headlong into the burning wreck of the apartment. She was shaking, tears streaming down her cheeks as she screamed, "Omar! Ayla! My loves! My loves!"

Bravo wrapped his rain-soaked jacket over his head, sprinted down the corridor, and, leaping over the blown-out front door, burst into the apartment. The place was an inferno. He could see the epicenter of the blast and, at once, his mind connected it with a hand-thrown explosive device—some sort of grenade. He spotted Omar lying facedown on the carpet, his clothes incinerated, his skin burned away, leaving a red-black pulpy mass. There was no sign of Ayla in the living room, and it was impossible to see into the kitchen or the bedrooms. He rushed toward Omar in an attempt to recover the body, but a beam crashed down, spewing flames and sparks in a wide arc. Still, he moved on, intending to leap over the beam, but the fire was so intense his jacket began to hiss and heat up as the moisture evaporated. Now flames danced across its drying surface. He was able to ditch it and get out of the apartment just in time.

Retreating down the hall, he arrived back at the stairwell, coughing, his lungs clogged, his throat raw and burning.

Dilara's eyes were opened wide and staring, her face a mask of anxiety and grief. "Omar? Ayla?"

"The fire is spreading; it's out of control," Bravo said. "We have to get out of here now."

Taking her hand, he tried to guide her down the stairs, but she resisted. "My family! I can't leave them—"

"Omar is gone. I tried to bring his body out but—"

"And Ayla? Tell me. What of my daughter?"

"I didn't see her." A horrendous cracking came from over their heads. The ceiling fractured and began to sag ominously. "Please, Dilara! Now!"

Even she, in her grief-stricken state, could feel the convulsions of the building, and at last she allowed Bravo to lead her down the stairs moments before the hallway ceiling caved in with a splintering groan.

At almost the same instant Bravo felt an arterial spray spatter the back of his neck. Dilara pitched into his arms, blood overflowing her wide-open mouth. The back of her head was nearly gone. Bravo looked up, saw an impossibly thin man on the stairs take aim at him. With his tombstone face and black, depthless eyes he seemed to fit the description of the man who had visited Maura Kite. A second bullet nearly took Bravo's ear off as he swung around. Letting go of Dilara's corpse, he vaulted onto the banister, then leapt, catching the gunman as he was about to fire for a third time.

With almost superhuman strength, the man slammed Bravo against the wall, stunning him. He stepped over him. Approaching Dilara, he stuck his gun in his belt, grabbed a fistful of hair at the top of her head, and, drawing a *wakizashi,* a Japanese short sword with an incredibly sharp edge, swung once, expertly decapitating her. In the next instant Bravo was on him. They tangled as the building groaned, cracked, and split around them, shards of fire-licked wooden beams raining down on them. Though aware of the destruction of his surroundings, Bravo kept his full concentration on his foe. Bravo's immediate objective was to wrest the weapons from the assassin. Grabbing Tombstone's wrist, he slammed the bottom of it with his knee. At the same time, he absorbed a blow to his midsection. A vicious chop to his kidneys almost made him lose his grip, but he swallowed the pain, then let it flow out of him as the training his father had put him through came to the fore, taking control of his mind and body.

Thought, pain, action, and reaction were now replaced by instinct. Bravo slammed Tombstone's wrist down on the banister —once, twice—until the fingers uncurled. The *wakizashi* slipped through nerveless fingers, dropping down the stairwell with a raucous clatter. At almost the same instant Bravo whirled his antagonist around, drove him back against the wall so hard his head snapped back and forth on the stalk of his neck. He drove a knee, seeking Bravo's groin, but Bravo had maneuvered just enough so the strike landed on the meat of his thigh. He chopped down with the edge of his hand, felt a collarbone give way, but Tombstone's eyes gave no indication either of pain or of trauma. Instead, he slipped his ankle behind Bravo's in an attempt to sweep him off his feet. He almost managed it. Momentarily off-balance, Bravo staggered, the small of his back smacking against the banister, then went down on one knee. One hand swept the floor, keeping him from falling over.

Drawing his gun, Tombstone hauled Bravo to his feet, bent him back over the rail. His jaws opened wide, his teeth gnashed, as he extended the muzzle of the gun toward Bravo. Bravo jammed the wooden shard he'd picked up off the floor into the gaping mouth. Tombstone tried to hold on but nevertheless loosed his grip. Bravo jammed a thumb deep into his left eye, twisting it. Tombstone made a sound somewhere between a shout and a moan. He turned, heading down the stairwell, which was now filling with smoke.

He crashed onto the next landing down, almost tripped over Dilara's corpse as he staggered out into the floor of her apartment. The hill of debris from the collapsed ceiling slowed him somewhat. Bravo caught up with him. He needed him alive, needed to know who he was, who sent him, and why. He lunged for Tombstone, grabbed his shirt, but with a violent twist Tombstone broke free.

Bravo saw him leap over the last of the debris, heading directly for the doorway to the Tusiks' apartment, which was by now rimmed in flames. He made one last attempt to run him down but was, once again, defeated by the intensity of the heat. However, Tombstone, unconcerned or perhaps driven mad by the loss of his eye, sprinted directly into the fire. Almost at once his clothes burst into flame.

Bravo called to him, but his voice was drowned out by the roaring of the fire and the building in its death throes. Tombstone turned. He stared at Bravo with his one good eye, and, curiously and chillingly, a smile broke out on his face. His shirt was now ash, fluttering off him in strips. Just before he was completely engulfed in flame, Bravo caught a glimpse of his bare chest; it had been marked by the sigil of the Unholy Trinity: a triangle inside a circle inside a square.

Then the entire floor dissolved into chaos and it was all Bravo could do to jump into the stairwell. He bent to Dilara, but she was headless now, no hope of carrying her out. Flames shot into the landing, forcing him to rear back. Then he was running down the stairs as fast as he could, trying to outrun the fire.

THIRTEEN

Rain and alarms, rain and shouts, and sirens piercing the night. Omar and Dilara's building was now completely surrounded by fire trucks, police vans, even a number of armored vehicles, a military presence, indicating the level of anxiety the explosion and fire had caused even the highest levels of the Powers That Be.

Bravo had emerged from the building just as the vehicles were arriving. He easily insinuated himself into the growing crowd of people who had gathered to watch the police, firemen, and emergency medical personnel arriving. Residents were staggering out of the burning building or sitting on the curb, head in their hands, only to be snatched up by helpful neighbors. Bravo, dazed and in shock, had tried everything under his power to rescue his friends, and there was a terrible pain inside him knowing that there was nothing more he could do for them. Nevertheless, he spent some moments comforting other victims, then stood aside to let the professionals do their work. He must have looked a fright, and his incessant coughing evidently caused a stir, because people near him looked startled. One of them asked if he was all right and tried to guide him to an open ambulance, but he balked, broke away, melted into the crowd. Still, he stayed close, watching carefully as more people were ushered out of the building either on their own two legs or on stretchers. He strained to see all the faces but could not find Ayla among the rescued. Wondering if perhaps she had already been taken away and he had missed her, he called the nearest hospital, asking for the ER. He described Ayla in detail and was assured that no patient fitting her description had been admitted that evening.

He made his way to the line of cafés overlooking the water, picking his way through the throngs for three blocks, retracing the route he and Ayla had taken earlier in the evening. There were two possibilities: either she was lying dead in her parents' apartment, a victim of the attack, or she had somehow made it out before he had. If it was the latter, where would she go? He did not have her mobile number, did not even know whether it, tied to a British telecom, was equipped to work here. He could spend the next several hours scouring the neighborhood, hoping to find her—a fool's errand if ever there was one—or he could go to the café where her father had taken her as a child, where she felt safe.

He hurried into the café. The place was all but deserted; Ayla wasn't there. He waited several moments, staring out at the people hurrying past, willing her to show up. Five minutes later a young woman entered, but it wasn't Ayla. Their eyes met and he saw her wince at the sight of him. Turning abruptly away, she sat at a table. As she was ordering coffee, he went past her to the men's room.

No wonder the young woman had winced. He scarcely recognized his reflection in the mirror. He spent the next ten minutes scrubbing ash, blood, brains, and debris off his face and clothes, all the while trying not to think what they were from. He sucked up mouthfuls of water, spit out as much of the smoke's choking residue as he could. His throat felt raw. He longed for a triple espresso, but he wondered if there was anyone left in the kitchen to serve it to him. He was trying not to think of Ayla, lying in the bathroom or bedroom, overcome by smoke, her body being consumed by the fire.

He looked in the mirror again and this time saw not himself, but his father. Dexter Shaw had been a man of considered thought, not action. He had, in fact, the mind of a chess grand master. Almost as soon as his son had been born he had worked out his future. The moment Bravo turned six, he had taken him by the hand and led him through the West Village, to a warehouse fronting the West Side Highway and, beyond, the Hudson River. In those days the area had yet to be beautified. There was no river walk, no parks or playgrounds, no manicured picnic areas or benches from which to watch the twilight slowly descend over lower Manhattan. There were only broken-down piers and the stubs of wooden pilings from the island's illustrious waterfront past, now rotting like an old man's teeth.

The door through which Dexter ushered his son was next to a late-night bar and club with the discreet sign THE WILD WILD WEST. When Dexter saw his son curiously regarding the sign, he had said, "Come on along, Son. We'll be late."

The enormous third floor was light and airy. The west-facing wall was almost all industrial windows. Wide mats lay on one part of the gleaming wooden floor, ropes thick as Bravo's wrist hanging from the ceiling, along with sets of metal rings. They were met by a short Asian man of indeterminate age named Todao, with skin like parchment and black eyes that, it seemed to the young Bravo, never stopped assessing his surroundings and those in it. Todao was as round as a rubber ball. He threw Bravo to the ground with such alacrity Bravo never saw him even move. The sensei stood over Bravo, grinning, held out his hand, helped Bravo to his feet. At once, Todao knocked him down again. Thus began Bravo's first lesson in the basics of physical warfare. Later he had been taken into the adjacent room, which was a completely silenced firing range, where he learned expertise in every form of bullet-spewing weapon.

The physical part of his training was only half of what his father had in store for him. Todao, as it turned out, was more than just a master martial artist: he was a scholar, as well, with a prodigious memory and an even more prodigious library of reference books on religious philosophy, archeology, Chinese,

Phoenician, Greek, Egyptian, and medieval medicine, myths, shamans, and spells, an entire panoply of the wisdom of ancient civilizations.

Bravo's mother had known none of this, of course. If she had, she would have tried to put a stop to it. She didn't understand, as Dexter had, the nature of the looking-glass war he was embroiled in. Or perhaps, Bravo suspected, years later, she was aware of much of what Dexter had planned for Bravo but chose not to think about it because it was far too terrifying. During his truncated lifetime, Dexter fought many battles against the Knights of Saint Clement, but he understood that it was the war that counted. And this war was changing not only its face but also its substance. Changes he was preparing his son to face after he was gone.

Bravo was convinced that his father had had intimations of his untimely death. Now, as Bravo looked into the mirror he stared beyond his smudged and dripping face, to the moments after the bomb had destroyed their Village town house. He had dragged Emma from the ruined parlor, but his father's corpse had stubbornly refused to be moved. He was lying on the ruined Isfahan carpet, to which he was firmly stuck. The Persian fibers had embedded themselves in the flesh of his back, as if enacting retribution against the Infidel.

Bravo blinked heavily, and his own face reappeared in the mirror. Bending down to the sink, he scrubbed the remaining soot off his face, but there wasn't much he could do about his clothes.

As he turned to leave, his mobile buzzed. Emma. *Oh Lord, she must be frantic.* Clearly, he wasn't thinking logically. He should have called her first thing when he got out of the building.

"Bravo, I heard the breaking news stories on local television. Are you all right?"

"I'm fine," he said, "but Omar and Dilara are dead."

"Dear God! What happened? The newscasters keep repeating that the explosion and fire was caused by a gas leak, but I don't know whether to believe them. Terrorism is number one on the list, as it would be in any major city in the world, when something like this happens. No metropolitan area is safe anymore; everyone knows that. But no one's prepared for an incident happening in their own backyard. Especially here in Istanbul, since the president has been doing his best to kowtow to the country's conservative Islamics. If you're with them, the theory goes, you're safe."

"It wasn't a gas leak," Bravo said.

"So much for that."

His adrenaline was still running him on overdrive. Fine, in action, but when you needed to think it could make you miss important details. *Concentrate!* he admonished himself. "The Tusiks were targeted."

"By the Knights."

"Possibly, but I'm not so sure."

"What do you mean?"

He told her about the eerie gunman, how he had run into the fire, about his strange smile, and about the meaning of the sigil on his chest.

"My God, that's the same sigil carved into the back of the gold crucifix Maura gave me," she said. "She said it had been a present to Val, but she'd never seen the sigil before. I haven't had time to research it." Bravo's sister did all his research, using her vast network of contacts both inside the Gnostic Observatines and in the outside world. She knew virtually everyone in their fields of religion, archeology, mysticism, and parapsychology, and everyone she came in contact with loved her.

"Don't bother," Bravo said. "It's the sigil of the Unholy Trinity." He told her what Fra Leoni had related.

"He claims it relates to Lucifer." She shook her head. "Well, he's a monk, after all. More deeply religious than we could ever be. I'll take that story with an entire pound of salt."

"I thought the same thing," Bravo said, "until I encountered Tombstone. Emma, I swear to you he was not of this world."

"Bravo—"

"Listen, Sis. We're under attack; that's without question. And if not from the Knights, then from some other group."

"A group we know nothing about."

"And if Fra Leoni is correct, then it's the worst-case scenario." Bravo had a brief coughing fit, still trying to clear his lungs as well as his head.

"Are you sure you're okay, big brother?"

"I'm fine, Sis. But I want you and Fra Leoni out of there. Take everyone with you. Get Antonio to keep a close eye on Valentin's widow. If the Knights did have anything to do with this, they may very well know that Maura is here."

"Where are you—?"

"No time now. Move it, Em!"

He had just enough time to close the connection when whatever he had been trying to keep down since he had Dilara's brains spattered all over him roared up. He bent over the sink vomiting, then retched bile when nothing of her delicious dinner was left. White and shaken, he ran the water, clearing out the sink, then rinsing his mouth over and over. He rested his forehead on his crossed forearms, willing himself to breathe slowly and deeply. But images of Omar and Dilara, like a sight from the interior of an abattoir, kept flaring in his mind.

Feeling a semblance of himself, he left the men's room, went down the short corridor and into the café. The bedlam on the sidewalk had scarcely abated, but in here there was still only one customer: the young woman, shoulders hunched over, head on folded forearms as his had been moments earlier. Thick black hair covered her head and neck, spread out over the shoulders. The woman he had seen before had had cropped hair.

He thought he recognized that . . . *Could it be?*

"Ayla?" he said breathlessly. "Ayla! You're alive!"

Her head came up, her eyes enlarged by tears, her mascara darkening the skin under her eyes. She looked as if she had been struck by a speeding train, which, emotionally speaking, wasn't so far from the truth.

He was about to sit down beside her when a pair of police officers passed by, and he was reminded of what was happening outside and the unwanted questions it might lead to if he was found here. "Your parents were targets," he said as she got to her feet. "We have to get away from this area. It's become a red zone."

"A what?"

"The danger is too great. Our enemies—"

"*Your* enemies, Bravo. My father was in the apartment when it exploded. And my mother?"

"She was with me, on the roof." He tugged at her hand. "Ayla, please come with me."

"Where is my mother?" She was rageful, and this transformation actually made her more beautiful. "What's happened to her? You're here and she's—"

"Dead, Ayla."

She struck him then, a hard blow with her balled fist. He took it, allowed her to expend herself, knowing even through his own multi-layered trauma that it was the right thing to do.

"Dead," she said breathlessly. "Dead dead dead." It was like a chant, an epithet rather than a prayer. "Dead dead dead." She was weeping again, bitter tears as much of rage as of grief. "And who's to blame? You, with your weird world, your weird enemies. We were fine until you—"

"We both know that's not true. Ayla, your mother told me about the trip to Lebanon."

"How much did she tell you?" Her tone was sharp, defiant, but there was also an edge of fear.

"She was only getting started when the explosion—"

"Oh, no. No, no, no." Ayla had recoiled away from him. "You're not going to get the story out of me. Keep away from me. You've destroyed their lives; I'll be damned if I'll let you destroy mine."

There were the cops again. It was only a matter of time before she and Bravo were noticed, and then the questioning would begin. Questioning he could not afford to get embroiled in. "If we leave now there's still a chance—"

Both her expression and her voice had turned steely with resolve. She had that in common with her mother. "I'm not going anywhere with you."

One of the cops had spotted them out of the corner of his eye, and as the police turned into the café Ayla at last noticed them. Bravo saw the spark of alarm in her eyes. Yet before it blossomed into fear he snaked his arms around her, pulled her close. "Hold me," he whispered just before he plastered his mouth against hers.

At first she resisted; then she put her all into it, her hot mouth open, her tongue questing. The kiss was as confusing as it was erotic. Nothing in either her words or her demeanor had given any hint of this twining of both tongues and bodies.

But when, moments later, the cops had moved on, she pushed him away, wiped her mouth with the back of her hand, and shot him a poisonous glare.

"Don't do that again," she whispered. "Never ever."

FOURTEEN

The beautiful fifty-seven-foot wood *gulet*, a traditional Turkish two-masted motor sailer with four sails, moved at a slow but steady pace, heading more or less away from the mainland, keeping its distance from the more heavily trafficked sea-lanes. The *gulet* was one of many used by the six or seven so-called lines that plied the waters from Bodrum to Marmaris, Gobek, and Istanbul.

Tonight, however, this particular *gulet,* the *Ajax,* was not in the business of the tourist trade. Being privately owned by members of the Gnostic Observatines, it was at Bravo's disposal whenever he wished or needed it. Now was such a time.

Four people sat on a sofa beneath the sun awning on the *Ajax'*s rear deck. The gleaming teak shimmered in the cool bluish moonlight. Turkish coffee had been prepared, poured from a silver pitcher into tiny porcelain cups. Plenty of sugar had been stirred into the sluggish liquid potent enough to cause heart palpitations in a human or resuscitate an elephant.

Bravo, along with Ayla, Emma, and Fra Leoni, sipped their coffee. The mood was somber, though hardly meditative. Following Bravo's orders, Antonio Bazan had taken Maura Kite to the safe house on the other side of the city. With Ayla's assistance, Bravo had already had Emma direct two Gnostic Observatines to stand guard over Dilara's sister and brother-in-law and their family.

"I've compiled enough firsthand evidence," Bravo said, "to

assure myself that we're dealing with an enemy other than the Knights of Saint Clement." For the benefit of Ayla and Fra Leoni, he reiterated his encounter with Tombstone, the man who had shot Dilara, possibly had bombed the Tusiks' apartment, before immolating himself.

"He sounds like the same man who came to see Maura Kite," Emma added. "The one who returned the strange crucifix to her."

"The strange crucifix?" This seemed to bring Ayla out of the semi-trance she had appeared to be in ever since she and Bravo had boarded the *gulet*. "What do you mean?"

"There's an engraving on the back. It's a strange symbol," Emma said. "I started to research it, but then everything started happening so fast—"

Bravo held up a hand. "Do you have it?"

Emma said nothing, neither did she move. Her mind was far away from Istanbul, lost in the dreadful aftermath of the explosion that had ripped apart her family's Greenwich Village townhome. Her father, Dexter, dead, her own eyesight gone. Her life as she'd known it snatched from her in the instant the bomb the Knights of Saint Clement had set was ignited. They had meant to kill Dexter; there could be no doubt of that. She was merely collateral damage. Half-dazed, half-maddened, she had crawled around on her hands and knees, blood runneled everywhere, until she had located her father. She was cradling his head when Bravo burst in, finding them, saving her.

"Emma?"

"Yes." She cleared her throat.

"Do you have the crucifix?"

Firmly relocated in the present, she dug it out of a pocket, held it out for her brother to take.

Bravo rose and, moving out from beneath the awning, held it up into the moonlight.

"Maura claimed to have given the crucifix to her husband on his last birthday," Emma said. "And yet she insisted she had no knowledge of the engraved symbol."

"Perhaps," Bravo said, "it was engraved afterward."

"By Valentin?" Ayla asked.

Emma shook her head. "Bravo, look at the engraving more closely."

Bravo drew out a penlight, played the narrow beam across the back of the crucifix. "The engraving is new," he said almost to himself.

"Tell us how new?" Emma asked.

"The cuts are still quite sharp. A tiny shaving is lodged in the bottom crevasse of the triangle." Bravo looked up. "I'd estimate less than a week old."

"Then Valentin couldn't have ordered it done," Emma said. "A week ago he was already in the mountains of Lebanon."

Ayla looked from one to the other. "What does this mean?"

"A triangle inside a circle inside a square," Bravo said. "It's the sigil of the Unholy Trinity, three objects that were cast out by God during Lucifer's fall."

"But this triangle is upside-down," Ayla pointed out.

"Precisely," Emma interjected. "Bravo, turn the crucifix upside down."

Bravo did as she directed. The holy symbol of Christ's death was now in the position historically preferred by Satanists.

"What d'you see?"

"The triangle is now right side up."

Istanbul was in chaos. Fireside found streets clogged, avenues blocked off, squares occupied by military vehicles. And everywhere the military vehicle that had been waiting for him at the airport crawled the city was teeming with soldiers in full riot gear. Fearful onlookers crowded the sidewalks, open-air cafés, and restaurants, and yet there were vast pockets of awful silence that was so unnatural it made the hair on his forearms stir.

He and his men had been met at the private jet area of the airport by Wul, Captain Balik's liaison officer, who had guided the cadre through Immigration as best he could. Even with his assistance, there was a delay because of the extraordinary lockdown measures the Turkish government had instituted following the incident at the Tusiks' building. Local news media, commandeering all the flat-screens at the airport, were reporting a gas leak and explosion.

"Except it wasn't a gas leak," Wul informed Fireside. "An apartment in the building was deliberately firebombed."

The instant Fireside heard that the apartment in question belonged to the Tusiks, he phoned Reichmann to update him. "Find out what happened and why," Fireside's boss had told him tersely. "Everything seems to be falling apart."

"Where is Captain Balik?" Fireside asked Wul as soon as he was off the line.

"At the site."

Accordingly, Fireside ordered his men to their hotel, while he instructed Wul to bring him to Balik.

The farther they moved into the heart of the city the better Fireside understood the extraordinary security precautions at the airport. The driver had his radio turned on. News reports of an explosion, of casualties—the dead and the maimed—without attribution streamed by like ghostly figures lost in a haze of verbiage and doublespeak—sound and fury signifying nothing. The news readers kept insisting the cause was a faulty gas line, but looking out the windows at the colossal military presence gave the lie to the official story.

At length, they reached the vicinity of the explosion. But by then the vehicle was so mired in stalled traffic they were obliged to get out. The air was so laden with ash, smoke, and diesel particulates Fireside could not stop coughing.

Following Wul, he wormed his way through the tightly packed crowd until they came up against a police cordon that might as well have been a brick wall. Showing his credentials, Wul ushered him into the area immediately surrounding the building.

It took them several minutes to locate Captain Balik amid the chaos he was trying to control. Policemen were swarming everywhere, moving in and out between the pulled-up fire trucks and army and police vehicles. All the ambulances had long since evacuated the injured and the dead.

At length, Captain Balik came into view. He was short and thin, his back ramrod straight. He was dark-skinned, with a long, saturnine face and hungry eyes. His lips were parted in a combination of stress and effort. He turned as Wul brought Fireside up. Balik nodded curtly, repeated Wul's briefing, though in slightly more detail: that ground zero for the explosion and fire was, indeed, the apartment of Omar and Dilara Tusik; Mr. Tusik had been killed in the initial explosion; the badly burned body of his wife, Dilara Tusik, had been found in the stairwell, presumably trying to escape. All at once, the flow of information stopped, replaced by a smug expression.

Fireside, who had been forewarned, knew the sonofabitch was holding out for more money. He gave it to him; it wasn't his, anyway. As it turned out, what he received was more than worth it. Preliminary forensics raised the possibility that the fire had been the result of a "propulsive incendiary weapon." In addition, a third body had been discovered just inside the blown-out doorway to the Tusiks' apartment. This was the item that interested Fireside most. For one thing, it wasn't the Tusiks' daughter. For another, and much more to the point, the male was "exceedingly strange."

"Strange in what way?"

Captain Balik shook his head. "Impossible to describe." Shouts and murmurs were coming from his men. His attention began to wander; he was needed elsewhere.

Fireside knew his window of opportunity was rapidly closing. "I need to see this strangeness for myself."

Balik was about to dismiss him when he received another massive fistful of banknotes. He counted them carefully, clearly keeping a running balance in his head. Then he glanced up at

Fireside, a sneer on his face. *This is my territory,* the expression said. *You play by my rules or not at all.*

"One hour," Balik said. "Remain in place."

Then, turning his back, he strode off into the smoke- and cinder-choked building.

FIFTEEN

"We've taken a tremendous loss," Bravo said. "Omar and Dilara were friends to us all."

"Good friends," Emma said, biting her lip.

"Yes." Bravo nodded. "Good friends. What's happened to them is a tragedy that's hurt us deeply, one we'll never forget. There will come a time for grieving and memorials. But if we stop to grieve now, if we do nothing but give in to our anguish, we're putting ourselves in grave danger. Someone's coming after us. We need to find out who and why. That's our first order of—"

He paused as Ayla got up abruptly and disappeared below-decks. His eyes locked with Fra Leoni's. The old man shrugged, shook his head. "What you said is right, of course. It makes perfect sense. Losing both parents at once . . . it's most difficult. We're all of us human beings, we all hurt in different ways, and it's often difficult to marshal resources in the face of unimaginable tragedy." His expression was solemn. "You have only to recall the reaction you and Emma had when your own father was killed by a bomb blast." He lowered his voice. "And speaking of your sister . . ." His eyes cut to Emma. She was hunched over, her face in her hands. Her shoulders shook spasmodically. "We can only keep our emotions in check for so long, Bravo," he whispered as Bravo passed him to sit next to Emma.

"Hey," Bravo said. The moment he put his arm across her shoulders, she turned into his embrace, her face pressed into his chest. "Hey, Sis. Come on."

Emma shook her head, but her sobbing had subsided. "He was such a great guy—funny and smart and interested."

"He was all that, Em. But is Omar the one you're grieving for?"

She made no response.

"Em, talk to me." He gave her shoulders a light squeeze. "Now's not the time for secrets."

Emma wrapped her arms around him, held him tightly, as he rocked her as she sobbed again in her grief and misery. After a time, she cried out in a hoarse voice, "You knew, didn't you? You knew from the jump!"

Bravo tipped her chin up. "About you and Val? Yes."

She stood apart from him. "Why didn't you say something?"

"It's your life, Em."

"Being with him always felt a little strange to me, but also, you know, transgressively exciting. I think because of who he was, a kind of double agent."

"He was also married."

"Our affair lasted five years, more or less."

"Then he couldn't have been happy with his wife," Bravo said levelly.

"He told me he wasn't. I never would have started up with him otherwise." She hesitated as a thought occurred to her. "Maybe I shouldn't have believed him."

"There's no way to know now," Bravo said gently. "Did you love him, Em?"

"I thought I did. Now I'm not so sure." Tears quivered in the corners of her eyes. "Do you hate me?"

"What? Of course not. Deep down you must know that."

"Do I?" She shook her head. "I always thought . . . After Dad was killed, after I lost my sight, I became tough as nails. I had to; I soldiered on. You needed me, and I needed me to be useful, to prove I wasn't . . . you know, an invalid." She gave a sharp, joyless laugh. "That I wasn't invalidated as a human being."

"Em—"

"No." She waved his reply away. "Let me finish. I need to say this." She took a shuddering breath. "But that wasn't enough for me. I hope you can understand this. You asked me before if I loved Val. I didn't, not really. But I *needed* him, in what I think now was a terrible, weak way. After this . . . Five years. I was screwing another woman's husband. Now I . . . I have to wonder what kind of person I really am. At night I lie awake, unable to sleep, wishing my sight back. I want that more than anything, Bravo; you have to know that. I want it back!" Her hands had clenched into fists, turning her fingertips white. "And knowing the one thing I want most I can never have is . . . I don't know . . . 'terrible' doesn't begin to convey how I feel inside. I don't feel whole. I realize I haven't felt whole since that dreadful day when I lost my sight. I think my affair with Val was a part of that, part of *needing* to be wanted, to be found attractive, to feel that I was . . . that I hadn't lost anything. . . . Now I think I was just being a selfish bitch. It's too much, Bravo. I don't know, I don't know . . ."

He wanted to say something, anything that would soothe her, but what could he tell her? Only platitudes and time-worn phrases that had lost their meaning. Still, he held her close again, felt the vibrations shudder through her body.

After a moment she broke away. She had always considered hugging, like crying, a sign of weakness, never more so than after she had lost her sight. But the recent tragedy had undone her natural reserve, her sense of feeling that an apartness was the only way to maintain her individuality, her essential Emmaness in a male-centric world.

"You think I'm only mourning Val, but that's not true. It's only now after he's gone that I realize how important Omar was to me," she continued, "how he treated me, as if I was sighted, as if there was nothing wrong with me. He used to take me shopping—did you know that?—on the way, he'd buy me little things, packets of fresh dates and pistachios or candied nuts, inconsequential but delicious. And he'd become excited by the sights we passed, describing the details in his excitement, including the history behind them, as if I were just another tourist. He never made me aware of my disability. He was so thoughtful. And that was wonderful, wonderful, but . . . now he and Val . . . it's all gone; whatever I had is gone."

She was weeping again. Bravo stroked her head, the back of her neck, wishing he could take away her pain, wishing he could give her back her sight. It occurred to him now that relocating from Manhattan to Istanbul hadn't been the best idea as far as she was concerned. They had been born and raised in New York; it was altogether familiar to her. Istanbul was another matter altogether, confusing to a sighted person; he could not imagine how baffling it must be to her. And there was another issue, pertaining directly to her gender. Day by day, Turkey was becoming less secular, more Muslim, a place where women were apt to be treated as second-class citizens, where she had no friends and very little prospect of making any. He made sure he took her out to dinner as often as he could, but hers was still a stifling regimen.

"I'm sorry, Sis," he said now, thinking he needed to make it up to her somehow. "I'm so sorry." He kissed the top of her head. "Maybe, after all this is over, we'll move back to New York."

"But why? Our work is here, at the crossroads of the old world and the new. You said so yourself."

He put a smile into his voice, so she would know. "It's possible I acted hastily. Anyway, let's hold it open as a possibility, okay?"

She nodded, slowly disengaged herself from him. "I'm okay now. Really, I'm fine." She produced one of her patented smiles. "You need to go after Ayla. She's belowdecks, isn't she?"

"Yes."

"She's the one who really needs you now."

I seriously doubt it, Bravo said wryly to himself, but in any event he blessed his sister for her empathy. "Maybe *you* should talk to her," he said half-joking.

"Coward." She pushed him playfully. "Go on now."

"Em, you don't know how prickly she can be."

"I know she's just lost her parents. I know she's a human being in the kind of pain we've both felt. That's all you need to think about."

As he came down the stairs, Bravo caught a glimpse of Ayla curled up in a fetal position on one of the berths. But the instant she heard his footsteps she leapt to her feet, wiping her eyes with her hand. Her skirt was rucked up around her thighs. Hastily, with no little embarrassment, she pulled the hem down.

"I'm going to get out of here. I need to see my aunt and uncle, reassure my nephews." She crossed to the sink, splashed some water on her face. She patted it dry with a bit of paper towel. "Tragedy is the time to be with family."

What a sad statement that was, Bravo thought. "I understand," he said. "But that isn't the brightest idea right now."

She glared at him. "*Now* you're concerned with security? You came up with that idea all by yourself?"

"I had help from you."

That stopped her. She stared at him wordlessly.

"Remember the kiss in the café."

She ran the back of her hand across her lips, as she had then.

"I did what I needed to do to save us both from being questioned. You would have been detained and I had blood on my clothes and stank of smoke and ash."

She turned her face away from him.

"I was trying to save her, Ayla. Your mother and I were up on the roof, talking. She had served us both *arak*." Of course Ayla understood what that meant. "She was about to tell me what happened to both of you in Tannourine when the explosion occurred. By the time we got to your floor the apartment was ablaze. I went in, found your father. I looked for you, but the fire was so intense . . . I tried to get her away, but you know your mother."

"Stubborn as a water buffalo and twice as strong." She took a deep breath, let it out slowly. "What happened? How did she die?"

"The stairwell was filling up with smoke. The hallway ceiling collapsed. Everything was chaos. I began to drag her down the stairs when . . ."

Ayla's eyes were as bright as beacons, their size amplified by incipient tears. "When what?"

"She was shot."

Ayla's hand flew to her mouth. "Shot? But . . . ?"

"I think the same person who set off the explosion shot her. Both your parents were targeted."

"But why?"

"I don't know."

"Yes, you do. You had recruited them."

Bravo knew he needed to press on. "The assassin and I struggled. I had him, but he slipped away."

"You let him escape?"

"He didn't escape, Ayla. He ran back to the apartment. He self-immolated."

"But . . ." She could scarcely speak. "None of this makes sense."

"That's what I have to do now: make sense of it." Bravo nodded. "So, like it or not, you're my responsibility."

"I *don't* like it; in fact, I hate it." Ayla shook her head. "Let no man write my epitaph."

Bravo rubbed his temples, decided to take another tack. "You and your mother went to Tannourine."

"Is that what she told you?"

Bravo just looked at her; there was no point in answering.

"Well, I have no idea what she meant."

"But you do, Ayla. You knew she was going to talk with me. You told me as much."

"I told you she would convince you to take me to Tannourine with you."

"*Back* to Tannourine."

The glare in her eyes was back. "I'm too polite to say what I'm thinking."

"In fact," Bravo said, "you're not in the least polite." His hand cut through the air between them. "But that's beside the point. You're off the hook; you have no more obligation to your mother or to me."

Her brows knit together. "What are you talking about?"

"I'm protecting you. You're out of this, as of now."

She laughed sharply. "Do you know nothing about obligations? This is my decision, not yours. Now tell me what's going on." This was said with a return of her old forcefulness. "I want to know."

He studied her while the silence built.

"Well?"

Still, he said nothing.

"Bastard, are you going to make me beg?"

"Frankly, I think you're constitutionally incapable of begging."

"You have no idea what I'm capable of. Now give."

Having brought her out of herself, he decided it was time to show her the crucifix. As she turned it over in her palm, he said, "As Emma said, Maura Kite told her she gave this to her husband on his last birthday but claims to have no knowledge of the engraving on its reverse."

Ayla turned the crucifix on to its back. "Maybe she's lying."

"No," Bravo said. "That symbol was made less than a week ago, while Val was in the Tannourine caves."

"How did she get this back?"

"That's the most interesting part," he said. "It was returned to her by the same man who shot your mother to death on the stairwell."

SIXTEEN

The glare of orange lights cast moving shadows on the walls and the floor both in front and behind them. A rustling of white-coated lab techs sounded like cicadas in the trees. Everyone wore latex gloves. Captain Balik escorted Fireside down corridor after corridor that stank of formaldehyde and carbolic.

Balik hadn't said a word during the car ride to the police mortuary. He and the driver were in the front seat, Fireside in the back. His face was blue-lit as he scrolled through screen after screen on his mobile. The driver kept catching a peek at Fireside in the rearview mirror until he lunged forward, opened his mouth wide, and snapped his jaws at him. After that, he was left in peace, the driver hunched forward over the wheel, studiously keeping his eyes on the snarled street traffic. Every now and then he switched on the siren, its high-low shriek blasting them a path through the city.

The mortuary was in the subbasement of the central police station, which, like everywhere else, it seemed, was crawling with armed soldiers. Fireside couldn't blame the central government, though he very much doubted they or the city had any reason to be concerned. Given what Balik had told him, this was not an act of international or home-grown terrorism. The Tusiks had been deliberately targeted; a message had been sent. But by whom? He frowned, worrying the question around and around in his head. He had already ascertained via text that the Knights of Saint Clement were not responsible. But if not them, then who? Of course Reichmann could be lying; he made an industry out of lying. But if he was, Fireside couldn't think of a logical reason. And Reichmann, inveterate liar though he might be, was nothing if not ruled by logic.

Around the next corner was a corridor shorter than the others, debouching at a set of swinging doors with round glass panels set at head height. They had reached the cold room and its strange occupant. Balik pushed open the doors as if he owned the place.

Even though the mortuary staff was dealing with the other fatalities of the explosion, including Omar and Dilara Tusik, both demurely draped by white cloths, the central table had been prepared for Balik and Fireside's arrival. The body—what was left of it, anyway—was lying on the slab. The first thing Fireside noticed was the teeth on the skull. They were elongated—too long for a normal human being—and he thought this was what Balik meant when he called the man strange.

"This is impossible," Fireside said as he bent over the cadaver.

Captain Balik, smirking, stood back. It was clear he had already observed the "impossible" anomaly.

At that moment, a portly man came through the swinging doors. When he saw Balik, he stopped dead in his tracks, his beady eyes taking in the entire scene. Fireside glanced up.

"Captain Balik," the portly man said at last. "To what do I owe this visitation?"

Quickly and quietly Fireside stepped over to where the Tusiks' bodies lay. Pulling aside first one cloth, then the other, he studied the corpses with the discerning eye of someone who had observed death in most all of its forms.

"This is official government business, Terzi," Balik snapped. "Get out of here."

"I'm the coroner," Terzi asserted. "This is my shop."

Balik took one threatening step toward him, and Terzi turned tail and, without another word, exited. By the time Balik turned back, Fireside was standing precisely where he had been when the coroner had so fortuitously barged in.

"Mr. Fireside, your time here is at an end," Balik said in the same tone of voice Fireside imagined he used ordering his troops around.

Nevertheless, Fireside returned his attention to the cadaver's face. At first, he had assumed he was seeing shadows, but on closer inspection, he realized, with a little thrill running down his spine, that the eyes were staring up at him from deep within their sockets. The lashes and lids had been burned away, of course, but how was it possible, he asked himself, that the eyeballs themselves were still intact?

Ayla regarded Bravo with a good deal of skepticism until he said, "Does the sigil mean anything to you?"

"I've never seen it before," she said so flatly Bravo didn't believe her. This woman had wrapped herself in so much psychic armor he wondered whether she could ever find her way out.

He watched her closely and was rewarded with the shadow of a flinch. Her gaze skittered away, to settle on a time and place he now believed she had spent many years burying. *You've seen this sigil before,* was what he was going to say. Instead, he bit his tongue and remained silent.

Nevertheless, she shot him a venomous look, as if he had tried to assault her person. Shaking her head, she produced the pack of her hand-rolled cigarettes, put one between her lips, flicked her lighter at the end of it, inhaled deeply.

As she blew smoke out her nostrils, Bravo leaned over and, so quickly she had no chance to pull away, plucked off the cigarette.

"If you're going to crush that out, so help me—" She stopped abruptly as he put the cigarette between his own lips and drew in deeply.

He exhaled, gave her back the cigarette. He said, deliberately mangling Shakespeare, "If anger be the spark of life, play on."

A burst of laughter escaped her, then, like a bubble popping on the surface of a lake. Bravo sat down heavily. "It's my fault, Ayla. I know it. I never should have involved your parents. It was a terrible position to put them in."

She took another drag deep into her lungs, watched him for a moment, smoke drifting around her. She slid into a chair next to him and held the cigarette out. As he inhaled, she said, "If I'm to be honest with myself . . ." She sighed deeply, ran a hand across her forehead, pushing back stray strands of hair.

"The truth is my father was thrilled to help you. He told my mom it was the proudest moment of his life. 'I'm fifty-six years old,' he said, 'and what do I have to show for it?' 'You have me; you have Ayla, your business,' she pointed out. 'You're a success, Omar; what more do you want?'" She took the cigarette Bravo passed back to her. "But he wanted something else, something more out of life, something he could neither articulate nor even define to himself. All he knew was that helping you scratched an itch that was driving him to distraction."

She took a drag; the smoke hissed out. "And as far as my mother . . . After her vision, she felt it was her duty—her obligation—to work with you, to protect you from what she saw was coming. Which is why she called me home yesterday."

"You could have said no."

She shook her head. "Not after what she told me. My mother rarely had visions, but when she did she was seeing the immediate future. Always."

Her eyes caught his in a direct look. "My mother's obligation is now mine. Which is why I have to . . . why I *need* to help and protect you."

"Protect me from what?"

She nodded as she ground the butt out. "You were right. I have seen that sigil before." She all but spit out the words. "My mother and I saw it in Tannourine. In the red tent of shadows."

"Do you know its meaning?"

Ayla's eyes cut away for a moment, then moved back to him. "I think we'd better go back on deck."

Fra Leoni was sitting, as if waiting for them to appear. He was holding Emma's hand.

"She's told you then," the old man said. His eyes held a sorrow too deep for human understanding. "The red tent of shadows."

Bravo nodded. "The question is, why are we seeing this sigil now?"

"I'm very much afraid that your friend Valentin's discovery woke the dead, so to speak. Lucifer's disciples have arrived."

PART TWO ☉

THE CEREMONY OF INNOCENCE IS DROWNED

ISTANBUL / MALTA / TANNOURINE

SEVENTEEN

Antonio Bazan, hunkered down in the Gnostic Observatine safe house, watched Maura Kite with the eyes of a hawk. The two of them were not alone, of course. Emma's call to arms had alerted the entire Istanbul Observatine cadre, which consisted of forty-odd men and women in all walks of life. It had galvanized those who held governmental positions—crypto-Catholics beneath their Islamic armor, though the Gnostic Observatines were humanists first and foremost, another reason they were anathema to the Church hierarchy.

The safe house occupied the fifth floor of a vast warehouse in the commercial and transport hub of Karaköy, Istanbul's oldest neighborhood. It was on the European side. The Galata Bridge, which took its name from the area's original name, connected it to Eminönü in the southwest.

Maura sat beside one of the windows, on a utilitarian wooden chair, staring out at the bridge as she absently picked at a bowl of vegetable stew spooned over rice, prepared by a member of the Order. From below, the hum and grind of forklifts and skid loaders could be heard through the wide, dusty floorboards, along with, on occasion, the grinding of gears from trucks coming and going. Diesel fumes worked their way into the air of the safe house.

Bazan was at a loss as to what to do with Maura. Currently he was fighting a strong impulse to break her free of Gnostic Observatine control and spirit her back to Reichmann in Malta. Bazan felt he needed to do this as soon as possible, even if it blew his cover, because he suspected there was more to this woman than she was letting on. Seeing that, for the moment, they were alone, he pulled up a chair. She seemed not to notice.

Looking for a way in, he said, "Once again, I'm so sorry for your loss."

"What d'you know about it?" she said without taking her eyes from the view out the window.

"I know what it means to lose someone you love," he said. "I had a brother. He was killed six months ago, on the border with Syria."

Still, she did not move. "What happened?"

"He was captured, by ISIS. They used his beheading as propaganda."

"That's . . . hideous," Maura murmured. "Those people have no souls." She put down the bowl of food; she had hardly eaten. "Tell me about your brother."

"He was the opposite of me," Bazan said. "He was always telling jokes; he said I was too serious."

"You *are* too serious," she said. "Without a sense of humor, there's no point in living."

"I've always had a hard time with that." He had her talking; soon, he hoped, he'd be able to open her like a can of beans. "Especially since my brother was murdered."

She turned to him, her gaze somehow heavy on him. She seemed different, though he was at a loss to understand how, or to make sense of it, because clearly she *looked* the same.

"Tell me, did you ever feel that what you see, hear, smell, feel is not enough, that there's something *more* out there?"

"Something more? I don't understand."

"No, of course not." She sighed. "Let me put it another way. I now feel I'm on the edge of something—something unknown, some new thing, something intensely exciting."

Bazan shook his head. "Perhaps it's just your grief. Grief colors everything, like a deep wound. It's all you think about, all you feel."

"And yet what I feel now is the opposite, an opening out. You see?" Seeing he didn't, she smiled sadly. "Val once told me that the only way to deal with grief is to laugh," she said in a voice both deeper and more authoritative than the one Bazan had become used to. "Do you know how to laugh? Do you know how to let yourself go? Do you know how to have fun?"

He frowned. What she was talking about was wildly inappropriate, considering the circumstances. In so many ways this person sitting across from him bore no resemblance to the one he had been guarding earlier. It was as if two people resided inside her body, as if something deep within her was struggling to the surface.

"Maybe we can laugh together." He licked his lips. "Maybe you could tell me—"

"A man walks into a bar with a roll of tarmac under his arm and says, 'Pint please, and one for the road.'"

Bazan stared at her. "I don't drink alcohol."

"Still funny, no? Okay. How about this: A man walks into his doctor's office. 'Doc,' he says. 'I can't stop singing "Green, Green Grass of Home."' The doctor says, 'That sounds like Tom Jones syndrome.' 'Is it common?' the man asks. 'It's not unusual,' the doctor replied."

Bazan looked blank. He was frankly dumbfounded by this new and inexplicable personality.

"Tough room. Okay, here's another." Something about her eyes drew Bazan like a magnet. "A woman gets on a bus with her baby. The bus driver says, 'Ugh, that's the ugliest baby I've ever seen!' The woman stalks to the rear of the bus and sits down, fuming. She says to a man next to her, 'The nerve of that driver. He just insulted me!' The man says, 'You go up there and tell him off. Go on; I'll hold your monkey for you.'"

Now Bazan did laugh.

"It took three jokes. You see, you are too serious," she said. "That's what comes of having two masters."

"Two—" Bazan's laugh faded. He felt a sinking feeling in the pit of his stomach. "I have no idea—"

"Don't, Antonio. Don't lie."

Had she ever called him Antonio before?

Her eyes narrowed. "It will just make things that much more difficult."

Bazan gaped at her. *What in the world—?*

"Val knew where your real loyalties lay. He confided in me just before he left. All the secrets and lies of his profession. As if he knew . . ." She closed her eyes for a moment. "He knew he wasn't coming back from that cave. He knew what he was going to find."

"Solomon's gold."

"You see, he'd had a visitation when he was five." She seemed not to have heard Bazan. "The shadow came to him; it spoke to him."

"Shadow? What shadow?"

"It prophesied that he would find the cave. That he would find the text used by King Solomon, the text that allowed his army of alchemists to succeed where all others had failed. Their formulae came from this text."

"What text?"

That was when he saw her eyes change: the white pupils, black irises, circled in red, and he felt paralyzed. He blinked and her eyes were normal again. Had he imagined it?

She reached out; the tip of her finger touched his chest. Gently, almost tenderly, she traced a circle, inside of which she traced a square. Inside the square, with an almost exquisite slowness, she drew a triangle.

Then she grabbed him with both hands and, with inhuman strength, hurled both of them into the window. The glass shattered with a sound like a gunshot as they burst through. Then they were in free fall, hurtling toward the tarmac below.

★

"I thought you said it was too dangerous for me to be out on the streets," Ayla said as they were driven, alarmingly fast, through the maze of traffic.

"I said it was too dangerous for you to be with your family," Bravo replied. "Besides, strictly speaking, we're not out on the streets."

"And if we're stopped by the police for driving at this insane speed?"

"Let me worry about that." Bravo leaned forward as the car took a left, went down a darkened side street. "Ah, here we are."

Up ahead, Ayla could see a heavyset man, hands plunged deep into the pockets of his suit, impatiently shuckling from foot to foot.

"Now listen," Bravo said. "I'm not going to introduce you as the Tusiks' daughter. That would only bring up questions—not to mention the police."

"I have nothing to hide."

"The regime has changed since you've been in London. Do you want to be stuck here for hours—possibly days—being interrogated? Besides, your parents were targets. I have no idea whether you are, as well."

Seemingly unfazed, she looked at him squarely. "I want to see my parents."

"Ayla—"

"This is not negotiable, Bravo," she said flatly.

"I'm going to introduce you by another name."

She lifted a hand. "Whatever." She was already looking past him, to the street and, beyond, the blocky structure of the police building.

He opened the car door for her to get out.

"Lena," Bravo said as they reached the sidewalk, "this is Damar Terzi, the city coroner. Damar, Lena is a forensic pathologist."

Terzi bowed his head. "A pleasure, madam." He swept his arm outward. "This way, please." He was a florid-faced individual with damp hands, sloped shoulders, and the poor posture of those whose work obliged them to be constantly bent over.

The coroner stopped them in front of two huge doors that opened outward. Presumably, this was where the bodies were brought in and taken out of the mortuary. He inserted a laughably old-fashioned key into the lock on a scarcely visible door within the larger ones, ushering them into a utilitarian corridor smelling of concrete, damp, and death.

As he hurried them along, Terzi said, "You won't have much time with the subject, I'm afraid. Captain Balik of the secret police has already made his interest known. I suspect he's about to take possession of the corpse."

"Lena wishes to examine the bodies of the Tusiks as well," Bravo said.

"Oh my!" Terzi exclaimed. "I hardly think she'll have the time to—"

"I wish a cursory exam," Ayla said with commendable steely calm.

Terzi nodded distractedly, but his air of nervous concern only increased.

They rounded a corner. Here the old smells were overridden by formaldehyde and strong antiseptic cleaners, tinged with a hint of fresh vomit. They passed through a pair of swinging doors, into the cold room. A wall of gleaming stainless-steel doors stored the cadavers until they were either released to the grieving families or, more often, disposed of. Two rows of three tables occupied the center of the room. Overhanging these were the articulated tools of the trade, like so many stalactites in a cave. The tables were empty, save one, on which the anomalous figure lay.

"My . . . The Tusiks first," Ayla announced.

The coroner hurried over to the wall of stainless-steel doors, opened first one, then another side by side. For a moment Ayla hesitated, and Bravo stepped toward her, worried that at the last she was about to falter. But then she squared her shoulders, approached the open tray-slabs, stared down at the burned and ravaged corpses of her father and her headless mother.

Ayla stared in shock for a moment. "You're absolutely certain this is them," she said. "Omar and Dilara Tusik."

"Yes, madam." The coroner's head bobbed up and down like a marionette's. "Quite sure." He coughed into his fist. "Dental records, you know."

Ayla rounded on Bravo, taking him aside. "You didn't tell me she was *decapitated*," she hissed. Incipient tears trembled in the corners of her eyes.

"You had enough on your plate without hearing every detail," Bravo said evenly.

"Decapitation is hardly a *detail*."

Bravo stared at her, wondering what was really going on behind her poorly tamped-down rage. Was that a touch of despair he detected? "I'm sorry, Ayla. Truly."

Without another word, Ayla turned her back on him and on them and, as Terzi rolled the bodies away, she stepped toward the other charred corpse displayed on the table.

What was she feeling? Bravo wondered. He watched for the small signs that were typical of trauma: the trembling hand, the welling of the eyes, the mouth hanging half-open as the victim took ever more shallow breaths. He observed none of these in Ayla. She was, so far as he could tell, the same as she had been before the viewing.

"How d'you account for the eyeballs being intact?" Bravo asked.

"I don't," Terzi said as he hurried back to them. "Frankly, there's nothing about this cadaver I can account for." He snapped on latex gloves. "Look here." He took up the right hand. "Easy to see that all the bones are unnaturally elongated."

"The teeth, as well," Ayla said as she scrutinized the skull.

The coroner nodded. "The teeth, indeed. But watch this." He broke a finger, tipped the piece so she and Bravo could see.

"The bone is hollow, like a bird's," Bravo said. "Could the marrow have been turned to a gas by the heat of the fire?"

Terzi took up a slender instrument from a steel tray, inserted the tip into the bone. When he extracted it, the end was completely clean. "Not without leaving a trace."

"Are all the bones hollow?"

"Take a look for yourself." Terzi led him over to a bank of backlit screens on which a series of X-rays had been clipped.

"All the same," Bravo said. "Hollow."

"Inexplicable as the eyes," Terzi said, leading him back to the table.

"These eyes," Ayla said. "It's not only that they were somehow untouched by the fire."

"Indeed, not," the coroner agreed.

"Their pupils are white, instead of black. The irises are pure black, but look at the rings around their circumference. They're bloodred."

"What are you talking about?" Terzi frowned as he bent over the cadaver. "All I see are two solid black eyes."

"Must be a reflection, the way I'm standing." But she threw Bravo a look.

Back out in the night, Bravo said, "Now tell me what's going on. I saw precisely what Terzi saw."

Ayla stared at him for a moment, then shook her head. "It was no reflection. The eyes were rimmed in red and in the center of each was a triangle inside a circle inside a square."

"You'd seen that sigil before." Now he needed her to come clean.

"I already told you." Her tone held an edge of annoyance. "In the red tent of shadows. When I was a young girl."

"Now you've seen it again."

Her eyes snapped to his. "Once again—"

"What you didn't tell me is that you know the significance of the sigil."

"I don't know what you're talking about." But her gaze had slid away from him.

"It's the sigil of the Unholy Trinity, Ayla. You know that."

When she gave no response, Bravo peered hard at her through the misty night. "We're not playing hide-and-seek, Ayla. You were the only one who could see it. That's incredibly significant. If you hold back now you're putting us all in mortal danger."

She nodded. "Later, when we returned home, when she finally came to terms with her defeat, my mother told me the meaning of the sigil."

"You being able to see it. Ayla, what does that mean?" But already she seemed beyond answering him.

EIGHTEEN

"The fall broke his neck?" Reichmann responded as he was given the news. "That's some bad luck."

"Valentin's widow landed atop him, driving his head into the pavement," Fireside said.

"And do we now have possession of her?"

Fireside sounded pleased. "That's what you asked for, that's what you got. My people are transporting her back even as we speak." He checked his wristwatch. "They should be there within the hour."

Reichmann dug his knuckles deep into Maximilian's fur. "I want her brought to me the moment she steps inside our walls."

Fireside nodded. "Of course."

"How did you do it, Collum?"

"To be honest, she walked right into our people."

Reichmann frowned. "You mean she got up and walked away from that fall?"

"As I said, Bazan's body cushioned her. Our *extramuros* cadre say they found her bleeding from a wound in her hairline. They assure me it's superficial. Otherwise, she appears unharmed."

"Remarkable."

Reichmann went to the window, staring out at the bruised sky. It was always raining lately, storms coming across from North Africa twice a week for the past three. Everything outside was dripping. Toadstools were popping up, and the smell of rot had begun to rise. Not for the first time, Reichmann regretted decamping from Paris to the Knights' ancestral castle here in Malta. The move was the pontiff's choice, not his. Reichmann regarded the papal order as a form of punishment for past failures regarding the Gnostic Observatines in general and Braverman Shaw in particular.

Shaw had placed the Knights on the downslope, an uncomfortable position Reichmann was bound and determined to reverse. With Anthony Bazan's death, Plan A had to be abandoned. Time for Plan B.

Turning from his contemplation of the storm, he gripped his mobile more tightly. "Find Captain Balik. Squeeze him for everything he knows."

"Done and done," Fireside said, severing the connection.

From his tower eyrie window, Reichmann watched the *extramuros* cadre that had been in Istanbul bring Maura Kite through the castle's massive wooden doors into the cobbled forecourt.

He felt the first threads of the tapestry he knew as victory resting in his open hand. Instinct told him that Valentin's widow was the key to finding the truth of what he had found in that cave. And, as Reichmann watched her being escorted into the castle proper, he felt sure that Valentin had communicated with her before he died.

Plan B was already fully formed in Reichmann's mind: He was going to use what God had given him, namely Maura Kite. He was going to squeeze her brain like a sponge, empty it of all useful information pertaining to Val and King Solomon's mine. And then Reichmann planned to load her up with disinformation about the Knights' immediate plans and movements, send her back into the bosom of the Gnostic Observatines. A better eyes and ears on the enemy he couldn't imagine—far better than that fool Antonio Bazan.

In the next five minutes before she was brought to Reichmann, he made all the arrangements he deemed necessary in his suite of rooms, so that when she was brought in to him he was ready for the cat-and-mouse game he was convinced she would play, just as she must have with Shaw and his accursed Gnostic Observatines when she went to them in Istanbul.

Reichmann was smiling broadly when she entered the room. Two of his men accompanied her, but the moment they stepped over the threshold he waved them out. They had taken good care of her, he saw. She was at least cleaned up, clad in a military jumpsuit, drab but utile. A small bandage at her hairline between her left eye and ear was the only reminder of her fall.

"My dear Maura," he said, stepping forward to take her hand, guiding her to a plush upholstered chair. "You must be exhausted from your ordeal."

"I slept on the flight over," she said with a smile, just as if they were old friends. "I was also well fed."

Reichmann sat down on a love seat directly opposite her. "How are you feeling?"

"I feel like I've started a whiskey diet. I've lost two days already."

Reichmann threw his head back, laughing. Maximilian would have reacted to his master's voice had he been in the room. He was nearby, however. Reichmann was keeping him in abeyance for the next stage of the interview. Reichmann enjoyed a good joke as well as the next person, but under the mirth he was frankly shocked to hear a woman who had just lost her beloved husband cracking jokes. Something felt off to him, and now he was determined to find out what it was.

Maura arranged her hands demurely in her lap. "I see that I've shocked you, Mr. Reichmann—and yes, I know who you are. But even though Val described you to me, he failed to mention your charisma."

Reichmann bowed his head slightly. "You do me honor, madam."

"Maura, please. If we are to be friends—"

"Then you must call me by my Christian name: Aldus."

"Such a handsome man, Aldus." Her smile was equal parts coquette and vamp.

Reichmann ignored her artless attempt to flatter him. "If you would be so kind, please tell me how you and Antonio Bazan came to fall through a fifth-story window."

Maura shrugged. "The story's simple enough. I didn't like that man, not from the moment I met him. He was coarse, abrupt, and his eyes were always running over my body as if he could see through my clothes."

Reichmann clucked his tongue sympathetically. "Go on."

"Well, there was some kind of emergency, I don't know what, and we were all hustled out of the building we had been in."

"Where was that?"

"I really couldn't say. Istanbul is a labyrinth to me."

"All right. Then what?"

"Bazan received orders to take me to a place that turned out to be above an active warehouse."

Reichmann leaned forward. "Where? What section of the city?"

"Again, I have no idea. Everything happened so fast, and I was very frightened. You miss all the details when you're frightened, you know?"

He ignored her babbling. "Did you see a marque, a street sign, anything?"

She shook her head. "It was all a blur."

Reichmann leaned back, sighing. "All right, then what happened?"

"I don't really know. I was sitting by the window. I could see a bridge."

"The Galatea?"

"Maybe." She shrugged again, her eyes glazing over as her mind reached back into the past. . . . "Anyway, Bazan drew up a chair close to me—too close for my comfort. He started asking me questions, but those restless eyes of his were all over me again, and I became uncomfortable. When I tried to stand up to get away from him he made a grab at me. I stumbled back, but he had hold of me and wouldn't let go. He began to squeeze my breasts. We crashed through the window. I don't remember much else, until your people ran across me and brought me back here."

"You know Bazan is dead."

Her eyes cleared, her gaze settling on Reichmann. "I didn't . . . I didn't look at him," she said. "I'm not sorry. That man wanted only one thing from me."

"You landed on him. He saved your life."

"Then his soul will be redeemed by the grace of God."

"What else can you tell me about your time with the Gnostic Observatines? Did you speak with Bravo Shaw?"

Her smile returned, and she looked around the room, at the marble fireplace, the Louis XVI ormolu clock on the mantel, the tapestried chairs and love seat, the fine wainscoting, the gleaming wood floor. "What strikes me is that here you are stuck away from the rest of the world in your high stone tower, lavish though it might be, while Shaw has all of Istanbul at his feet." She cocked her head. "What a sad, solitary life you must lead."

The interview had abruptly jumped the track it had been on; she had hijacked it. "You haven't answered my question," Reichmann said in an attempt to regain control.

Maura stood. Rain rattled against the windowpanes. She opened the window, stood, back arched, arms spread wide, as the rain struck her, making her jumpsuit cling to her body. She closed the window and turned back to him, her figure revealed through the sopping material.

"You see how easy it is, even here, to expose yourself to the elements, to embrace life."

"My vows . . . All my earthly needs are fulfilled here."

She held her smile in place. "And what of your spiritual needs?"

"The Vatican sees to those," he said, surprising himself with his honesty. "On occasion they send a high-ranking official—Cardinal Duchamp—to make sure of my fealty to God and to the pontiff."

Maura pursed her lips as she returned to the tapestried chair. Reichmann did not offer her a towel to dry herself off. "I find it telling that you used the medieval word 'fealty,' rather than the one I might have used."

"And what word would that be, my dear?"

Abruptly her eyes grew large, her nostrils flared. "I am no one's *dear*."

Reichmann's smile was growing thin and strained. "Not even Valentin's?"

"I would have said that this Cardinal Duchamp was dispatched to ensure my *allegiance*."

Reichmann's smile vanished like the sun behind clouds. "And what would you know of allegiance?"

"For those who believe God has a plan for us, they willingly give Him their fealty."

"I see you've excluded yourself from those who believe in God. Valentin was a good Catholic. Are you, then, apostate?"

"Oh, I believe in God," Maura said. "I believe in Him most powerfully."

"But you won't give Him your fealty."

"That is not something I have ever given out."

"Even—as I asked before, in a somewhat different fashion—to Valentin."

"It would never occur to Valentin to ask for my fealty. He loved me. That was enough for him. It should be enough for any man."

"And did *you* love *him*?"

"More deeply than you could ever fathom; with all my heart." She regarded him for a moment, as if considering how far she wished to take this topic. "And I have to wonder whether you can understand that, Aldus. Looking at you makes me think you've never given your heart to anyone, or if you have you've successfully ignored it."

Once again they were on uncomfortable ground. He felt as if he had been led off the prescribed path, only to find himself in an area of quicksand. "Why would you think that?"

"Because a man like you—"

"What would you know about a man like me?"

"A man like you would consider falling in love a weakness. Love would render you vulnerable, and that, I believe, is anathema to you."

She was right, of course. The first woman who had pegged him. How on earth had she done it? he asked himself. But he had no answers. It was only perhaps fifteen minutes since she had entered the room. Surely she couldn't have summed him up so quickly.

"As it happens, I've never found what your Valentin did. A woman like you. My work precludes me from—"

"Don't, Aldus. Don't lie."

Again he was taken aback. To his chagrin his palms were moist. A single bead of sweat snaked its way down his spine. Perhaps, he thought, it was time to bring Maximilian into the picture. Sooner than he had planned, but then this interview was nothing he could have imagined, let alone have planned for. He had been expecting a grieving widow, vulnerable and pliant in her depression. Either that or a woman with her back up, angry at being abducted, even if his people have saved her from the clutches of Braverman Shaw and the Gnostic Observatines.

He shrugged now, more nonchalant than he felt. "What would you have me say?"

Maura's gaze was unwavering. "The truth."

Reichmann spread his hands. "As you wish." He pressed a button and with an audible click a door in the rear of the room opened. "But first I'd like you to meet someone."

Pushing the door aside with his massive shoulder, Maximilian padded into the room. Reichmann was used to people being intimidated by his dog the first time they met him, often after that, as well. But Maura didn't flinch, didn't raise her eyebrows in surprise.

"This is Maximilian," Reichmann said, somewhat non-plussed. He disliked the way Maura Kite kept him off-balance; it was a position he was unused to. "Max, go over and say hello to Maura."

As if the dog could actually understand his master, he came across the room, passing Reichmann without hesitation, to stand in front of Maura. His head was at the same height as her breasts. She leaned forward. Most people would have put their hand out tentatively, even pulling it back when Maximilian moved. Not Maura. She put her face on a level with his, said, "Hello, Maximilian, how are you feeling today?" Maximilian shifted his weight slightly. She glanced out the window, then back to the dog's face. "I know. I don't much care for storms, either. But I do like the rain. I know, but maybe I could teach you how to enjoy it." She smiled, but it was a different smile from the one she had presented to Reichmann. And, to his astonishment, Max appeared to recognize something special for him, because he put his head in her cupped hands, making a deep and contented sound in the back of his throat.

"What a perfect teddy bear!" Maura exclaimed, kissing the animal on his shaggy forehead.

NINETEEN

"It's a disaster, pure and simple," Bravo said.

"Not Bazan's death, surely," Fra Leoni said. "He was Reichmann's creature from day one."

"And that's why I gave him a long leash."

From a safe distance Bravo looked along the street through powerful field glasses, the police cars, the swarming officers, spearheaded by an officious, fierce-looking leader. That must be Captain Balik, if Damar Terzi's description was accurate. Above them, the smashed window seemed to smile at Bravo, mocking him.

"The devil you know. I knew Bazan; I knew what mattered to him, how to control him and, therefore, control the flow of information to Reichmann." Bravo shook his head. The three of them were on the roof of a building diagonally across the street from the former safe house. "We'll get past his death." Due to quick thinking and perfect discipline Bravo had been able to clear the safe house of the half-dozen Gnostic Observatines before the police showed up. "The real disaster is Maura Kite's disappearance."

"You think she has more information than she's given you?" Ayla asked.

Bravo handed the field glasses to Ayla, fingered the crucifix with the symbol engraved on its reverse. "In retrospect, I think she was lying about everything." He lifted up the crucifix. "Even this."

"What d'you mean?" Ayla asked, taking a break from scanning the police activity.

"I don't think she gave it to Val," Bravo said heavily. "I think he gave it to her."

"But the inscription was engraved while he was in Tannourine," Fra Leoni said.

"Precisely. That's why I think Valentin is still alive."

"Then why did his wife come here?" Ayla asked. "Why didn't she go to him? That would be the logical response, wouldn't it?"

"Yes." Bravo nodded. "But I suspect that logic has nothing to do with the situation." He turned to her. "You, of all people, can understand this, Ayla, having seen the red tent of shadows."

She shuddered visibly, ran her tongue over her lips. "My mother and I were inside it."

Fra Leoni studied her intensely but said nothing, preferring to reach his conclusions from observation.

"It's past time you told us what happened," Bravo said.

Ayla sighed, nodding. "After everything that's occurred I can't disagree with you." She looked up at the sky, a Turkish green, lush and luminous, from the lights in the streets, cafés, shops staying open late in the hopes of luring in one more group of tourists.

"There was a storm that night. One of those wild, frightening furies you sometimes experience in North Africa. Anyway, we were caught in the deluge, thunder and lightning all around us. We had been on our way back from an archeological dig, but in the darkness and chaos of the storm we had lost our way. The rain came down so hard it was like a sheet of opaque glass, driving my mother off the road. In the shallow ditch, the car wallowed in mud the color of tar.

"My mother got out to survey the damage, then climbed back in without saying a word. We sat in the car for a bit; then as the rain seemed to be letting up, she took me away from there, out of the ditch and along the road. I fell, scraped my knees badly. I remember crying, my mother trying to lift me into her arms, as she had done when I was a child, but I was too big, too heavy.

"Soon enough we set off again, but moments later the torrent reasserted itself. We slogged on, then abruptly stopped. I'm sure that by this time my mother was completely disoriented. Perfectly understandable, of course."

Across the street, the police were packing it in, the floodlights switched off one by one. Captain Balik went to his unmarked car, climbed into the rear. Birds wheeled overhead, still curious about the commotion or perhaps attracted by the flash and glitter of the lights off the shards of glass that still lay in the street, spattered with Antonio's blood. His corpse was long gone, taken by ambulance to the police morgue.

"We must have walked for an hour or more after that," Ayla continued. "Until, all at once, it seemed, pinpricks of light appeared through the downpour. They weren't stationary; they bobbed and weaved. 'At last!' I remember my mother saying, the first words either of us had spoken in hours."

Balik's car moved off, followed by the remaining official vehicles, leaving the street looking denuded and abandoned.

"There were five of them," Ayla was saying. "Lebanese tribesmen. Three men, two women, and they all looked like pilgrims. As it turned out, they were. They took pity on us, mostly, I guess, because I was injured, but also because my mother was fluent in idiomatic Lebanese."

"They took you to the red tent of shadows," Bravo said.

"That's right."

"Where you were sheltered from the storm," Fra Leoni said, "and tended to."

"I hear the skepticism in your voice," Ayla said. "But I was very ill. That's what happened."

"I am not gainsaying anything you tell us," Fra Leoni said. "But listen to me, the red tent of shadows is said to have been created by King Solomon's army of alchemists. Legend has it that the majority of alchemists did not want the assignment, even though it came as a direct order from their king. In fact, a good number of them left, trooping out of Israel. The ones who remained had their own doubts, so much so that they delayed the project again and again, until Solomon's death. Their relief was overwhelming, for they were convinced that was the end of it; they could turn their undeniable talents to other projects that had been vexing them for decades. But they were wrong, for shortly after the king was interred in the City of David his son, Rehoboam, appeared before the alchemists and bade them finish the creation of the red tent of shadows under penalty of death. One supposes he had good reason to feel more than a stab of panic. With his father's death, the power that resided in Solomon began to crumble. The peoples of his vast empire began to rise up. The rule of Solomon's son was suddenly in jeopardy. He needed the power that resided inside the red tent of shadows. Unlike his more trusting father, Rehoboam suspected the alchemists of dragging their feet. Accordingly, he set up camp in their cavernous laboratory, watching them like a hawk day and night until their task was completed."

Below their eyrie, pedestrians, as if sensing the evil vibes, hurried past without venturing near the warehouse. No lights shone through the windows; the fifth floor was dark.

"By all accounts—and, please remember, this is a myth, an incredibly fanciful one at that—the cadre of alchemists was successful. The power Solomon's son craved so desperately was brought into being inside the red tent of shadows." Fra Leoni's eyes were glittering in the greenish streetlights. "But the power was beyond his imagining. All the fears of the alchemists who had fled Israel in terror, defying their king, rather than be party to the creation, were borne out. The power of the shadow was a dark power—the darkest, in fact—for inside the red tent of shadows the alchemists had summoned Lucifer."

Fra Leoni cleared his throat. "History records that Rehoboam failed to hold on to his father's empire. He went to war with the

Kingdom of Israel, and then with the invading Egyptians. Soon enough Solomon's empire crumbled, sliced into sections, then vanished altogether."

"And the son," Ayla said. "What happened to Rehoboam?"

Fra Leoni leveled his gaze on her. "History records that he ruled Judah in a constant state of war for seventeen years, and that when he died he was laid to rest beside his ancestors in Jerusalem. However, recent archeological work with X-rays and other modern equipment quite beyond my comprehension indicates that his burial site is devoid of a body."

"Looters," Ayla said.

"A reasonable conclusion," Bravo said. "But . . ." He looked to the old man.

"But," Fra Leoni concluded, "the legend records that there came a time when Rehoboam stepped into the red tent of shadows, and vanished, along with the tent itself and whatever unholy presence was inside it."

"What if the police left guards behind?" Ayla asked.

"They haven't," Bravo replied. "Everyone's gone." He pointed to the warehouse across the street. "All the lights are out."

Ayla looked dubious. "Still."

Fra Leoni was still as granite beside her. "Even if there are guards," he said in a thin, reedy voice that sent a chill down her spine, "they will not see you."

Bravo and Ayla left him on the rooftop, staring sightlessly into space. Down on the street, nothing moved, save one end of the ribbon of police tape that had come untied. It rose and fell like a banner as they moved past it into the deeper shadows of the warehouse.

Ayla never did discover how Bravo defeated the lock on the side door, but moments later they were inside. Bravo switched on the flashlight app on his mobile. They climbed the filthy stairs to the fifth floor and found themselves in a vast open space.

There were no walls, not even a partition. Off to her right was a kitchen of sorts: a cooktop, a half refrigerator, its door open, revealing a pair of empty racks. Whatever had been in there had been cleaned out.

As Ayla moved around the room, she saw no evidence of phone jacks, Internet modems, or the like, though there were electrical outlets spaced around the baseboards. The floorboards were of an even color, she saw, so no rugs or carpets had been laid down, no scrapes that might tell of hastily moved furniture.

"Your people did a good job of removing all traces of themselves."

"They are well trained," Bravo replied.

There was, however, a bowl and spoon, upended on the floor near the window from which Antonio Bazan had jumped or been pushed.

Ayla stuck her head out the window. "It's a long way down."

Bravo knelt beside the smashed window, looked at the contents of the bowl spilled across the floor, then the windowsill.

As his gaze lowered again, he spied a crude drawing on the wall. "Look at this."

Ayla stepped closer. "What have you found?"

"The sign of the Unholy Trinity again. A triangle inside a circle inside a square."

"Who d'you think drew it?"

"I can tell you that it wasn't any of my people," Bravo said, rising to his feet. "That leaves us with only two choices: Bazan or Maura."

TWENTY

It was only during the latter stages of a magnificent dinner, sitting across a gleaming table from Maura Kite, that Reichmann began to feel the warm glow of satisfying victory. Maximilian sprawled under the table midway between them, snoring. Collum and his cadre were in Istanbul. Both Omar and Dilara Tusik, two of Shaw's key informants in Istanbul, had been killed in an explosion the Turkish government was at a loss to explain.

In addition to this intel, Reichmann had gained possession of Valentin's widow. After dinner, he led her up to her bedroom with its large en suite bath. The room itself was sumptuous, expensively furnished, with an antique four-poster covered with a striped silk canopy with fringe all around and tassels on the corners. He left her there, saying good night, and went straight to his bedroom suite, which was at the end of the hall. He performed his ablutions, then padded back into his bedroom, where Max lay on the floor at the foot of the bed with his head on his paws. Max's eyes followed him faithfully as he moved around the room. As he was turning down his coverlet, he heard a noise or thought he heard a noise out in the hall. Max's head had come up and, as Reichmann wrapped himself in his silk dressing gown, the dog rose onto all fours, ready to accompany him. Signaling the dog to remain where he was, Reichmann emerged from his room, peered down the dimly lit hall. It was deserted.

He hesitated for a moment, listening hard, but heard no

more sounds. Nevertheless, he proceeded along the runner on bare feet. The door to Maura's room was ajar. He could hear the shower running. He hovered in the oblique shadows of the wallpapered hallway, his face blank in the flickering light cast by the old-fashioned gaslit wall sconces. At once, he became immersed in the sound of water splashing against bare flesh.

As he entered Maura's room he felt as if he were floating, as if he were dreaming. But then transgressions were nothing new to him. Stepping across the Persian carpet, he picked up a snippet of an unfamiliar tune and wondered whether that was the sound that had somehow made its way into his room.

At the threshold to the bathroom he stopped. His position was such that he could see the shower reflected in the mirror. However, the mirror was opaque with steam. All at once the melody came to an end; the water was turned off. Maura was a shadowy blur as she stepped out onto the floor mat. He sensed rather than saw her reach for a towel, heard the unmistakable whisper of terry cloth against damp skin.

Then the shadow reached out, toweled off the mirror, and Maura Kite stood revealed to him. She was staring at her reflection in the mirror, but Reichmann had the eerie sensation that she was watching him over her right shoulder as he watched her. Her hands came up, fingertips tracing the contours of her temples, her cheeks, her neck. When they reached the level of her breasts, her fingertips traced the lines of what appeared to be a reddened welt between them. Her hands moved, cupped her heavy breasts, lifting them up and out. She rolled her erect nipples back and forth, and a Mona Lisa smile transformed her face. Her eyes turned dreamy. Everything about her relaxed as a pinkness suffused her skin. Her hands left her breasts, moved lower, made circles on her lower belly. It was flat and hard, like an athlete's, and it took Reichmann's breath away. Her hands lowered farther still until they were lost to his view, but by the rhythmic rocking of her hips he knew what they must be doing. The skin at the small of her back flushed a deeper pink.

All at once, and to his surprise, her hands reappeared. They gripped the edge of the sink as she raised herself up on her toes. The juncture of her legs was now level with the sink edge. She rolled her hips forward, then lifted and fell, lifted and fell, like the tide over ancient rocks. He heard the sharp intake of her breath each time she rubbed herself against the smooth, cool porcelain sink. Her head arched back, her neck extended, the cords on either side standing out. Her nostrils flared, her mouth hung open, her breath coming in short, explosive pants. Then she gave a little cry, her hips jerked inward, her buttocks contracting. Her body shivered as her cries continued, so swiftly one upon another, they finally merged into a long-drawn-out groan.

Then her head came down, her shoulders fell, and she leaned against the sink, weight on her forearms. Reichmann, overcome with sensations, stared at the knob at the top of her spine, where it joined her neck, and he thought he had never seen anything more erotic.

Later, as he lay in bed, staring at the darkened ceiling, he experienced again the incredible longing that had almost impelled him into the bathroom. He could feel himself coming up behind her, his robe parting as he clasped her breasts, his erection slipping into the crease between her still-quivering buttocks.

Thrusting himself out of bed, he knelt before the seventeenth-century gilt and wood image of Christ on the cross, bowed his head, and prayed for serenity in the face of a temptation he knew would lead him astray. In this way, with the divine help of Christ, he was able to rein in his earthly appetites. He prayed to keep in the forefront of his mind the long days and nights ahead, interrogating her, mining the data he required out of the recesses of her brain. He could not afford for his mind to be clouded by lust. His task was clear: extract her knowledge of Val and the location of King Solomon's mine. Nothing must be allowed to stand in his way.

With that thought in mind, he closed his eyes and, soon enough, plunged down into a deep sleep in which he dreamed that the image of the crucifixion in his room was jolted off the wall and broke into a thousand glinting shards.

He awoke in the low hour before dawn. The moment his eyes opened, the trajectory of the day was formed crystal clear in his mind. Energized, excited, even, he bounded out of bed, slapped water on his face, and dressed. It was his habit on interrogation days to shower only when his work was done for that particular cycle. As he inhabited close quarters with blood, sweat, and fear, there was no point in doing otherwise.

His anticipation made him hungry, but he decided to adhere strictly to his schedule and start Maura's interrogation at once. As the Gestapo had proved, there was a tremendous psychological advantage in dragging subjects from their beds, starting in on them while their minds were still muzzy with sleep, their bodies ripe with cortisol, their psychological defenses down.

He stepped into the hall, turned down toward Maura's room, but was halted in his tracks by the sight of Maximilian, strung up, head down, in a star pattern. Max's tongue, gray and dry, hung from between his black lips. His eyes were glazed over. His blood had sunk into the runner below him, turning it black.

Reichmann felt his insides rebel, his gorge rising, but before what was left in his stomach could make its way into his mouth he smelled smoke and the first tongues of flame entered the hallway like an invading army.

Emerging from them was a figure out of nightmare. It was Maura, but distorted almost beyond recognition. Her hair was the color of flames, her skin as dark as a dreamless sleep. She wore no clothes—his semi-paralyzed brain registered that they must have been incinerated in the conflagration—instead was wreathed in flames, which licked about her person as if alive and responsive to her will. The weal between her breasts glowed as if with an inner life, and now he saw it was a strange and unfamiliar sigil: a triangle inside a circle inside a square.

She grinned, her teeth sharp and shimmering in the ghastly firelight. And then she was sprinting directly for him. He had just enough time to see how demonic her eyes had become before he turned and fled.

TWENTY-ONE

"Remember that time you beat the crap out of that guy who was bullying me?" Emma said as they sat in the backseat of the car heading to the airport at top speed. Ayla was sitting in front. Emma didn't know whether she could hear them, but she didn't care.

"Your junior year in high school," Bravo said. "Sure, I remember."

"Well, I never told you that a couple of weeks after that he asked me out."

Bravo turned to her. "He did what?"

"We dated for a while." She laughed. "I'm imagining your expression." She put a hand up, her fingertips delicately roaming his face. "And I was right!" She looked beautiful, the passing buildings throwing her alternately into light and shadow. "It turned out he was very sweet. His hassling me was a form of flirting."

"Some flirting!"

"Each to his own," she said.

"What happened?"

Her face darkened. "His sister . . . I don't know; something happened to his sister."

"She died?"

"No, I don't think so, but something else . . . Anyway, the family moved away. I got a postcard from him once, from Lake Placid." She put her head on Bravo's shoulder. "I always get a bit melancholy when you go off like this."

He put a protective arm around her.

Forty minutes later, they arrived at the airport. Emma grasped Bravo's forearms in their traditional Roman leave-taking. "Three things before you go."

"Always," he said softly.

She smiled up into his face she remembered so well but hadn't seen in two years. Had he aged? Did he look tired, careworn? What had the last two years, Jenny's unexpected death, done to him? She had only his tone of voice to go on, and hypersensitive as she was, she knew he had become expert at hiding his fears and anxieties from her. In many ways the death of their father had brought them closer together, but in another, wholly unexpected way it had estranged them from each other. They were now both reluctant to share their innermost feelings. Emma suspected some, if not all, of this was a result of her disability. Did Bravo secretly pity her? How many sleepless nights she had prayed that wasn't so, but she could not bring herself to ask him for fear that, even if he lied, she'd know it. She knew his pity would devastate her, would undo all the struggles, all the hard work she had put in repairing her psyche after losing her sight.

"Keep your eyes open, even when you sleep," she said now. "Keep your mind open to the improbable as well as the impossible." She pulled him to her, kissed him on both cheeks as she wrapped her arms around him. "And go with God. You're all the family I have, and I love you most fiercely."

"Don't worry, Em." He stroked her hair. "Nothing's going to happen to me."

One of the half-dozen private jets the Order owned was waiting for them on the tarmac. Bravo followed Ayla up the steps into the interior, the stairs were pulled up, the door closed, and they were shown to their seats. The car with Emma in it had already driven away.

When the jet was in the air, Bravo unbuckled his seat belt. "Fra Leoni lied." The flight attendant had just offered them a choice of fresh-squeezed blood orange juice or champagne. "Or, more accurately, he judiciously edited his description of the myth of the red tent of shadows."

"Why would he do that?" Ayla sipped her juice. Bravo had no idea whether she would drink champagne. Had she made the secret conversion from Muslim to Catholic as her mother had?

"Frankly, he doesn't trust you." A sly smile crept over Bravo's face. "Don't take it personally. The only people he trusts are me and, I think, Emma."

"You and your sister are close."

"We always were, but our father's sudden death cemented our relationship in an entirely new way." He was brought up short, realizing that he had entered delicate territory. "I'm sorry; I didn't mean . . ."

She waved away his words. Her expression was inscrutable. This was one of the things he realized belatedly that he admired most about her. It was also the most maddening. Reaching to alter the mood, he said, "You know Em used to tell this story: One winter we had a lot of snow, so Dad got out our sled for Em and me to use. A couple of hours later, when he came out to check on us, so she says, Dad told me not to be selfish. 'Let your sister use the sled half the time.' To which she says I replied, 'I do, Dad. I use it going down the hill and she gets to use it coming up!'"

That got a laugh out of Ayla, as it was meant to do. "True story or not?"

Bravo shrugged. "I suppose it depends on your point of view."

"Another mystery unresolved."

"You're a good one to talk."

She seemed to absorb that well enough.

Outside the clouds slid past, ribboning, until the plane rose into clear, thin air.

"Okay, what did Fra Leoni leave out?"

"A crucial element—I wouldn't call it a fact, because this is all from a myth."

"A myth Fra Leoni clearly doesn't believe in."

"On the contrary."

She shook her head. "You could've fooled me."

"He gets like that—contrary and edgy—when he's frightened. The truth is, you frightened him—or, rather, what you and your mother claim to have seen in Tannourine."

"We *did* see it."

"Well, you've yet to tell me exactly what you saw."

"First tell me what Fra Leoni left out."

Bravo let out a slow breath. "He told you that Solomon's son entered the red tent of shadows and vanished along with the tent itself."

"That's the myth as he told it."

"Well, it's not quite right. There was, in fact, something left, in the aftermath."

"What?"

"A book, a testament, call it what you will—but, in any event, a manuscript known as the Testament of Lucifer."

"The what?"

"The Book of Deathly Things. It's part of the Unholy Trinity."

"I had no idea what it constituted. No wonder Fra Leoni is afraid."

"The Greeks identified four elements: earth, air, fire, water. The Pythagoreans claimed to have discovered a fifth element they called aether. Alchemists know it as the Quintessence. By either name it's the pure energy of the universe, Light and Life itself.

"For untold centuries, a clandestine search has been under way to find the Quintessence. No alchemist was able to create it." Bravo's father had found the Quintessence, had in fact left a tortuous trail for Bravo to follow to find it, following his death. That Bravo had, indeed, found it was not something he was prepared to tell Ayla.

"A far less well-known, but connected, legend concerns the

Book of Deathly Things," he continued. "It's the first of what we've been referring to as the Unholy Trinity, relics of an age so ancient it has been all but forgotten. The Catholic Church categorically denies the existence of the Unholy Trinity. The Vatican has gone so far as to forbid its constituents to speak of it, labeling such talk heretical, blasphemous, and anathema.

"The Book of Deathly Things contains the very essence of evil shadows, death, and that which dwells in the abyss that lies beyond all darkness. The spells and incantations detailed in it are, it is said, the writings of Lucifer himself. That Testament, then, is the very antithesis of the Quintessence, allegedly able to annihilate it and, with it, life itself, so you understand Fra Leoni's terror of it. To this day, it has never been found, nor has there been any verifiable evidence that it's anything more than mad legend and superstition."

"Until now," Ayla said.

A curious silence settled over them, as if each, harboring secrets, was reluctant to push further into forbidden territory. But within hours they would be setting down in Tannourine, and then all secrets would need to be revealed. Before then a more secure lifeline of trust would have to be established. Bravo was all too aware that the issue of trust was causing Ayla to hold back. Clearly, her parents had trusted Bravo with their lives, but from her point of view that trust had been misguided. Omar and Dilara had been killed because of their involvement with him. That it had been their choice did not, he suspected, mitigate against his culpability so far as Ayla was concerned. Whether she would always hold this failure against him even he couldn't yet know, but he knew that their relationship required deepening before it could be mended.

As he turned to her, she said, "Please, don't try to win me over with stories about your childhood. That's a ploy for bad films and TV shows. What's known as shortcuts to characterization. There are no shortcuts to knowing someone, not in real life, anyway. Only in a screenwriter's mind."

"I was about to tell you something about your father, but you have a knack for short-circuiting conversation."

"I don't want to hear your paeans to my dead parents. Can I be any clearer?"

After that, they lapsed into silence. After a decent interval, Bravo rose, went to the rear of the plane to talk to the steward, have a bit to eat, and clear his mind. Being in close proximity to the wreckage of Ayla's psyche was becoming toxic.

"Girl trouble?" the young flight attendant said as she looked up from the meal she was preparing. Her name was Lida, and, like all of the crew, she was a member of the Order. Unlike the Knights, the Gnostic Observatines admitted women to their Order. "You two seem to be working at cross-purposes." She blushed as she handed Bravo a cup of freshly brewed coffee. "Sorry. It's a small cabin. I couldn't help overhearing."

Bravo sipped meditatively. "I admit she has me baffled. Talking with her is like doing battle with a porcupine."

Lida put a hand over her mouth to stifle a laugh. "I have a sister just like her," she said in a whisper.

This interested Bravo. "How do you deal with her?"

Lida rolled her eyes, which had the effect of both lightening the mood and making her look like an adorable cartoon character. "I learned from hard experience, you leave her alone and try not to let her draw too much blood."

Bravo contemplated the wisdom of this advice while he finished his coffee. As he was about to turn away, Lida poured another cup.

"Do you know how she—?"

"Two sugars, no cream."

"That's a start." Lida balanced a small spoon on the saucer, stashed two packets of turbinado sugar in his breast pocket, gave him an encouraging smile, and went back to preparing their meal.

Ayla did not look up from the magazine she appeared to be reading until he proffered the coffee. Then all she said was, "I take two sugars."

She seemed slightly taken aback when he plucked the packets out of his pocket, laid them on the rim of the saucer.

"Thank you," she said, the words escaping her lips before she could think about it.

She put down her tray, set the saucer on it, ripped open the packets, slid the sugar into her coffee, and stirred. Instead of sitting beside her, Bravo moved up to the row in front, slipped into the window seat, stared out at nothing. The sky was an oyster gray. Clouds skimming by blocked out everything below them. If only he could block out his memories of Jenny. How simple life would have been had his father never assigned her to protect him! And yet he fell asleep thinking about her, wishing she were sitting here beside him, and he dreamed he was on an Order jet, flying away to Mauritius or the Seychelles, perhaps, wild as the wind howling by outside.

When he awoke, someone was beside him. Still lost in the last tendrils of his dream he thought it was Jenny, but then he smelled Ayla's perfume, and something else.

"Nice nap?" she asked in a voice dry as a glass of five-hundred-dollar champagne. She dropped his tray-table, slid the food Lida had prepared in front of him. When he glanced at her, she said, "I already ate."

"I was dreaming." The moment he said it he regretted it, but he had still been half-asleep. He didn't want to tell her anything personal now, not this creature who inexplicably blew hot and cold, as if she had a multiple personality disorder. Or possibly it was the temporary derangement of having lost two parents in one dreadful instant.

"I hate dreams," Ayla said, surprising him yet again. "I always dream of the past; I dream of things I'd rather forget."

"Me too," Bravo said, letting his gaze roam over the food. It smelled good, but he found he had no appetite.

"For god's sake eat something. You'll need all your strength once we land in Tannourine." When he didn't reply or take up his knife and fork, she said, "What did you dream about?"

Bravo stared out the window for a moment. The clouds had parted; the blue-gray mountains below meant they had crossed over into Lebanon while he was asleep. They were nearing Tannourine. The plane banked, and rays from the setting sun struck the Perspex window. Bravo pulled down the shade, throwing both their faces into deep shadow.

"I dreamed I was lying beside a woman named Jenny," he said, contravening his own decision not to reveal himself. "When I woke up I thought she was sitting beside me." He paused for a moment. Why was he doing this? What was it about Ayla that drew him, despite all her sharp quills?

"What is it?" she asked.

"I'm waiting for you to say, 'Disappointed?'"

She smiled grimly. "That sounds like me." But then she kept quiet, and he began to feel a change in her, so subtle most other people might not have picked it up.

"My father assigned her to protect me, when I was first learning about the Order," he went on. "She succeeded, but in the process she was wounded—badly. We thought she was recovering, but then she took a turn for the worse."

"She died."

"Yes."

"I'm sorry." She sounded like she actually meant it. She took up his fork, put it in his hand. "I want you to know . . . I mean . . ." She paused, biting her lip. "Look, I know I've been acting like a bitch ever since I met you."

"It's understandable, what with your parents' deaths—"

"Listen to me, please." She held up a hand. "I don't want to talk about my parents. Not a word."

Their deaths were like open wounds. Bravo could empathize. He still thought about that nightmare instant on the smoke-filled stairwell when pieces of Dilara's brain were spattered on the wall. He could taste the hot spray, smell her insides, and he almost gagged. He put down the fork.

Ayla apparently noticed his extreme distress; she did not

implore him to eat but signaled for Lida to come take the tray away. When they were alone again, she said, "I want to tell you what happened inside the tent of shadows." When Bravo made no comment, she pressed on. "As it turned out, I was injured rather more severely than we had thought. Possibly walking so far had exacerbated the problem.

"In any event, I had lost a lot of blood by the time we reached the clearing where the tent had been pitched. It was very large— as big as a house, or so it seemed to me—but I was just a child, so my perspective might have been off. One thing I do recall clearly: it was perfectly square.

"I was carried inside by two of the people we met. There was a straw pallet in one corner a baby had been sitting on. Someone lifted off the baby and they laid me down. By this point I was feverish. Someone—an old woman—started to attend to me. My mother tried to stop her, but they pulled her away. Still, she stood over me, eyes fixed on the old woman's hands. I don't know what she did—I couldn't see—but at first there was a searing pain, so bad I arched my back. Someone screamed, but I don't know whether it was me or my mother. Almost immediately, though, the pain subsided. When it disappeared completely it was replaced by a sense of euphoria. I felt as if I were swimming in warm water.

"I looked up toward the top of the tent, the first time my vision was clear since before they brought me in. That was when I saw the sigil: the triangle inside a circle inside a square. It was as large as the moon, or so it seemed to me, and there was someone standing directly below the triangle, as if he were in it, a part of it. He was in shadow. I couldn't see his face; I only knew that he was very tall—taller than anyone else inside the tent. He opened his mouth and I heard the wind howling. At first, I assumed that it was coming from outside, but the tent walls were still, so I knew it must be calm—the storm had finally moved on. But the howling kept up, and now everyone else in the tent formed a circle. The circle inside the square, you see, yeah? And inside that circle was someone, some *thing* that represented the triangle."

"When you say . . ." He frowned. "It was a man, you said."

"I said it *looked* like a man—a male figure in shadow, anyway."

"Did you hear him speak?"

"I saw . . . I saw the circle billow out in one place, as if in response to an order, but if it was spoken either I didn't hear it or I can't remember. One of the people had the baby in her arms; she lifted him up high—higher than the heads of the adults. Something moved out from that central shadow. Maybe it was a finger; I don't know. It pressed against the baby's chest, the baby started to cry, and I smelled something."

"What did you smell?"

"I don't know." Ayla screwed up her face. "Something like . . . oh, like meat frying." The sudden pallor she had taken on seemed to luminesce in the shadows of the cabin. "I . . . I caught the briefest glimpse of the baby as upraised hands lifted him out of the circle. It looked—I know you won't believe this—it looked like something had been tattooed on the baby's chest."

"Could you see what it was?"

"No, not really. But when I saw that sigil in the present something stirred in my mind, something that had been hidden; maybe I had hidden it from myself. It became clear, and I knew that's what had been burned on to the baby's chest."

The plane started its descent. Lida came up the aisle to remind them to fasten their seat belts, then went back near the kitchen and strapped herself in. Bravo cleared his ears twice as the rough-shouldered mountains rose up to meet them. The plane dipped and rocked through a number of air pockets and sudden wind gusts.

"What happened then?" Bravo asked.

Ayla closed her eyes for a moment. "Then they took my mother. From where I was lying I couldn't see past the backs of the people forming the circle. I tried to lift myself up to a sitting position, but almost immediately I was overcome by dizziness. The old woman tending to me pushed me down by the shoulders. She was far stronger than she looked. Either that, or I was far weaker.

"Inside the circle, the shadow rose up. I could imagine my mother being pushed toward him as the baby had been. I think she was meant to be tattooed, too."

"But she wasn't?"

Ayla shook her head. "I don't know what happened, and even long afterward my mother wouldn't speak of it. Of course, my father never knew a thing; she swore me to secrecy."

They were nearing the runway now, or what passed for it in this godforsaken area—a narrow landing strip of packed earth with portable landing lights and a tiny shack at the far end. If there were people around, Bravo did not have a view of them from his angle of sight out the plane's window.

"What d'you think happened?"

"It was my mother," Ayla said. "Somehow she fought him off—she fought them all off. And then the entire tent was on fire. There was screaming and smoke and a stampede as of panicked animals. I remember my mother scooping me up, and then she was running with me in her arms. I saw sparks flying through the air. I thought they were lightning bugs and began to laugh, trying to snatch them out of the air. Then the dizziness became too much for me and I passed out. When I awoke, sunlight was pouring through the thick canopy of trees. My head was in my mother's lap. She was singing an old song she used to sing me to sleep with when I was sick or had too much halvah to eat after dinner.

"'Where are we?' I remember asking her.

"'In a distant land,' she said, and then sang me back to sleep."

The jet touched down, a slight bounce along the packed earth; then the engines were howling in reverse as the plane headed for the far end.

TWENTY-TWO

"He spit the bit."

Cardinal Duchamp, in the middle of the chapel, whirled. "I beg your pardon?"

"When it's deemed that a horse is untrainable, it's said to have spit the bit," Collum Fireside said. "This is what's happened with the *Nauarchus*."

"Then it is wise you have come to me, Collum," Duchamp said.

The two men walked down the deserted central transept. Fireside's *extramuros* cadre had not been allowed inside the walls of Vatican City. They had repaired to a nearby restaurant, from where the Holy Father ordered his pizzas, to await word from their leader. They were well trained. They did not gossip among themselves or speculate on where they might be headed or what they might be ordered to do. Theirs not to reason why.

"In all honesty, I didn't know what else to do," Fireside said.

"Don't play the naïf with me," Duchamp said sharply. "You are too long in the Knights' employ and too far up the hierarchy not to be adept at the Order's particular form of politics. You have coveted Reichmann's position almost from the moment he recruited you."

Fireside was properly chastened. "I found the decision decidedly peculiar, if I may say."

"You may not." The cardinal's hands were clasped at the small of his back, his torso tilted slightly forward, as if he were facing down a headwind. "One does not question the decisions that come from on high." He pursed his lips. "Still, considering the dangerous path Reichmann has chosen, one cannot help but wonder whether this was the Holy Father's purpose from the first. After all, one cannot ascend until one has fallen as far as one can."

"Rest assured, Your Eminence, I will do whatever is asked of me—"

Duchamp held up a forefinger, listening to the choral chanting that had arisen from parts unseen. "Kyrie eleison. Christe eleison. Kyrie eleison." *Lord have mercy. Christ have mercy. Lord have mercy.* "Magnificent, isn't it? When we hear human voices lifted in unison by their faith, when we are in the presence of the hymns to God, we feel deeply our humility before Christ. We see the path to salvation; the channel to redemption is as clear as the air we breathe, purer than any earthbound substance. And we are in awe at the fragility of life."

The hymn continued, growing in both volume and joyous piety. The cardinal turned to Fireside. "Do yourself a favor, Collum; refrain from any assumption. From this moment forward, your work for the ministry of God, for the Holy See, for us in particular, will be followed, evaluated, annotated, and, if need be, modified." A slow smile spread across his face. "We must be clear, Collum, we value tradition over all else. We will not favor too many modifications."

Fireside bowed his head. "I am humbled, Your Eminence. And at your service, as always."

"We are pleased to hear this, Collum. And yet, we are inclined to need more than spoken pledges, the Knights having become, shall we say, unstable."

"With all due respect, Your Eminence, it's not the Knights, per se, who have become unstable."

Cardinal Duchamp worried his lower lip. "We take your point, Collum. The recent quarterly fiscals have been alarmingly disappointing."

"Reichmann has allowed his obsession with Braverman Shaw to overshadow his more mundane fiduciary duties."

"Mundane they may be, but they are our lifeblood," Duchamp said. "The businesses set up shaded from the sunlight of the Holy See are vital to our interests." He frowned so deeply his eyebrows fairly met. "What precisely has the current *Nauarchus* ordered you to do?"

Fireside, who thrilled at the modifier "current," nevertheless decided not to tell the truth. Mentioning Maura Kite's involvement would by necessity bring up subjects even he didn't want the cardinal to know about, such as Reichmann's theory that Valentin Kite had found the entrance to King Solomon's mine. He, himself, did not give it much credence, believing the idea was part and parcel of Reichmann's growing mania. Instead, Fireside's agile mind concocted an answer that would please Duchamp. "I and my *extramuros* cadre have been dispatched to terminate Braverman Shaw."

"Reichmann told me this was a near-impossible task," Duchamp said.

"We have received word that Shaw is on the move. This is an ideal time—indeed, possibly the only time—he may be vulnerable."

The cardinal nodded sagely. "We are not opposed, but we are of the opinion that you have been given only half your assignment."

Fireside's ears pricked up, just like his Arabians when they knew he was near.

"We have come to the firm and unshakable conclusion that the Knights require a certain, ah, pruning," the cardinal said. "Operating outside the bounds of Holy See canonical law set down in the Knights' original charter is reprehensible. It cannot be tolerated."

That was a joke, Fireside thought. Under Cardinal Duchamp's stewardship, the Knights of Saint Clement were almost always operating outside of those bounds. The half-dozen lucrative banking businesses in Switzerland and Cyprus were proof enough of that. But, of course, Fireside said nothing of this.

"In light of these findings, we wish never to encounter the current *Nauarchus* again." The cardinal ceased his pacing, turned to Fireside. "The alternative is a visitation by the pope's chosen representative to clean house, from the ground up. And, Collum, we do believe that neither one of us wants that, are we correct?"

"As always, Your Eminence."

"Then make it so, Collum. Accomplish your tasks and we will look most favorably upon you when Reichmann's replacement is named."

Bodies. Bodies everywhere, strewn helter-skelter in the hallways, on the stairs, in the parlors, sitting rooms, offices, and library downstairs. Reichmann sprinted as fast as he could, the fire and the awful thing that had been Maura Kite hot on his heels. He could hear her laughter echoing through the fog of smoke and rapidly increasing heat. He had pulled his robe over his nose and mouth to help filter out the smoke and fire particulates he knew could lay him low within minutes.

How in God's name, he wondered as his desperate flight continued, could all his men have been killed so quickly? Some were burned to death, others curled and shriveled, as if they had been brined or pickled; still others lay bared to the bone, their flesh seemingly melted away.

As he ran through the living nightmare that had overtaken his castle while he had been peacefully sleeping, his only imperative was to escape. The idea of turning to confront whatever Maura had become, even if he'd had a weapon, which at the moment he did not, never entered his mind. He was all about getting free, staying alive. Nothing else mattered.

Heading toward the scullery door, he was flying past the kitchens, where oatmeal was still bubbling on the burners, fresh scones piled high, sausages burning, and fried eggs curling into cinder from the outside in, when a shadow stepped in front of him.

Maura!

For the first time, he saw that the eerie symbol of a triangle inside a circle inside a square had by some alchemical process been imprinted on her irises. Her eyes opened wide, but not as wide as her mouth. He caught a briefest glimpse of an inhuman tongue flicking out before he reversed course, sliding a bit on the slick floor, then running for all he was worth, sweat flying off him like rain blown by tempest winds.

He felt something icy touch the center of his back and crawl upward for a heart-stopping instant like a gigantic thousand-legged insect. With a terrified shout, he broke away, dove left, then right, through the library, then the drawing room, bodies everywhere, the castle turned into a veritable charnel house, the stench of roasted human meat sickening him. He navigated the maze-like downstairs at top speed, praying that Maura, even in this hideous, unknown state, wouldn't have his familiarity with the layout. That pipe dream was almost immediately shattered when he rounded a corner, saw her standing spread legged, blocking his way to the front door.

She opened her mouth, and it seemed to him that it contained more teeth than was normal in a human mouth. "I am ill met by sunlight." The words came out as a kind of screech, like a child running a bow across violin strings for the first time.

Again he reversed course, but this time, leaping over more corpses, he was able to wrench open a narrow door in one of the back hallways, step onto a tiny, unlit landing, and pull the door firmly shut behind him. Quickly but carefully he descended the staircase he knew so well down to the stone cellar, with its wine storage, heating units, and utility niches. Counting treads in the darkness brought him into the cellar without incident. Above him, he thought he heard a rattling of the door.

Down here, it was still cool. Neither the fire nor the attendant smoke had penetrated the thick stone underfloor or the massive interlocking wooden joists, but he knew it was only a matter of time before the smoke, at least, would begin leaking through, as the roof and then the upper floors collapsed.

There was a cellar exit, if only he could get to it in time. But already a flood of light illuminated the stairs; then a figure, interrupting that light, began to descend. With it, the stench of burned wood and bodies, tendrils of smoke writhing like snakes in the air. The cellar began to heat up at a terrifying rate.

Reichmann, heading for the short flight of stone steps up and out into freedom, froze, pressing his back against the wall. The presence was now in the cellar proper. Too late to make a run for it, he'd be caught out. Was there nowhere to hide? And then he remembered the cold meat locker. It was fairly new— he'd had it installed to his own specifications—and was hidden behind a panel in order to keep tight inventory control of some of the more expensive cuts, especially the dry-aging beef.

Removing his slippers, he picked his noiseless way to the locker. The lever presented yet another problem. He knew from experience that it made a definite click when it was opened. He stood before the locker, as if paralyzed. The skin on his back prickled. Was that heat he felt through his robe? He shivered involuntarily. He had to make up his mind, and fast. Gripping the stainless-steel lever in one hand, the end of his wide belt in the other, he began to ease the lever out toward him. As soon as there was enough room he slid the end of his belt between it and the catch to stop the noise.

With the door open a crack, he withdrew his belt end, slipped into the locker, shut the door behind him. Retreating to the far end, he hunkered down, already shivering with the intense cold. In the darkness, he strained to hear the slightest sound. A tense silence reigned for some moments, while cold sweat slithered down his spine, moistened his armpits. The silence was so absolute that when the distinctive click came, even damped from hearing it from this side, it sounded like a crack of thunder. Reichmann scuttled behind a rack of hanging sides of beef.

The smell of congealed blood filled his nostrils, but there was another scent he couldn't readily identify, but which he associated with the thing that had been Maura Kite.

Through a slivery gap he saw a shape enter—a shadow darker than the darkness. Her legs scissored. She quested around, clearly searching for him. Maura's eyes blazed briefly as her head swung in his direction. He did not move a muscle, not daring even to breathe. Could she hear the thudding of his accelerated heartbeat, the rushing of blood in his ears? He closed his eyes and, for the first time in many years, prayed. *Heavenly Father, protect me from this demonic presence. Christ Lord, grant me an escape and I will be your faithful servant forever and ever.*

Time passed, slow as molasses poured in winter. Reichmann's lungs cried out for oxygen, and still he refrained from taking a breath. Even the momentary cloud of his breath would surely betray his presence to this thing. His temples throbbed painfully; a vein stood out in the center of his forehead. Lights danced crazily behind his closed eyelids.

When he could bear it no longer, he opened his eyes. The peculiar scent was stronger, the legs, straight as posts, nearer. In fact, he saw, to his horror, that Maura was standing no more than two feet away, the thick sides of beef the only thing between them. He could hear her breathing, like the sigh of a great engine. The blaze of her eyes briefly sparked in the darkness. At any moment now he expected one of her hands to be thrust through the narrow gap in the meat, to feel her fingers constricting his throat. *How ironic,* he thought, *and how dreadful to be burned alive in a refrigerated meat locker.* But, to his great surprise, nothing of the sort happened. In fact, nothing happened. Still, he was so panicked that it was some time—how much it was impossible to say—before he realized that he no longer smelled that peculiar scent. Not only that, but he sensed he was alone in the locker.

Taking a long, shuddering breath, he rose on legs made

shaky by compressed joints. He waited, heart pounding, but he could see nothing, hear nothing. Cautiously, he moved out from behind the sides of beef. From the meat locker it was only a short distance to the steps up to the cellar exit and to freedom. He opened the locker door, immediately smelled smoke. He heard a crash from overhead, and the entire castle shuddered. Time was running away from him. No matter what, he knew he had to make a last-ditch run for it.

Taking several deep breaths, he set off, sprinting through the hazy darkness, trying his best not to cough as smoke entered his lungs with each indrawn breath. At last, he mounted the stone slabs, unlatched the thick oaken door, frantically pushed it open, and burst out into a morning luridly glowering with enormous tongues of flame. Sparks showered and flew in all directions. The sky itself seemed on fire. Too, the air was thick with the castle's groans as it entered its death throes. He did not waste time looking back over his shoulder, certain that that bitch Maura Kite had managed to destroy his home completely. Even with the flames licking higher and the column of smoke broadening out like a canopy, help would be too late in coming. The castle was far away from the nearest town.

He made a beeline for the stables. Apart from the restless horses, the interior was deserted. He chose Neptune, his favorite, led him out of the paddock, and swung up onto his back, grabbing on to his mane.

Then Reichmann rode, bent far over so that Neptune's flying mane sometimes obscured his vision. No matter. As the horse pounded over the moors, directed by pressure from his knees, Neptune knew precisely where to go. He had ridden him to and from the private airfield many times, taking so much pleasure in riding that he preferred this mode of travel to reach the airstrip where his plane and helicopter waited. Now he thanked God for his horses—for Neptune in particular—for he had seen no sign of the Land Rover anywhere.

The airfield came into view. The helicopter was gone, having taken Fireside and his cadre on the first leg of their assignment, but the Learjet was standing by, as it always was. The crew was outside, on their mobile phones as they stared at the castle going up in flames. But they soon pocketed these, as they recognized Reichmann, pulled him off Neptune, and under his command hustled him up the stairs and into the plane's interior.

The pilot and navigator went immediately to the cockpit to start their abbreviated preflight checks while the flight attendants scrambled to fetch Reichmann clothes to wear.

Moments later all were strapped into seats, the Lear's brakes came off, its engines roared, and it sped down the runway. Even as they left the ground, Reichmann refused to look at the castle. A past too terrible to contemplate. A future altogether unknowable, but without doubt frightening.

TWENTY-THREE

Even on the brightest days, when the Italian sun was at its zenith, Valentin Kite carried his shadow around with him like an invisible cloak. Inevitably, there were times when he wondered if this weightless entity, which nevertheless straddled his shoulders as if he were Atlas holding up the weight of the world, belonged to him. In those moments, he felt keenly the presence of another, the sensation moving through him like a serpent uncoiling.

But, in truth, these moments were few and far between. He had arrived in Capraola via a circuitous route he now could no longer remember clearly, as if the journey had been taken by someone other than himself. Since setting foot on Italian soil he had scarcely given his shadow a second thought, and when he did it was with a feeling of admiration fed by a sensation of power growing inside himself like mushrooms in moonlight.

That metaphor would appeal to Saint Bella dell'Arca, he thought: *"I am ill met by sunlight."*

Up ahead, at the crest of the hill, was the stone edifice of the convent of Saint Angelica Boniface. Amid hornbeam trees, he passed through rising plateaus of coltsfoot, nasturtium, iris, and lavender. The scents were quite pleasing, but when they burst inside him something shuddered. Midday had passed dark and dank with scarcely a breath of wind to stir the treetops. Valentin was returning from the village with local foodstuffs in a mesh sack. A loaf of stone-ground bread under one arm.

He spied Malus the moment he crested the last rise, standing hands loose by his sides, as if he had been waiting for hours for Valentin's return. It wasn't until Valentin had closed the distance between them that he saw the backpack strapped over Malus's shoulders. A tiny thrill of guilt and lust eeled through Valentin at the thought of being left alone with the nuns of Saint Angelica Boniface.

"I must be off," Malus said in his curiously accented Italian.

Was he originally from eastern Europe or the Levant? He'd never say, being understandably vague about his origins. Like all good masters, he maintained an air of mystery that played into his power and enhanced his stature.

"How long?" Valentin asked.

"No more or less than is necessary."

Valentin was still acclimatizing himself to Malus's patterns of speech. The patterns of his thinking seemed, for the moment, beyond him.

"And in the meantime?"

"In the meantime, prepare yourself."

Malus was very young, not more than twenty or so, Valentin judged. He was tall and slim, ascetic looking, had copper-colored hair, thick and long, curling behind his ears, obscuring the nape of his neck. The whisper of a red beard shadowed his strong jaw. If he had been thicker of build he might have been mistaken for a Viking, for it was surely true that he did not appear to belong to the modern world. The shape of his face, the way he wore his hair, above all the look in his eye—one more lambent than the other—marked him as someone born out of time. Like everyone he knew, Valentin had looked at old photographs of ancestors—fathers and mothers, grandmothers and grandfathers, great-grandparents. The further back in time these people had lived the stranger they looked as compared to modern-day people. Discounting the way they dressed or combed their hair, their faces were different, could not be mistaken for someone of Valentin's generation. This was how

Malus appeared to him: as if he were looking at a tintype photo shot and developed a long time ago.

"Prepare myself," he said now.

"And our sisters." Malus's inscrutable gaze weighed heavily on him. "Our enemies will be upon us shortly."

"How can you know this?" Valentin said, though it had become clear to him days ago that Malus knew many things, though it was impossible to understand how.

"Because I have sent for them."

"And they will come?"

"Oh, indeed yes."

"But how can you be sure?"

Malus smiled his feral smile. "I never knew my parents. My mother died giving birth to me. By that time my father was already gone, less than a memory. When I was seven I ran away from my foster parents, not because of anything they had done—it was clear to me that they loved me. And when, six months later, I finally realized that I couldn't run away from myself, I came back. 'How do you know they'll want you back?' my younger foster brother asked me when I found him playing in the dirt outside their house. 'Human nature,' I told him."

Malus shifted the weight of his backpack to a more comfortable position against his spine. "The war is almost upon us." He laid a hand on Val's shoulder. "The war you and Maura are a part of, the war that is the beginning of the end."

Watching Malus walk away down the hill, Valentin shuddered.

Bravo had much to consider as they deplaned in the Tannourine area. The mountains were all around them; the air was perfumed by the enormous cedar forest of over sixty thousand trees. Sunlight sparked off the cliff faces and the virtually perpendicular waterfalls that spilled like pale ribbons from high above them. All seemed so tranquil and calm it was impossible to imagine the religious war being fought over every acre.

It wasn't just that he found Ayla's story of the ritual performed inside the red tent of shadows to be incredible—he himself had been witness to a number of advents that defied rational explanation, not the least of which was the existence of the Quintessence his father had discovered and then secreted away for his son to find. It was that he was hearing in her story childhood remembrances, and memories, as he well knew, were problematic, since with every successive remembrance of an event one recalled not the original memory but the latest memory from the last time you retrieved it. And so with each remembrance the original was subtly altered by your current emotional state, intervening occurrences, reactions to experiences. On top of that, he was hearing the memories of a child injured, on the verge of passing out, terrified for herself and for her mother. With these givens, could anything Ayla said be taken at face value? That was the conundrum Bravo was pondering as they made the short walk downhill into a village, so tiny, so remote, it had no name anyone could recall. It was nothing more than a couple of intersecting streets along which dispirited people trudged with bowed backs and, occasionally, elderly vehicles creaked and crawled like old soldiers, long invalided by an unknown and unseen war. A distinct air of incipient disaster seemed to hang over the place like the discharge of a hunting rifle.

Ayla took him into a run-down building that seemed like a private home but was actually a bed-and-breakfast of sorts. They were the only patrons in the place. They were seated at a table overlooking a wall mural of what Ayla told him was the convent of Saint Shallitah, one of a pair of Maronite Christian monasteries in the Tannourine vicinity.

They ate black-eyed peas and chard stew, diced chicken with red pepper sauce, meatballs with stewed cherries, and *zaatar* salad, made by the proprietor's wife, a tiny woman with a grim expression and nothing to say. The proprietor himself was a man in the shape of a question mark, with the outsized hands and feet of a farmer or a day laborer. Though taciturn, he was friendly enough.

Off the plane, shedding his recent memories like a snake its dried skin, Bravo found his appetite, had second helpings of everything, and scraped his salad down to the plate. The owner, who served them himself, hovered in the doorway to the kitchen, shuckling back and forth from one foot to another.

"Your friend there looks so nervous he might pee himself," Bravo said.

Ayla gave him that wry smile that made her seem almost approachable. "Not many visitors up here these days. Judging by the mural, he's Maronite Christian. I could be a Muslim spy for all he knows."

Bravo grunted, a poor substitute for a laugh, but that was all he had at the moment.

"The cave that Val found," he said in a break between courses. "We're in the area where he told me it's supposed to be. He was supposed to send me the exact location if and when he found it, but of course that never happened."

Ayla scooped up some stew with a triangle of warm pita. "Relax. I called someone who's bound to know."

"What about the rebel cadres? These mountains are infested with them."

"I told you to relax."

"Without weapons?"

Afterward, at Ayla's behest, he rented a four-wheel-drive car from the proprietor, along with food and water, a tent, a portable Coleman stove with fuel, and backpacks suitable for hiking. While she was in the bathroom, he made a secondary deal with the man. For an exorbitant sum, Bravo was able to procure a 9mm Beretta in excellent working order, along with two boxes of ammo. By the time Ayla was back, he'd squirreled them away on his person.

He drove, but Ayla navigated with only the occasional aid of the GPS on her mobile. Heading out of the village, she directed him onto a narrow, snakelike road that wound up and up into the mountains. It was paved, after a fashion, but was punctured by so many potholes their speed was greatly diminished. The farther from the village they drove, the higher the elevation, the worse the road's disrepair became. Now entire sections were composed of nothing more than gravel, which spewed like a boat's wake from beneath the nearly bald rear tires. Farther on, Bravo was obliged to maneuver perilously around what appeared to be a mortar crater, now partially filled with greenish water over which insects, clad in what appeared to be warlike metallic armor, luminously skimmed and hummed. On their right the mountain continued its vertiginous ascent, but on their left an exceedingly dense jungle pressed oppressively in, from which now and again emanated bursts of eerie birdcalls and animal grunts.

Nevertheless, in just over two hours, they came around a hairpin bend and, at last, saw just above them what Ayla said was the abandoned village of Ain-Al-Raha. Legend had it that the village, whose name meant "Source of relief," had been a protected place for injured Christian Crusaders during the wars that lasted from the eleventh through the thirteenth centuries. Ain-Al-Raha was the home of several sixth-century and Crusader-era churches.

"There are a group of historians who believe these churches to be incontrovertible proof of the early presence of Christianity in the Upper Levant," Ayla said.

The afternoon was waning. The slanting sunlight threw long shadows across the stone façades and their own bodies as they clambered out of the vehicle. The air was cool and crisp. The sporadic rattle of far-off automatic fire came to them as if a warning.

"Come on," Ayla said.

They struck off toward the middle of the deserted village, which nevertheless held an eerie sense of watchfulness, an anticipation of an event yet to take place. As was often the case with abandoned buildings—and even more so with entire villages—

the presence of history could be felt in the form of the ghosts of inhabitants alive in ages past, reluctant to leave their ancient surroundings. The scent of stone dust, of centuries, crumbled beneath the relentless boot of time, infused the dusky air.

As the distant gunfire to the east subsided, the setting sun winked out in an apocalyptic moment and the muffled cannon fire of thunder arose in the west. A fork of lightning fluoresced the darkening clouds advancing like an army between the gaps in the foliage-choked mountains.

Ayla was looking around as if she were in Leicester Square waiting for her date. Bravo, right hand underneath his light jacket, folded his fingers around the butt of the Beretta he had jammed into his waistband at the small of his back. Not that it mattered. One moment they were alone in the village square; the next they were surrounded by a dozen men armed with Kalashnikovs.

The man directly facing them was clearly the leader, tall and darkly bearded, with the wiry muscles of someone used to difficult climbs, hard labor, and not much food to show for either. He was dressed in the robes of a jihadist; a length of cloth, dirt stained and grubby, circled his head. He was thin as a rail, with knobby shoulders and knees, and yet, as was true of all charismatics, he radiated an undeniable strength of purpose. Sadly, with his sharp beak-like nose, wary eyes, and thick lips he also exuded the air of someone who saw what he wanted to see and nothing more. This tunnel vision was endemic to fanatics of all religions, creeds, and stripes, Bravo had found. Whatever did not fit into their particular worldview was dismissed or, better yet, unseen.

"Tell your companion to take his hand out from beneath his jacket," the leader said in Lebanese Arabic, "before it is shot off." He bared his large teeth, yellowed and damaged. "My people are known for their short fuses."

"Does that mean you do not have full control over them?" Bravo asked.

This brought a scowl to the leader's face. "You are only alive at this moment because of my friendship with Dilara and Ayla."

"Bravo," Ayla hissed under her breath, "what the hell are you doing?"

"What's his name?" Bravo whispered back.

When she told him, Bravo addressed the leader. "Nasir, Protector of the Faith, are you aptly named?"

This brought Nasir up short, a curious and not altogether friendly look on his face. "Ayla," he said, "what is this? Why have you brought this infidel here? What d'you want?"

Before she could answer, Bravo released his grip on the Beretta, showed both his hands, palms toward Nasir. "We're here to hasten the demise of those who shot Dilara to death."

Nasir's eyes opened wide, their whites seeming to shed lamplight. "Ayla, is this true? Is your mother dead?"

At that moment the first fat drops of rain carpet bombed them. A rushing in the air like bats' wings, a heightened smell of stone dust as a sudden wet gust caused dust devils to rise in a feat of levitation, presaged the deluge.

They all trooped into the nearest building—one of the Christian churches—and Bravo could not help thinking he and Ayla were being herded like cattle. But once inside, Nasir ordered a fire be made from the stacked cordwood next to the enormous fireplace in what had once been the refectory.

As they were drying off, he approached Ayla. He smelled not very different from a camel. "Your mother," he said softly. "She's dead? Someone killed her?"

"Shot to death, as Bravo said," she affirmed. "My father was burned to death in the fire they started."

Nasir managed to look both startled and angry. "And who are these people?"

"We're hoping to find that out here," Bravo said.

For the first time Nasir regarded him directly. "You are not Muslim, like Dilara and Ayla."

"I respect all religions," Bravo said.

A small silence sprang up around them, even while the downpour continued to detonate against the tile roof and stone façade, abruptly broken by Nasir's laugh, raucous as a cockatoo's. "Your friend has the soul of a politician, it seems, Ayla. An answer that deflects and reflects at the same time."

"Bravo's right in what he says, Nasir."

Ayla turned to dry her clothes on the opposite side. The cadre was spaced about the room, some standing, others leaning against walls, still others hunkered down on their haunches, rifles lying on their tensed thighs.

"We need to find out who killed my parents, and we believe the starting point is in a cave high up in these mountains."

Nasir shrugged. "What makes you think that?"

Bravo took up a stick from the rubble lying on the floor, drew the symbol in the dust of the floor: a triangle inside a circle inside a square. "Have you seen this before?"

Nasir gave Ayla a penetrating look.

"It's all right," she said softly. "I've told him the story."

Nasir's eyes narrowed. "All of it?"

"As much as needs to be known."

He gave a brief nod, looked at Bravo again, and, for the first time since they had entered the church, spoke to him directly. "You need my"—his arm swept out to encompass his men—"*our* help."

"It's the Tusik family that needs your help, Nasir."

"You owe my mother—and me—a debt," Ayla said.

Thunder rolled and through the windows—sills afloat in water—every now and again, sheets of lightning could be seen shedding electric blue light into the jungle on the descending edge of the mountainside. The rain was like the roar of an attacking horde—hoarse and primeval.

"The nature and form of my debt," Nasir said, "were between your mother and me. It concerns no one else."

"Dilara is dead, Nasir. You must get that through your head. I will not stand idly by and allow her murderers to go unpunished." She eyed him, her face flushed with the blood of anger and revenge. "You, of all people, know the meaning and importance of punishment."

At the sound of the word "punishment," the jihadist cadre came to life, rising from their haunches, pulling away from the walls, forming a circle around their leader and the two intruders. But Nasir, lost deep in thought, seemed unaware of their movements. Instead, he raked his fingers through his beard meditatively.

At length, he nodded. "Yes. You're right. I owe what I owe. There can be no question of Dilara's worth to me over the years. So. I will do as you ask. I will help you if I can." He looked from Bravo to Ayla and back again. "Where is it you wish to go?"

"To the Cave of Shadows," Ayla said without hesitation.

TWENTY-FOUR

Light was draining away in the long afternoon. Soon Istanbul would be shrouded in darkness. Lamps would be lit; lights would blaze. As they had been all day, the streets were overflowing with jostling crowds as they wended their way through spice-laden markets, along shop-lined streets, avoiding the ubiquitous beggars and touts running wild, or simply sat at minuscule tables, cheek by jowl with their neighbors, sipping Turkish coffee and popping delicate sweetmeats into their mouths.

Reichmann, miles away, high above in the arc of the world, had just exited the jet's cockpit. He had been huddled with the pilot and navigator, instructing them to make for Alexandria, Egypt, then bending over the charts as they plotted the best air route. Now he punched in a number on his mobile phone and, as he took his seat, heard the male voice say, "Captain Balik."

"Are you free to speak, Captain?"

"Mr. Reichmann?"

"Indeed."

"Give me a moment."

Reichmann heard the sounds of a chair creaking as Balik rose from his desk, then the low murmur of voices speaking official-ese, which was the same in any language, and finally a kind of hollow silence.

"I'm in the stairwell," Balik said at length. His voice sounded a bit echoey. "We can speak freely."

"What have you discovered?"

"It seems possible, perhaps even likely, that the man who fell or was pushed to his death—Antonio Bazan—was responsible for the explosion and subsequent fire that ripped through the Tusiks' apartment and an adjoining section of the building."

"What evidence do you have?"

Balik's tone remained neutral. "It's our working theory."

"In other words, you have nothing." Reichmann had lost whatever respect he might have had for this man. In any event, Reichmann had more important things on his mind than the captain's incompetence. "Why have you omitted the fact that Dilara Tusik was shot to death?"

"You know about that?"

"I know many things, Captain. A fact of life you would do well to keep in mind. In any event, I pay you enough to keep it in mind."

"I have no dispute with that," Balik said grudgingly. "But as of this moment, we are assuming that Bazan shot her as she was escaping the apartment. We found the murder weapon on the stairwell. I didn't deem the detail important. If she hadn't been shot she would have been burned to a crisp. I will be wrapping up the case today. I have far more pressing matters to attend to that involve the security of the state."

Very convenient, Reichmann thought morosely. *These people are as thick as a brick and shun hard work as if it were the plague. Well, perhaps to them it is.* He understood all too well that a quick and tidy wrap-up suited the government best. Still, he could not suppress the contempt he felt for their incompetence. Balik clearly had no idea that Maura Kite had been with Bazan, that she had most probably killed him because she had discovered Reichmann had turned him from the Gnostic Observatines to the Knights. But why should she care? And yet very clearly she did. Hadn't she just tried to kill him, as she had with the rest of his castle contingent?

Thinking back to Fireside's report following his visit to the police morgue, Reichmann was convinced that the strange corpse found in the doorway to the Tusiks' apartment had been the perpetrator of their demise. Further, it now seemed clear to him that that corpse was somehow connected to whatever it was Maura Kite had become. And in this Balik's laziness might very well suit his purposes.

"Collum Fireside will come to collect that body in your morgue," he said in a neutral tone.

"What? My forensic team is about to—"

"It isn't a forensic expert you need, Captain," Reichmann said. "It's an exorcist."

"I don't understand."

Of course you don't, Reichmann thought. *You're a Muslim.* "In any event, Fireside will relieve you of the corpse."

"Impossible." Balik was making a show of bristling, but Reichmann wasn't buying it.

"Nothing is impossible, Captain. You, of all people, ought to know that."

"Please. There are limits to what money can buy."

"Calm yourself, Captain. My suggestion—and it's only a suggestion—is for your own good as well as mine. I assure you that my people will discover more about that corpse than your forensic team ever could. Imagine how their findings will enhance your stature inside the Turkish security apparatus." He paused. "So will the extra twenty thousand dollars that will be deposited in your offshore account."

The security captain grunted his assent and that was all there was to it. Well, not quite. "One more thing, Captain. I want you to find Ayla Tusik, the victims' only child. I have it on good authority that she was in Istanbul during the incident."

"And if she's no longer here?"

Reichmann rolled his eyes and counted slowly to ten. "Find out where she is now."

Without waiting to hear if Balik would comment he cut the connection and called Collum to inform him of his newest task.

TWENTY-FIVE

"What happens when they come through that door?"

"They'll see me and be charmed," Emma said with her best professional smile.

"How do you know they'll come?"

"I know the way the world works." She turned her sightless eyes on him, large and still a beautiful cornflower blue. "By the way, I'll just bet you look spiffy in that Savile Row suit Bravo bought you."

As it happened, and as Emma rightly sensed, Fra Leoni stood looking at himself in the mirrored back wall of the Salinas Holdings, Ltd., reception area. Salinas was another of the Gnostic Observatines' secular corporations. He was only half-aware of the vaguely bewildered expression on his face. "It fits me perfectly," he said with a tinge of wonder.

"Well, of course it does," Emma said. "The company took four fittings, remember?"

"I remember many things, Emma—far too many for a human brain, I often think!—but clothes fittings aren't one of them. After all, I'm used to robes." He sighed. "Well, I imagine it's to be expected. Even I, cloistered as I am amid the Gnostic Observatines, cannot avoid the modern world creeping in now and again." He frowned. "But how on earth did you tie my tie so perfectly? It's got that dimple in the center of the knot I see in all the men's fashion ads."

Her laugh was like the tinkle of sleigh bells. "I've had plenty of practice with my brother."

"You know," he said, turning his head from side to side, frowning at his pink cheeks, "I feel positively naked without my beard."

"And yet," Emma said lightly, "it makes you look fifty years younger."

Fra Leoni chuckled appreciatively. He had become very fond of Braverman's sister. She was keen of mind and generous of spirit; even better, she was possessed of a sense of humor he found irresistible.

At that moment an electronic squeak like a mouse whose tail had been stepped on sounded, and Fra Leoni's gaze went immediately to the monitor that showed images from the four security cameras placed in strategic locations both outside the building, which Salinas owned, and within.

"Front door," Fra Leoni said redundantly, as all four had different sounds so Emma could distinguish them as if she were sighted. "One man."

"Interesting. Still. He looks like a government stooge," she said as she buzzed their visitor in, "right?"

"You would know better than me," Fra Leoni said. "But if I had to make a wager my money would be on you."

Emma laughed again. "Do you remember who you are today?"

"Ralph Waldo Emerson."

"Now is the time to be serious," Emma said.

"Right. Sorry. I am Percival Dockery-Smythe," he said in perfectly accented upper-class British as he threw his shoulders back, military-style. He shook his head. "My goodness, the Brits still have names like this?"

"Indeed, they do," Emma said. "And you're *Sir* Percy. You were knighted twelve years ago."

"Ironic that, being a knight." Fra Leoni's gaze switched to the CCTV camera in the elevator. "He's on his way up."

"Places, everyone," Emma said, which was Sir Percy's cue to head into the director's office. "Break a leg," she added just before he disappeared through the doorway.

Precisely three minutes later, Captain Balik walked through the door.

Mortal terror has a way of exhausting you on every level, Reichmann thought behind closed eyelids, as he tried to sleep. But every time he began to drift off he'd start awake with an icy shiver, the image of whatever it was Maura Kite had become reaching out for him between the hanging sides of beef. The stench of whatever was oozing out of her pores mingled with that of the cold locker. Earlier he had been served a grilled steak, potatoes gratin, and creamed spinach. His nostrils had flared at the scent rising from the plates, and with his first bite of meat, rich with fat and bloody as a knife slash, he had disgraced himself, vomiting all over the food.

Now in a different seat, the acrid smell of disinfectant in his lungs, he popped a couple of Ambien and waited for the drug to roll sleep over him like a comfy blanket. And yet no comfort was afforded him. Instead, he was drowning in the rising tide of his last moments inside the castle—choking on smoke, singed by flames, pursued by a creature that would have seared the pages of any number of tomes on demonology he had read as a young man. But never in his life would he have imagined that demons were real, let alone that he would come face-to-face with one that wanted him dead.

He was now beginning to wonder just what it was Valentin Kite had stumbled across in the last cave he and his crew had visited in Tannourine. Of course, Reichmann had read the ridiculous legend that King Solomon had ordered his cadre of alchemists to protect the hoarded gold they had conjured up for him in some magical manner. But now he had to wonder about something that should have been obvious to him from the outset: if, indeed, the king's gold mine did exist, if indeed it contained gold that had been laced with the Quintessence and was thus as different from the normal precious ore as a peacock was from a wren, then why not the protection, as well? Was that what had happened to Val and his people? But even if so, then how could that have affected his wife? She had been nowhere near Tannourine, let alone the cave.

Unanswerable questions revolved in Reichmann's head like a Ferris wheel—a circle, always moving, but without end—dizzying him, frustrating him, and, not the least, frightening him. What he had experienced in Malta was outside his ken. There were no satisfactory explanations in the rational world—or in his own intra muros world for that matter. The Church had trained him not to believe in demonic possessions, in exorcisms, in magic of any kind. And yet his predecessor had believed in the existence of the Quintessence, a substance, if not magical, then surely alchemical and, thus, anathema to Church doctrine. Did that mean it didn't exist? Had Reichmann's predecessor been chasing a ghost? Was the discovery of the Quintessence simply a shard of disinformation released by Braverman Shaw's father to confound and befuddle the Church and, by extension, its strong right arm, the Knights?

And, for that matter, what of King Solomon's gold? Was its existence legend or myth? Because, as Reichmann knew full well, the two were not synonymous. Legends, on the one hand, had a way of turning out to be true, albeit in the most inopportune of times, at least in his experience. Myths, on the other hand, were just that. Wild tales handed down over the centuries becoming more improbable, more exaggerated, with each retelling.

For so long, he had neatly placed the story of King Solomon's alchemically altered gold squarely in the category of myth, and therefore it held no interest for him. Then Cardinal Duchamp had come to him with what he had believed to be a harebrained scheme. Scraps of ancient documents and what appeared to be maps of what the cardinal's cartographers had identified as the mountains in Tannourine. Gradually, it dawned on Reichmann, though Duchamp was scrupulous in not saying as much, that the search for Solomon's gold was strictly a private matter, which, like the half-dozen businesses the Knights had set up and were running for Duchamp, was unknown to the pope or the other cardinals inside Vatican City.

And so Reichmann had recommended Valentin Kite, and the rest was recent history. What should have been a straightforward exploratory mission that Reichmann was certain would amount to nothing turned out to be anything but: deaths, mysteries, and an inexplicable transformation had followed Val's entry into that last cave.

What to make of all of it? Reichmann would have asked himself this question had he not finally plunged into a slumber so complete that he had to be shaken awake upon his arrival in Egypt.

"Good afternoon," Captain Balik said as he approached Emma's fortress of a desk. "I hope I'm not interfering with the end of your business day."

"There is no end to Salinas Holdings' business day," Emma said with a neutral smile. "We do business all over the world."

"And what precisely is your business?" Leaning forward, Balik pressed his fists against the desktop. "If I may ask?"

Emma, feeling the change in air pressure, smelling his distinctive odor as he neared her, kept her smile unchanged. "And you are?"

"Iman Balik, Captain, Millî İstihbarat Teşkilati." The Turkish intelligence organization.

She could hear him reaching into his suit jacket pocket, flipping open his credentials, holding them up for her to see. She kept her head still, her eyes staring straight ahead into the greater darkness of his head and chest.

"If you are, indeed, MİT," Emma said, "then you've done your homework and know exactly what businesses we are engaged in. If you need me to tell you then you've come here unprepared."

Balik frowned at her seeming lack of interest in his ID.

It might be that he hadn't yet worked out that she wasn't sighted. "Humor me, Miss . . ."

"Ms. Shaw. Emma Shaw," she said. "But to be truthful, I grow weary of telling you what you must already know."

"Import-export of rugs and home furnishings which you manufacture, global transshipping for smaller manufacturers. How am I doing?"

"It's a beautiful thing. How can I be of assistance, Captain Balik?"

"I am continuing my investigation of the recent explosion and fire near the Golden Horn."

"A tragic gas main leak; so the local media informs us." She spread her hands. "How does that concern us?"

"I understand that your brother, Braverman Shaw, was acquainted with Omar and Dilara Tusik, the victims at ground zero."

"A number of us here were, Captain. Including me. Do you wish to ask me questions concerning our relationship?"

"I'd prefer to talk with your brother."

She cocked her head. "Why?"

"Ms. Shaw, where is Braverman Shaw? Is he currently in Istanbul?"

"He is not, Captain."

"Could he be on the company jet that took off earlier today?"

"That I could not tell you."

"And was the Tusiks' daughter, Ayla, on that same plane?"

"I don't know," Emma said truthfully. "I've never met her."

"Nevertheless," Balik persisted, "you are Mr. Shaw's sister."

"A fact we've already established."

"His confidante."

"My brother's life is his own, as is mine," Emma said easily. "He's away on business; that's all I know."

"Come now—"

"I have been entirely forthcoming with you, Captain Balik. Should you have further questions you may ask them of our CEO, Sir Percival Dockery-Smythe."

Balik produced a sneer that Emma could sense, though, of course, she could not see it. "And I suppose Sir Percival is away on business, also."

"As it happens he's right here in the office." Emma picked up the intercom headset, murmured into it for a moment, then set it aside. "Salinas Holdings wishes to cooperate with the MİT as fully as is possible. Sir Percival will see you now."

Over the centuries, Fra Leoni had become a master of many arts, trades, and skills. Over those same centuries he had been forced to deal with officious overlords of every type and stripe—from popes to magistrates, kings, queens, and princes, doges, tsars, and, more latterly, modern-day presidents and politicians. In short, he knew how to talk with them, to them, over them, and through them, foiling their tasks and short-circuiting their will. Captain Balik was no exception.

Stepping through the doorway, he was shown through a maze of offices, down a corridor of dove-gray carpeting and black-and-white photos on either wall of old Singapore, Hong Kong, Penang, and Istanbul itself, at the end of which was a double door made of teak planks polished to a high sheen.

"Ah, the constabulary!" Sir Percy cried, rising and coming around from behind the desk.

"The what?"

Bewilder 'em with savvy jargon, give 'em what they think they came for, then finish 'em off. "The strong arm of the law." He extended his hand. "That's what you are, Ms. Shaw tells me." Not waiting for a response, he clasped Balik's hand in his, squeezing in jocular bonhomie. "A distinguished member of the MİT—not unlike our own MI6, eh what? I've a couple of those chaps in my club just along Whitehall." He was still gripping the captain's hand. "Long ways from there, at the mo', I can tell you. I love your country, sir, love Istanbul especially, but one does get a bit homesick now and again, doesn't one?"

"I wouldn't know." Balik had managed to pry his hand from the other's grip, and now his face held to a desperately baffled scowl in the manner of a drowning man grasping on to the last broken spar in his vicinity. "I came here to—"

"Yes, yes, to ascertain the whereabouts of my illustrious colleague Braverman Shaw. Fact is, sir, he flew out this morning. Headed for Lebanon, so I'm given to understand. Well, is it any wonder? Our forest holdings are under siege now by any number of insurgent bandits who feel no compunction whatsoever in burning everything to the ground, including our property." He shook his head, his jowls wobbling. "Can't have that, can we, old boy, no, we jolly well can't!"

"About Ayla Tusik," Balik said, sensing the slightest break in the verbal assault.

Sir Percy frowned. "Yes, Devil's own business, that. Losing one's parents—both in one swell foop, as it were."

The captain's bewilderment deepened. "What?"

"I mean to say." Sir Percy returned to his desk, flipped open a humidor, selected a cigar. He turned to Balik. "Care for one? No? Pity." He clipped off the end, stuck the cigar in his mouth. "My Lord, these little Cubans are heaven on earth." Snatching up a heavy silver lighter, he flicked on the flame, got the cigar going in a thick cloud of aromatic smoke.

"About Ayla Tusik. You were saying?"

"Was I?" Sir Percy puffed away, eyes half-closed in a kind of ecstasy. "Well, I mean what more can one say? The poor child." He shook his head dolefully. "I would counsel her to see a grief therapist, wouldn't you? I mean it's the only humane suggestion one can make, given the dreadfully tragic circumstances."

By now, the captain's eyes were fairly crossing in frustration. "Have you seen her?"

Sir Percy's snowy brows knit together as he puffed away like the enormously entertaining Caterpillar Alice ran across in Wonderland. "Who?"

"Ayla!" Captain Balik fairly shouted. "Ayla Tusik!"

The eyebrows rose as if on stilts. "Should I have? Is she here in Istanbul?" He reached over to the intercom, shouted, "Ms. Shaw! Is Ms. Tusik in these parts? Have I breached protocol by not contacting her? Find out where she's staying immediately and order flowers."

"The card, sir," came Emma's electronic voice.

Sir Percy blew smoke like an overexcited engine. "The what?"

"The condolence message, Sir Percy."

"Oh, you know." He waved a hand in the air. "The usual. 'Our deepest sympathies, sorry for your loss, anything we can do to be of assistance,' in that vein."

"I'll get right on it," Emma's voice said.

"There's a good girl!"

Sir Percy turned once again to confront the man from MİT, but the captain, irritated beyond endurance, had already beat a hasty retreat.

TWENTY-SIX

Rain beat down the dark-emerald leaves. They bobbed and weaved like a boxer trying to avoid pelting blows. Lamps secreted inside the church, presumably by Nasir's cadre, had been lit, their glow only vaguely penetrating the gloom of night. Caught between the mountains and the strangling jungle, the abandoned village seemed on the verge of being repopulated by cedars, strangler vines, and species of moss so thick and virulent they might have been a form of extraterrestrial life.

There was food in their vehicle, along with a Coleman stove, Bravo reflected, but in this torrential downpour both would be ruined before he could get them back to the church. Plus, despite the rather tenuous relationship between Ayla and Nasir—at least so far as Bravo could determine—he was not at all sure the jihadist leader would allow him to leave the church unaccompanied. One saving grace was that he hadn't been patted down; he still had his 9mm Beretta, safely stowed away at the small of his back.

They ate a sparse and unappetizing meal. The jihadists seemed uninterested in food other than to sustain them. The dangerous energy of the zealot burned within all of them. Each time Bravo looked up, he caught one or another of them staring at him with a furtive and altogether hostile glower. Going forward, he'd have to keep that in mind, as if this mission weren't fraught with enough peril.

After what passed for the dinner meal, Nasir came and

hunkered down opposite Bravo and Ayla, who, perhaps by unspoken mutual consent, had made themselves as comfortable as could be expected, separate from the cadre.

"The rain will end by midnight," Nasir said as if he were a shaman. "It is the time of the month of the full moon. We'll be guided by its light and, Allah willing, we will make the climb to the cave near dawn."

They all dozed then. Bravo wanted to talk with Ayla, but any start he made was met with desultory one-word responses. She had once again withdrawn into herself, and though there was no telling what was on her mind, he suspected she must be reliving her desperate time inside the red tent of shadows. He still had no idea how much—if any—he should believe of what she remembered. Anyway, as he drifted off into a shallow and restive sleep he had his own ghosts haunting him, beginning with the terrible events in the stairwell, his inability to save Dilara, his enormous guilt at her cold-blooded murder, for which he must take much of the responsibility.

He awoke to find Ayla squatting next to him. "How can you sleep?" she said when she saw his eyes glittering in the torchlight.

"It's a gift."

He meant it as a joke, but she just looked away from him. He waited for some time, aware that there was something she wanted to tell him.

"I'm not like my mother, you know."

"It never crossed my mind," Bravo said. "You left home. You made your way in the Western world."

Her gaze swung back, her eyes burning. "You don't know. I never forsook my heritage."

"And I respect that," Bravo said. "These days, it isn't easy being Muslim in the Western world."

"How would you know?"

"You're right, of course. I'm a Catholic."

She studied him for a moment. Then, as if making up her

mind, said in a voice significantly lower, "What happened to us here in Tannourine changed her irrevocably."

He nodded. "She told me it caused her to cross over to—"

"No, no," Ayla said quickly. "You don't understand. The incident undermined her entire belief system. She no longer had a rock to cling to in turbulent times. She was cast adrift in the sea of night."

"I'm sorry to hear you say that," Bravo said. "She told me she had found her faith again in Christ."

"I can't believe she ever said that, but if she did, she lied."

"Why would she do that?"

"Why d'you think? She knew you needed me with you. She also knew you would resist. It would be just like her to exploit your weakness for a fellow Christian—especially one who had converted from Islam." She cocked her head. "That would be irresistible to someone like you, wouldn't it?"

Bravo sighed. "I believe it would, yes."

Ayla favored him with a tiny smile. "Don't be downcast, Bravo. She genuinely cared for you." Ayla murmured a laugh, still mindful of waking those asleep and of being overheard. "Something of an anomaly for her, believe me."

"It seems your mother remained a mystery to the end."

"Trying to understand her was like trying to catch lightning in a bottle. Her uncanny dreams of the future didn't start until sometime after we returned home." She cocked her head like a bird listening to human conversation. "Until this moment, I don't think I ever connected the two. I can't think why; it seems so obvious now."

True to Nasir's prediction, as if a spigot were turned off the torrent of rain let up just before midnight. One instant it was pouring; the next the sky was revealed as the dense cloud that had been pressing down on the mountains lifted like a curtain in the theater, revealing the stage with its magical silver light shimmering upon the dripping leaves, in the pools of water, stirring the muddy open spaces.

Killing the fire and the lamps, they stepped outside to a world of pure black-and-white. The cold coin riding high in the heavens turned both foliage and mountains into walls of jet black, pressing in even more oppressively than they had during the day.

Nasir, leading the way, chose a steep path, luckily for them more rocky than muddy. Yet it was narrow, twisting back on itself like the coils of animal intestines, shimmering wetly in the moonlight.

They moved in single file, silent amid the metallic insect buzzing and guttural animal chatter. The higher they ascended the nearer the dense jungle grew until they were, now and again, brushing elbows and hips against encroaching foliage. The cadre carried their Kalashnikovs as if they would be required to use them at a moment's notice, an observation that did nothing to give Bravo confidence. However, the ineffable beauty of their surroundings was inescapable. Moonlight fell in dreamlike ripples, making sharp-edged patterns. Their shadows were distinctly outlined, inky animations.

A bit over three hours into the hike, the way briefly leveled out, then took an abrupt left-hand turn. They plunged headlong into thickets of foliage. Then, all at once, the lowering moon winked out as the jungle's canopy closed over them like a shroud. Here and there tiny lozenges of moonlight crept stealthily through the leafy branches, but for the most part the darkness was nearly absolute. In this blackness, the chittering and growls of the jungle inhabitants were magnified far beyond normal, echoing and reechoing off the granite outcroppings, mossed-over rock faces as sheer as any city skyscraper. The noises combined with the often foul stench of what must be rotting foliage but smelled more like flesh to wrap them more securely in the bosom of the jungle.

At this point, both Bravo and Ayla, who was walking just ahead of him, were completely dependent on the men in front of them, who were, in turn, dependent on Nasir to lead them safely up the mountain to the Cave of Shadows. Bravo could hear the fall and splash of a waterfall—one of many in this area of Tannourine—but he couldn't see it through the walls of blackness that continued to press in on him.

They took a turn to the right and then, almost immediately, to the left, after which Ayla halted abruptly.

"What is it?" Bravo whispered.

"They're gone," Ayla breathed back.

Peering over her shoulder, he saw that she was right. No figures, no patches of movement in the darkness. He turned around, discovered that the two men who had been following him had vanished as completely as those who had been ahead of them.

"Nasir," Ayla called. And then with more vocal force: "Nasir!"

The jungle chittered and screamed; insects whirred around them, wings ablur. They moved cautiously forward and soon enough saw a small patch of moonlight up ahead where lightning had felled and burned a number of trees.

As they picked their way toward it, Bravo heard what sounded like a snuffle, though it was so brief he couldn't be sure. His attention was momentarily distracted by the sight of Nasir standing in the clearing. He appeared to be looking back at them, but as his face was in shadow it was impossible to tell for sure.

At that moment a horrendous crashing approached them from out of the blackness. Ayla, just in front of Bravo, froze. He glimpsed a black shadow bursting from the underbrush, thundering directly toward Ayla as if the Devil himself were on its tail. It passed through a small patch of moonlight, and Bravo glimpsed small eyes glowing a lambent gold, open jaws revealing monstrous upthrust tusks, used to root for food or to impale other animals—like Ayla. Then the wild boar disappeared into the absolute darkness.

Out of the corner of his eye Bravo saw Nasir cradling his Kalashnikov as if he hadn't a care in the world. Bravo shoved

Ayla out of the path of the charging boar. At the same time, Bravo drew the Beretta, the 9mm a seemingly puny weapon against four hundred pounds of racing muscle, hooves, and fangs. Nevertheless, the handgun was his only option. Dropping to one knee, he squeezed off one, two, three shots, but he was firing blind. He could have sworn he hit the beast squarely, and yet, improbably, demonically, the boar kept on, closing the gap between them with astonishing speed. Bravo managed to fire once more before the beast was on him, eyes maddened as if in pain, his saliva-drenched jaws yawning, the nauseating stench released by his innards like a whiff of hell itself.

"So," Fra Leoni, still in his Sir Percy persona, said, "how did I do?"

"Like Lawrence Olivier on the London stage," Emma said. "Captain Balik blew out of here as if his pants were on fire."

Fra Leoni laughed. They were sitting in Sir Percy's office, alone since the entire staff had been temporarily moved out of the city following the crisis at the safe house. They were sipping celebratory gin and tonics, which Fra Leoni had concocted from Sir Percy's sideboard. The real Sir Percy was safely ensconced in his baronial home outside Cambridge, on a well-deserved vacation.

"High praise, indeed"—Fra Leoni's eyes twinkled—"especially from you."

"What was that?" Emma said, feigning offense. "Am I so judgmental?"

"My goodness, you're not judgmental at all, my dear. Simply —and quite rightfully, in my view—difficult to please."

"I believe that runs in the family."

"Indeed." Fra Leoni took a sip of his drink, then rose off the sofa on which he had been reclining. "You know, I think this triumph over state control calls for a celebration." He smiled. "How about I take you out to dinner. Anywhere you want to go."

"How about Mikla?"

"That's my girl." Fra Leoni set his glass down. "I'm going to change and make a reservation for us to dine al fresco on the terrace. Back in a jiff."

Emma laughed. "Since you're still in Sir Percival Dockery-Smythe mode why not keep those duds on?"

"Too restrictive. My neck is already red and raw from this collar."

Emma heard him bustle out. She was in the process of savoring the excellent gin and tonic he had prepared for her when, without warning, the front door of the offices swung open and someone stepped into the reception area.

"Emma?"

"My God." She rose at once. Setting her drink down, she made her way out into the office entry.

"Maura."

TWENTY-SEVEN

The boar's jaws were wide open, but they never snapped shut. Instead, they remained gaping open as the gold in his rageful eyes slowly turned to ash and his great shuddering body gave one last spasm as he died.

The boar was at rest now, half atop Bravo, who lay on his back, dazed, his thoughts in chaos, having teetered on the knife-edge between life and death. He looked up at the solid roof of the jungle, unable to move. A single drop of rainwater splashed onto his cheek, bringing him back to himself.

Then he became aware of lights bobbing all around him, figures bent over him, lifting the great stinking beast off him. As they did so, he caught a glimpse of a deep gash in the boar's flank. He recalled in vivid, terrifying detail the animal's maddened eyes, and he began to see a pattern, a plan as awful in its design as in its execution.

It was Ayla who held out a hand, and he took it, feeling her surprising strength as she helped him up. She gave him some of her water, which he gulped down gratefully.

"Thank you," she said when he handed back her container, and, leaning in, kissed him lightly on the cheek, pulling away, it seemed to him, as fast as she could.

Looking past her, he saw Nasir had come to the near edge of the clearing. Behind him, he could hear the cadre starting to skin the boar.

Bravo still had a grip on the Beretta, which he held at his side. "You did this on purpose."

"What?" Ayla looked from him to Nasir and back again.

"You heard me, Nasir."

The jihadist shook his head, his expression sorrowful. "I don't know what the infidel's talking about."

Ayla turned to Bravo. "What *are* you talking about?"

Bravo addressed Nasir directly, even if the other wasn't interested in speaking to him. "We were in plain view. You heard the thrashing of the boar as he beat down the underbrush. But you knew he was coming even before that, didn't you?" Nasir's expression did not change. "It was the boar's grunting that sparked your plan. You heard it and got the idea. First, you somehow signaled your men to abandon us."

Nasir laughed. "What, in this darkness? How would I possibly signal them?"

"It was preplanned. At a certain time, at a certain point, whichever, your men had standing orders to break away."

"Preposterous!" Nasir spread his hands. He was still looking at Ayla. "Why would I do that?"

"To test us," Bravo said. "No, strike that. To test me."

"He gives himself such importance—"

"If it wasn't going to be the boar, what was it going to be, Nasir? A near miss with a bullet? A knife fight in the darkness?"

"Like all infidels, this one is paranoid about us, Ayla."

"The boar's presence so close by was sheer luck. You had a couple of your men run him down. One stabbed him deeply in his hindquarters, maddening him; then he was sent off in our direction."

"But that would've been right at me!" Ayla cried.

"At last!" Nasir nodded. "You see the insanity of his ravings!"

Bravo took Ayla's hand, led her through the jungle to where the men had almost finished skinning the beast. "There," he said, pointing to the upraised flank. "You can clearly see where he was slashed."

"An old wound," Nasir said, coming up beside them. "Ayla, don't let him sway you."

But she was already squatting, peering at the knife slash. "The wound is fresh."

"So? One of my men, in skinning—"

"No, Nasir." Her fingertip came away with fresh blood. "The boar was knifed before Bravo killed him." She wiped her finger on a fallen leaf. "He's right, Nasir. I could have been killed while you stood there. What were you thinking?"

The jungle stirred all around them, but quieter, more subdued, as if the creatures within it were holding their collective breath. No air stirred. In front of them, the bloody carcass was being dismembered, layers of fatty meat being sliced away from the bones.

"You were never in danger," Nasir said with a sullen expression. "One of my men had the boar in his sights at all times."

"But you would have risked Bravo's life."

"He's an infidel."

"But he's important to me, Nasir."

"He might have been deceiving you, Ayla. I had to find out the truth."

"You didn't trust me," she said hotly.

"On the contrary," he said. "But you know how these infidels are. Lies are second nature to them."

"Not this one," Ayla said. "Don't ever try something like that again."

What light filtered through the canopy in the glade had subtly changed. It was less icy, warmer. Dawn was not far off, and neither was the Cave of Shadows.

"Maura!" Emma felt a surge of conflicted emotions as she rose. "What happened to you? After you disappeared, we feared you had been taken by the Knights."

"I was." Maura, sounding very much herself, came and took Emma's hand. The two women embraced, then sat down side by side. "First, I have to tell you that Antonio Bazan was working for Reichmann. Once he was alone with me in the safe house, he tried to get me to talk, but I saw through him. I knew him for what he was, and I was stupid enough to tell him that I was going to turn him in to you. That was when he tried to kill me."

"How did you two go out the window?"

"I . . . I don't really know. I was sitting by the window. Someone had given me a bowl of food. I took a bite, but then my appetite just evaporated. That's when Bazan came over. He started crowding me. I was pushed off the chair, up against the window. He swung at me, I ducked, and then . . ." She massaged her forehead.

"And then?" Emma prompted.

"I don't remember. The next thing I knew I was on an airplane, but everything is hazy and I have no specific memories until I got to the castle."

"The Knights' castle in Malta?"

"That's right."

"Then what?"

"I was cleaned up, given fresh clothes, and escorted to dinner with Reichmann, which was a bit of a nightmare. He promised to torture me. He seemed to be looking forward to it."

"I don't doubt it. Did he torture you, Maura?"

"No. I escaped before he could lay a hand on me."

"How on earth did you manage that?"

"I started a fire. In the smoke and chaos I ran out, made my way back to you."

"Thank God," Emma said, squeezing her hand.

But in the now familiar darkness of her world Emma felt something alarmingly wrong, the smallest hint of something out of alignment, something that had warped the texture of the woman she had come to know.

"Maura, what is it?" Emma tried to rear back, to withdraw her hand, but it seemed to her as if she were in the grip of an iron vise. "Maura?" And, then, as she felt the woman's breasts press against hers, she called out. But as if she were in a dream no sound came out of her mouth.

Something was squirming its way toward her, swimming in the ether that was visible only to her, something that had lodged itself inside Maura. It grew in size and scope. With all her might, Emma tried to separate herself from Maura, but she could not. An icy wind had penetrated her, making her movements sluggish, indecisive. It was as if her brain had been disconnected from her body.

"You think I didn't know. But I did."

Terror flooded Emma—the kind of primitive dread familiar perhaps to her ancient ancestors, but which had not often been felt in humankind for centuries. Frantic, she wondered desperately where Fra Leoni was, how he was allowing this to happen. But while she could sense the invading presence, her senses to the outside world had been shut down as tightly as a bathtub tap being closed. Not even a single drip of sensory perception of the office in which she assumed she still sat was available to her; she might as well have been floating in the farthest reaches of outer space, airless, lightless, free of gravity.

"I knew about you and Val—*my* Val. What you two did together . . ."

And then, in the next dreadful instant, Emma sensed the thing squirming its way toward her. It reached out a shadowing finger that pulsed like a heart. She screamed as the long talon on the end of it etched a square onto the space between her breasts. Inside the square it drew a circle. Inside the circle it drew a triangle.

Emma screamed again, but whatever it was that had scored her and now had entered her was the only one who heard her.

Why? Emma howled. *Is this your punishment?*

Punishment? No. This is happening because it is written, came the reply that reverberated through every bone in Emma's body.

She seemed to be melting and coalescing at the same time.

Written? Where is it written?

In the Book of Deathly Things.

Her bones ached with every word "spoken" back to her.

Pain erupted through every nerve ending, as if her very essence was being torn asunder.

The Book of Deathly Things, the Testament of Lucifer.

PART THREE

SHADOWS OF INDIGNANT
DESERT BIRDS

ALEXANDRIA / ISTANBUL / TANNOURINE

TWENTY-EIGHT

The Royal Library of Alexandria was once the greatest repository of knowledge in the world. It was built at the beginning of the third century BC during the reign of Ptolemy II of Egypt. Though it at first contained the entire writings of Aristotle, Ptolemy III sought to widen the library's knowledge. In those days, Alexandria was a booming port, visited by peoples from the lands of the known world. Ptolemy cleverly decreed that every visitor to the city was required to surrender all books and scrolls in his possession; these writings were then swiftly copied by official scribes. The originals were put into the library, and the copies were delivered to the owners.

The library grew vast. Here in ten great halls, each embracing one of the divisions of Hellenic knowledge, ranked spacious *armaria,* numbered and titled, gathered like nesting gulls the myriad manuscripts containing the wisdom, knowledge, and information accumulated by the known world. Alas, the great library was destroyed, in what conflagration no historian can say for certain.

All of this history flashed through Reichmann's mind as he made his way through modern Alexandria's teeming streets. What he knew, and most others did not, was that, contrary to general thought, the great library was not one vast structure, but many smaller ones scattered throughout the ancient city. And while it was true that there was a main building and that this building was indeed burned to the ground, either by Caesar's troops, by uncivilized vandals, or by the terrified elders of the budding Catholic religion, during the riots to destroy the Cult of Isis, a small handful of the other, more distant structures survived.

It was to one of these—the library that housed the eleventh division of knowledge, unknown to historians and archeologists alike—that Reichmann now approached in the full bloom of Alexandria's rosy, hazy dawn.

The building on the outskirts of the Al Hadrah district was unprepossessing. In fact, it virtually disappeared, owing to the fact that it was built into the side of a low hill. Possibly this was one of the reasons it had been spared the destruction visited on the main library. The main reason, however, was that because of the controversial nature of the material it housed, it had never been officially listed in the Hellenic archives.

The curator, an old man with a head like a watermelon whom Reichmann had known for years, though not by name, answered the ancient verdigris bellpull. Stepping into the library was like entering a monastery. The air was cool and hushed; the musty, vaguely fruity scents of books, manuscripts, and the olivewood vitrines in which the sheaves of papyrus were kept in temperature and humidity-controlled conditions perfumed the interior.

The old Alexandrian was the guardian of this long-forgotten slice of history. Who paid him and how he managed to live was anyone's guess, and none of his business, Reichmann had long ago decided.

"SabaaH il-xeir ya ustaaza, Reichmann. Ana taHt amrak ya fendim?" *Good morning. How can I be of service?*

Reichmann told him; the curator pointed, then melted away into the gloom behind his great age-scarred desk, to resume whatever he was doing before Reichmann had darkened his doorstep.

Reichmann was confronted by a large space divided into eight separate areas, all lined with niches for books and documents.

Between these, three spiral staircases led to the upper reaches of the building—the so-called wings. As directed, Reichmann took the left staircase and ascended, his shoes pinging lightly against the metal treads. At one time the staircases had been made of stone, but these had collapsed some time ago in an earthquake that had threatened the very structure itself. If not for the welcoming arms of the hill into which it had been dug, the library would surely have been in shambles.

The upper level was hot and dusty. It seemed clear that hardly anyone had been up here, including the guardian. This filth and clutter reassured Reichmann rather than repulsed him. So far as he was concerned, the fewer people accessing this part of the library the better.

The space was five sided. Each wall contained shelves filled to the brim from floor to ceiling. A rolling stepladder rose in one corner. To Reichmann's experienced eye, some tomes had yet to be archived, and considering the guardian's advanced age, they probably never would be.

There were no electric lights and, of course, no implement with a flame was allowed anywhere inside the library. However, each section was equipped with battery-powered lanterns that gave off an eerie greenish glow guaranteed not to in any way deteriorate the precious paper and papyrus holdings. There were, of course, no windows, as sunlight was the mortal enemy of paper and papyrus alike.

The center of the room contained a long wooden refectory table and a number of straight-backed wooden chairs, adding to the sense of being in a monastery. Switching on a lantern, Reichmann spent the next half hour scouring the shelves for the book he felt sure would help him.

Following the horrendous incident in Malta, he had come to this library in Alexandria in hopes of discovering the strange and disturbing glyph he had seen incised into Maura's burning flesh and, even more shockingly, in her eyes.

The triangle inside the circle inside the square.

Because there was now no doubt in his mind that he was dealing with a form of demonic possession. How it had begun, why it had enwrapped Maura Kite, he had no idea. But instinctively he knew that he would never discover the answers to those questions until he solved the riddle of the sigil's meaning.

He had been too much in shock and terror for his life to think of it in the moment, but on the plane ride here he had drawn deeply from the well of his memory, certain that he had encountered that sigil before, sometime in the distant past. But where? Try as he might, he could remember neither context nor meaning.

And then he had it. Like a great fish surfacing from the deep he saw himself sitting in the Canonic Club in London's posh Belgravia. He and the cardinal were sitting on either side of the enormous fireplace, drinking brandy, smoking Cuban Montecristos, the process of Reichmann's recruitment into the Knights of Saint Clement a fait accompli. A break in the leisurely conversation, the cardinal's Romanesque head tilted back as he released a cloud of fragrant blue smoke. As the cloud dissipated, Reichmann noticed the sigil, incised into the marble mantel over the hearth at the Canonic Club, small, almost insignificant in the midst of the enormous slab carved with an equal number of cherubs, the eagle that had been Saint John's constant companion, the dragon that Saint Michael had slain, clusters of grapes, and reverent heads, eyes lifted skyward. The cardinal began to speak of Reichmann's removal to Malta, of his specific duties, and Reichmann's momentary curiosity was forgotten. Until this moment many years later in Alexandria.

Reichmann started, as if he had been suddenly roused from a drunken stupor. The sigil had been on his doorstep all this time, floating amid the debris of his memories, waiting for its moment to be recalled.

Turning around, he saw a figure sitting at the refectory table. Reichmann had not heard him come in, nor had he sensed him. This last alarmed Reichmann; he was an adept at sensing changes in his immediate surroundings. The man, younger than Reichmann by far, appeared completely immersed in a thick tome that lay open before him. He did not look up when Reichmann passed behind him and removed a book on the history of the Canonic Club.

Seating himself at the far end of the table, he ventured a brief glance at the newcomer. His hair was a pale copper, thick and curling, long at the back. His brow was wide and straight, his skin sunburned a deep reddish brown. With his head down this was all Reichmann could see of him. Already disinterested, Reichmann turned his attention to the book, *A Tangled Web, Being a Complete and Factual History of the Canonic Club*. It was written by someone named Alastair Gordon IV, whom Reichmann had never heard of.

According to the author, the Canonic Club had a long and twisted history. Founded sometime during the reign of Elizabeth I, Tudor (the precise year of its founding, 1559, 1560, or 1561, has been obscured by the fog of English history), the club was composed of just a handful of powerful landowners and businessmen. Although it was ostensibly a gentleman's club, like Boodle's and the rest of its ilk, it seemed that the Canonic Club's real business was in trying to place the imprisoned Mary Stuart, Queen of Scots, Elizabeth's cousin, on the throne of England, thus bringing Catholicism back to the country and wrenching control from the Protestants.

Added funding was provided in an almost constant stream from both the Vatican and powerful forces in France and Spain, both of which at that time were virulently Catholic. In fact, a majority of ousted English Catholics had fled or were exiled to France at the beginning of Elizabeth's reign. The one thing the founders did not do, though their benefactors abroad begged them to, was actively plot to assassinate the queen. With feet on the ground and ears to the walls of the most important meeting rooms in London they knew all too well that Elizabeth employed the largest and most sophisticated spy network of the time. All around them would-be assassins were being cut down, tortured, and eradicated by this canny network.

Instead, theirs was a cabal of long-term planners. In fact, they had no dog in the vicious and bloody hunt of Catholic versus Protestant. What they lusted for was power. Indifferent— even contemptuous—of the raging religious wars, they used the funds from abroad to further their exploration of matters that had been hidden from the eyes of men for centuries. As their ranks grew, the founders were dispatched singly or in twos to the Levant, the war-torn lands of the Ottoman Empire, in search of what Alastair Gordon IV called "unholy artifacts" from the dawn of civilization. Even with all his training, had Reichmann not encountered the thing Maura Kite had become he might easily have accused the author of ridiculous hyperbole. Instead, Reichmann read on, becoming more and more engrossed in the history of the club into which he had been recruited.

TWENTY-NINE

Following orders to the letter, as he always did, Collum Fireside rented a van, along with the paraphernalia he would need, and took two of his men to the police morgue to take possession of the strange corpse. He had already hired a small jet to ship it back. Though he found it slightly odd that Reichmann wanted it in Alexandria and not Malta, Fireside was not the sort to ponder imponderables, finding action and physical work a far more productive use of his time and energy.

While his men prepared the vehicle for the body, Fireside made his way to the morgue. Though he passed various official personnel in the hallways, the morgue itself was void of life. The corpse lay on a gurney, encased in a body bag. Evidently, Captain Balik had more important matters to attend to, as did the coroner. Fireside shrugged. Well, who could blame them? Fireside himself wouldn't choose to spend any more time here than was necessary.

Approaching, he unzipped the body bag halfway in order to make certain that that devious bastard Balik hadn't pulled a switch at the last moment. But, peering into the bag, Fireside saw the right corpse. The lidless black eyes stared straight up at the ceiling in disconcerting fashion. He wondered what Reichmann would make of this thing and what he was going to do with it. What could one do with it?

He was zipping the body bag back up when he heard a noise from behind him, as if someone had dropped a flask. As he turned, something grabbed hold of him. Whipping back, he discovered his right forearm pinioned by a hand, bluish white though it was, of what must be flesh and blood. The black carbonized shell that had encased it lay in fragments, and he realized vaguely it was the sound of the shattering chrysalis he had heard, though why it had seemed to come from behind him he didn't know. The other forearm rose and fell, the carbon likewise shattered, and then the newly freed hand rose to the thing's face and ripped off its black covering.

Fireside's blood turned to ice as the black eyes turned in his direction. The mouth hinged open to an unnatural width, exposing the long teeth. He thought he saw the nostrils flare, but because there was so little of them left he couldn't be sure. He tried to free himself, but the elongated nails pierced his skin and flesh. As they severed veins blood pumped out, running down his arm, filling his hand.

He knew he should chop down with his free hand, break the bones of the reanimated wrist, but he was somehow paralyzed, as if this were happening in a dream. Then the thing's other hand shot out, and the long nail of the forefinger punctured his throat. He gagged, blinked heavily, felt himself sinking into the floor, though when he looked down the floor was as solid as ever.

But what he did see was the nail, red with his blood, incising a triangle into his skin, then a circle enclosing the triangle, last a square enclosing them both. Somewhere, not too far away, children were playing, shop vendors were hawking their wares, tourists were being fleeced like lambs, and old men sat in cafés drinking tea and playing chess. But Fireside's world had been reduced to several square feet, no larger than a prison cell, from which it was altogether impossible to escape. With all the strength left him he once again tried to fight back, tried to defend himself, could not. Then he was struggling simply to breathe. It was all he could do to inflate his lungs. His last thought was: *Is this what it means to die?* And then . . .

A heartbeat later, the world winked out.

"This is the last lap," Nasir said, but by this time Bravo didn't believe a word he said. Ahead of them lay a natural stone bridge. On either side, an abyss of indeterminate depth yawned, beyond which the almost sheer sides of the mountain rose up, disturbing in the first glimmers of dawn light. The bridge was completely covered by vegetation, as were the mountain cliffs. They walked across gingerly, on the lookout for tangles of brush or arcs of roots that could catch an unwary traveler as effectively as any man-made snare.

On the other side of the bridge, the way constricted into what could only be thought of as a tunnel, the shadows closing in around them, swamping them in twilight. A turn to the right brought the path to an abrupt end at a rise far too steep to attack without ropes, pitons, and crampons. Then, as Nasir's men cleared away the brush, Bravo saw what appeared to be an ancient staircase chipped out of the living rock. The steps were worn and shallow, the space between them irregular.

"Is there no other way up?" Bravo asked.

Without a word, Nasir began to mount the stairs, his men following. Bravo had insisted that none of Nasir's men remain behind them, so he and Ayla started their climb last.

The way was arduous in the extreme. The staircase was as steep as any he had climbed in Capri, and far more treacherous. It was narrow and, on either side, a steep falloff of tangled foliage and rubble-strewn bare spots, the result of rockslides, made any sideways movement perilous and, possibly, lethal. Here, in this remote spot, even a broken limb could be a death sentence. The steps were often covered by lichen, slippery in the perpetual dampness where the sun never penetrated. Some were cracking or broken off entirely, so that the climbers had to concentrate on each step upward, looking only at the staircase itself and nowhere else. Doubtless this was why they missed the small sounds from just below them until an explosion, a short spray of bullets cutting through the air beside Bravo's head, froze them. The bullets shattered three steps just above him, separating him from both Ayla and the jihadists.

He suspected this might have been deliberate because the next short volley completely obliterated the steps above him. Pulling out the Beretta, he twisted his torso, squeezing off a shot, then, glimpsing the figure who had shot at him, put two bullets in his chest. The figure threw up his arms as he fell backward, taking the man behind him with him. More shots were fired, this time in panic and at random. Nevertheless, Bravo crouched down as best he could, using one hand, fingers grasping shattered rock, for balance while he fired again and again, slowly, carefully. *Be judicious with your shots,* Todao, Bravo's sensei, had counseled. *With bullets, as with the movements of your mind and body, timing is everything.* Another man collapsed, pitching off the staircase. *Be prepared for each shot to find its mark, but anticipate nothing.* A fourth man turned sideways, Bravo's bullet missing him by millimeters. He leapt upward, aiming his AK-47 directly at Bravo's heart. *If you keep your mind free of expectation you will be able to act and react without constraint and in perfect freedom.* Bravo hurled his gun. It struck the man flush in the face. Blood exploded from his nose, his split upper lip. Chips of teeth flew. He staggered back, his eyes red rimmed, lips pulled back as he spit out a gob of blood, saliva, and teeth. He brought the AK-47 up to bear, but Bravo was already on him, driving one knee into the man's groin. Bravo snatched the AK-47 out of his hands as he pitched off the staircase. But at the last instant he made a desperate grab for the weapon. His fingers found purpose; Bravo felt himself losing balance. At once, he let go of the AK-47 and the man hurtled down, his back breaking on a rock outcropping before pinwheeling from sight.

Bravo was left teetering on the brink of following him. He had let go of the weapon too late, his equilibrium was lost, and, even though he reached back, his fingertips slipped off a moss-encrusted step. There was nothing for it; he was going over, the same fate of his assailant awaiting him.

At the last instant something jerked at him, arresting his fall. He slipped on a step but recovered his balance in time to see Nasir racing back down the steps as lithely as a mountain goat. He heard shots fired, was about to go after Nasir, when Ayla's arms surrounded him, drawing him back against her.

"Steady on," she whispered in his ear as their bodies pressed hard against each other. "Don't get the wrong idea; I still hate your guts. But I meant it when I told you I honor my obligations."

With some difficulty he turned to face her. Her arms were still around him holding him, but not as tightly as before. "Holding on to the hate—any hate—will rot you from the inside out."

His gaze held hers for a long moment. Pressed together, they had begun to unconsciously breathe in unison.

"That bit of Taoist wisdom from your father?"

"My father was too busy trying to save people."

"He didn't hate anyone or anything."

"Not in that way, no."

"Even injustice."

"He fought injustice."

"Even the Knights of Saint Clement."

"He may have pitied them. But hate, no. Hatred would only have blinded him when the branchings of his path presented themselves."

"Where d'you get off talking like that?"

At that moment Nasir appeared, clambering up to where they waited. He handed Bravo the Beretta. "Reload this first chance you get," he said as he resumed his assault to the ledge where the cataract hid the Cave of Shadows. Bravo knew that was as close as Nasir would ever come to giving him a compliment.

THIRTY

Emma stared down at the husk of what had once been Maura Kite. There was scarcely anything about the thing that lay on the carpet that spoke of being human. What lay before Emma's gaze looked like the shed exoskeleton of an unnaturally large insect: paper-thin, dry, brittle, devoid of muscle, cartilage or, even, bone. She lifted up one foot, brought it down, and the thing that had been Maura crunched beneath her sole like a dried-up beetle. She kept stamping until the husk was nothing but ash ground into the carpet.

It was only then that Emma realized that her sight had returned. Her head snapped up as her heart thundered in her chest. She looked around the room at the objects, colors, sheens, hues, shadows, pools of light. The richness of the walls, golden and deep red, the jewel-toned swirl of the carpet pattern, the curve of the leather task chair, the desktop, filled with worksheets in Braille that had been brought over from the other office, an ear bug that translated what was on the computer screen into speech. For several moments, she was mesmerized by the phosphorescent pixels on the computer screen, the colors so bright, the fall of light from the task lamp, the moldings around the doors, the plaster cornices at the place where the walls met the cream-colored ceiling, the steel etchings of Ottoman Istanbul before it was Istanbul, the black cross-hatching making the buildings seem three-dimensional. *My God,* she thought, *how is this possible?*

But in the next beat of her overexcited heart the thing that had entered her, having migrated from Maura to her, asserted itself in her mind, imprisoning it in a steely death grip. The essence of Emma, what was left of her, struggled against the darkness that had invaded her, but already she could feel the strength leeching out of her, another will imposing itself upon hers, pushing her down, down, down, into a dark, dank place so deep inside her mind she was already lost in the unknown of herself, the unexplored territory of every human psyche too terrible to look at, let alone touch. And there she was imprisoned, shriveled into a fetal ball, unable to move or even reason. Pure terror engulfed her, making her incapable of rational thought. And, like a spike driven through her skull, it threatened to alter her forever.

But more harrowing than anything was that she—Emma—was aware of every thought, every movement, every call to action, incited by the entity with no body, no soul, that had entered her. She had become a puppet—a prisoner in her own mind, powerless, utterly helpless, a horrified observer as, she now suspected, Maura had been. It was like being swallowed alive by some monstrous creature out of nightmare.

The soulless thing's thought now turned to Fra Leoni, and Emma's bones turned to water. Her frantic thoughts tried—and failed—to imagine what dreadful fate it had in store for her friend. She wanted to cry out, to warn him in some way—any way—but she remained bound to her wheel of psychic pain.

She heard herself calling to Fra Leoni, the last thing she wanted to do, saw herself striding through the back offices to find him, though she wanted to run as far away from him as possible. And yet, to her dismay, she was mesmerized by her returned sight—she couldn't help herself; it was such an incredible gift. But then she was inundated with guilt, shame, and dread at the appalling cost to her and to those closest to her.

She saw Fra Lèoni now—the first time she had actually seen him, though she had formed a picture of him in her mind's eye.

He was far more imposing, far more striking in a timeless way. His pale-blue eyes seemed like sunstruck pools of water. His wide lips curved up in a smile as soon as he saw her.

"I'm ready!" He wore lightweight sea-blue slacks, a white collarless shirt, the sleeves rolled up, revealing tanned forearms, ropy with veins.

But almost instantly his expression turned to one of consternation. *He's seen the difference in my eyes,* she thought. *Good for him.* But to her horror, the soulless thing inside her, having anticipated his revelation, lunged at him. With a nimbleness belying his extreme age, he sidestepped her attack. His eyes darkened as they narrowed. Had he always been able to do that? she wondered. Spinning her around, the entity guided her left hand as it lashed out, just missing him. He stepped forward, violating the circumference of her defensive circle.

He wasted no time asking her what had gotten into her. She had the distinct impression that he knew—that, furthermore, he'd suspected all along something like this would happen. He engaged with the soulless thing, concentrating on her eyes. *They look different; they must look different,* she thought. *What do they look like?* Emma wondered, realizing that she had not yet seen herself in a mirror. *What does he see there? Can he recognize the soulless thing? Does he know what it is? Can he see me trapped here in my own skull like an embryo in a womb that will never open?*

The struggle between her body and her friend was like nothing else she had ever experienced—as much psychic as it was physical, perhaps more. He was most careful to keep away from the tips of her fingernails, which she used as micro-knives to poke and slash. What would happen to him if one of them drew blood? Would the soulless thing migrate to him, leaving Emma's corpus a hard, empty husk? Was her fate to be the same as Maura's? Emma could only imagine what a combination of the soulless thing and a human immortal might create. If only there were some way for her to prevent it. But she was so securely imprisoned she could not even stir her psyche. She would have wept had she been left the capacity to cry.

But now it looked as if she needn't have worried. Fra Leoni had grasped her corpus at the nape of her neck. Even Emma, buried so deeply, felt the electric shocks spark through her body, disconnecting thoughts from one another. She felt like an infant being shaken by her hysterical mother. Everything was being concussed—action, reaction, offense and defense, strategy and tactics all being agitated at such a rate that they were no longer assets.

The soulless thing that had taken possession of Emma was halted in its tracks; a certain babbling in a terrifying language unknown to Emma streaked through the room like a flurry of dark stars. It grated on her, rubbing her nerves raw, sickening her. It sounded all wrong, as if it were emanating not from her mouth, but from a pit that had just opened up in the floor. The room grew dim with it, as if each word were drawing on the invisible horrors lurking in deepest night. The sentences, cadenced like an incantation, caused the space around her to become gelid, oppressive. It was as if a series of heavy iron doors were being slammed shut, one by one, and she realized that the soulless thing was conjuring up another prison cell just like the one she had been thrust into, that it meant to imprison Fra Leoni. She couldn't allow that to happen, but how to stop it?

And then she heard the chanting from Fra Leoni, and, from her incessant reading as well as from long conversations with her brother, she recognized the words as Tamazight, a three-thousand-year-old language, the human race's oldest. She wasn't fluent, could only understand a word here and there, but she sensed that it was directed at the soulless thing, that he was meant to entrap it, imprison it, just as Emma was imprisoned. She longed to cry out, to ensure that Fra Leoni knew she was still inside her own mind. *Kill it!* she cried soundlessly. *Kill it!*

Fra Leoni had Emma's body well in hand. The incantation spread around her like an invisible net, each word he spoke sparking like a firework. She could feel the soulless thing writhing, could feel death shimmering, closing in on it, beginning its death grip. She was at once elated. *Soon I'll be free,* she thought.

But then a new terror seized her. What if in killing the entity Fra Leoni killed her as well? What if he thought she was already dead, as Maura seemed to have been? Emma thrashed around in her prison. *I don't want to die!!!*

With the soulless thing being churned to chaos, its grip on her weakened just slightly. Gathering herself, Emma struck with a Herculean feat of willpower. She felt her mouth opening, her own words squeezed out of her: "Fra Leoni! Help!"

He started, his head whipped around, and, in that instant, he lost control of the entity. The nail on its middle finger pierced the small of his back. His torso arched, his eyes turned the color of opals, their pupils lost, and he fell to the floor, unmoving.

No! Oh, no! Emma screamed soundlessly. *God in heaven, what have I done?*

THIRTY-ONE

"'Inevitably,'" Reichmann read, "'one cannot write a complete history of the Canonic Club without addressing the numerous rumours, legends, and myths surrounding the Gothic institution.'" It transpired that, at the beginning of the Industrial Revolution—the first two decades of the 1900s—the name was changed to the Antaeus Club. The founders were, of course, long gone, their long-range plans disrupted by rebellious or disinterested grandchildren and great-grandchildren. In that decade of social upheaval, coal-dark skies, and rampant unemployment, the Antaeus Club became a haven for a fist of high intellectual men involved in the occult secrets of the ancient world—a potent anodyne to the terrors of a world, born in the blood of workers, squalling its advent, torn off its axis, and stood on its head.

After twenty years, a man by the name of Raphael Goldoni intervened in the club's history. Where he came from was impossible to say, though it was safe to say that he was of Italian extraction. He appeared one evening, claimed his position as the last living male heir of one of the six founders. He had traveled from afar, so he claimed, to take his rightful place at the head of the club, sweep away the occultists, and return its name to the Canonic Club and reestablish its original mission. He had the documents and the money to back up his desire, as well as a charismatic personality that seemed to charm everyone he encountered, even, apparently, the great poet-philosopher William Butler Yeats.

So in the third decade of the twentieth century, Goldoni led the newly revivified Canonic Club back to its roots. And what precisely were its roots? This was the essential question that Alastair Gordon IV spent six years of his life trying to find out. Was the Unholy Trinity myth, hyperbole, a dream like King Solomon's mine or El Dorado, a lie used by the founders to further their personal explorations of the Levant and maintain their positions in the power centers of Elizabethan England? Or was it real?

To Reichmann's bitter disappointment, the author had no definitive answer or, if he had, he had not chosen to share it with his readers. Closing the book, Reichmann glanced up to find that the young man was gone. Again Reichmann had not been aware of him rising and leaving, and he could not fathom how that was possible. The strange fellow had, however, left the book he had been studying open on the table at the place where he had been sitting.

Reichmann rose, stepped down to the other end of the table, slid into the chair the young man had occupied. It was strangely cold, as if it had been set in a meat locker before being placed in this room. That was, of course, impossible, so Reichmann dismissed the notion, setting his mind to examining the book. Strangely, it had no title, nor was there any author attribution. The second thing he noticed was that it was very old, the pages almost translucent, dusty with age, and, in places, brittle. Pages could easily fall apart if the reader was not exceedingly careful. The third thing Reichmann noticed was that the book was handwritten in several different languages, often more than one to a page. This was highly unusual. The only time he had come across a book like this was an ancient text on the origins of religion in a dusty, ill-used corner of the Vatican Library. The text was a jumble of languages: Hebrew and Phoenician, Sumerian, and Arabic, Greek and classical Latin. Different-colored inks had been used and it was clear to him the writing was from many different hands.

Then he came upon a section that looked like Greek crossed with mathematical symbols, a language that, it seemed to him, had been created by aliens, rather than the mind of man. Pages and pages of this strange language until in the precise middle of the fourth page he came upon a language-free space devoted to a large single sigil: a triangle inside a circle inside a square.

Reichmann's head snapped up. Pushing the freezing chair back with a squeal, he rushed downstairs, through the labyrinthine stacks to the front of the library. The curator sat on his high stool, perusing the daily newspaper. A tiny cup of coffee sat by his right elbow.

"That young man," Reichmann said breathlessly.

The curator looked up. "What young man, *ustaaza* Reichmann?"

"You know. The one with the long copper-colored hair."

"*Ustaaza* Reichmann," the curator replied softly, "there is no young man. You're the only visitor the library has had all morning."

Thunder rode through the canyons, broke against the stone steps they were climbing like a roaring, storm-invigorated sea against sheer cliffs. The vibrations from the cataract now filled their world with an excess of sound not unlike that of a rock concert, rendering speech all but impossible. Nasir, using hand signals, let Bravo and Ayla know that it wouldn't be long now until they reached the ledge beyond which the Cave of Shadows waited, mouth open, to devour them.

Another forty minutes brought the staircase to an end. At long last they had reached the ledge and the cave. By this time they were all thoroughly soaked from the cataract's mighty spray.

"This is as far as we go," Nasir said. "My men will not venture inside the cave."

"What about you?" Bravo said.

"We will guard you," Nasir replied obliquely. "No one will get by us."

They were standing to one side of the cave mouth. The stone was slippery as a sheet of ice. The remnants of Val's expedition were still scattered about: backpacks, ripped open and empty, half of a portable tent, half a dozen candy bar wrappers lodged into the cracks between rocks. A bedraggled head scarf fluttered limply. Something unrecognizable that, on further scrutiny, appeared to be a human femur, burned to a crisp, lay nearest the cave mouth.

"Lovely," Ayla said.

Bravo was aware that Nasir and his men gave the grisly artifact a wide berth. Some of them refused to look at it, preferring to stare out at the cascading water and the blue-green mist it threw up.

As Bravo and Ayla stepped into the shadows, Nasir said, "We'll be here when you return. But don't expect us to come in after you."

"It's not one of ours."

Reichmann pushed the book farther toward the curator. "I don't understand."

"I know every book and manuscript within these walls," the old man said. His hooked finger stabbed out, nail as yellow and horny as a macaw's beak. "This isn't one of them."

With extreme care, Reichmann opened the book to the place where the odd writing began, turned it so that it faced the curator. "Is this language known to you?"

The old man's rheumy eyes hesitated for a moment; then his gaze dropped. "That, *efendim*, is Tifinagh, the world's oldest language. Tamazight, the spoken equivalent, is still spoken today among the Amazigh tribes from the Canary Islands in the Atlantic, the Siwa oasis in Egypt, and from areas in North Africa to the Niger River in the Sahara. The Phoenicians appropriated parts of it, then the Greeks."

"Can you read it?" Reichmann asked, heart pounding.

"No," the curator said. "Very few can."

"Give me a name."

The curator tapped his chin reflectively. "I personally only know one, *efendim*. A man who has come here from the time he was six years old, brought by his father. I loved that man, his father."

Reichmann closed his eyes, counted to ten. "Curator, please. The name."

"Well, you won't like it, *ustaaza* Reichmann."

Reichmann leaned across the curator's desk. "What I don't like," he said, biting off each word as if it were a morsel of food, "is this procrastination."

The old man's head bobbed up and down. "As you wish, *efendim*." His eyes seemed to echo an exhaustion beyond words, to contain countless decades of truth and deception in their hazy depths. "If you want those passages translated the man you seek is Braverman Shaw."

"Shit, shit, shit." Outside, in the burning Alexandrian sun, the book tucked under his arm, protected from the dazzling light, Reichmann punched the speed-dial number of Fireside's mobile. The call went straight to voice mail. He had given Collum orders to terminate Shaw. Now in one of life's most ironic clusterfucks he needed Shaw's help. Amid the incessant clatter and wail of the city, he hurried down the street. "Shit, shit, shit."

THIRTY-TWO

"It's Reichmann," Fireside said, checking his mobile.

"You no longer work for Reichmann." Emma looked at him with her changed eyes—eyes black and white, rimmed in crimson. Looking into his eyes was like looking into a mirror. She held out a hand. "You are his enemy."

Fireside gave her his mobile, nodded deferentially, the thing inside him bowing to a greater power—the hierarchy of the Unholy Trinity of which they were now both an integral part. "My men are inside; we're ready to take off."

"I have filed a false flight plan," she said. "No one will know where you've gone."

They were standing at the foot of the stairs that led up to the private jet in which Fireside—a completely different Fireside—had arrived in Istanbul a day before.

"Use your resources wisely," Emma said. "Your new path is complicated and delicate."

"I understand."

"I doubt you do." Emma smiled sweetly. "But that's of no consequence. You have your orders."

"Have no fear," Fireside said. "They will be fulfilled."

"You are new to this life," Emma told him. "We have no fear. Emotions are as alien to us as sunlight, the passage of time, friends. We are part of something larger, more powerful, eternal. We have no need of anything else."

★

Bravo and Ayla switched on powerful LED Maglites. Whatever light seeped into the cave mouth vanished ten feet in.

"What do you expect to find here?" Ayla said as they moved forward into the musty darkness.

"The same thing Val found."

"Have you any idea—?"

She stopped so abruptly that Bravo, several steps ahead of her, turned around. "What is it?"

Ayla shook her head. "I . . ." She rubbed her bare forearm with her free hand. "I don't know."

She shivered, and Bravo, noting that her breathing had become rapid and shallow, stepped to her, said, "Take it easy. It's all right." He waited a beat, until the haunted look in her eyes receded. "Now tell me what's going on."

She took a deep breath, exhaled a little too quickly. "I know this sounds crazy, because I've never been here before, but I'm getting an overwhelming sense of déjà vu."

"The red tent of shadows."

She nodded, licked her dry lips. Her voice was thin and reedy. "I feel as if ants are crawling all over me. Fire ants."

"There's nothing on you."

"I know that." Said a bit too sharply. "Obviously. Rationally."

"The feeling isn't rational."

"It isn't, no."

He nodded. "Good."

She looked startled. "What?"

Bravo gave her a small, tight grin. "It means we're in the right place, we're on the right track." He studied her for a moment. "You all right to go on?"

Her eyes blazed as she rose out of her funk. "Don't think for a moment I'm a liability."

"The thought never occurred to me."

"I'll bet." Her reflexive defenses suddenly up again.

"Why would I lie to you?"

"All men lie."

What did they do to you? he wondered. *Something unforgivable, I'm betting, because one thing you're not is a drama queen.* And then: *Do I scare you as much as they do?*

"I want to tell you something."

He waited, patient, knowing that she was walking a figurative knife-edge, that any move or vocalization might tilt her away from him.

Her voice deepened, darkened in pitch. "There were four things in life that frightened me. With my mother gone, there are three. One is what happened in the red tent of shadows." She drew a breath. Her eyes were glittery in the pools of light that surrounded them like an aura of white fire. "The second is you."

"Me?" Bravo was taken aback. "What about me?"

She shook her head, her expression troubled. "I don't know."

They watched each other for some time, wary as feral animals. *What is it between us?* Bravo asked himself, unable to come up with an answer. It was like there was a membrane that allowed some things to pass through, while keeping them blind to each other. He was about to turn away when she stopped him.

"There's something else."

The third fear. She looked different now, as he imagined she might have as a little girl, when her mother brought her to Tannourine.

"I didn't come home just because my mother asked me to."

"But you would have."

"Of course." She hesitated, a tiny tic starting to semaphore at the corner of one eye. "I got bounced."

"From your job."

"Terminated with prejudice." She gave a brittle laugh, as if she were a girl trying to make light of skipping over a crack in the sidewalk.

He waited. It would not be politic to ask her the cause. Plus, he knew she would tell him if she wanted to. It turned out she did.

"There was a group of four men at the bank. They were trading in currencies, taking money from clients' accounts, creating false ones, and establishing what's called flash-trades. Heavy orders that are pulled almost immediately. But you know what happens; it's like getting caught in an undertow. Traders looking for any edge they can follow the big trades in, then you bet against those trades and make money off the momentary price dislocation."

"No one at the bank saw this?"

"Yeah," she said. "I did. E-mails like 'If you ain't cheatin' you ain't tryin'.'"

"Which is why you got bounced."

"No one wants a whistle-blower at a major bank."

"The gang of four?"

"Let go slowly and quietly, one at a time, no questions asked."

"And you?"

"What about me?" she said sharply.

"You amassed damning evidence. You could have gone to the regulators."

"Only if I wanted to be blackballed from the business for all eternity."

"Still . . ."

"I'm in checkmate. They threatened to implicate me."

"But the evidence would—"

"As a spy."

"What?"

"I'm Muslim. A Muslim in Britain. In international banking. With that Conservative government, most of whom are their friends."

"Jesus." Bravo regarded her with a new respect. "Time to find a new profession."

"I was damn good at my job. I have the skillset for that one thing."

"Maybe," he said. "Maybe not."

They moved farther into the cave, the way sloping downward, a chill rising up from the lower depths to grip them. The odors of rock, minerals, water seepage, were laced with a man-made tang—that of fear.

"Smell that?" she said softly.

"A very old fear," Bravo said, voicing the continuation of both their thoughts.

As they penetrated deeper, an unsettling feeling overcame Bravo. He felt the air thicken, until it was like fog, though it was clear enough ahead. It seemed to him that with each step they were moving back in time, not a matter of days or even months. It was as if the years, centuries, were falling around him like dry leaves. The cave had immersed him in the desolation time wreaks on all things mortal. Once, he had been in an office tower in Shanghai. For a moment the elevator he was in had slipped an electronic cog, and he was sent hurtling down, until he slammed the red emergency stop button. That same sickening sensation of falling fast and out of control gripped him now.

At length, they arrived at the painting that had so captivated Val. Bravo was grateful for that. Slowly, methodically, they played their flashlight beams over the entire mural from beginning to end. He had the immediate sense of seeing the painting through a kind of veil, but that seemed background to an even stronger feeling.

"It's like it has been waiting," he said. "Waiting for us."

To his surprise, Ayla nodded, for once in complete agreement with him. She hadn't taken her eyes from the mural from the moment it had surged out of the darkness, illuminated like a lambent scar.

"A procession," Bravo said.

"A royal one," Ayla added, "judging by the figure on the throne with the gold band encircling his head."

"King Solomon." As he peered more closely, Bravo's voice had shrunk to a whisper. "My God, the gold circlet, the way he's dressed, the shape of his beard. It's him, all right."

Ayla was right beside Bravo. "And who's that behind him?"

"What?"

She pointed. "Right here. This shadowy figure."

Bravo frowned. "I don't see a shadowy figure."

"Really?" Ayla's finger traced the outline. "His face is blurred or has been scratched away."

Bravo rubbed his temple. "I'm not seeing anything. Okay, let's take a figurative step backward, look at this clearly. You say you see something—"

"I *do* see it!"

He lifted a hand. "Hear me out. You say you see this figure; I don't." He turned to her. "You remember the last time something like this happened?"

"Of course. In the police morgue in Istanbul. I saw the eyes of that burnt creature differently than either you or the coroner."

"Ergo, these two instances must be linked in some way or other."

"But why should I see these things and not you or anyone else?"

"Anyone else we know of," Bravo corrected her. "In any event, I can't answer you."

Ayla shivered again as she returned her attention to the mural. "Okay, but we agree we both see the man on the throne."

"King Solomon, yes."

"What about the round object? Do you see that?"

Bravo moved the beam of light slightly as he leaned closer to the painting. "Yes, but what is it? It's not a disc, not a circle. It's something other, a shape clearly beyond the ability of the painter to depict."

"Perhaps that's not surprising. The shadow figure is handing it to King Solomon."

"As if he's the power behind the throne."

"And there's the sigil of the Unholy Trinity." Ayla frowned. "What's that writing near it? I can't make it out. It looks like a child's scribbling. Is it even a language?"

"It is." Bravo squinted. "It's Tifinagh, a language that's three thousand years old."

"Older than time."

"Just about."

"Can you read it?"

"Just a moment." Bravo's lips moved silently, translating the writing in his head. Suddenly he reared back. "Christ!"

Alarmed, Ayla said, "What is it? What does it say?"

"This is impossible," Bravo said, worrying his lower lips. "Completely impossible."

"We'll both be the judge of that."

"It's the last words uttered by the controversial sixteenth-century sainted martyr, Bella dell'Arca," Bravo said.

Ayla shook her head. "Saint Bella dell'Arca. I've never heard of her."

"Unsurprising. She died very young—at fifteen years of age, if I'm not mistaken."

"How did she die?"

"Burned at the stake, a victim of the Protestant inquisition." He hesitated a moment. "Fra Leoni knew her."

"What?" Ayla exclaimed. "That's crazy."

"Pay attention," Bravo said, "and it may become less so. She was a strange woman by any stretch of the imagination. The official line is that she died for her religion, her pope, and her God. Which brought her sainthood. But there were rumors, softly making the rounds, that she stretched the word of God, twisting it to serve her own purpose. People whispered of men— and women, nuns—taken to her bed, children born, raised outside the precincts of Catholicism. It was said their expulsion was a necessity because they were different."

"Different how?" Ayla asked.

"Fra Leoni didn't say," Bravo said.

"Didn't," she said, "or wouldn't?"

Bravo looked at her sharply. "The last words universally attributed to her as the flames crisped her feet and licked at her thighs were, 'Give me strength to catch the Light before it dies.' But that isn't quite right. According to Fra Leoni, what she actually said was, 'Of a sudden I am ill met by sunlight.'"

"A completely different meaning," Ayla said.

Bravo nodded. "One the Church would neither countenance nor wish to be entered in its history."

It was at that moment that they heard a sound. Something was coming at them from deep within the belly of the Cave of Shadows.

THIRTY-THREE

Valentin was on top of Sister Agnetha—or, more accurately, in her—when he heard the master return. Maybe "heard" was not the right word; "felt" was more like it. There was a sense of merging in Valentin's head, an expansion, as if, as he was looking up at the sky the clouds had rolled away to reveal the moon and impossibly distant stars.

A surge of joy rocked him, so inexpressible it moved him to tears. Feeling the wetness on her naked breast, Sister Agnetha mistook his emotional spasm for a physical one and moaned in disappointment. As Maria Veniera, the *madre vicaria*, had taught her when she had taken Agnetha into her bed, her spirit would not be able to receive the seed of the Lord if she did not reach climax. The intimate liquid spilled from Maria Veniera when she was in the throes of religious passion was equal to the seed of the handpicked males such as Malus and Valentin.

Then, as Valentin's movements inside Agnetha escalated into an aggressive thrusting motion, she moaned in pious thanksgiving that he was allowing her the opportunity to be once more one with Jesus Christ.

As if to echo her thoughts, Val began to chant, "The body of Christ receives you, the body of Christ loves you; the body of Christ receives you, the body of Christ loves you. . . ." The chant sent Sister Agnetha into an ecstasy, physical and religious, the one being the same as the other, as Maria Veniera preached. Agnetha's arms and legs splayed wide to afford the

Christ surrogate deep and complete access to her body and, thus, her soul.

Afterward, the moon seemed as if it were coming in through the window. The shadow of a nightingale, passing through the treetops, played over Agnetha's sweat-sheened body as she lay, collecting the last few remnants of what Christ had just offered her. Her mouth was hanging open, her nostrils flared. Her pupils were enlarged. Then, coming out of her sex-induced stupor, she looked down at herself, saw her erect nipples, and, with a soft cry, drew the sheets up over herself. She stared straight up at the ceiling.

"My God," she whispered. "My God."

"Yes." Valentin sat on the edge of the bed, his bent spine to her. The knobs of his vertebrae were deeply shadowed. It astonished him how little pleasure sex with her gave him. He coupled with her because it was required of him, but in truth he divorced himself from his body, his mind far away across the Mediterranean. Finally, he heard himself intone the litany: "You're a Catholic. You inhaled shame along with your mother's milk."

"I'm not ashamed," Agnetha said, though when she sat up she held the sheet to her chest. "I am enrobed in God's glory." Reaching out, she touched his shoulder, then tapped on each knob as if they were snare drums. "When I joined the Church, when I took my vows, I married Christ, but never in my wildest dreams did I think I would be so exalted to be allowed into his presence."

Valentin, head up, stared out the open window, wishing the nightingale would return, so he could imagine himself flying away, back to Emma, whom, he was quite certain, he would never see again. Not only was Agnetha a child when it came to having sex; she was a child in her thinking also. Her belief in the Church, in Christ, was so absolute she was as easily manipulated as a three-year-old. And yet it was what Malus asked of him. He was in it now—all the way down in the well—

and he knew there was no climbing out. There was only deeper to drop, further and further away from Emma.

The cloister was a fine place at night. It was hidden away from the more public areas of the convent, including the church where they sang the hours. It was at the center of the private space where the nuns spent the bulk of their time, where on the second floor ringing the square space the nuns slept, cell by cell. Unless Maria Veniera, *madre vicaria*, called them to her bed for the blessed union with the holy fluids of Jesus Christ.

At one corner of the cloister a lemon tree rose; at the opposing corner, a Valencia orange. At the center crouched an ancient stone well, sculpted with bas-relief arches that mimicked those that held up the second story and marked the covered walkway that girdled the cloister. The well was dry now, had been for a number of decades, but once it provided freshwater for the cloister's inhabitants and visitors alike. Nowadays visitors were few and far between. Maria Veniera saw to that.

Valentin and Malus strolled the paths side by side, from lemon tree to Valencia orange and back again, making a figure-eight circuit. The sky above them was clear, the wind almost nonexistent.

"How went your journey?" Valentin asked.

"Well," Malus murmured. "As all journeys must."

"It's good to have you back."

"Maria Veniera?" Malus said, intuiting his thoughts.

"Despite all efforts, we remain intruders in her territory."

"Leave her to me, then."

Valentin dipped his head, relieved. Truth be told, Maria Veniera gave him the willies. Though he would never dare admit this to Malus, there were times when Valentin started to believe in her powers to reach through the ether, commune with Jesus Christ. The things she could get up to! He shrugged off these dark thoughts, concentrated on what Malus was saying.

"Valentin, you must think of humans as composed of building blocks. The more carefully you rearrange the blocks the more useful humans become."

"I assume that includes Maria Veniera."

Malus's thin lips curled into a cruel smile. "Very shortly now, we will be dealing with people far more difficult than the current *madre vicaria*."

"And how will we deal with them?" Valentin asked.

"Tonight, after dinner, repair to the viewing room. There you will see how I deal with Maria Veniera."

Howling like a pack of wolves, a sudden rush of wind. Whatever was coming was headed directly toward them at such a speed that turning and running back toward the cave mouth was out of the question; they'd be overtaken before they went five yards.

Bravo's LED illuminated a crooked sliver of deep shadow. He grabbed her hand. "This way!" Leading her to the left, where the narrow cleft in the rock afforded them a place to slip sideways out of the main cave. The enclosed place echoed back the eerie howling, increasing both its uproar and power. He kept going, urging her onward with a kind of controlled desperation.

The howling seemed to be following them. He could feel icy ripples at his back as the air turned turbulent ahead of the onrushing force.

Now it was her turn. "Up here!" she whispered fiercely, taking a long step up, rapidly vanishing into the darkness overhead.

Bravo risked a glance down the defile, saw nothing, felt buffeted by the rising wind, and launched himself up the rock wall, following her onto a ledge formed by the millennia-old impact of one rock face against another. They lay together, entwined like lovers in the low, narrow space. He could feel the beating of his heart, then realized that he could feel hers as well beneath the swell of her breasts. They dared not speak, stared instead into the darkness as the howling reached an almost earsplitting pitch, seeming to come from all around them, to oppress the air, giving it weight, heft, and menace.

The howling grew to an extended ululating crescendo. Bravo felt Ayla begin to tremble, and he held her tighter. Her face was in the crook of his shoulder. He sensed that she might be weeping, and he held her tighter still. He felt naked and afraid—exposed to forces he was unprepared to face. With a cold shiver, he realized he was completely out of his depth. Had Dilara known what he would find here? Had she seen it in her prophetic dream? The extreme peril of the path he was on was at last brought home to him. He thought of his grandfather and suddenly felt so close to him he might be able to reach out and touch him, and oddly it was to Conrad his soul fled, not to Fra Leoni. He sensed that death was close at hand, perhaps only an arm's length away, and suddenly his only thought was to protect Ayla, to protect her from whatever was to come. He enclosed her body with his, and for once she didn't shrink away, didn't push him aside, but lay quietly within his arms, weeping still.

The howling became a bellow of rage and resentment, the raw, ripping sound an outcry, as if in grievance for past injustices. And for just that instant, Bravo was certain he could make out words—Tamazight words, the spoken analogue to Tifinagh, the writing above the object that Ayla said was being handed to King Solomon by a shadow figure only she could see, the world's oldest written language immortalizing the last words of Saint Bella dell'Arca, who died in the ides of autumn, 1546, words only someone who was there at her death would have known.

The hair on his forearms stirred, there was a prickling at the back of his neck, and his pulse raced despite all efforts to keep calm. What in the hell was down there? he asked himself. Whatever it was, he was quite sure it was not of this world. What would his father have made of this situation? His father, who from the time he had hit his teens had taken him twice yearly to the hidden library in Alexandria to read crumbling texts in Tifinagh, telling him that the most important occult histories were written in this ancient and all but forgotten language, the language used by, among others, the cabal of alchemists assembled and driven to distraction by King Solomon. *Tifinagh is the language of magic, or what in ancient time was thought of as magic,* Dexter Shaw told him, while with cotton gloves turning the pages for his son. *Your grandfather Conrad was fluent in Tifinagh—well, more than fluent. He claimed to be an alchemist himself, the last of his kind; so he used to tell me. He was very old by then, and I confess that I took these ramblings with more than a grain of salt. I made the mistake of assuming his mind was slipping into dementia when he said that he had actually read a number of the texts King Solomon's alchemists wrote as they attempted to conjure for his son the thing he desired most: alchemical gold, imbued with the power to make him supreme and uncontested ruler over what is now the Middle East. He claimed to have memorized them, but, really, Bravo, who could believe that?*

After the old man died, Dexter, trying to rid himself of an itch he could not scratch, returned to the Alexandria library. But try as he might, he couldn't find the texts, *Nihilus Inusitatus,* Conrad had claimed to have read and memorized. They were not there, if they ever had been.

The soul-ripping howling was so close now it was a physical thing, like a storm battering a ship's sails. Ayla's hunched shoulders began to shake in earnest, and Bravo began to whisper in Tifinagh. The howling continued but did not seem to draw any closer. And then, as quickly as it begun, it vanished, leaving a hollow, quaking silence in its wake.

THIRTY-FOUR

Everything around them was cloaked in utter darkness. The silence was deafening, his ears ringing as if in the aftermath of a bomb detonating.

As he brushed Ayla's hair off her face she said, "What happened?"

"We're alone," Bravo said. "Whatever was in the cave is gone."

Disentangling herself from him, she rose up on one elbow, keeping her head bowed in order to keep herself from a painful smack from the roof of the niche. She peered down, then switched on her Maglite. Rock and more rock. Nothing to suggest anything had been there.

"Could we have imagined . . . whatever it was?"

"Anything's possible," Bravo said, to humor her. "But I doubt it."

They clambered down into the cleft, followed it back out into the cave proper.

"Two paths," Bravo said. "Farther into the cave, or out."

Ayla looked at him in the peripheral glow from her Maglite. "I think we know what's waiting that way." She pointed into the cave.

"So you don't think what we experienced was dual halluc-ination."

"Do you think what we went through is something to make fun of?"

Darkness had fallen by the time they emerged. Had they been inside for so long? But the stars and moonlight making the cataract glitter and spark were real enough. The ledge outside the cave mouth was deserted.

"No sign of a fight," Ayla said, looking for blood.

"They heard the howling, too." Bravo began gathering twigs and bits of branches. "They've fled. The noise scared them witless."

With Ayla's help, he started a fire. Because of the mist in the air, it took patience and some doing. At length, they sat cross-legged, watching the flames shoot up, listening to the wood snap and crack, the comforting sound almost but not quite lost in the roar of the waterfall. Smoke rose, mixed with the mist, was swirled away in the cataract's backwash.

"I have questions," Ayla said after what seemed a very long time.

"So do I."

"But I'm willing to bet I have more."

He dipped his head. "All right."

"First, what the hell happened back there?"

"I was hoping you could tell me."

She stiffened. "What?"

"Have you forgotten your feeling of déjà vu? You told me you had the same feeling you had in the red tent of shadows."

"I was a child. Who knows what I felt?"

"I don't believe that for a minute," he said, "and neither do you."

She glared at him for a moment. Then, in the next second, that part of her armor melted away. "The howling . . . yes, the howling . . ." She turned away, stared out into the rushing water, as if it might cleanse her of her memories. "For so long I told myself I had dreamed them, that they were nightmares I used to scare myself. And, believe it or not, for a time—a long time—I had convinced myself of that. It was one of the ways

I comforted myself when present problems threatened to become overwhelming."

She picked up a stone, threw it distractedly into the flames. "It's fire, you see."

"What's fire? You're not making sense."

Her gaze swung back to meet his, held it fast. At long last, she did not seem intent on pushing him away. "There's no point in burning them at the stake, as they used to do during the many inquisitions that took place in England, France, Spain, the Levant, as well, as soon as the Crusaders crossed the Mediterranean." She took a breath, went on, convulsively now, as if, having started down this road, she now had to run as fast as she could. "In the red tent of shadows what I thought I saw, what I dreamed I saw—what I *did* see . . . The figure at the center of the group burned that baby after marking him with the sigil—the triangle inside a circle inside a square."

"The figure *murdered* the boy? Sacrificed him to, who . . . Lucifer?"

"Oh, no. The baby didn't die. Not at all. When the flames withdrew, the figure held up the baby. He was black, as if crisped to charcoal. But then the figure began to peel away the charcoal and, as if it had been a wrapper, it fell away to reveal the boy . . . alive . . . with these, I don't know, these preternatural eyes that looked at each person in the tent, including my mother, including me—especially me, I'm sure of it—with the gaze of an adult."

"And that's when the real fire started."

"Yes."

"And your mother spirited you away."

"An interesting way to put it." She nodded. "I was half-delirious by then. There was poison in me or, at least, a terrible infection. A raging fever. Her attention returned to me completely. Without her, I think I would have died hours or days afterward."

Bravo took some time to digest what she had finally allowed

herself to share with him. At length, he said, "Whatever ruled in that tent—"

"The dark figure."

He nodded. "The shadow figure," he said meaningfully, his gaze heavy on her. Could it really have been the Sum of All Shadows? he asked himself. Could she have seen the Devil?

The significance of what he'd said took a moment to sink in. Then she gasped. "The shadow figure behind King Solomon."

"The shadow figure only you can see, Ayla. Why is that, do you think?"

"Because I was in the red tent of shadows. I was there when—"

"When the burned and branded child fixed his eyes on you. The knowing eyes of an adult."

"That wasn't all." Ayla's eyes grew dull, the flames turning them opaque. "The baby boy pointed to the mark that had been incised into him and said, 'Nihil.'"

"He spoke."

"I told you."

"He said, 'Nihil.' Ayla, are you sure?"

"I couldn't forget a word like that. Why?"

"When I was a teenager my father took me to one of the untouched remnants of the ancient library in Alexandria, Egypt. That's where I learned to read Tifinagh, through the manuscripts there. But all the time, my father was searching for a book his own father claimed to have read. He never found it, though."

Ayla hunched forward, her frame tense. "What was the name of the book?"

"Nihilus Inusitatus."

The evening meal in the convent was its usual somber affair; the nuns were enjoined from speaking during meals. It took place late, after the nuns sang the Evening Office, concluding with,

"Iam ad occasum solis et nos vidimus et Hesperum, canimus Dei Patris et Filii et Spiritus Sancti. . . ." *Now that we have come to the setting of the sun and have seen the evening star, we sing in praise of God, Father, Son, and Holy Spirit. . . .*

Eight nuns on each side of the refectory table, Valentin seated next to Sister Agnetha. Malus occupied the chair at one end of the table. At the other end sat Maria Veniera, *madre vicaria*. She was possessed of large, heavy-lidded eyes, sultry lips that needed no help to be a luscious cherry red. She projected an aura of sexual malice. It seemed to Valentin, if not to Malus, who remained the only person in the convent unmoved by her physicality, that Maria Veniera was naked even when fully clothed. She moved like a nude, gestured like one, watched him in her sultry fashion as if it were prelude to sexual intercourse. Her power in this realm and ability to wield it was an astonishment to him. Malus merely curled his upper lip in contempt and passed on.

Not this evening. Tonight was to be different. Valentin's heartbeat quickened to imagine what Malus had in mind for her.

Malus had ordered lamb, served so rare it lay bloody on the plates before each diner. Sautéed potatoes, green beans, barely passed over steam, and, later, a salad fresh from the garden, speckled with shards of crimson-skinned radishes. Wine from the cellars below them and a spectacular tiramisu, a specialty of the kitchen.

Sated, the nuns returned upstairs to their individual cells, where, after performing their nightly ablutions, they lay on their pallets, their bodies quivering, each one hoping to be called to the *madre vicaria*'s bed and an ecstatic union with the sacred fluid of Christ.

Well below this small village of hope and unconscious lust, the cellars of the convent exuded the must of ages. Stone dust lay atop the bottles of wine and liqueurs, stacked horizontally in wooden berths, like slumbering sailors aboard a ship. The cellars were vast and, beyond the shelves, mostly unexplored.

Here is where Malus had set up shop, so to speak, where the real business in which he indulged was alive in ongoing experiments. It was to one of these rooms beyond the borders of the convent as it was known to its permanent inhabitants that Malus took Maria Veniera. He had intercepted her as she was following her flock out of the refectory. The novices who had served dinner and had subsequently cleared the table were in the kitchen, eating their dinner of congealed leftovers.

The cellars looked like crypts. In fact, in Roman times, to which the convent traced its founding, they very well might have been, though, apart from the venerated crypt of the controversial Saint Bella dell'Arca, there was no evidence of the remains of anyone. The ceiling was composed of a series of interlocking stone arches, massive and brooding as the storm clouds that occasionally rushed south from upper Tuscany.

Valentin would dearly have loved to have been a fly on the wall during Malus's conversation with Maria Veniera, but he was left on the outside watching covertly as Malus miraculously diverted the *madre vicaria* from her nightly rounds of the nuns' cells and, without a fuss, accompanied her down to the cellars. He hung back at a safe distance, allowing them to disappear through the oaken door and down the winding stone stairs into the cool, damp understructure. He could not hear their voices, could hear nothing, in fact, but the slow drip of water somewhere in the pooled shadows.

By the time he arrived at the viewing room, Malus and Maria Veniera were already installed in the adjacent chamber. A one-way mirror had been set into the chamber's stone wall, allowing Valentin to see everything that went on next door without himself being seen. Microphones high up in the walls where they met the ceiling spewed the conversation into the viewing room.

The air inside the dim viewing room was still and stifling. There was nothing much in the way of furniture, just a single wooden straight-back chair, stained umber. Cherubs gamboled across its back, trailing sacred streamers. In the chamber where

Malus stood facing the *madre vicaria* it was quite different. Tapers burned in wrought-iron wall sconces; a trio of lit candles rose from a serviceable wooden table, on which was set a tray of flasks and beakers, the contents of which Valentin was entirely ignorant. He had never seen them before. A matched pair of chairs, as elaborately carved as those of a royal family, backed against opposite walls.

"Do you really believe that you'll be successful in taking control of my girls?" Valentin heard from one of the speakers.

Maria Veniera faced Malus, hands on hips. She was clearly unafraid of him. *Such a terrible mistake,* Valentin thought with some relish. He was fairly trembling in anticipation of seeing her brought low.

"My girls love me," Maria Veniera went on. "They venerate me as much as they do Saint Bella dell'Arca. And why not? They believe I am her reincarnate."

"It seems odd to remind you that the Church does not recognize reincarnation," Malus said. "In fact, as far back as AD 553 the Second Council of Constantinople made clear its condemnation of Origen, an early Church writer who believed souls exist in heaven before coming to earth to be born."

A slow smile spread across the *madre vicaria*'s vulpine face. "Do not preach to me of the Church's early days, when priests commonly married and had children." She tilted her head to one side, making her even more virulently desirable. "Do you know how celibacy came to the Church? No? Like everything else in the Church, it came down to money. When they took their vows, priests gave over their money and lands to the Church. Many of them were quite wealthy. But what do you suppose happened when they married and produced progeny? Why, the children inherited their money and lands, leaving the Church out in the cold. So the venal decision was made, leading to the Church's burgeoning wealth and an unnatural and sometimes tortured life among its ordained practitioners."

"So you have taken it upon yourself to rectify this wrong."

"I have judged myself blameless. I bring relief as well as ecstatic union to my girls."

But not to Valentin. Maria Veniera had resisted all his advances. Fucking Sister Agnetha was all well and good, but it was still always Emma Shaw's face he saw, not hers. He had thought that Maria Veniera's outright sexuality would cure him of his longing, but now he saw her in this venue he knew that he was condemned to heartache. Emma was out of his reach now; he had chosen a path that was anathema to her.

"The ecstatic union," Maria Veniera was saying now. "That is a truly loving gift."

Now here comes the hammer, Valentin thought, his malicious smile reflected back to him in ghostly fashion in the glass this side of the one-way mirror. But to his astonishment, Malus said, "I could not agree more, Sister. I commend you for your resourcefulness as well as for your initiative."

"If you are an honorable man, if you really mean what you say, then protect me from my father confessor. He is continually sticking his snout into the convent's business, as if he were a pig in search of truffles. Sooner rather than later he will surely upset the delicate balance I have created here."

"That is within my power," Malus said. "But first I require you to confess."

Maria Veniera laughed unpleasantly, as if anticipating his response. "Confess what?"

Malus gave her a penetrating look before he said, "The union you provide your girls . . . it isn't with God; it isn't with Christ."

"No? Who are you to say?"

"Let us come at this another way. You claim to be the reincarnation of Saint Bella dell'Arca."

Maria Veniera pulled herself up to her full height. "I do."

"And I say that's a lie."

"You don't know what you're talking about."

"No, of course not," Malus said with a Mona Lisa smile.

"Well, then . . ." Stepping to the central table, he picked up one of the flasks, poured the contents over his left hand and forearm. Maria Veniera wrinkled her nose at the acrid smell. Setting the flask down, Malus stepped to the wall, lifted a taper out of its sconce, and, tipping it, set fire to his arm. Whatever was in the flask must have been some form of accelerant, because it burst into flame.

Maria Veniera gasped, jumped back, a hand to her mouth.

"Do you remember?" Malus said, coming toward her, flaming arm held high. "Do you remember what the flames felt like as they burned through the branches on which you stood, set fire to your clothes, and then . . . do you remember the feel of your skin crisping as it peeled off your flesh?"

"Why?" Maria Veniera said.

Even in the viewing room Valentin could smell the scent of roasting meat.

"Why are you doing this?"

"Why are you not reacting as most people would?" Malus asked. "You should be appalled by the stench. Anyone else would be gagging, retching. But not you, Maria Veniera. Why is that?"

She made no effort to answer. Malus seemed both unsurprised and unperturbed. Returning to the table, he said, "I think we've had just about enough of this, don't you?" Taking up a different flask, he poured what must have been water over his flaming arm, dousing the fire. What was left was a hand and forearm burned to a crisp.

Lord in heaven, Valentin wondered, *what is this?*

As if to answer him, Malus slammed his forearm against the edge of the table so hard Maria Veniera jumped. The charcoaled exterior broke apart like a shell, revealing his flesh underneath, opalescent as a baby's new skin, but unharmed.

"Look familiar?" He was smirking openly at Maria Veniera.

She was staring wide-eyed at the arm. Then slowly, inexorably, her gaze inched upward to Malus's face.

"'I am ill met by sunlight,'" Malus said. "These beautiful words saved you."

Again, as slowly as if time itself was being stretched like taffy, she fell to her knees, her hands clasped before her.

"Lord, it is you," she whispered. "My prayers have been answered."

Malus stepped toward her. As if mesmerized, Maria Veniera unbuttoned the top of her habit until a pale V of her bare flesh was exposed. On her chest, shining in raised weals, was the sigil: triangle inside a circle inside a square. As Malus placed his renewed hand on the top of her head, the sigil turned red, blood running beneath the surface. It pulsed as if with a life of its own.

When he took his hand away, he held it out for her to take. Both his expression and his voice were unutterably tender as he said, "Rise, Bella dell'Arca, Black Saint. Your long wait is at an end."

THIRTY-FIVE

"We're sitting ducks here; you know that."

Bravo stirred the fire with a stick half-charcoaled. "In the darkness no one will make the climb, and if they're foolish enough to try, we'll hear them."

Ayla turned, looked back at the cave mouth. "That thing . . ."

"Will not bother us now."

Her head swung back. "How can you be sure?"

"It doesn't want to hurt us—at least, not at the moment."

She shook her head. "I don't understand."

He took out water and sticks of dried meat from his knapsack, handed her some of both. She chewed without apparent interest while he spoke.

"Consider the quote on the disc," he began. "The mural is very old, there can be no doubt of that, but the inscription on the disc being handed to King Solomon is not."

"But you said it was written in—"

"Tifinagh, a three-thousand-year-old written language, yes. But you see, Ayla, that message, quoting Saint Bella dell'Arca's actual last words, was newly written. Whatever was originally on the disc has been obliterated by, I suspect, the same hand that wrote the new message."

"I don't understand. If the message is new, why would it be written in such an arcane language?"

"Most messages are meant for a specific person." Bravo stirred the coals, glowing like animal eyes in the darkness. He had taken some water but was disinterested in the food. "This one is no exception."

She laughed uneasily, putting aside her unpalatable dried-meat stick. "What are you saying? That the message was meant for you?"

"You can count the number of people who can read Tifinagh on the fingers of one hand, and there are only two—me and Fra Leoni—who would understand the translated message." He had set the stick on fire. For a moment he watched it burn down toward his hand. "My father used to say that when all other explanations fall apart believe the one that's presented to you."

"Your father—"

"He was a very wise man."

"I'm bored already." Then, perhaps to mitigate the sting of her words, she added, "What about your grandfather?"

For several beats, Bravo was silent. Then he said, "I never knew my maternal grandfather, but Conrad, my father's father—I knew him in old age. Though his mind was completely intact, his body had given out. He was confined to a wheelchair. He liked when I pushed him around. He could talk to me endlessly."

"What was he like?"

"Truthfully? He was the proverbial black sheep of the family."

"He didn't head the Gnostic Observatines?"

"Oh, yes. But he took them in . . . questionable directions. Through a friend, he became involved in the Canonic Club, a notorious gentleman's club in Belgravia. The founders were staunch Catholics, though their religion had to be hidden away to protect their lives and the lives of their families. That was long before Conrad became involved. During the time he was there, the name changed to the Antaeus. There were lots of wild stories, rumors, even, once, a police raid, though they found nothing untoward.

"My grandfather's interests had turned to the occult. He was in excellent company at the club, which, at that time, was infested with explorers—courageous men who braved life and limb in their search for ancient wonders. When they returned to London, they were like wild men—women, opium, who knows what else. They badly needed to let off steam.

"It was during that time that one of my grandfather's compatriots returned from Lebanon with a book he claimed was bound in the cured skin of a virgin."

"The *Nihilus Inusitatus*."

Bravo nodded. "Yes. According to Conrad, he didn't have possession of the book for long. The man who found it, an inveterate gambler, needed money to fund his next expedition. Though Conrad begged him not to, he sold the book for what would even today be an exorbitant amount of money."

"But your grandfather had time to read it?"

"He read it and, according to him, memorized it."

Ayla looked skeptical. "Do you think that's possible?"

"I inherited my eidetic mind from him, so yes, I'd say it was eminently possible."

"And your father, hearing that it had found its way into the library at Alexandria, took you there, combining lessons for you with his attempts to find it. Did your grandfather pass down the information he'd memorized to your father?"

"Sadly, no. The two didn't get along. At all. My father felt Conrad had turned heretic when he involved himself in Antaeus. He didn't want any part of him."

"He let you see him."

"Sure," Bravo said. "At the end of Conrad's life. But that was more my mother's doing."

The fire was slowly dying out. Bravo took up another stick, stirred the embers as Ayla threw an armful of twigs onto them. She waited until the fire was going again. "Back to the writing. Assuming you're right and it was put there recently, my question is why?"

"Bread crumbs," Bravo said.

"Come again."

"It was put there for me to follow."

"Follow where?"

"Saint Bella dell'Arca is still venerated in one place: the convent of Saint Angelica Boniface, in Capraola, Italy. That's where I have to go."

"That seems like a long shot to me."

"You're not in my line of work."

"But I might soon be." She grinned. "Explain, please."

Bravo sighed. "I wish I could. All I know is that someone— or some *thing*—wants me at the convent."

"And you're going to go? Dance into the mouth of the lion unprotected?"

THIRTY-SIX

Emma landed in Rome at night. The arrivals hall bloomed with a cool and dazzling light. She felt as if she were swimming through an overlit aquarium. Travelers with dead eyes, towing wheeled suitcases, wandered to and fro as if lost in a maze. She had never felt her apartness more keenly. Conjured from fire and darkness, she was a true wanderer, bereft of a body, chained and bound outside of time. If she had been any other kind of creature, she would have wept for herself and all the things denied her. As it was, tears were nothing more than a concept to her. If she could have wept would she feel some form of release, some surcease to her confinement?

Outside, the night was mild. A feckless wind caught at her hair, and she brushed it back from her face. As she waited in line for a taxi, she watched the people streaming out of the arrivals hall: businessmen, couples starting their holidays, tourist groups, their leaders with little flags on handheld poles, mothers with babies asleep in their arms, their harried mates maneuvering luggage and strollers collapsed for the journey. This was not a city of hard edges, of glass and steel. It was a city of time-worn stone, of domes and catacombs, a soft city, always teetering on the edge of its past. Above all, it was the nexus of the Catholic Church, of its struggles to survive in the postmodern world, to remain relevant in the face of the rising waves of change, beating against it faster and stronger. Cradle of Christ, crown of corruption: it was, in all, a good place to be.

It was a curious thing, she thought, hunched in a corner of a taxi on the way into the city. Unlike other major capitals like New York, Paris, or Tokyo, which glowed and flashed at night like high-tech jewels, few of Rome's public buildings were lit up. Rome was a dark city, with a dark and bloody history. She felt at home here; at least there was that. Or she had in the past; now she was on the cusp of something new, as strange as if there were two moons rising over the rooftops rather than one.

Without baggage or encumbrances of any kind, she roamed the city streets. At first, they were packed with tourists and Romans alike. Later they emptied out until a few drunk teens and an abundance of trash cans overflowing with gelato cups and pizza rinds were her only companions.

She crossed the Tiber on the Ponte Sant'Angelo and found herself on the Borgo Santo Spirito, which tickled her funny bone. More fun was to come.

The high gates of Vatican City were closed and guarded, but neither of these safeguards was an impediment to her. As she passed into the Vatican she felt the familiar tidal pull. It constantly fascinated the entity inside her that for centuries Lucifer had used Saint Peter's Basilica as a kind of second home. She suspected he fed on the multi-stranded corruption that was part and parcel of the power the Vatican continued to amass. Cardinal, archbishop, pope, banker—sooner or later all fell prey to the human frailty of the lust for power and money. The Church couldn't save them from their own humanity. The delicious irony was a source of Lucifer's pride.

She roamed the basilica at will, alone—always alone. She felt Emma—the real Emma, the past Emma, coiled and still resistant—stirring inside her metaphorical cage. Despite her blackest instinct, this Emma intrigued her. She was not like the others she had inhabited. She was stronger, more resourceful, wily as a fox. She was also patient. This surprised Emma. She felt the past Emma biding her time. She felt watched, judged, but, disconcertingly, not hated with the bitumen-like bitterness of her previous hosts. What she felt from this one was pity. Even more disquieting, she was recognized as a denizen of a lost world. This Emma felt her *aloneness*—and understood. Her disability had removed her from the world of sighted humans. She could not see them, admire their clothes, their makeup, their hairstyles, their expressions, their movements. She could not see the colors of the day, nor the multitude of blues and black of night. All visual cues to human behavior, to the world, were denied her. And unlike those who had been born sightless, she felt keenly what she was missing.

Centuries ago, when in the body of a child, she recalled squatting at the edge of a lake, watching water spiders glide over the surface without causing even the shadow of a ripple. Now she felt herself to be a kind of water spider, gliding over the surface of life, never dipping even a metaphorical toe into the turbulent currents and whirlpools of life. She felt neither the elation nor the heartache of the human experience. She lived in an obsidian castle, impregnable, silent as her own eternal death.

Now, seemingly out of nowhere, a tectonic shift had occurred.

It was disorienting to feel a kinship with a host. A sudden surge of joy jolted her, causing her to cry out. But no one was around to hear her, the echoes falling on stone and marble, while the image of Christ looked down on her with blind eyes and numb mind.

But almost as soon as the flash of joy moved her it vanished, replaced by her fear of Fra Leoni. She had been clever but lucky, she knew, as well—very lucky. Still, all she could manage was to paralyze him. Though she tried, she was powerless to kill an immortal. Previously, she had thought them a myth. Knowing the truth somehow diminished her, made her ashamed of what she was. She lifted her hand, stretched out her fingers. The nail that had penetrated the base of his spine was already black, rotting away. She had no idea whether it would grow back. All she knew was that what she had done had caused her pain—not the past Emma, not the coiled Emma, but she who now inhabited Emma's corpus. How this was possible she was at a loss to explain. She had not experienced pain in many centuries. The thought of it even more than the physical discomfort unsettled her.

She left the basilica as quickly as she could, the visit not at all what she had imagined. Dawn was still some hours off, but she had to be gone from Vatican City before the light rose on another day.

Valentin watched, nose pressed painfully against the mirrored glass, as Malus pulled Maria Veniera to her feet. *But she wasn't Maria Veniera at all,* he thought, *was she?* She was Saint Bella dell'Arca. In either identity, her dark, alluring sexuality should have cut him like a knife. How many times since coming to the convent of Saint Angelica Boniface had he glimpsed the lush body beneath the robes, the globular breasts, the narrow waist, once the powerful thrust of her thighs as she disrobed in one of the nuns' cells at night? None of it stirred him the way Emma had. She had ruined him for anyone else, including this shining beacon of lasciviousness.

Now he watched as Maria Veniera and Malus stared into each other's eyes while she unbuttoned her habit all the way, stepped out of it. She was naked; she wore not a stitch of undergarment. And she was as magnificent as Valentin had imagined—and of no interest to him whatsoever.

He saw her in profile, but just for a split second before Malus turned her so her back was to him. Malus bent her over the table, breasts compressed, her arms straight out above her head. Valentin's erotic eye focused on her powerful buttocks in the moments before Malus stepped up behind her. She must have opened herself to him because, without ceremony, he plunged into her.

Valentin turned away, but he still heard them going at it, just as Malus wanted. Malus was taking possession of someone he assumed Valentin desired. He was marking his territory, as well as exhibiting his complete dominance. Valentin laughed bitterly as he banged his head against the far wall of the viewing chamber, trying to find that nightingale to take him far, far away from this place he had come to fear and to despise.

"I can't sleep."

"Think of the cataract as rain," Bravo said. "The sound of rain always brings sleep."

"Not always." Ayla lay by the fire, head pillowed by hands pressed together as if in prayer. "It rained all day and all night after my mother took me from the fire that engulfed the red tent of shadows. Not surprisingly, I was unable to sleep. I trembled and cried. I couldn't stop shaking."

"You had a high fever."

"That was part of it, yes."

She was quiet for some time. The crackling of the fire, now and again lost in the rumble of rushing water, might have reassured anyone else but her. Bravo watched the rise and fall of her side and knew she was still very much on edge. In its waning hours, the night seemed to have closed around them as if it meant to crush them. The atmosphere was heavy and oppressive, seemingly with no relief in sight.

"What happened," he said, "in the rain?"

She was silent for so long he wondered if she had heard him.

"I remembered," she said at last, her eyes half-closed. "After that, sleep was out of my reach. It became a stranger to me, and no amount of cajoling or rationalizing could coax it back."

She sighed deeply, and for a time he thought she might have at last drifted off to sleep. Then she twitched, like an exhausted child who wills herself to stay up to listen to the adults.

"I set the fire, you see. The red tent of shadows burned up because I took a twig from the fire and set the burning end against the tent's material, down low, where it met the ground, where no one would notice until it was too late."

"You must have been very frightened."

"'Fright' doesn't begin to cover it." She sat up suddenly, her eyes bright and glittering. "Most people, I think, have at least one incident in their past they'd like to forget. The thing is, for them, no matter how traumatic, it *is* in the past. But not for me. I tried to extinguish it with fire, but that didn't work, did it? Whatever was in the tent still exists. It wants revenge. It's killed my parents, and now it's after me."

"I don't think so," Bravo said. "If that was the case, it would have killed you when we were inside the cave."

"So if it didn't want to kill me, then why did it come after us?"

"I think it was protecting what's still deep down in the cave, past the place Val explored."

"In that case, we should go back inside."

He shook his head. "What we experienced was a warning, a fraction of its power. I don't yet have the tools to combat it. We'll save that for another day. For now, we need to concentrate on the platter's inscription."

She nodded. "The bread-crumb trail, you called it. I remember."

"I told you before that I think it's driving me toward the convent."

"I remember that as well."

"I was wrong," Bravo said carefully, gauging her expression with every word he spoke. "It seems clear to me now that it's *you* it's driving toward the convent."

THIRTY-SEVEN

When Captain Balik, Millî İstihbarat Teşkilati, was first notified that Sir Percival Dockery-Smythe had been found unconscious or dead at the offices of Salinas Holdings, Ltd., he was at first disinclined to go, preferring to fob it off on one of his junior officers. After Balik's wild and wooly interviews with the starched Emma Shaw and the mad as a hatter Dockery-Smythe, he'd had just about enough of the Salinas top echelon. But then, unaccountably, the stricken old man instituted a chord inside him. After all, now he thought about it Dockery-Smythe was not so far from his own father, dotty in his last declining years.

When he arrived at the offices, the open door was being manned by two uniforms, who parted like the waters of the Red Sea when he showed them his ID. An EMS team was on-site, but no one had moved the body, as per his orders.

He consulted with the sergeant in charge of the first-response detail, then sent him and his men off to canvas the tenants on the floor as well as those on the floors above and below to see if anyone had heard or seen anything untoward. He didn't expect them to come up with anything—it was make-work—but he wanted them out of his hair while he examined the body.

The entrance was clean, save for what appeared to be spots of cigarette ash ground into the rug. In one of the inner offices, the old man was on his back, staring at the ceiling, looking like he had had a heart attack or a stroke and had fallen backward.

Balik squatted down beside the body. The first thing he did was scoop his hand under Sir Percy's head, checking for wounds, abrasions, lumps, any or all of the things that would be in evidence had he been struck from behind. Balik found nothing of the kind, but as he was feeling around the old coot opened his eyes and said in his plummy upper-class British accent, "My dear captain, I didn't know you cared."

When he had finished being astonished, Balik called for the EMS personnel. With their help he got Sir Percy up off the carpet. As they set him on a sofa, Balik noted that there were no bloodstains on the carpet, nothing in fact that would lead him to believe that the old man had been attacked.

One of the EMS workers took the old man's blood pressure, while another fed him some water from a bottle.

"Normal," the pressure taker said, unwinding the cuff.

"Why should my blood pressure be anything but?" Sir Percy said, looking from one man to another and finally settling his piercing gaze on Captain Balik.

"Sir," Balik began, "we found you on the floor, unresponsive. The first responders thought you were dead." He frowned. "In fact, they told me you had no pulse."

Sir Percy harrumphed. "Clearly, they were mistaken."

Balik found it impossible to refute this statement. "Sir, can you tell me what happened?"

"Tell you what happened?" Sir Percy snapped. "When?"

Balik, acknowledging that he had once again fallen down Alice's rabbit hole, heaved a sigh of surrender. "I should like to know how you came to be lying on the floor of the office."

"How the devil should I know?" Sir Percy said, his annoyance growing. "I was insensate."

Talking to this man, Balik thought, was like trying to herd cats. He took another stab at getting somewhere reasonably sane. "Who was the last person you saw before you became . . . insensate?"

"A woman."

"Yes?"

"Maura Kite."

"You know this woman?"

"I thought I did." Sir Percy looked Balik straight in the eye. "I mean to say, if she did me some harm, then clearly I got her bloody well wrong."

Balik cleared his throat. "Why would this woman . . ."

"Maura Kite."

"Yes. Why would she do you harm?"

Sir Percy looked up at one of the pressure takers. "Could someone please fetch me a spot of tea?" His gaze returned to Balik. "And you, Captain, what's your pleasure?"

"Nothing for me, thank you."

"Oh, come on. A coffee, I expect, yes?" Sir Percy gestured to the pressure taker. "We have all the fixings. Through that door, down the corridor. Second door on your left. Off with you now. The captain and I need a parlay."

"Ah, parlay. That word I know," Balik said, looking pleased with himself. "I saw *Pirates of the Caribbean*. Twice." He nodded to the man, who vanished through the door.

Captain Balik returned his attention to Sir Percy. "Now about that parlay."

"Ah, yes. I think, Captain, that we can be of service to one another."

"Really? I had you pegged for *zirdeli*—something of a, what is it you Brits say?—ah, yes, a nutter."

"I'm as crazy as anyone else," Sir Percy said. "Though I daresay quite a bit saner than most."

"In that event, tell me about Maura Kite. Why would she do you harm?"

"Oh, that." Sir Percy considered a moment or two. "Maura Kite had lost her husband, you see. Only days ago. Very sudden, it was. She was half out of her mind. She believed that we owed her some money over the death."

"You're an importer-exporter."

Sir Percy produced a genial smile. "Insurance, as well, as it happens."

The pressure taker returned with two paper cups. "Thank you," Sir Percy said, took a sip, then went on. "Are you covered, Captain? A man in your position—well, I mean to say one can't be too careful. You *do* have a family. I can offer you a very fine policy at a most competitive price, too."

"I'm fine, thank you." He put his coffee aside. "You said we could help one another."

"I believe so, yes."

Balik steepled his fingers. "Please tell me how."

"Well, I need your help and I think you need mine."

Balik bared his teeth; they were very white against his dusky skin. "With what, may I ask?"

"Your murder investigation."

"Which one?"

"The only one that really counts, Captain. The murders of Omar and Dilara Tusik."

"But that's already been solved."

"I assure you," Sir Percy said, "it hasn't."

Balik's tone hardened. "The case is closed."

"Reopen it." It was Sir Percy's turn to insist. "Trust me when I say that you'll be glad you did."

Balik eyed him for some time. "What's your angle?"

"I told you. We can help one another."

Balik sat back. "All right. Let's say I agree. Then what?"

"Then I ask you to have one of your men fetch the gun you found in the stairwell—"

Balik's eyes narrowed. "How did you know about that?"

Sir Percy waved away his words as if they were gnats. "He fetches the gun and brings it to us at your morgue."

"And why would we be at the morgue?"

"To take a look at the unidentified body you found in the Tusiks' apartment."

"I've already looked at it," Balik said. "Twice."

"Like Captain Jack Sparrow, yes? But you've missed something vital."

Balik's eyes narrowed again. "Are you saying this unidentified man is the one who killed the Tusiks?"

Sir Percy rose to his feet. "Why don't we go to the morgue and find out?"

"Because the body is probably gone by now." Balik stood to face Sir Percy. "It's being taken by a man named Fireside."

"Collum Fireside, I presume."

"That would be the one, yes."

"And where would Mr. Fireside be taking the body?"

A slow smile spread across Captain Balik's face and he waggled a forefinger. "That's what you want to know, isn't it?"

THIRTY-EIGHT

The fire had died down for the second or third time; Bravo had lost track. He was bone tired, weary in body and in spirit. It had been a monstrously difficult journey to get to the Cave of Shadows, and what he had found inside had, frankly, sent an arrow into his chest. He was not a man easily frightened, and this fact more than any other brought home to him how desperate and perilous his quest to find out what had happened to Valentin had become.

Despite Bravo's weariness, he put more wood on the fire, throwing more kindling under the larger pieces of wood, which he had stacked up in a pyramid. The fire-flare illuminated Ayla's face. In the solemn repose of sleep her features looked perfect, her face luminous. She was not yet dreaming. All the care and worry lines for the moment vanished with the extinguishing of her conscious mind.

He settled back, palms outstretched to the heat; then, his hands warmed, he jammed them into his trouser pockets to warm himself further. That's when his fingers encountered the gold crucifix given to Emma by Maura Kite. He brought it out, firelight glimmering off its sculpted surface.

A memory rose into his mind, bright and shiny as new, as memories often will when triggered by a sight or sound, smell, or touch. He was very young, pushing Grandfather Conrad in his wheelchair. It was a cold, clear day in December. He remembered the crows in the trees, lifting and cawing at their approach, pure black against the robin's-egg-blue sky. Far off, over the hill, a dog was barking. The comforting drone of bees. Conrad's white hair, still thick this close to death, spiked up like a crown of thorns.

"It's good to be away from London," Conrad said. "At last."

"What d'you mean, 'at last,' Grandfather?"

"Too many dark days, too many darker nights." The old man's large-knuckled hands twisted on his blanket, with which Bravo had covered his lap before starting out. "Those were evil times. Your father was right; I never should've gotten involved. You remember that, Braverman."

"Involved in what, Grandfather?"

"Hellfire and brimstone is real enough; I'll tell you that," the old man said, and then commenced to mumble, ruminating to himself. Bravo, having become familiar with these episodes, knew better than to keep querying his grandfather, who would either ignore him or castigate him for transgressions he himself had made.

They pushed on toward the old apple tree, its gnarled trunk and branches brutalized by time. It was his grandfather's favorite resting place on these excursions. When he died, he told his family, he wanted to be buried beneath the canopy of labyrinthine branches.

In the dappling of sunlight and shade, as Conrad continued his incomprehensible monologue, Bravo saw that his fingers were twisting back and forth, that they held something between them. To Bravo's shock he saw that it was a crucifix. His father had already branded the old man a heretic, a man cut off from God.

Bravo waited until the monologue had drifted to its inevitable end before asking about the crucifix. Whether it was because they had reached the sanctuary of Conrad's favorite spot or because his mind had returned to a state of the perfect clarity of his younger years, the old man spoke to him as if Bravo were his confessor.

"This—see how I cannot even say its name—has become my touchstone, my long and narrow pathway back to God. My one chance home." He held it up by its delicate chain so that the image of Christ swung back and forth from sunlight to shadow and back again. "But it also frightens me, Braverman. There are moments when it singes me, when I am certain that it will be the instrument of my death." With a snapping gesture he enclosed the crucifix in his fist. It trembled, as if with an ague that now would never leave him. "I have strayed so far, and fallen so very, very fast. . . ."

His voice trailed off, and no attempt on Bravo's part could rouse him. They stayed like that for some time, the boy and his grandfather, silent, contemplative, strangers to one another, yet bound in some extraordinary manner unfathomable to both of them. It was only years later that Bravo realized that his grandfather's palms and fingers had been covered in blisters.

Bravo was startled out of his reverie as his sat phone suddenly came alive.

Having excused himself from Captain Balik's presence on the pretense of having to urinate, Fra Leoni went back into the office's entry, Emma's domain. It was here the infernal confrontation between Emma and Maura must have happened. If he was right, there would be some form of residue; there always was. For a moment he stood perfectly still, his keen gaze taking in every last detail. At length, he knelt on creaky knees on the rug. His hand reached out as if to touch the rough circle of ashes that had been ground in, but he quickly drew it back as if burned.

"Deus vel in caelo," he whispered. "God in heaven."

He pulled out his mobile phone, punched in Bravo's sat phone number.

"It's about your sister," he said softly enough so Balik couldn't hear. "Emma's been compromised."

"Compromised how?" Bravo's voice sounded thin, metallic, not at all human.

"All I can say now is that she has become something else. When Maura Kite unexpectedly showed up at the Salinas offices she was not herself. She was possessed."

"By a demon?"

"Call it what you will, Bravo. The point is whatever possessed her is now inside Emma."

"What?" A brief stab of panic shook him to his core, followed by sorrow, then rage. "I can't believe . . . A demon? Fra Leoni, tell me how is this possible?"

A terrible silence ensued, within which was implied a finality that caused a second wave of anxiety to well up in Bravo.

At the other end of the connection Fra Leoni closed his eyes for a moment, trying to remember what it was like being so young, so unprepared. So human. "Bravo, it is time for you to put aside all skepticism and simply listen."

Bravo closed his eyes, felt the trip-hammer beating of his pulse in his carotid, against his closed lids, a terrible tolling for his sister, perhaps also for himself. "All right," he said at length. "But first, one question: Do you know where she is?"

"I do not."

"I think I might." He told Fra Leoni about the inscription he had found on the wall painting inside the Cave of Shadows.

"The convent of Saint Angelica Boniface, in Capraola."

"Yes."

"Worse and worse. Emma is already in extreme danger; in days she will be beyond all help."

"Meaning?"

"Whatever has taken up residency inside her will have destroyed the Emma you and I know and love."

"Then there's no time to lose. I'm going after her."

"Be still, Bravo. Listen. Your own danger is imminent. If you become compromised as she is now you will be unable to help her. Worse, you will become part of the growing danger. So. There will come a moment, sooner rather than later, when Emma or, if as you posit she is indeed on her way to the convent of Saint Angelica Boniface, a creature of her ilk will try to get to you. Recall the strange body you saw in the morgue. Remember particularly its long nails. Stay away from those nails. The penetration of flesh. That is the method the creatures use to possess human bodies." He paused for a moment to catch his breath. "Do you understand me, Bravo?"

"Yes, but—"

"No ifs, ands, or buts. Do as I tell you." He heard Balik's restless tread. "I must go now."

"When—?"

"We'll speak soon. In the meantime, protect yourself at all costs."

"What kind of man knows all these secret things?"

"The kind of man," Fra Leoni said, still in his Sir Percy guise, "who has lived a long time, who has made many friends in many walks of life."

They were approaching the side entrance to the central police building, the shortest way to the morgue. Captain Balik's sleek car had negotiated Istanbul's early-morning streets like a ghost, never blocked, never challenged.

"And, one presumes," Balik replied, "the kind of man who has made a certain number of enemies."

"Now we're getting somewhere, Captain."

"Ah, but I think not, Sir Percy," Balik said as they stepped out of the car. "Mr. Fireside's van is gone, as are his men. They have already taken the body. We're too late."

"Let us suppose a different reality," Sir Percy said, opening the door and stepping through into the stench of sweet decay and bleach.

One of Balik's men was waiting for them just outside the swinging double doors to the morgue. He had a hangdog look that seemed to set the captain's teeth on edge.

"Well, do you have it, Dolman?"

Dolman held up a plastic evidence bag. It was filled with what seemed to be bits of charred metal.

"What is this? I ordered you to bring me the murder weapon."

"But, sir, this *is* the murder weapon," the unfortunate Dolman said like an oft-beaten cur.

"What d'you mean?" Balik snatched the evidence bag from him, squeezed it here and there. "What did you do, Dolman? Is this some form of joke?"

"I'm afraid not, Captain," Sir Percy said before Balik's minion could answer. "What you're holding is all that's left of the handgun used to shoot Dilara Tusik."

Balik glared at his man. "I demand an explanation."

But it was, again, Sir Percy who answered him. "It's waiting for us inside the cold room."

They passed through the doors. Hours ago, Balik had given orders sealing off the cold room to staff while Fireside and his men maneuvered the strange corpse out. Actually, Balik had just been reiterating Reichmann's orders to him.

To Balik's evident surprise, the body still lay on the table. To his eye, it looked untouched. "I don't understand," he said, abruptly bewildered.

"Soon enough," Sir Percy said, "you will." He gestured. "Put on a pair of those latex gloves, if you would, Captain."

As if he were sleepwalking, Balik did as he was asked. He never took his eyes off the corpse. Sir Percy led him over to the table. They stood beside it, staring down at the carbonized body.

"Now," Sir Percy said, "touch the breastbone with the tip of your finger."

Balik, still mesmerized by the body, said, "What is going to happen?"

"It's a surprise," Sir Percy said. "Go on now. It won't bite. Not now, anyway."

Balik shot him a confused look, then returned to his study of the corpse.

"Captain, you would be the first to admit that there was nothing normal about the Tusiks' murders, yes?"

"Privately, I would," Balik said. "But not in my official report."

"Well. It's just us chickens here."

"What?"

"The breastbone, Captain, is waiting."

Slowly, cautiously, Balik stretched out his hand. Extending his forefinger, he gently touched the corpse's breastbone. The moment he did so, the body collapsed into a heap of blackened ash. Severely alarmed, Balik jumped back. "What in hell—?"

"Yes," Sir Percy said, "at last you've caught it precisely."

THIRTY-NINE

Putting the sat phone aside, Bravo turned the gold crucifix over, looked at the sigil of the Unholy Trinity engraved there.

Protect yourself at all costs, Fra Leoni had cautioned.

Bravo dug into his backpack, took out a small folding knife. Opening it, he placed the edge of the blade against the golden back and started his work to first efface the sigil and then obliterate it completely.

Much later, in the departures lounge of Atatürk Airport, Fra Leoni sat at a café, sipping a cup of tea, hot, strong, and bracing. He was reliving his show-and-tell at the morgue, going over each detail, no matter how minuscule or seemingly unimportant, because at this moment in time, when everything had changed, nothing could be deemed unimportant.

"You can see for yourself that the body has disintegrated just like the murder weapon," he had told Balik. "This creature's grip broke down the gun's metal components."

"How?" Balik had looked dazed and confused. "How did it do that?"

"The how isn't relevant to your case," Fra Leoni had said, "is it?"

Balik had shaken his head. "I've never . . ." His voice trailed off as if he had lost all breath.

"None of us have," Fra Leoni said. "Until now."

Convinced that the thing that had inhabited the body gone to ash was the one that had murdered the Tusiks, the captain had told Fra Leoni what he had wanted to know, namely that Reichmann was behind the shipping of the body and that he had ordered it sent to Alexandria, Egypt, where Fra Leoni was now headed.

Fra Leoni looked around him at the milling throngs, completely unaware that they stood on the brink of annihilation. He turned, stared out the window at a city that was suddenly alien, alive with menace. He rubbed his temples, wanting to think clearly before he took action. To do that, he knew, he had to work through the incident, step by step. The small of his back still ached around the place where the possessed Emma had stuck him with her nail.

There could be no doubt that the war for humankind's collective soul had commenced. *But so soon? God help us all.*

He needed to figure out why Emma's possession had come about. Why Emma, of all people? This was why he had agreed to take the Quintessence. His mentor, far wiser than he, had foreseen this battle for the End Times, though clearly not the point at which it would commence. But then this was why he had kept himself alive long after his zest for living had faded like a photograph too long exposed to the sun.

One step at a time, he told himself. First, he needed to pinpoint the reasoning behind the possession; he knew that any mistake he made now would invariably lead to mankind's ruin.

FORTY

At first light, gray and ashen, Fireside led his men through the dense forest toward the last and steepest assault that would bring them to the cave behind the Baatara Gorge waterfall. When they encountered the stench of rotting flesh, Fireside signed to his men to up their vigilance. Closer, a swarm of buzzing filled the air. Several paces on, they came upon a number of bodies. Though they were bullet riddled and bloody, those on their backs looked like they were still alive, their stomachs rising and falling in the rhythm of breathing. Closer still, Fireside and his men saw the thick mat of black flies feasting on the chunks that had been torn out of the corpses' bellies. Nearby lay a wild boar carcass, which had been systematically stripped of its meat with knives, so by humans, not animals.

Fireside surveyed the scene with a calculating eye. His cadre, of course, had no idea what had happened to him, and he gave no outward sign that would signal a change had occurred. In any event, they were fixated on the job at hand. Any small slip he made would pass over their heads like the raucously crying morning birds.

His only real concern was the infestation of jihadists hiding, training, and staging in and around Tannourine. But the sprawl of the recent dead encouraged him; cadres had been here and moved on. As he and his men ascended, insects buzzed around them, lit on their shoulders, drew blood from their sweating scalps and necks. The roar of the cataract was a constant, growing in volume until it blocked out the animal screeches and cacophonous birdcalls. Fireside liked this least, and he was proved right when the last man in line arched back and fell down the cliff. He hadn't even heard the gunshot.

His men reacted as they should, firing into the tangle of vines and foliage even though they lacked visible targets. But clinging to the steep and narrow staircase they were at a distinct disadvantage, and in ones and twos they were picked off. By this time, Fireside had swung onto a thick vine and, hiding there, reassessed his situation. He couldn't go on knowing the hidden snipers would shoot him as they had his men, and he couldn't stay on his precarious perch indefinitely. Time to take the initiative.

He swung down, making a twisting descent vine by limb. He knew they must be searching for him. From the way they had ambushed his cadre, the expertise of their sharpshooters, he knew he was up against well-trained jihadists. They would have made a count of Fireside and his men, would now know they had killed all but one. They wouldn't risk leaving even a single soldier alive. Moreover, they knew these mountains far better than he did.

Once upon a time that would have made a grave difference, perhaps a fatal one. But that was then; this was now. Fireside was no longer Fireside. He was at once something more and a great deal less. He had no fear of death; he was a wreaker of destruction, a black angel of death.

He came upon the first sniper, nestled into the foliage, well hidden from afar, but not from him. Had someone been able at that moment to look into his eyes, they would have seen the change: the crimson rims around the iris, the sigil imprinted upon the pupil. Now, with his vision enhanced and from his vantage point above and to the right of the sniper, he could see how the jihadists had aligned themselves, each one three feet farther down in the mountain foliage, a well-documented military formation. He was both impressed and contemptuous.

How vulnerable they were to an enfilade counterattack: raking fire down the line of men crouched, tense, waiting for him to appear far above the place where he actually was. His eyes and brain vectored the line of five men, calculated distance and speed.

Then he leapt.

His extruded fingernails, his bared elongated teeth, slashed into one jihadist after another. Blood flew as necks were slashed, raised arms bitten down to the bone, carotid arteries severed. Fountains of blood. He was covered with it when, finished with the four, he came face-to-face with Nasir.

"Who are you?" Nasir's voice was a guttural sound, akin to that of an animal at bay.

"More to the point," Fireside said, "*what* am I?"

His head and upper body flashed forward in a blur. His teeth fastened on to Nasir's throat and he began to shake his head back and forth with such force that Nasir's entire throat came away in a spray of blood and gore. As the last of the jihadists fell away from him, Fireside turned and headed back up, eschewing the staircase, sticking to the vines and twisted branches, ascending in great leaps. As he went, he moved farther to his left, away from the thicker sprays from the cataract. The blood began to coagulate on his skin and clothes. Mammals and birds fled in his wake.

FORTY-ONE

The early-morning mist had risen as Emma, miles to the north of Rome, outside the village of Capraola, approached the convent of Saint Angelica Boniface. The sun shone on the treetops, speckling the earth beneath. As she stepped out of the rental car, shadows gathered around her like a murder of crows. It was as if she absorbed the sunlight, as if it vanished into her, as water swirls down a drain. Larks left their perches, flew south to more hospitable climes.

Something was happening to her. Something unexpected, something important. It made her heart thump almost painfully against the cage of her ribs. Or was it the old Emma, imprisoned deep inside her, who was thumping? She could no longer tell, and this both frightened and exhilarated her.

For a long time she stood perfectly still, one hand on the half-open car door, one hand at her side, fingers lightly curled, preparing for something ahead of her that was already stirring but which she could not yet see.

I am not who I was, she thought, *and I am not yet who I will be.*

The sunlight struck her as it would a sightless person, with a physical force that transcended heat or brilliance. She recognized it for what it was, a doorway to step through, and she slammed the door behind her, set off down the path to the convent's front door with forceful strides.

Inside, it was cool and dim, which suited her better. At least it once had; now she was not so sure. Placing the notion aside, she set out in search of Malus. She found Valentin instead.

He was standing just beyond the open doorway to the refectory, where meal settings were being placed on the table in perfect silence. He was brought up short. The skin around his eyes turned white. "Emma." He looked like he had been punched in the gut.

"Emma is gone," Emma responded, and was shocked to find that somewhere inside her tears were being shed. *What is this?* she asked herself. *What's happening to me?* Shielding this inner monologue, she smiled. But it seemed false, even to her. "You haven't asked about your wife." Remarkably, the memory of grinding Maura Kite's husk to dust didn't thrill her as it should have. It was as if a gray veil of mourning covered her from head to foot. A spasm of rage racked her. Nevertheless, she kept that hateful smile in place. "You said my name as if you were old friends."

He leaned forward, peered into her eyes just as if they were hollow, affording him a glimpse into what lay beyond. Again something stirred inside her, stronger this time, muddying her thoughts with unwanted emotion. Never before in all the centuries had she felt anything like this stirring inside her. There had always been the utter stillness of the grave, a dense and weighty essence that served as her anchor. She did not have that now; she floated on dark and unknown seas. Had she been other than what she was, she would have been filled with fear.

"It's good to see you," she said from somewhere deep inside her. "At last."

Valentin's eyes opened wide, his mouth forming an O. "I thought you said Emma was gone."

"She's gone, and she's never coming back," she said with a spit of venom. Inside, she was so dismayed, she turned her back to him and, without another word, stepped away.

The grounds, silent save for the contented humming of

insects, gave way to cool stone passageways that debouched on the colonnaded cloister, which ran around the sun-drenched quadrangle. Valentin opened the black iron grate, crowned with a cross, and they passed silently through. Birds lifted and vanished at their approach, as did a pair of nuns, who hurried away, their heads down. Fat bees buzzed somnolently as they went about their hunting and gathering. On the other side, a nun, hands folded into the sleeves of her habit, passed onto and out of the cloister, on her way to some inscrutable mission. Emma waited until she was out of sight.

"What a little shit you are, Valentin. You certainly don't miss your wife. But your darling Emma, ah, that's another story." Her tone was acid. "Is that your problem?"

"I don't have a problem," Valentin snapped, then realized what he had done. He sighed, staring out into the molten dazzle of sunlight. "You won't like what's happened here since Malus returned from Alexandria, either."

Again she dripped contempt. "In other words, he's already mastered the *madre vicaria*."

"You know?" He seemed taken aback.

"I've been around him a long time." There was now a note of triumph in her voice. "Virtually all his life." She subjected Valentin to an astute inspection. "But I see that he's misjudged you."

Valentin started. "What d'you mean?"

She turned to face him, an expression of contempt on her face. "Sister Maria Veniera has gotten under your skin."

"What're you talking about?" All his defenses were up.

Emma gave him a slow, steely smile. "She has a certain magic, that's unquestioned. Look how all the sisters here have fallen under her spell. But you . . . well, Malus wouldn't have expected it from you." She raised an eyebrow. "But I would."

"You don't know me at all."

"You're weak, easily manipulated." Her thin smile held not one iota of warmth. "Emma didn't need her eyes to see that."

He reared back, clearly stung. "You know less about Emma than you know about me."

"I know men, Valentin. A long, long line of men, and they're all the same." Her anger at him was threatening to get out of control. "You're no exception."

"I was chosen."

"You fool," she almost shouted. "Only the weak, the insecure, are chosen; don't you know that?"

Aware that Valentin was studying her with a curator's care, she said hastily, "Malus hasn't chosen anyone in this convent, the *madre vicaria* included."

"You didn't see him rutting with her as I did."

"Well, at least you used the correct term," she said tartly, still struggling to regain her equilibrium. "Do you imagine he'd choose someone with whom he ruts like an animal?" She tilted her head, but Valentin remained mute. "No, he's waiting."

"For what?"

"Not for what. He awaits the woman who, like you, was chosen at a young and tender age."

"Why wouldn't that be the *madre vicaria*? She isn't Sister María Veniera," Valentin blurted.

Emma placed her hands on her hips. "Who is she then?"

"Saint Bella dell'Arca."

Emma laughed again. "Really. Saint Bella dell'Arca was burned to death centuries ago."

"She was saved." Reaching out, he exposed the sigil on Emma's chest. "She has this, just like you."

Emma stepped back. Shaking off the effect his fingers had on her, she said, "So he raised her up."

"Unless what I saw was a mirage."

"The Resurrection of the Dark."

"You see. She *could* be the one he's been waiting for."

Emma scarcely heard him. The Resurrection of the Dark had happened to her, several times. It was hardly pleasant, but sometimes there was no other way. But Bella dell'Arca, that was unexpected. What was Malus up to? What hadn't he told her?

Plenty, said a voice deep inside her. The hair at the back of her neck stood on end. It was not her own voice.

Bravo was the first to see the figure almost literally emerging from the verge of the waterfall. He could see the man was shouting as he staggered forward, but the roar of the water drowned out whatever he was trying to say.

Bravo shook Ayla's shoulder to wake her from the unpleasant dream within which she had been restlessly twitching. Her eyes snapped open, bringing intense spots of color to the drab surroundings. *What?* she mouthed.

"Someone's here."

She sprang up in time to see the figure stumble up the last steps and fall to his knees on the ledge. She and Bravo both headed toward the man, his head hanging down on his heaving chest, but at the last moment he raised it. Bravo reared back, recognizing Collum Fireside. He reached out to grab Ayla, pull her back, but it was too late. Fireside had come alive, his eyes alight. Wrapping Ayla in a viselike grip, he pinioned her arms against her sides, pressed her hard against him.

Ignoring her ineffectual kicks, he grinned past her, his over-bright eyes fixed on Bravo.

"Looks like I arrived just in time," Fireside said flatly.

Bravo noted the crimson ring around Fireside's irises. In Bravo's peripheral vision the length of Fireside's nails stood out like a downed live wire, flashing extreme danger.

Sooner rather than later, Fra Leoni had unerringly predicted.

As in Acts 9:18, "And immediately there fell from his eyes as it had been scales: and he received sight forthwith," all skepticism fell away from Bravo. He believed in every word that Fra Leoni had told him. He believed in what his own eyes were seeing. He believed in Lucifer and his minions come to earth. And, in that moment of blinding clarity, he believed in his grandfather absolutely.

"Step to the lip of the ledge," the thing that was Fireside said. He turned, and Ayla with him, as Bravo began to obey his command. The thing had one long nail at her throat. There was something subtly wrong with what Bravo was seeing, but as yet he couldn't figure out what, except that it was such a small thing. And yet so vital.

"Keep going," Fireside said, his teeth bared, canines showing, as long as a werewolf's. "Your fall will be a long and painful one."

Just like Grandfather Conrad's, Bravo thought.

He was no more than two paces to the space between the ledge and the cataract when three gunshots pierced the thunder of the waterfall. Fireside jerked left, then right. Letting go of Ayla, he spun around, confronting the man, who shot him again, this time in the chest, with the long-barreled .357 Magnum. Fireside was driven half a step backward. But this wasn't Fireside, after all. No blood appeared at the bullet entries. Bravo, desperately searching for Ayla and not seeing her, spotted instead the black holes in Fireside's back, fabric flayed away by the impact where the bullets had entered. Ayla was nowhere to be seen, but past Fireside's bulk Bravo glimpsed Aldus Reichmann, *Nauarchus* of the Circle Council of the Knights of Saint Clement, his nemesis. He was dressed in a sweat-stained trekking outfit, beads of water in his hair and on his face. Strapped crosswise to his back was a black cylinder that might have been a quiver had it not been firmly capped.

In a blur Fireside took a stride forward, kicked out hard with his left leg, sending Reichmann reeling backward. The heel of Reichmann's climbing boot caught on a slight outcropping of the ledge, and he lost his balance. Magnum spinning away, arms splayed wide in a vain attempt to regain his balance, he started to topple over the edge into the watery abyss.

Bravo leapt forward, sliding on his stomach. He caught

Reichmann's wrist just as he went over. The weight almost pulled him over, too. He slid, caught at the outcropping that had upended Reichmann, grabbing it for dear life to halt his forward momentum.

The two men, bitter adversaries who had never met before this but had inflicted grievous mutual damage, stared into each other's eyes.

This isn't going to work.

Bravo lip-read Reichmann's words, the vibrating air too saturated with noise for voices to be heard.

Hang on, Bravo mouthed. *I'm going to pull you up.*

Reichmann frowned. *Why should you try?*

Bravo didn't waste energy on an answer Reichmann lacked the capacity to understand. Instead, Bravo hauled on his enemy, but with only one arm available and his own position precarious he couldn't make any headway at all.

You can't, Reichmann mouthed. *You see? You can't save everyone, and why should you try? What's wrong with you? It's a weakness, not a strength. A terrible flaw.* He smiled. *In any event, I'm not worth saving.*

Shut up! Bravo kept at it, but try as he might, he couldn't find a way to draw Reichmann to safety. To the contrary, all Bravo's efforts were having a negative effect on his own position as he slipped closer to the edge.

But there is something worth saving here. Reichmann rolled his eyes up. *The container strapped across my back. Take it.*

What? Bravo, astonished and bewildered, stared down at his enemy. What was Reichmann's game? *What d'you mean?*

Something happened. I . . . the castle . . . Malta . . . she burned it and everyone in it.

She? Bravo felt like the dream boy who came to class for finals not having studied. *Who?*

Take it, you fool, before it's too late!

Too late for what? Bravo, sliding another few inches over the edge, had to make a decision now. Either retrieve the quiver or take the long fall with Reichmann. Bravo let go of the outcropping, desperately snatched at the cylinder's leather strap. When he had it in his hand, he was still reluctant to let Reichmann go. Reichmann, in a last effort, bit his hand, and Bravo at last released his grip.

Reichmann fell, vanishing into the cataract as Bravo squirmed his way back onto the ledge and into Fireside's implacable grip.

FORTY-TWO

What would make the world's colors go smeary? What would bleach those colors gray as a dishrag? Could it be the laceration on her collarbone, leaking blood? Was that what caused her legs to buckle? Was that why she was on hands and knees, head hanging down?

She was aware that Bravo was in trouble but could not regain her feet, let alone contemplate coming to his aid. The breath sawed in and out of her lungs as if she were an asthmatic caught without her inhaler. With the agonizing slowness of a praying mantis she moved one leg, then the other. Her knee kicked something in front of her—a black cylinder. Grabbing it by its cord, she dragged it along after her. She had no idea where she was headed, only knew she had to get away from the big man who had scraped her with his hideously long nail. She knew, she knew. A certain coldness invading her she didn't want to think about. She couldn't. Not now. Not until she was safe. Maybe not even then.

Like a wounded animal she sought the darkness, deep shadows in which to hide. Hide as, in a sense, she had always hidden since she and her mother had returned from Tannourine. How far she had traveled since that day, but she could not outrun herself. Wherever she found herself, there she was—all the despised parts of her.

She had lied to Bravo, as she had lied to everyone but her parents. From them she could not stay hidden. They had made her, after all. At least, her mother had. She crawled into the cave mouth, found a pitiful form of comfort in the darkness, all she had now. Afraid even that was slipping away. The slash on her collarbone. There was no pain, but there was something else far, far worse.

She had lied to Bravo, but she had come so close to telling him the truth, and this terrified her more than anything. Almost. She closed her eyes, a moment from her past swimming into the theater of her mind, out at the café in Istanbul she had taken Bravo to, the café where she had shared secrets with her father. The one and only time.

"My darling Ayla," her father began, "I know you think I'm ignorant." He raised a hand palm outward to forestall her intended outburst. "Please. Let me finish."

She subsided, but she found herself trembling with expectation. Or was it anxiety? To this day, she couldn't be sure.

"I know you think I'm ignorant of your inner life with your mother. I'm not. I know . . . well, I know everything. What she wouldn't tell me, which is most, I managed to glean for myself." He smiled weakly, and she realized that he was as nervous as she was. "Your mother isn't the only one in the family with sources."

He turned his tiny coffee cup between blunt fingers, around and around. "She never should have taken you to Tannourine. I know she had to, but still . . ." Around and around. "You're *my* daughter, too."

He sighed. "Ayla, she did a terrible thing. She took you away while I was in Bodrum on business. She knew my mind. She knew I'd try to stop her. She knew I had a say in this, but she chose to ignore me. You're my daughter, too."

Ayla stared down at her coffee. She could not answer him, could not even meet his gaze.

"I know what you must be feeling, but you must never be ashamed of who you are." He took a breath. "Or what you are."

That's when she had begun to cry.

Now, in the darkness of the Cave of Shadows, she tried to touch her wound but snatched her hand away. The heat was like a furnace.

"Ayla, we are, all of us, like phyllo—layer upon layer—and it may be that sometimes these layers, lying one atop the other, are in conflict. We are complicated beings. We can feel terror and wonder, pleasure and pain, love and hate at the same time. And we can be coward and hero all at once. We are both good and evil."

Her father's words resounded in her ears as she opened her eyes, lifted her gaze to the ledge outside the cave mouth, where Bravo and the big man were in the midst of their life-and-death struggle. She had been wounded; she was too weak to come to Bravo's aid. But her shame was this: even if she hadn't been slit by that thing's nail she would have backed away from the current conflict. She knew what it was that Bravo battled; she had encountered it before. Her terror of it paralyzed her.

Now, curled into a fetal position, the cylinder pressed to her breast like a teddy bear, she could at last weep for herself, for everything she had lost.

The fire, having been stoked by Bravo, flared up, crackling and snapping, crowned in a diadem of sparks. It was a thing of beauty, blazing and symmetrical, providing perfect light and heat. Until, that is, Fireside and Bravo crashed into it, scattering the burning twigs every which way.

Fireside, wasting no time, struck Bravo with his massive fist, rocking his head backward. His hair began to hiss and smolder. Bravo drove a knee into Fireside's groin, loosening his grip. He immediately chopped down on the side of Fireside's neck, but either he missed or the cords of Fireside's neck were so thick they protected the nerves beneath like an armadillo's carapace.

Fireside heaved Bravo out of the fire, slammed him down on his back so hard Bravo momentarily lost his ability to breathe.

His lungs labored, momentarily paralyzed. A terrible blackness, fluid and depthless, squirmed at the edges of his vision.

Grinning hugely, canines bared, Fireside launched himself at Bravo, straddling him as he landed on knees and haunches. Bravo withdrew the gold crucifix, dangled it by its chain in front of Fireside's face.

"Really?" the creature growled deep in his throat. His laugh was like the guttural warning cough of a lion as he batted the crucifix out of Bravo's hand. It tumbled through the air, landing in the hottest part of the scattered fire, where the red-hot embers glowed like predators' eyes in the darkness between the cataract and the cave mouth.

He grabbed Bravo by the throat, throttling him. Bravo's mind had been divided. He wanted to know where Ayla was. He wanted to know she was all right, that she hadn't been struck by one of the Magnum's bullets. But he could discern no exit wounds on Fireside. It was as if his body had absorbed them entirely. Bravo's worry for Ayla had diverted his attention, allowed him to fall into Fireside's grip, and now he was paying the price.

Concentrate! he heard Todao saying as his sensei tossed him again and again to the practice mat. *To concentrate is to gain power over your attacker.*

Bravo, on the verge of passing out, concentrated every ounce of energy on Fireside. *An empty mind is a victorious mind,* Todao had said. *A crowded mind drowns in defeat.* Bravo was not going to drown. He emptied his mind.

And saw his way in. Just in time, as Fireside, believing he had subdued Bravo, had extruded the nail on his right forefinger. It was yellow-black, filthy looking, coming closer and closer to Bravo's throat. He could not let it penetrate his skin.

Emma, Fra Leoni had said. *If you become compromised as she is now you will be unable to help her.* Emma. *Worse, you will have become part of the growing danger.*

Writhing like an eel in mud, Bravo drew the Beretta from beneath him, placed the muzzle against Fireside's right shoulder joint, fired three times in succession. Bravo had no illusions that the bullets would bring the creature down, but the percussions sent Fireside reeling backward on his knees. The top of his head scattered more ash, burning twigs, and flames, none of which appeared to faze him in the least. Just beyond, Bravo glimpsed the crucifix, glowing as cherry red as the embers on which it had landed.

Bravo knew there was only one desperate measure to try. Experience had shown him that no amount of pure physical force or discharge from a handgun could kill the infernal thing that had taken possession of Fireside's corpus.

Leaping onto Fireside, Bravo stretched out, grabbing the crucifix's chain, drawing it into his hand. His teeth gritted at the scorching pain, but in his emptied mind there was ample room to put it aside. Fireside was reaching up for him, one hand cupped at the base of his neck, pulling him down toward the extended fingernail.

Bravo pushed the glowing crucifix into the center of Fireside's forehead. The creature's eyes opened wide. Bravo pressed it down harder. Fireside's mouth gaped wide, saliva draped across huge glistening teeth. Bravo kept pressing, harder and harder, the flesh of his palm smoking, the agony beginning to fill up the entirety of his mind. This had to work before that happened or he would surely pass out and all would be lost.

Beneath him, Fireside's body was thrashing, the heels of his boots beating such a thunderous tattoo shards of rock shattered, spinning off in all directions. Dimly, Bravo felt one rip into the back of his jacket. Nevertheless, he was not to be deterred. Using his thumbs he ground the crucifix into Fireside's forehead until it disappeared completely in a searing wound.

With an inchoate cry the thing that was Fireside threw Bravo off him, stumbled to his feet, staggered toward the lip of the ledge and the cataract beyond. The two ends of the gold chain hung down incongruously over his eyes. Bravo launched himself up and out, following Fireside.

A step before Fireside lurched over the edge, Bravo grabbed the two ends of the chain, pulled with all his strength. Like a stopper popping out of a drain in which it had been lodged, the crucifix came away from Fireside's forehead. His eyes dimmed, lights were extinguished throughout his mind; his body was just getting the message as he vanished into the torrent, whirling like a snowflake in a storm.

Bravo, lying prone on the ledge, turned over on to his back. He ached in every part of his body. His breath came hard and fast. His mind was reeling as he stared up at the crucifix he held dangling above his head. It was pitch black.

PART FOUR

A GAZE BLANK AND PITILESS
AS THE SUN

ALEXANDRIA / CAPRAOLA / TANNOURINE

FORTY-THREE

When Fra Leoni appeared out of the sun dazzle, framed in the doorway to the library at Alexandria, the curator looked up from the local newspaper he was reading and, with a huge smile, took up his cane, and hurried around from behind his high desk.

"Ahlan wa sahlan, mawlānā!"

"Ahlan bīk, Aither."

"How does this morning find you?"

Fra Leoni smiled wanly. "We shall see, old friend." He pointed to the cane. "And what of you?"

"My hip. I fell off one of the sliding ladders three weeks ago." He grinned self-deprecatingly. "I fear I've become a clumsy old fool."

"In three or four weeks I have no doubt you'll be your old self again."

Aither's grin widened. He took the old man's hand in his and bowed.

"Enough of that, *habibi*. We know each other too long."

"It's because of our long history that you are venerated here, *mawlānā*." He stood up as straight as he was able, leaning on his cane. "How can I be of service?"

"Stay here while I climb the stairs," Fra Leoni said. "Come only when I call you."

"My hip will not deter me on the stairs, be assured."

"Then come quick as you are able."

"Ya saatir." *May God protect us.* The smile wiped clean

by the old monk's sober words, Aither nodded. "What has happened?"

"It's not so much what," Fra Leoni said, beginning his ascent. "It's how bad."

He felt the chill the moment he reached the second floor. He stood quite still, gasping like a fish just landed on the slanted boat deck. It was as if something had sucked up all the oxygen. And there was a certain dimness that would not abandon the rooms no matter how many lamps he lit. He felt a clawing at his insides, as if some invisible rodent, having invaded him, was now trying to claw its way out.

Instantly Fra Leoni's worst fears were realized. He knew what had been here, and his heart turned to ice. His hands trembled and a tic started up at the edge of his left eyelid. He glanced behind him. He told himself he did so to make sure Aither hadn't followed him, but another, deeper part of him knew it was his fear response at work. He needed to make certain the thing wasn't still lurking about.

Having assured himself, he stepped forward, past the place where Reichmann had been running his fingertips across the spines of the shelves of books, past the chair where Reichmann had sat, reading while clandestinely observing the figure at the far end of the table.

The closer Fra Leoni came to that spot the more slowly he moved, until his progress was no faster than a slo-mo camera shot. He turned his head, heard his cervical vertebrae crack, a pistol shot in the dense and smothering silence.

Every nerve ending seemed to be screaming: *Here, here is where it sat, shoulders hunched, head down, reading what? A manuscript, an open book?* His gaze rose, swung toward the shelves. His vertebrae cracked again, another gunshot. Which book? Why was it here? What was its purpose? The infernal creature—forever enslaved to the Sum of All Shadows—never did anything without a specific reason.

The silence was so absolute it was like a living thing, pulsing with the beat of its own heart. But soul? No, there was no soul here, just a yawning void into which both sound and light were sucked as if down a drain. Fra Leoni felt this growing vortex, felt himself starting to vibrate to it, and at the last instant understood the void wasn't merely the residue of the creature's residence, but a trap laid for whoever came after, whoever might want to track it. Whether that might be specifically him he didn't know and had no time to contemplate the question. The undertow had become a rip tide. Trying to strip him of energy and will. He saw the rise of the darkness out of the void at the center of the place where the creature had crouched like a spider, spinning its invisible web. Worse, he felt himself pulled toward it. The force of it increasing exponentially, his power to resist it eroding alarmingly, as if, stripped of defenses, vulnerable again, he had returned to his adolescent state.

At once terrified and bewildered, he began his chanted prayers, as he had been taught, but stumbled over certain words, forgot others completely, his terror on the verge of panic before he had the good sense to call for Aither, his vocal cords aching with the strain.

He was being dragged farther along, closer to the void. He could see the energy forces swirling, feel their mesmeric pull, and he stumbled to his knees. This was the position in which Aither found him as he sped into the second-floor room, as light and nimble and speedy on his feet as any dancer in his prime.

Having been primed by Fra Leoni's concern, he took in the situation at a glance and immediately spoke in a strong, clear voice: "Exsúrgat Deus et dissipéntur inimíci ejus: et fúgiant qui odérunt eum a fácie ejus!" *Let God arise and let His enemies be scattered: and let them that hate Him flee before His Face!* He raised his arms from his sides, as if slowly lifting a heavy weight over his head. His voice carried strong and true into the heart of the spinning black void. "Sicut déficit fumus deficiant; sicuit fluit cera a fácie ígnis, sic péreant peccatóres a fácie Dei."

As smoke vanishes, so let them vanish away; as wax melts before the fire, so let the wicked perish at the presence of God.

A shift, small but seismic, buffeted the room. In the hellish dimness there appeared sparks of light. The rustle of a breeze stirred their hair. Now Fra Leoni staggered to his feet. His face was still white as bone, but his eyes had regained a semblance of their ferocious brilliance.

Together, the two men continued the chanted invocation: "Proeliáre hódie cum beatórum Angelórum exércitu proélia Dómini. . . ." *Fight the battles of the Lord today with the Army of the Blessed Angels, as once thou didst fight against Lucifer, the first in pride, and his apostate angels; and they prevailed not: neither was their place found anymore in heaven.*

A howling arose from the abyss, of frustration, venality, and envy, then of intense agony such as no man has ever suffered.

"Sed projéctus est dráco ílle mágnus, sérpens antíquus, qui vocátur diábolus et sátanas. . . ." *But that great dragon was cast out, the ancient serpent, who is called the Devil and Lucifer, who seduces the whole world. And he was cast unto the earth, and his angels were thrown down with him.*

Fra Leoni drew from his pocket an incense stick, lit it with a trembling hand. The air seemed to writhe as the scintillating sparks of light doubled and redoubled. The smell of sulphur and burning incense mingled.

"Deprecáre Deum pácis, ut cónterat sátanam sub pédibus nóstris. . . ." *Beseech the God of Peace to crush Lucifer under our feet, that he may no more be able to hold men captive and to harm the Church. Offer our prayers in the sight of the Most High, so that the mercies of the Lord may quickly come to our aid, that thou mayest seize the dragon, the ancient serpent, who is the Devil and Lucifer, and that having bound him, thou mayest cast him into the bottomless pit, so that he may no more seduce the nations.*

The light was coming, seeping in from all directions, and such was its strength, such was its power, that it began to overwhelm the void, filling the infernal darkness with a bright dazzle, too blinding for even Fra Leoni and Aither, and they had to avert their eyes, as their voices rose to a crescendo of sound and power: "Váde sátana, invéntor et magíster ómnis falláciae, hóstis humánae salútis!" *Begone, Lucifer, inventor and master of all deceit, enemy of man's salvation!* "Holy, holy, holy is the Lord, the God of Hosts."

In a flash the room was as it had always been for centuries, before the invasion. Fra Leoni, exhausted and sick at heart, sank into a chair, head bowed, arms crossed over his chest.

"Mawlānā!" Aither cried, stepping toward Fra Leoni. "I pray to God that you haven't been grievously injured."

"Not grievously, no." Fra Leoni lifted his head. His eyes, enlarged and watery with incipient tears, stared into Aither's knowing gaze.

"Mawlānā, please."

Fra Leoni took a great shuddering breath. "Coming here, I feared the worst, *habibi.* I prepared myself. And yet, I was almost defeated. Without your help, I fear I would have been."

The curator shook his head. "This I cannot credit."

Fra Leoni, his heart aflutter like a wild caged bird, said, "The reliquary. It's safe? It's intact?"

Aither's eyes opened wide as he reared back. "No, *mawlānā!* You can't be thinking—"

Rising, Fra Leoni said, "Take me there."

"It's too dangerous, my old friend. Even for you."

"I was almost overtaken, Aither. You know what that means. His army has awoken and is on the march. The moment foretold when Lucifer rises again to reclaim what was once his is at hand."

"But for that the Infernal would require the Unholy Trinity— the book, the salver, the engine. Only when they are together again can the Sum of All Shadows be summoned. God, in His infinite wisdom, made it impossible for him to touch these things again."

"As is his wont, Lucifer has found a way around the problem. He has tasked three humans to find and retrieve the Unholy Trinity. The first—the Book of Deathly Things—has been found."

The curator's face, drained of blood, looked like a death's-head. "Has it been brought to—?"

"I believe it has." For once Fra Leoni looked every year of his advanced age. "But there's only one way to be sure."

"The reliquary." Aither almost choked on the words.

"Now." Fra Leoni had not raised his voice, but all the same his command was incontestable.

Aither, knowing when to concede, nodded unhappily, led the way through dusty corridors to the opposite end of the second floor. There he paused before a large breakfront that held an imposing basalt statue of Anubis, jackal-headed Egyptian guardian of the underworld. Anubis held a staff with which he guided souls from life into death in one hand and an Ankh, the breath of life, in the other.

Aither stood back. "Last chance," he said softly.

"I have been attacked twice in two days," Fra Leoni said. "I am severely weakened. This is our only chance. The final storm is almost upon us. Without me, Bravo will not survive."

With a small gold key he wore around his neck, Fra Leoni opened the door to the breakfront. As Aither watched, he reached behind the statue, pressed a tiny section of the breakfront base hidden by the plinth on which Anubis was set. A tiny click, and the breakfront swung easily away from the wall. An arched entryway beckoned, and the two men stepped through to the chamber beyond.

"Without your key, no one has been in here for centuries," Aither said in a hushed voice. "Even me."

The room was almost claustrophobically small, circular, with a domed ceiling. Aither went immediately to light a lamp, and slowly the contents of the chamber became visible: a series of five vitrines positioned in a star pattern. They were waist-high, with clear sapphire tops, rather than glass. Each was hermetically sealed, which meant opening one was a final operation. Once the atmosphere of the modern world was allowed in, the damage to ancients of ancients would be done: they would turn to dust.

One vitrine held the partial skull of Saint John; another, the forefinger of Saint Paul; the third, the skeletal foot of Saint Peter; the fourth, the shriveled ear of Saint Matthew. Within the fifth, over which the two men hovered in trepidation, were a pile of bones—not human bones, but those of a large avian.

"Antiphon," Fra Leoni said. "Hello again, old friend."

"Please, you can't do this," the curator pleaded. "It's too dangerous."

"Stop wringing your hands like an old woman." Fra Leoni, so close now, was on edge, but there was a resignation in him that he did not wish to deny.

"But, *mawlānā*, the idea of destroying even one of these relics is anathema to the Church."

"My friend, if the Church knew what was in here we would be cast out as surely as Lucifer and his dark angels were cast out of heaven."

Aither bowed his head. "Is there no other way?"

"You know there isn't." Fra Leoni clasped the curator's shoulder. "We have been through many adventures, some filled with the light of God and Christ, others deep and dark. But none have been as dark as what we face now."

"Yeats."

"Yes. William Butler Yeats. One of the most influential members of the Antaeus Club during the first decade of the twentieth century. It was to Yeats that Bravo's grandfather was drawn and with whom he became close friends. Conrad Shaw recognized Yeats for what he was: a diviner of the future. '. . . everywhere / The ceremony of innocence is drowned; / The best lack all conviction, while the worst / Are full of passionate intensity,'" Fra Leoni said, quoting from Yeats's most storied poem, "The Second Coming." "Conrad Shaw understood that

Yeats was not speaking about his own age, but prophesizing what was to come in future generations. But now the time of Yeats's Second Coming has begun. 'The blood-dimmed tide is loosed . . . / Surely some revelation is at hand.'"

"Yeats's philosophy of the two opposing gyres."

Fra Leoni nodded. "And in that widening gyre, the falcon can no longer hear the falconer. The old gyre—Yeats's spiral—is ending. Mankind's trajectory along the widening gyre of science, democracy, and heterogeneity has been failing since the millennium. The next one—the opposite gyre—will be one not of science and democracy, but of the primal power of mysticism, the rise of tribalism, the resurrection of what Yeats called the 'rough beast.'"

"Lucifer." There were tears in Aither's eyes. "I understand. It must be done. The unthinkable, yes."

Fra Leoni placed his hand on the corner of the vitrine that contained Antiphon's bones.

"The eagle of Saint John, his constant companion."

"His familiar."

The curator smiled. "I can only imagine how that would send the Church elders into fits of apoplexy."

"In the time of the Apostles, the Church had not yet been born. It does not get to rewrite this part of history, Aither." He fingered the vitrine. "You see, Antiphon is the falcon of Yeats's prophesy. The first gyre began with Saint John and Antiphon, falconer and falcon. Now, at the end, the falcon had flown so far it can no longer hear its falconer. Their power is ending as a new power rises.

"This room, these holy relics, have been the source of our Order's light and strength in the long struggle against the dark. Now, in our hour of greatest need, one of them must be unlocked; one of them must transfer to me its light and its strength so I can return to the struggle renewed. Otherwise . . ."

"Yes." Aither nodded. "Otherwise the darkness will surely prevail."

"So," Fra Leoni said, straightening with difficulty. "I will require your assistance."

"I am here," the curator said as he moved to a place just behind and to the right of Fra Leoni. "I am always here."

Pulling on the curved handle of his cane, he drew out a thin Damascus steel blade in a practiced sweep. He swung it hard and fast. Even as Fra Leoni was turning, the blade sliced through skin, flesh, muscles, arteries, and finally bone. Such was the force of the killing stroke that Fra Leoni's head flew across the chamber, struck the stone wall, bounced to the floor, leaving a bloody smear.

Aither had stepped back, avoiding the arterial spurts fountaining out of the severed neck. For long eerie moments, the body stayed on its feet, swaying like a drunkard. Then, like an exhaled breath, it collapsed onto the floor in front of the bones of Antiphon. With the legs still twitching in galvanic response, Aither let go of the blade, bent over, snatched the gold key from Fra Leoni's hand.

Squatting on his hams next to the head, he stared down into Fra Leoni's open eyes, frozen in an expression of surprise at the moment of death.

"Yes, I'm sure you're shocked. I suppose I would be, too, were I in your shoes. But, you know, betraying you was easier than I had expected. Of course, certain people greased the wheels, but still . . ." He contemplated the key, turning it over and over. "You would never let anyone else have this. And I, stuck in this graveyard for so very long, was not even allowed into the reliquary. I wasn't trusted, was I?" Aither laughed at the irony, then rose, turning away.

Using the long-sought-after key, he methodically went from vitrine to vitrine, opening each one up, standing over it, as the air of a new century was sucked in, as the relics of the four Apostles, of Antiphon, the ancient power of the Gnostic Observatines, turned to piles of gray powder. These he swept onto the floor with the back of his hand, until all five vitrines were empty, the power of the reliquary broken, destroyed utterly.

Without a backward glance, he went out of the chamber, replacing and locking the breakfront. Downstairs, he returned to his accustomed spot behind his high desk, his gaze dropping to the article he'd been reading when Fra Leoni had appeared. When he had finished the article, he drew a mobile phone from a drawer, stepped outside, and, beneath a burnished sky, initiated the call he was obliged to make.

FORTY-FOUR

Valentin was hard at work in the convent scriptorium, writing in a cribbed hand with pen and ink on sheets of fat-colored vellum, when Emma entered. He was sitting on a stool, drawn up to a wooden table with a top angled toward him, much like those draftsmen used to use before the advent of CAD.

The scriptorium was an immense space: two stories of books and hand-bound manuscripts behind the wire-fronted doors of massive cabinets that rose from floor to ceiling. The heavy, leaded-glass windows faced north, ensuring no direct sunlight fell upon the scriptorium's precious contents, while allowing in enough ambient light to keep the room from feeling like a cave. In one corner, a narrow spiral staircase led up to the second floor.

On this first floor, where Valentin labored, seven life-size marble statues were arrayed in niches between the cabinets. Behind him were three figures from the Old Testament. First was Cain. Beneath his feet were carved the words of God: "Your brother's blood cries out to me." Second, in the middle of the scriptorium, was Job. Beneath his feet were carved his own words to God: "And repent of dust and ashes." Third, at the far end, was Moses. At his feet, this quote: "And we smote him, and his sons, and all his people." In front of Valentin were the four Apostles: John, Peter, Mark, and Paul. At the feet of each was carved his respective symbol: an open book, keys, a scroll, a sword and closed book.

Valentin glanced up when Emma's shadow fell across his writing but then immediately put his head down. The fingers of his right hand were ink stained. A cup of water, half-empty, sat just beyond his left elbow.

"How far along are you?" Emma picked up the leaves of vellum Valentin had finished, scanned them with an avid eye. "The Book of Deathly Things." Her eyes sparked. "The Testament of Lucifer." She put down the top sheet. "How *fortunate* are you to have the entire manuscript in your head."

"Like fire written across the sky," Valentin said in a carefully neutral voice, so that Emma wouldn't know whether he was being reverent or facetious. She sat beside him. He felt her as strongly as if she were a stoked furnace. A tingling sensation starting in his scalp worked its way down his neck, into his spine, making him shift from one buttock to another.

"Am I disturbing you?"

"It's her voice." Valentin forced himself to keep writing. "You know that, don't you?"

She said nothing. Her head was down, her eyes on his writing.

"I wonder why that is, Emma."

"Don't get smart with me," she snapped. "You're an initiate."

"I was an initiate at the age of six," Valentin corrected her. "I'm more than that now."

Emma thrust the sheets back on the table, sat glaring at him while at the same time her heart thudded against her ribs. "I don't . . ." She looked away, then back down at her busy hands in her lap. "I don't know—"

She halted abruptly, her head coming up, watching Malus, who had stepped into the scriptorium. His blazing eyes took in the two of them as he snapped closed his mobile phone. He gestured with his head, and, without another word, Emma rose.

"You little shit, keep your grubby hands off me," she snapped while slipping Valentin a bit of paper, folded into almost nothing.

Malus watched her storm out of the scriptorium before he approached Valentin. Drawing up a chair, he sat, arms crossed over his chest. "Your work is meticulous, Valentin."

"Thank you."

Abruptly Malus leaned forward, his voice more intimate. "Still, I can't help but wonder. . . ."

Valentin paused in his writing, his pen hovering over the beginning of the next word. "Wonder what?"

"Whether the *pace* you have set for yourself is, how should I put it, *maximal*."

Valentin grunted, began to write again. "It is what it is."

Malus pursed his lips. "Such a reflexive sentence does the truth no justice."

"And what would you know of the truth?" Valentin asked as he dipped his pen into the inkwell.

Malus's face worked its way through a grimace. "Well, *I've* no need to prove my worth."

Valentin was about to respond, then shut his mouth. All at once it occurred to him that Malus was jealous. It was he, Valentin, who had been chosen to stare into the fire of the Testament of Lucifer, to have each and every word imprinted on his brain, to be the messenger—more, to be the curator and the active agent, to set the Book of Deathly Things back down in writing, where it would be read by the growing ranks of disciples.

"But you," Malus continued in his soft purr, "what will happen to you when you've finished your task, when the Book of Deathly Things is completed?"

Valentin had already considered that. "Perhaps the Testament of Lucifer will never be finished." He shrugged, setting down his pen. "After all, neither you nor anyone else can force me to finish it." He cracked his knuckles, then tapped the side of his head with a forefinger. "Imagine, Malus, if a paragraph, a sentence—even a word—is left out of the manuscript. What will happen then, hmm?"

Malus stared at him for a moment. Then, without warning, he grabbed Valentin's left hand, squeezed so hard Valentin was forced to open his fist. His eyes locked with Valentin's, Malus plucked up the bit of paper Emma had left him.

"Do you think me a half-wit?" his purr sprouting thorns. "Do you think what you've entered into is a game?" Unfolding the paper, he held it out for Valentin to read. "What did she write?"

Valentin, swallowing hard, transferred his gaze from Malus's eyes, hard as marble, to the slip of paper. "'Three AM. Misericord,'" he said aloud.

"The Misericord, where the nuns are disciplined. How appropriate." Malus's eyes twinkled malevolently. "At first, I was gulled by her anger. Who wouldn't be? I know Emma far longer than you do. But this." He pointed at the note. "This is something different, something I've never before encountered." He cocked his head. "What d'you suppose she wants, Valentin?"

"I haven't the vaguest idea."

Malus's lips twisted in a sneer. "Yes, well, be that as it may, you will follow her instructions. At three this morning you will meet her in the Misericord."

"And then?"

"You'll listen to what she has to say."

"And then report back to you."

Malus gave him a pitying look. "Walk with me," he said, rising.

Valentin stretched his aching back as he accompanied Malus along the scriptorium. They stood before the statue of Moses, staring up at the patriarch.

"You see up there," Malus said, pointing. "The horns on Moses's head. All the ancient paintings and statues of Moses are the same. Horns. Why is that, do you suppose? Did Moses really have horns?" Malus's laugh carried a malicious edge. "It was a mistake, Valentin. A *translation* mistake made so long ago no one can remember when it happened. But I do. The word was actually 'halo.' But the translator saw it as 'horns.' Lucifer made it so. Do you see? No? How much prejudice arose from that one mistranslation? Like a pebble skipped across the pond, a constantly widening gyre, spirals of hate spread outward. That's all Lucifer had to do. Religion and wars are man's creations. Territory and sovereignty are man's creations. Jealousy, venality, intolerance are man's creations. Lucifer only had to sit back and watch, laughing."

"And now he wants more," Valentin said. "He wants to return to the place where he was cast out."

"Heaven? God?" Malus's laugh ripped the air like the slash of a knife. "No, no, Valentin. Lucifer wants what became his after the Fall. He wants dominion over God's corrupted creation here on earth; he wants the allegiance of every single human being."

"It won't come off."

Bravo opened his eyes, saw the once-gold crucifix swinging above his head. Several drops of water landed on his hairline, slid down either side of his forehead.

"Look!" Ayla said, swinging the crucifix into the spray from the cataract. It vanished, only to reappear, dripping wet, still black as tar. "The black is permanent."

Bravo felt dizzy. The world seemed fragile, made of spun gossamer. Even the rock faces, shimmering in wet, leaden sunlight, appeared insubstantial. Inside a dream, he looked up at Ayla, and the moment he did the world snapped back into sharp focus, colors so bright and saturated even here in the waterlogged shade he was forced to squint.

She crouched beside him. "What happened?"

"Are you all right?"

"You can see for yourself. I protected myself inside the cave mouth." But her face was ashen, her cheeks streaked with the remnants of tears. Her lower lip quivered quite out of her control. "Tell me what happened. Where are—?"

"They're dead." Bravo sat up. His head felt split in two and his muscles as if they had been put through a wringer. "Reichmann and Fireside both went over the edge into the maw of the waterfall."

"Did you cut Fireside's head off?"

"What?" She hadn't asked if he was all right, now this bizarre question. "No."

"Then we can't be certain he's dead. We have to find him and decapitate him. That's the only way."

He stared at the crucifix, silky, glimmering darkly. "I pressed it into the center of Fireside's forehead. It went in. All the way in. As he toppled backward, I pulled it out. Now it looks like . . . that." All at once, he transferred his gaze. "Wait. How d'you know about decapitating these . . . things?"

Ayla shook her head. That was when he saw the gash on her clavicle. It was still bleeding. He rose up, held her by the biceps. "How did that happen?"

"This?" She glanced down at her wound. "The man you called Fireside. His fingernail scraped me. When he was shot, I wrenched myself away. It must've happened then."

Bravo scrutinized her, looking for any change in her, no matter how seemingly insignificant. He could find none. And yet Fra Leoni had warned him to stay away from the creatures' nails. One thing Bravo had learned about her was that however she presented herself was the polar opposite of what was going on inside her. Why she was doing her utmost to clamp down on her jangling nerves could be put down to her close call with Fireside. An encounter like that would scare the pants off anyone. But why she had been crying was another matter.

A thought occurred to Bravo and he glanced around. "Reichmann had a sealed cylinder with him. He insisted it was important."

She handed it to him.

He stared at her, then at the cylinder. It was made of some plastic, thick and hard. On either end, the caps were sealed with waterproof neoprene gaskets. Clearly, Reichmann had gone to great lengths to protect whatever was inside.

He was about to open the cylinder when Ayla started to tremble all over.

"The quicker we get from this cave the better." He got them both to their feet, hefting the 9mm. "It's a long way down, and who knows what the hell we'll encounter on the way."

"Hell" seems like the right word, he thought as they set out.

FORTY-FIVE

They reached the nameless village, their starting point, just as dusk was settling over the valley. It seemed even more sad and enervated, as if someone was already digging its grave. On the steep descent, they had encountered plenty of dead bodies, but none living. At Ayla's insistence, they had spent a fruitless hour searching for Fireside's body. As Bravo pointed out, if the thunderous cataract and the turbulent currents it produced in the river basin at its foot hadn't churned both bodies into paste, then the sharp-toothed rocks had certainly shredded them. Bravo and Ayla had stopped twice for water and toilet breaks and once for food. He found himself ravenous, but he had to force her to take even a mouthful of dried meat and stale bread. She chewed distractedly on the meat, nibbled around the mold on the bread, then refused to eat any more.

The high peaks were still gleaming in sunlight; otherwise, blue-green shadows reigned. The village, drained of energy and purpose, was dotted here and there by people trudging their way home, food shopping in desultory fashion, their minds seemingly as blank as a broken TV screen. Though the village was tiny, it seemed an almost painful quill of civilization after their concentrated time in the mountains. The sulfurous atmosphere was hazed with smoke and diesel fumes. The particulates in the air made them cough.

The proprietor, welcoming them indifferently, escorted them to a room on the second floor. It had one bed. It was the only room he had. Neither Bravo nor Ayla had the energy to search for another place to stay. Ayla took a shower first, the lukewarm water like a heavenly bath. Layers of mud, dust, blood, sweat, and tears sluiced off her, forming a dark grainy whirlpool as they were sucked down the drain. She toweled off, climbed into a clean cotton shirt and jeans the proprietor had provided both of them for a usurious sum. She was half-asleep, head nodding on her chest as she sat in a ratty upholstered chair, when Bravo emerged from the bathroom, his skin shiny, hair slicked back off his forehead, clad in new clothes. By that time, the delicious odors of cooking food called them downstairs. He smiled at her, and she decided she liked the stubble that was on its way to becoming a beard.

The proprietor's wife had prepared a feast the likes of which astonished them. Extracting a large hunting knife from its scabbard at the small of his back, the proprietor cut up fresh pita into small, bite-sized triangles, then expertly cubed grilled lamb with the serrated blade.

This time, Ayla ate her fill, stuffing her mouth as if she had been incarcerated for a month. She said not a word. Bravo observed her as if through the wrong end of the telescope. He could not escape the suspicion that something had happened to her in the cave mouth, a significant crack in her psychological armor. And yet she remained as stubbornly unreadable as ever. He was still searching for any alteration in her personality due to the wound on her collarbone but finally gave it up. Too much time had passed without her being affected. He chewed on that conundrum for a while, adding it to the growing stack that surrounded her.

When, at length, they were finished, the proprietor reentered the dining room to bid them a pleasant night. They trudged up the stairs, where Ayla collapsed on the bed. Besides the bed there was the chair she had been sitting in and, at right angles to it, a small desk with a wooden, spoke-backed chair. A moth-eaten rug covered perhaps a third of the floor. A single window overlooked the main street, where, currently, a dog was barking as if his life depended on it.

"I'll take the chair," Bravo said.

"No, no." She slid over. "There's room for both of us." She laughed. "Don't worry. I won't take my clothes off."

Unlacing his boots, he lay down beside her. Soon enough he heard her breathing slow and become regular. He was exhausted; he felt her against him, her eyes closed, her mouth barely open. Lamplight gleamed on her cheeks, got lost in her long lashes. He closed his eyes, willing sleep to come, but the image of Reichmann calling to him, falling into the thunder of the cataract, made sleep out of his reach.

For a while, he simply lay there, staring at the shadows on the ceiling. As a small child he had done the same, half-believing the shadows stretched across his bedroom ceiling would come alive after he fell asleep. He thought of Ayla, then, calm and fragrant beside him. She was an undeniably beautiful woman, with the kind of charisma that compelled even men like Nasir, accustomed to the company of only other men, to listen to her. She was lovely, but there was also a current of violence in her, the fire of rage. And so her nature was contradictory, a very human trait, except her contradictions were extreme.

Silence, and the slow plodding of time.

Rolling off the bed, Bravo padded to the desk, settled into the chair, and broke the neoprene seals, unscrewed the cap of the cylinder. He slid out a manuscript, the title of which stirred the hairs on his forearms: *Nihilus Inusitatus,* the book his grandfather Conrad had read and memorized, the book his father had been searching for in the library at Alexandria. Setting it in the pool of lamplight, Bravo opened it, saw on the first page the sigil of triangle inside circle inside square. It was called the Nihil, according to the manuscript. It was the sigil of the Unholy Trinity.

Bravo's heart pounded painfully in his throat. He could scarcely draw breath. *At last,* he thought. *At last.* He began to read, translating in his head from Hebrew, Phoenician, Latin, Greek, Arabic, Sumerian. And then he came to the section that had stopped Reichmann in his tracks, written in Tifinagh.

Bravo pored over the pages. It was agonizing work, especially in his state of overadrenalized sleep deprivation and with the physical pounding he had taken. Every so often he had to massage out a cramping muscle. Precisely when he dozed off it was impossible to say, but at some point his brain had had enough hyper-stimulation for one day and it shut down. He slept, cheek on the strange, alien-looking Tifinagh glyphs.

Was it the tiny noise that roused Ayla from her deep slumber or was it a function of her sixth sense, inherited from her mother? Either way, Ayla opened her eyes to a room full of shadows. In the glow of lamplight, she saw Bravo slumped over the desk, fast asleep. The ghost of a smile played across her lips.

Then one of the shadows detached itself from the others, took a step toward Bravo. A shard of light showed her Bravo's gun in the shadow's hand. The figure brought the barrel of the gun to bear on the back of Bravo's head. Ayla was up and across the floor in one movement. The figure had just enough time to turn its head. The proprietor's face looked at her, but the crimson-rimmed irises told her it was no longer the proprietor she was looking at.

Without a second thought she ripped the knife from its sheath at the small of the proprietor's back, grabbed a handful of hair with her left hand, drew the wide blade of the knife across his throat. Blood erupted. The thing kicked out, slamming into the chair. Bravo awoke with a start. He twisted, his gaze falling on a face now unrecognizable as the proprietor's. The crimson line that circled his irises was bleeding into the whites, staining them a rich, final rose.

Ayla was struggling with the creature, holding it close against her while she slashed deeper and deeper. The knife's serrated teeth pierced cartilage, muscle, struck bone. The thing became hysterical as she began to saw away at the bones. Its elbows struck her over and over, but she held on for dear life as if she were riding a Brahma bull. Bravo leapt up, pried his gun away from the proprietor's grip. He had to break two of his fingers to do so.

"Clear!" Bravo called, waving Ayla back. She swung her blood-soaked arm away, and he fired point-blank into the side of the thing's neck. The percussion rocked all three of them. Blood, bits of skin and viscera, shards of bone exploded in a dense pink slurry. Immediately Ayla dove back in, like wading into a muddy pit. Her teeth were bared, her nostrils flared; a deep animal grunt came from her as she swung the knife in a shallow arc, sawing through the shattered vertebrae, the nerve bundles, completely severing the head from the body.

Only then did she jump back, covered in blood, panting, teeth still bared, watching as the head rolled into a corner, the body unnaturally still, as if it lacked a human autonomous nervous system.

"Goddammit, I told you," she snarled at Bravo. "Now look what you've made me do."

Dropping the knife, she pounded her fists against Bravo's chest, screaming and crying all at once. He did nothing to stop her, recognizing the dam that finally burst, her panic-stricken rage too great now to contain. He let her rail against him, hurt him even because he figured she deserved to, the nature of her rage, the ragged edge of panic terrifyingly familiar to him, and, anyway, he thought, *I care about this woman deeply. I care what she thinks and what she does. I care what happened to her and what will happen to her. I want to keep her safe. I want to do for her what I failed to do with Jenny.*

Ayla's fists beat at him, working to a crescendo. At the moment she cried out, blood and tears flying in equal measure, her fists uncoiled, her rage turned to anguish, and she fell against him, her face buried in the hollow of his shoulder, her body shaking all over. His arms came around her. This time she did not flinch away but buried herself deeper into him. He held her tight. He kissed the top of her head, heard her sigh as he picked her up, carried her into the bathroom, where she allowed the water to inundate her without for an instant letting him go.

FORTY-SIX

"Where is God in this scenario of the Second Coming?"

"That's what you asked?" Emma shook her head. "You have balls, I'll give you that." She took a step closer to him though they were alone in the Misericord. "And what was Malus's reply?" she said in a voice just above a whisper.

"He said God had stepped aside," Valentin said, "that He had grown ashamed of the transgressive failures of his greatest creation."

"So God can feel shame." Emma's eyes glimmered in the Misericord's gas lamplight. "It's not just us Fallen."

"If you choose to believe Malus."

Valentin looked around the underground chamber. It was irregular, as if it had been carved out of the convent's leftover subterranean area. Great stone pillars rose to arches that supported the thick-walled structure. The entire convent seemed balanced above them. The chamber's only furniture was one long table at waist height, narrower than a traditional table. From iron hooks embedded in the walls hung an array of whips, bloodstained horsehide belts, and flayers, lending the Misericord a dour medieval aspect. The air was thick with the odors of repentance and pain.

He stood so close to Emma he could feel the rise and fall of her breasts. A certain heat rose inside him, but her face appeared eerily placid.

"Malus knows we're here," Valentin said.

"I find that unsurprising."

"Really?"

She produced a Sphinx-like smile.

"I get the impression that he no longer understands you," Valentin said.

"Also unsurprising." Her lips were half-open. "I no longer understand myself."

Valentin's heart nearly escaped his rib cage. "Tell me." He dared to place a hand on her upper arm.

She stared at his curled fingers as if trying to figure out their intent. "She has imprinted herself on you"—Emma's glittery knowing gaze rose to his—"hasn't she?"

"I forsook the woman I thought I loved for her."

"Forsook?" Emma's eyes held a modicum of amusement.

"In many ways I'm an old-fashioned man."

"Does that mean you were brought up to hate and fear women?"

"It means the opposite." He peered at her, his grip tightening as his tension ramped up. "Where is Emma?"

The woman he was facing turned, went from shadow to shadow, assuring herself that they were alone. Malus was nowhere to be seen. Perhaps he was with his newest protégé, Saint Bella dell'Arca.

"You know where she is." Emma's voice was low and hoarse when she returned to Valentin. She stood very close to him so her voice would not carry. "Inside me."

"Inside you how?"

"She should be dead." Emma's lips opened slightly as if to receive a kiss. "But she isn't." For an instant a dark cloud of fear raced across the lenses of her eyes. "I don't understand."

"She's strong," Valentin said. "Stronger than you are."

"That's impossible."

"And yet you have doubts. In fact, you know it is true."

Emma's eyes closed for an instant before flying open again. "I feel her, coiling and uncoiling like an adder. I'm afraid to fall asleep."

"She'll rise up in a second coming." He used the phrase deliberately, both for its irony and for its force. "She'll overwhelm you."

"I brought her sight."

"Don't be ridiculous," Valentin said. "You've imprisoned her."

Emma seemed to be breathing hard, her focus going in and out, as if the internal guerrilla warfare with the real Emma was ongoing. "I don't . . . I don't want to change places with her. I can't bear the thought of being locked up . . . inside."

Valentin's grip moved up her arm to her shoulder. "Maybe there's another way—a third possibility."

"What?" Emma said, reaching up to him on the balls of her feet. "What is it?"

"I loved my mother so very much," Ayla said. "And I hated her more than I've hated anyone else in my life."

"Rest now," Bravo said, sitting next to her in the Order's airplane that had brought them to Tannourine. It was refueled and ready to go. They had found the proprietor's wife lying in her bed, face empurpled, throttled to death. Her eyes were open wide, their horrified gaze watching the slow plod of eternity. Reaching out, Bravo had closed her lids while Ayla examined the charcoaled husk curled like a serpent beside her: whatever had been left of Collum Fireside had crawled out of the churning river by the superhuman effort of the thing inside him, before transferring itself to the Lebanese proprietor.

"I don't want to rest," Ayla said. "I want to talk." Her restless gaze fell at last on Bravo. "There are things I have to tell you." Then slid away again. "I'm not who you think I am."

"In the end, we're all strangers to ourselves, Ayla."

Her gaze snapped back at him. "You don't get to make this easier."

About to reply, he thought better of it, subsided back, watching her with a perfectly neutral expression. Turning her head, she put her hands up over her eyes, cupped her fingers. When she took them down and turned back to him, he almost gasped out loud.

Her eyes were no longer coffee colored; contact lenses nestled like a tiny egg cracked open in the palm of one hand. On her pupils were etched the Nihil, the sigil of the Unholy Trinity.

Tearing away from his grip, Emma took an unsteady step backward. "I can't do it," she said, clearly horrified. "I *won't*!"

"Then you're a prisoner already," Valentin said, "locked in an endless battle." He reestablished their close proximity. "I know her. She won't curl up and die like the others you've possessed. She'll fight and keep on fighting. And, who knows, in the end it may turn out that she's stronger than you are."

Emma laughed. "Don't be absurd!"

But there was no snarkiness in her expression, none of the condescension she projected like the quills on a porcupine. Valentin detected a sliver of apprehension, the first questioning of her dark faith.

"You cannot have these thoughts," Emma said. "You cannot be talking like this." Her eyes darted back and forth as if seeking shelter. "You are chosen."

All around them fireflies rose and fell like waves upon an ink-dark sea. A sweet scent, like a baby's breath, reached them— night-blooming jasmine, perhaps—and then was swept away.

"The falcon no longer hears the falconer."

Emma, eyes opened wide, stared at Valentin. "Where did you hear that?"

"I don't know," he said. "It just came to me. It's what I feel, deep inside."

"'Turning and turning in the widening gyre / The falcon cannot hear the falconer; / Things fall apart . . .' The first lines of William Butler Yeats's poem 'The Second Coming.'"

Valentin lifted his chin. "How d'you know it?" And when

she hesitated, he said, "Emma recited it to me once. She was obsessed by it."

"Emma."

"You see?" He grinned at her as he stepped closer to her. "It's as I told you. The battle has been joined."

"Indeed, it has."

They both started as the figure of Malus coalesced out of deepest shadow. In the space of a heartbeat he crossed to where they both stood, ran his fingernail across Valentin's throat. Blood erupted; Emma gave a shout, jumping back. Malus paid heed to neither. Instead, he took Valentin's head in his hand, gave it a terrifying crack, severing the neck at the spot between the third and fourth cervical vertebrae. Another pass with his fingernail, and he was holding Valentin's decapitated head by the hair, sweat still streaming down its face, contorted by astonishment and fear, as the body collapsed onto its side.

FORTY-SEVEN

"There are no crimson circles," Bravo said, trying to keep himself together as he peered into her newly naked eyes.

"Nor will there be," Ayla said. "I'm not like *them*."

"Clearly."

"Neither am I possessed."

He was moving away from her, into the aisle. All his muscles seemed to have contracted at once.

"Bravo," she said softly, "you held me in your arms—twice. I would not harm you."

"You may have no choice in the matter."

She shook her head. "You misunderstand the situation. No harm will come to me."

"Because—?"

"I am chosen."

Her eyes held a strange glitter that despite himself alarmed him. They sat on opposite sides of the aisle, like strangers who have struck up a wary conversation mid-flight. Outside, it was still dark. The plane crouched at the foot of the runway, inert. The pilot did not deem it safe to take off until dawn light. There were runway lights, but they weren't working.

"This is what my mother did to me. This is why I hate her."

Bravo deflected Ayla's words. "You claim you were chosen— by whom?"

"You know by whom." Her eyes were bleak. Her head was down; she was trembling with long-withheld tension. "Now I will tell you the story—the real story." But she stopped then, as a novice diver will do at the end of the board, at her first real look down. "Don't look at me like that."

"Like what?"

"With such revulsion."

"After what I've seen—"

"I told you we needed to find the thing you knew as Fireside. I told you we needed to decapitate him. It's the only way."

"Only way?"

"Bravo, I couldn't bear it if you hate me."

"Answer my question."

She regarded him with the look of someone caught too far out on a limb. "To stop them moving from host to host. To kill them."

"And who exactly are *they*?"

"The Fallen."

His eyes opened wide. "You mean the angels who were banished by God, who fell with Lucifer?"

"Maybe. I don't know. My mother never told me."

Dilara. Bravo realized that ever since her death it was Dilara who had been standing ghostly and powerful between them. And then the memory of her bizarre and bloody death returned to him in full force. "Your mother—she was beheaded." That was why Ayla had been so upset at the morgue—angry with him for not telling her. "But Dilara—she wasn't one of the Fallen; she couldn't have been."

"No." Ayla shook her head. "She wasn't."

"Then why did the demon decapitate her?"

"My mother was very powerful—more powerful than you know. She told me once when I was a child that she had lived many lives, that she remembered these lives in astonishing detail. I think her dreams were somehow memories extracted from her past."

Now Bravo understood. It wasn't reincarnation Dilara had been talking about with Ayla. Like Fra Leoni, she was an immortal. Which made her daughter—what? Something Other. Something even Fra Leoni might not recognize.

He took out the crucifix, black as tar and just as slick and shiny. "If the power of God through Christ couldn't stop the thing inside Fireside—"

"Well, it did stop him," Ayla pointed out. "It couldn't kill him because the power of Christ had been corrupted by the Nihil engraved into the back."

"I whittled it off," Bravo said, "during the night, while you were sleeping."

"I wasn't sleeping. I was guarding you."

"You say the Nihil corrupted the crucifix's power of Christ; hasn't it done the same to you?"

"The crucifix is a *thing*," she said. "A thing manufactured by man, a thing without a soul. You were right. We are being led back to the convent of Saint Bella dell'Arca."

"Why?" Bravo said, though in his deepest soul he was afraid he knew.

And then Ayla confirmed his worst fears. "My mate is there. The thing that marked me in the red tent of shadows. The infant has grown into a man."

Bravo thought about this for some time. Then, slowly and gingerly, he recrossed the aisle. He heard her deep-felt sigh when he settled into the seat beside her.

"Bravo, you must believe me. I would never hurt you. I would never let anything . . ."

"You made sure the proprietor was dead."

"Yes."

"You looked like you'd had practice."

Her eyes slid away from him. Her nostrils flared, and he felt the stirring of the animal, wild and powerful, prowling beneath her human surface, the animal that had sliced the head off the proprietor.

"That gunshot . . . ," she began, before her voice faded out.

"We did it together," he said softly.

"Yes." She wet her lips with the pink tip of her tongue. "Together." She seemed reanimated as she turned back to him. "You see now."

"I don't think I will, Ayla, at least not all of it, until you tell me your story."

Still she hesitated. "You understand how difficult this is."

"As much as I'm able, I do."

She tilted her head back slightly, her eyes slowly going out of focus. She stared out the Perspex window. "Do you think it will get light soon?" But she was talking to herself, and Bravo made no move to answer. Then she nodded, as if giving herself permission to continue.

"When my mother brought me to Tannourine, she thought she knew what she was doing. We didn't come across the red tent of shadows by accident; it was our destination all along."

Lida, on her way to serve them tea and toast, was waved off by Bravo. She turned on her heels and went back to the galley. Ayla continued on, too wrapped up in conjuring the past to notice.

"She had a plan in mind. Maybe it was a good plan, maybe not. I don't know. What I *do* know was it was bold. My mother entered the red tent of shadows with me in hand. Her plan was to harness my nascent powers with hers. Her aim was to destroy the shadow at the center of the tent." Ayla shook her head. "Hubris. How could she think that she could defeat the Devil?"

"That wasn't the Devil in the red tent of shadows."

Ayla stopped her narrative with her mouth half-open. "What?"

"I doubt your mother would ever have attempted such a thing. Certainly she wouldn't have exposed you to such a threat."

Her eyes snapped back into focus. "But that's precisely what she did!"

"No." Reaching out, he took her hand. "Ayla, listen to me. The manuscript in the cylinder is the *Nihilus Inusitatus*. I couldn't figure out why Reichmann would bring it to me, until I started reading it. The most relevant section is written in

Tifinagh, a language I can read, as you know, but he can't. He needed me to translate it for him."

Ayla shook her head. "What does this have to do with—?"

"The middle section of the *Nihilus Inusitatus* speaks of the Unholy Trinity. Each element—in this instance we're speaking of the Testament of Lucifer, which I believe Val discovered—has been assigned a Guardian. The thing you saw in the red tent of shadows is the book's Guardian."

"The shadow."

"No. I believe the shadow figure was merely a manifestation of its power," Bravo said. "The Guardian was the infant you saw, the one who marked you with his stare. He was the one your mother wanted to destroy. What happened?"

"It's just as I told you." A horrified expression had come over Ayla, paling her to the color of chalk. "His stare terrified me. All I could think of to do . . . I set the fire. I burned the tent down. What did I do?"

Bravo squeezed her hand. "You were ill. You were protecting yourself and your mother."

"But I screwed it up. Her plan went up in flames."

"Have you considered that it might never have had a chance?"

"No." She answered instantly, automatically. Then, after a moment of consideration: "No."

"I believe she had foreseen the day when Val would find the Testament of Lucifer. She took you to Tannourine, into the red tent of shadows, in order to keep the Book of Deathly Things hidden."

"Killing the . . . the Guardian would have done that?"

"I don't know, and I don't think she did, either. But changing the present would certainly affect the future, and she was hoping that if, with your help, she was successful what she had foreseen would not then happen."

Ayla was silent for so long Bravo feared that he had lost her to her own complex inner world, a world into which he had inadvertently strayed. Or had he been shoved there by Dilara?

Had Dilara foreseen this possibility? She had warned him that he never would return alive from Tannourine without Ayla's help, and she had been right about that.

"We need to get off this plane," Ayla said, rising.

"But Ayla—"

"Now." Grabbing her backpack, she stepped past him, down the aisle toward the door. "Before the dawn comes."

FORTY-EIGHT

"Well, he's served his purpose." Malus looked from Valentin's severed head to Emma. "He got the ball rolling with a bang, didn't he?" Malus smiled, almost dreamily, dropping the head. "Come morning, this will give the sister quite a start." He gestured. "Walk with me."

They strolled out of the garden proper and along the pillared cloister itself. No one was about, but it was that hour when the birds start their clatter. The wider world, however, was still steeped in the web of slumber. Even the night breeze seemed to have fallen asleep.

And all the others inside the convent *were* asleep, save one. Sister Agnetha, having missed her divine nighttime visitation, had tossed and turned on her narrow bed, had even done the unthinkable, touching herself between her moist thighs, groaning through the hand she had clapped across her mouth. But she couldn't find release that way; she required the probing hand of God, the flow of His divine liquor, to satisfy her. But her arousal was such that she was obliged to rise from the damp sheets, hastily don her habit, and leave her cell. That was when she heard the voices, so soft that they might have been mistaken for the chirr of insects. Descending the stone night stair, she reached one of the arched doorways leading to the cloister just in time to see the *madre vicaria* exiting the garden with a peculiar gait. Almost a swagger. She passed through the cloister on the other side and vanished into the nighttime shadows.

Creeping out beyond one of the spiral pillars, Sister Agnetha peered into a jumble of starlight and deep shadow, but there were two shadows on the ground, both lumpen, one large, to which her curiosity directed her.

It was only when she was close enough to stumble over it did she recognize Valentin—or, rather, his decapitated head. She did not have to turn to look to know that the larger shadow contained his body. She looked around wide-eyed. No one there, but there had been, just moments ago. Maria reveling in all the glory of her power.

Jamming her fist into her mouth to stifle the scream that bubbled up inside her, she dropped to her knees, weeping, distraught, bewildered, and utterly devastated. A dreadful litany circled in her mind, repeating in baleful echoes: Valentin was dead. A terrible chill passed through her, then. Wrapping her arms around herself, she rocked back and forth, crooning softly.

"Oh, Lord," she whispered, "why hast Thou forsaken us?"

Even as Sister Agnetha prayed in confusion and terror, Malus was on a roll. "What Valentin also provided was an insight into the impossible situation you now find yourself in."

"Give me a sister," Emma said crisply. "Pick one—any of the nuns will do." She held up a hand, the nails extended. "I'll dig my claws in and transposition. This body will wither and die and, along with it, whatever remains of Emma."

"According to Valentin, there's plenty of her left—all of her, I'd judge."

"And you believed him?"

"One thing one must say concerning Valentin was that lying wasn't his, shall we say, forte."

"Then let me be rid of her. Let us *both* be rid of her."

"Situations are never that simple." Malus strode, hands

clasped at the small of his back, for all the world like any cleric whose mind is absorbed in the word of God. It was a pose in which he found pleasure for that very reason. "I need this body —Emma's body."

The thing inside Emma shuddered. "For how long?"

"Only a short time now. Then you will get your wish. As a reward you can transposition into anyone you choose."

"Why?"

"Why do I need it?"

"Yes."

"As a lure."

"I don't understand."

"Allow me to illustrate. I have ceased to receive reports from—." Here he used a word in Tamazight that had no analogue in the English language, or any other known language, for that matter. "One must assume that his existence is at an end. One must further assume that Braverman Shaw decapitated him."

He stopped, and the Fallen inside Emma with him. "This is no ordinary man. He is directly descended from Conrad Shaw, and we all know about *him*. However. With the deaths of Dilara Tusik and Fra Leoni—Braverman Shaw's two immortal protectors—I have isolated him. Either he is on his way here or he will be shortly. The corpus you now inhabit will play a key role once he arrives."

"I want to transposition into him," she said.

Malus gifted her with a malevolent smile. "Of course you do. If he survives, he is yours to do with as you will."

The Fallen eyed Malus with a good deal of intelligence. "You don't believe he will survive."

"My dear, I *know* he won't."

The Fallen sighed. "And in the meantime, what about Emma?"

"Yes, Emma." They began their walk again. The first streaks of daylight were limning the hills to the east. The wind had picked up and the birds had unaccountably fallen silent. "Well now, I have devised a method of dealing with her. Like a surgeon with a scalpel I will cut her again and again, and extract her from you bit by screaming bit."

"Farther. No, farther," she said. "We're not far enough away."

"From what?" Bravo asked.

"From everything."

They were on the far side of the runway. The village with no name had faded into the distance. They were surrounded by trees and undergrowth, but still Ayla pushed them onward. Through the forest, which grew denser with each yard they traveled. Somewhere the sun might be edging toward the eastern horizon, but here it was still the dead of night. Insects buzzed and whirred. Bravo thought there must be a beehive somewhere close by.

"This will do," Ayla said.

"Will you please tell me what's going—"

He stopped abruptly. She had turned her back to him. Now she was shedding her shirt and undergarments. Then he saw her bare shoulder and back, and he remembered her saying, *Don't worry. I won't take my clothes off.* Now he knew why.

She stood before him naked to the waist. Along her left shoulder, down that side of her back to the bottom of her rib cage crawled a complex network of scarred flesh, raised and dark red, as if the blood that had oozed out had petrified in place.

Bravo, horrified, reached out, his fingertips brushing lightly against the dark web. "Ayla, what happened?"

"The fire." Her voice was a hoarse whisper, obliging him to step closer to her before the wind took her words in its beak and flew away. "The fire I set."

"A plastic surgeon would—"

"You don't understand."

He heard the anguish in her voice and kept his thoughts to

himself. She dug into her backpack, handed him a small flask. It appeared to be made of black glass.

"Unstopper it," she instructed, "and pour the contents over the scars."

"Are you in pain?" Bravo asked. "Will this take it away?" She shook her head, mute. The flask's seal must have been airtight; he heard the rush of air as he popped it open. The liquid inside was viscid, oily, acrid.

"Make sure all of the scars are covered."

He touched her, ran his fingertips over the jungle of knotted flesh, viny, turbulent, indignant.

"Have you emptied the flask?"

He handed it back to her. Instead of dropping it into her backpack, she threw it into the underbrush.

"Step away," she said.

"What's going to happen?"

"Please, Bravo."

The anguish in her voice compelled him to comply. "All right."

"Now stand still," she said. "Whatever happens, you're not to move. Yes?"

"Okay."

"Promise me, Bravo."

His heart was pounding. He had a terrible intimation of what was to come. "I promise."

He heard a quick sound, like the scratch made by the claws of a small mammal. The flame at the head of the wooden match wavered over her shoulder. When she touched it to the slickly glistening web of scars, Bravo gasped. What he had poured onto her was an accelerant. The fire spread instantly over the entire expanse of her scars.

"Ayla!" he cried.

"Remember your promise!"

Her skin seemed to be crawling, as if alive. The flames ate at her, crisping the thickened scars, and the stench of roasting meat made him gag. It was all he could do not to rush at her, put out the fire with his body, depriving it of oxygen. Instead, he stood rigid as a wooden soldier, his heart beating so hard and fast he had to turn his concentration inward to calm himself.

At length the fire died out, as if turned off with an invisible switch. During the entire ordeal Ayla had neither moved nor cried out. How could this not have been agony for her?

"You see the charcoaled area," she said.

"Yes." Bravo, stepping closer, could not believe his eyes. "It looks hard, like a shell."

"That's exactly what it is," Ayla said over her shoulder. "Now hit it."

"What?"

"Hit it with your fist."

"What? No. I don't want to hurt you."

"The fire didn't hurt me, Bravo. Neither will your fist. The shell protects me."

Stunned, Bravo did as she requested. The shell fissured, cracked open, the shards falling at her feet, all that remained of the unnatural fire. The new pink skin of a baby, unblemished, satin smooth, glimmered among the leaves and branches. The web of scars was completely gone.

FORTY-NINE

When she had regained consciousness after the bomb explosion was detonated in Dexter Shaw's Greenwich Village town house Emma had felt nothing. She couldn't see, hear, or move, but the shock endorphins her body was pumping out by the pint dampened the devastating pain. It was only thirty or so hours afterward, when she had resurfaced in the hospital, that the tsunami of pain crashed over, causing her to shake all over, her face to blanch, and the nurses with the crash cart to come running, shouting, "Code Blue!"

Emma had thought that extreme level of pain, at the threshold of consciousness, was the worst she would ever endure. She had told herself it would never get any worse, and this thought, if not consoling, carried her through until the morphine kicked in, until the doctors brought her back from the brink of what she had come to think of as the long sleep into which her father had been so shockingly hurled.

And yet. And yet that level of pain, only dimly recalled now, in the magical realism of her nightmares, was nothing compared to what she felt now. She was swimming in a sea of agony. Though she had no body, all her nerve endings were on fire, sending signals that made her brain boil like water on a hot pan. She wanted to curl up and die. An instant after she had that thought she realized that that was just what was about to happen to her. A release-wish fulfillment. The only way out was the easiest, the path of least resistance. A nihilist's dream come true.

And she began to die—cell by cell, neuron by neuron. . . .

But that wasn't the worst of it. The worst of it was knowing that there would be no sweet surcease, no end to the crushing pain, a pain so terrible it was all but inconceivable until moments ago. A nihilist's gospel come true.

The word "nihilism" forcefully coerced a reaction in her brain's autonomic chain of command. Something she had picked up, like static from a far-off station, from the thing possessing her.

Nihil. The name for the sigil of the Unholy Trinity.

In a thunderbolt of insight she understood what was happening to her. Into her head now came a short story she had read when she was a teenager that had stuck with her into adulthood. And now the title became her battle cry. *I have no mouth,* she thought, *and I must scream.*

She tried to scream but could not. If she could have wept she would have, but she couldn't do that, either. All she could do was lie in the womb into which the creature had roughly shoved her while her skull was slowly, agonizingly crushed. There was no respite, no surcease. Even unconsciousness was denied her. This wasn't life, nor was it death. Death offered an end to pain and torment. This all-encompassing torture was now part of her until the end of time. And, as Malus had foreseen, slowly, inexorably she began to slip down the treacherous slope into insanity.

When Ayla turned back to him, her eyes blazed so flatly, so finally, that Bravo took a step backward.

"What are you doing?" Her arms were crossed over her bare breasts. "Don't." Reacting to the horrified look in his eyes. "I told you that I'd never hurt you."

"I don't . . . I can't believe you'd be able to make good on that promise."

Bravo held up her shirt between them, as if it could shield him from her, what she had become, what she was. A thing unknown to him, a creature who had seduced him into trusting her, with whom he thought he had grown close.

"It was all a lie." His whisper was hoarse with shock. He threw the shirt at her. "Everything you've told me, everything you've done."

"No, it isn't true! Bravo, you've got to believe me. I'm standing in front of you, naked in a way I've never dared to be in front of another man my age, vulnerable as only my parents have known me."

He shook his head. "It's gone. Ayla, whatever we had before —whatever I thought we had—is gone. It was a mirage, a clever one, I grant you. But you won't fool me again."

She pulled on the shirt, buttoning it. "What are you talking about?"

"You know very well what I mean: your eyes, your ability to see the demon inside the dead husk at the morgue. You saw the shadow figure handing the object to King Solomon on the wall painting in the Cave of Shadows. You're able to regenerate through fire. Your mother was an immortal. You didn't know that; she didn't tell you. Now I'm wondering why. Are you immortal or are you demon, angel or devil?"

"I'm neither." She took a step toward him and he retreated two steps. "Bravo, please."

He stared at her suddenly unable to think clearly.

She didn't know whether to laugh or to cry. She did neither, alighting her gaze on him as streaks of dawn light lit the eastern clouds in ruddy pastels. Birds were calling to each other high over her and Bravo's heads. All around them leaves rustled as if stirred by an invisible hand.

"Your relationship with your mother was adversarial. She hid things from you, the most important things about herself. And now I find myself wondering whether everything you've told me was a lie to gain my confidence, to find out my plans."

"Stop it! Oh, my God, please stop!" Her voice lowered as she saw the Beretta pointed at her. "And just listen—"

He dropped his gun hand, turned away, heading back toward the airstrip where the plane was waiting.

"Bravo, if only for a minute." She came after him. "Listen, why d'you think I had those scars ever since the fire I set?"

"Your thought processes are quite beyond me."

"Do you think I'd want to go through life being disfigured?"

"Some people might, to remind them of the sins they've committed."

"I've committed no sins!"

He said nothing. Seeing her regenerate through fire had severely unnerved him. She had witnessed the baby—the Guardian—regenerated through fire. He had marked her. Whose side was she on?

"Don't you see? It was you, Bravo. I couldn't get rid of the scarring without you."

"Please." They were almost back at the verge of the airstrip. The plane hunched like a silver bird at the end of the runway, ready to make its getaway.

"I don't blame you for not believing me." She was almost trotting to keep up with him. The underbrush tore at her as if with wicked fingers, as if wanting their separation to increase. "Honestly, I wouldn't, either, if I were you. But my mother . . . you knew my mother."

"I'm beginning to wonder if I did."

"Whatever you might think of me, you know she wasn't evil. She loved you, and so did my father. Bravo, what I'm telling you is the truth."

"You've lied to me from the beginning—about who you are, about *what* you are."

"That's just it. I don't know what I am. I've always been afraid of—"

The edge of his hand cut through the air between them. "Keep still now. Not another word."

He advanced up the ladder. Half inside the open door he turned, and for a terrible, heart-stopping second she feared he wouldn't allow her on board. But she held her ground, just this side of defiance, and knew she was on a knife-edge, that the next moment events could go either way. But she would not give in to him, would not show him the terror that gripped her heart. A moment later he looked at something over her head, the sun rising, perhaps.

"I'll take you to your betrothed." He did not look at her. "You two demons were made for each other."

She wanted to say so many things to Bravo, things that mattered to both of them, but there was no point. He'd made up his mind. She was beyond redemption.

Still without looking at her he vanished inside.

Shaken, sick at heart, she stepped into the interior. Her hands were trembling and her knees felt weak. She started at the sound of the stairs being pulled up behind her. She took a seat as far away from him as possible. The Beretta lay on the seat next to him. He was staring at her. For just a moment she met his gaze, but it was so cold, so utterly hostile, that her heart sank and she was forced to look away. Lida gave her an icy glare that threw her more than it should have. She had just enough time to strap herself in before the plane's brakes came off, and they were galloping down the airstrip, lifting off into the pink-and-gold air.

Sitting back, she closed her eyes. She felt her pulse in her temple, at the base of her throat. She felt her gorge rising and forced herself into a semblance of calm. All was lost now; she knew that. Perhaps this was always the way it was meant to be, that what had begun long before she had been born was doomed to fail. Now her last chance was gone. Now she had no choice but to go to her dreadful fate.

Outside the window, far away, a falcon was rising on the thermals, turning and turning in a widening gyre.

FIFTY

Toward evening Malus took a break. Not for him, for Emma. He'd been at it for hours—though for him time was relative; an hour could be a day or a minute. Years had no meaning. The body on the table before him was twitching with heightened galvanic response. It was expected; it could not be helped. And though he hadn't wanted to stop—why cease to feel pleasure?—there was a certain toll exacted on Emma's body, even though Emma, the original Emma, was incarcerated in a black place, solitary confinement, you might say, or a sensory deprivation tank, deep within the living brain. He could not afford Braverman Shaw seeing his beloved sister damaged. That would not do at all.

"Here, I brought you sustenance."

Malus looked up, the details of the Misericord coming back into focus. He saw the Black Saint holding out a mug filled with a dark liquid, thick as mud. It was neither hot nor cold. He took it without comment, drank it down.

"You've been at this a long time," Bella dell'Arca said. She had never been more alluring. Sex oozed out of her every pore along with her sweat. Malus's infernal work had caused a rapid rise in the Misericord's temperature despite the fact that it was belowground.

Malus gave her a flat stare. "It makes no difference to me."

"There you're wrong." She took the mug back. "This work takes a great deal of effort, even from you."

He watched her, silent, inhumanly still. Before him, Emma

lay on a stone slab not unlike the ones the Aztecs used, when their priests ripped the throbbing hearts out of sacrificial virgins. Her eyes were closed; she was barely breathing, as if in a state of suspended animation.

"Why, Malus? Why expend so much energy on this one woman? We already have her."

"We don't yet have her brother."

"Braverman Shaw. What makes him so special?"

"Dangerous, Bella. Exceptionally dangerous."

"To us?"

"*Especially* to us," Malus said. "He is Conrad Shaw's grandson."

Bella dell'Arca blanched, her lips pinched. "I thought we were done with him. Finally."

"We managed to turn the father against him. Not that it mattered. Dexter Shaw, Braverman's father, possessed none of Conrad's . . . extraordinary powers."

They were alone in the Misericord, but just beyond Sister Agnetha crouched by a small spy hole in the wall, one eye open wide and unblinking. She drank in the scene like a draught of poison. The tracks of her tears had not yet dried on her pallid cheeks. Her lips were cracked and raw from chewing on them. She could hear every word, and every word made her grind her teeth in an agony of disillusion. The disillusion ceded to despair. Despair was colonized by rage. And the rage grew into a terrible, towering thing, too overwhelming for her to make sense of or to manage.

"What are you saying Braverman does?" Bella dell'Arca shook her head. "How is that possible?"

Malus stared down at the inert figure of Emma Shaw, his enmity and malice growing with every breath he took; he did not know the answer, and this void in his knowledge vexed him no end. "We were fortunate with Conrad Shaw." He ran his fingertips along the inside of Emma's forearm, a caress that struck the Black Saint as somehow obscene. "An accident crippled him, confined him to a wheelchair. With him sufficiently weakened, we were able to destroy him."

"Ancient history."

He turned his angry eyes on her. "You."

"I was burned to death. That's all ancient history means to me."

Unfortunate for you, Malus thought, losing some of his respect for her, for what she had endured in the name of Lucifer. *After all,* he thought, *we all suffer at our Brother's hand. That is our fate; that is how we achieve our end; that is how we will enslave the humans. Nothing else matters.*

"There is something you're not telling me, something between you and Braverman Shaw," she said.

"I fear he is his grandfather incarnate."

"What makes you think that?"

"We had the Quintessence in our hand . . . almost. We had infiltrated a female into the Order's Haute Cour, spent years grooming her, matching her to Dexter Shaw. He had the Quintessence. She was going to get it for us. But then the fools at the Knights of Saint Clement blew up Dexter's town house and him with it. So we adjusted the female's agenda to the son, Braverman. Dexter had hidden the Quintessence, had left it for Braverman to find. That he did—he's an exceptionally resourceful fellow. We were certain he'd use it on this woman—what was her name? Oh, yes, Jenny—because he was in love with her, as Dexter would have been had he lived. But he didn't. He showed the same unique control as his accursed grandfather."

"Then Conrad Shaw wasn't an immortal like Dilara Tusik."

"No," said Malus, "he was something quite different, quite extraordinary. We were lulled into a sense of security when his son turned out to be ordinary."

Bella lifted the back of her hand to Malus's cheek, stroking gently. "All this hard work has made you morbid." Her hand slid down, taking his. "Come. I'll give you what you need."

She led him out of the blood-heat of the Misericord, into the wine cellar, where she slipped to her knees before him.

Thus distracted, Malus fell from extreme vigilance, unaware as Sister Agnetha rose from her painful crouch and stole into the Misericord. As Agnetha stood over Emma a harrowing sorrow overcame her. Tears overflowed her eyes. She felt hollow inside. Worse, she felt bereft of God's love. He had turned his face from her, from the entire convent, and she knew what that meant.

"My dear," she whispered. "Oh, my dear, what has he done to you?"

Emma's eyes popped open, causing Agnetha to gasp. "Where is he?"

"With the *madre vicaria*."

"They're not talking."

"They're . . . you know."

Emma closed her eyes for a moment. "What are you doing here, Sister Agnetha?"

"They killed Valentin." Agnetha's voice had been reduced to a sandy whisper. "Cut off his head, left him lying in the cloister garden. An unspeakable desecration."

"What happened to Valentin's body?"

"God has forsaken us." Agnetha was weeping freely. "We're damned. Even here, so close to God, we're damned."

"Answer my question." Emma's voice was soft, a velvet caress.

It had the desired effect. Agnetha came back to herself. "I buried him, beneath the lemon tree."

"All by yourself?"

"We do what we must. It was the Christian thing to do."

Emma blinked. "Speaking of. You being here, now, at this moment."

"I was spying on them." Agnetha reached out to touch Emma, hesitated, thought better of it. "I want to help."

Emma's gaze was fixed on the sister's hand, hovering over her, trembling. "Are you sure?"

"I don't want to be damned."

"You want to be redeemed."

"Yes."

"You want to be seen again in the eyes of God."

"I want His grace to shine again on me."

"I know a way."

Agnetha frowned, as if remembering something important. "You're in league with him."

"Once I was."

Agnetha's frown deepened. "What's happened?"

"I know the way to salvation. The only way."

"I shouldn't trust you."

"Then you're surely damned, Sister."

Agnetha squeezed her eyes shut, as if to block out a nightmare. Then she shuddered. She opened her eyes, saw her situation for what it was. "Help me. Please."

"You will do something for me."

"Anything."

"It won't be pleasant."

"Nothing has been pleasant since these men came," Agnetha said truthfully, "since God has shown us the back of His hand."

"It will take all your courage, Sister."

"To return to God, I have courage in spades."

"All the way to the end."

"I am not afraid of death," Sister Agnetha said. "Lead me to heaven, and not to hell."

Emma smiled. "All right, then." She gestured. "Lean over me. That's right, as if you're about to kiss me. Bring your lips nearer. Nearer." Emma stared up at the milky arc of Agnetha's throat. "You beautiful creature."

Emma lifted her head off the slab, bared her teeth, took a bit of Agnetha's tender skin and flesh between her teeth, bit down hard. Agnetha shuddered but didn't make a sound. Neither did she pull away. Blood began to flow, hot and rich, into Emma's mouth, coating her tongue, dripping down her throat. Agnetha's hand found Emma's, fingers twining, the pressure and warmth of reassurance.

The connection had been made, different from the puncture that built the bridge to transposition. This process was not a one-way street; it was a two-way artery, requiring the freely given consent of both parties. It was a correspondence, not a conversion and so, strictly speaking, not of Lucifer's realm. For Emma, the danger was incalculable. If she was to be found out . . .

But she could not consider that now. She directed her full attention on the correspondence, the give-and-take, the reclamation of Agnetha's soul. And in return Emma would receive—

Her keen ears, attuned to even the slightest change in her immediate environment, picked up the sounds of heels clicking against stone, the whisper of approaching voices that now burst like fireworks into the Misericord where she lay, where Sister Agnetha bent over her, offering her sacrificial blood. In an instant Emma would be found out, she would be undone.

Her mouth filled with Agnetha's blood, Emma closed her eyes. Even so, tears like glittering diamonds appeared, trembling on her cheeks. Every nerve inside her was screaming for her to act, and yet for the space of a heartbeat she hesitated. Then, with the rough voices of Malus and Maria Veniera, lovers, co-conspirators, rising like a sandstorm, she kissed the wound she had made in Agnetha's vulnerable throat. Emma's lips moved against the bloody flesh. Raising her hand to Agnetha's chest, Emma pierced skin, flesh, viscera, and muscle with her elongated fingernail, opening her up from stem to stern.

Emma would not look as Sister Agnetha's eyes popped open, her mouth stretched in an O of shock in the endless second before she fell away, her lifeless body slithering off Emma, collapsing by the side of the stone table on which Emma still lay, ostensibly wiping the blood off her face but in fact erasing all evidence of the tears that had stained her cheeks as well as her heart.

FIFTY-ONE

Rome came and went as if in a dream. Save for Bravo stopping at several shops for purchases they headed straight for the Roma Termini train station. What Bravo bought remained a mystery to Ayla. He insisted she stay in the taxi both times, and each time he returned with carefully wrapped packages. Neither of the exteriors of the shops gave her a clue as to what he might have purchased.

On the train north, they sat opposite each other without exchanging a word. Bravo stared out the window. All during the flight he had immersed himself in the *Nihilus Inusitatus,* studying page after page scrawled with what appeared to her to be alien writing. She itched to know what he was learning, but there was a barrier between them now that she felt incapable of breaching.

Wearied from him icing her out, she turned her attention to a pair of college girls on the other side of the railcar. The one facing her was extraordinary looking, with long dark hair, smoky eyes, inviting lips, a Pre-Raphaelite face. She wore a black leather jacket, her hair below her shoulders. She was what had come to be known as a plus-size, a term Ayla found offensive. She found herself wondering whether the girl was too beautiful for fat shaming from her peers. Certainly, her companion was thin enough, though Ayla could only see the lower halves of her legs, her stockinged feet, crossed at the ankles, propped up on the seat beside her girlfriend. Both were busy on their mobile phones, their thumbs blurred as they texted or e-mailed. A large map of Florence and its vicinity was unfolded between them, but neither of them paid it any attention. Once the Pre-Raphaelite girl facing Ayla looked up from her mobile and laughed at something her friend must have said. Ayla envied them, wondering what it was like to live a life so carefree, so free of adult anxieties and responsibilities. Suddenly she felt a surge of profound love toward these two girls. How was it possible, she wondered, to love someone when you didn't know her at all? How strange and wonderful life was sometimes.

But not for Ayla. Life had been reduced to a series of mistakes, missed opportunities, withholding when she should have been forthcoming, and vice versa. All leading to this moment. When she and Bravo should have been inseparable they were estranged. He no longer trusted her, if he ever had. It was clear to her that she had damaged what had been a terribly fragile alliance, one that she had never wanted, had fought tooth and nail against, but had been dragooned into by a mother whom it was impossible to deny. Poisoned. Born and bred on Fate, Ayla had ingested blind obedience with her mother's milk. All leading to this: an ending in which Ayla and Bravo both might very well die.

She rose, made her way through the swaying car, down the three stairs to the lav. When she emerged, the girl with the Pre-Raphaelite face was waiting. They smiled at each other. Ayla opened her mouth to say something but didn't know what that might be. Then the moment was gone; the girl entered the lav, closing and locking the door behind her. Ayla fell back against the wall, eyes closed. Nothing she had recently experienced brought home to her with such immediacy the barrier between her and the rest of the world. She felt marooned, a stranger in a strange land that followed her wherever she went. She was stuck; Fate had decreed it. She would never be like the Pre-Raphaelite girl, never feel the normal feverish rush and pull of hormones, never agonize over texts to boyfriends or BFFs, never feel the world crashing down over a breakup, only to be lifted to Olympian heights, sparks flying, with the next boyfriend.

And in return what did she have? Opening her eyes, she climbed the stairs, stared down the car at Bravo. As if sensing her gaze, he turned from his silent contemplation of the passing countryside, locking eyes with her. She wanted to smile, tried to, but it was as if her mouth were paralyzed. Were they enemies? Were they friends? Well, they had never been friends, not really, and now not ever. What were they then? She knew, but he did not, and now the moment was long past and she was terrified to tell him, terrified of his reaction. But she had to tell him before they entered the convent, didn't she? Had there ever been any other choice?

The Pre-Raphaelite girl emerged from the lav, ascended the stairs with her thick, powerful thighs, her young, thrusting breasts. Her glimmering red nails.

"Are you all right?" she asked Ayla, poised on the stairs.

In that breathless moment, an impenetrable glass wall between them, Ayla did not know how to answer her.

Bravo sat, muscle tensed, brain locked, staring out the train window. He focused on the close-up. The blurring of the world soothed him, provided a balm for the sense of betrayal that had brought him low. Far worse, it had dislodged his focus, had dislocated him from the job at hand. The danger to him, to the Order, perhaps to mankind itself, was now incalculable. Whatever forebodings he had harbored had been magnified a hundredfold by what he had read in the *Nihilus Inusitatus*. He wished Fra Leoni were here but then quickly recalculated. He had tried to raise Fra Leoni on the phone after he had called warning Bravo about Emma. Bravo's people said that they had been monitoring police activity at the office. Apparently, Fra Leoni had fainted and some idiot cop thought he was dead. Clearly not, since he had subsequently flown to Alexandria.

This was not, it itself, concerning; the old man was often gone on secretive trips and he was adamant about not telling anyone where he was going, but in this instance Bravo was worried. Why hadn't the old man told him that he had fainted? What if the episode wasn't so benign? What if he had been attacked by the creature that possessed Emma? After all, he and Emma had been together in the office.

As for Emma herself, or more accurately the creature she had become, Fra Leoni had surmised that she had gone to the convent of Saint Angelica Boniface. Her mobile was either off or out of juice. Come what may, Fra Leoni could take care of himself, but Bravo was terrified about his sister. What if he couldn't save her? What if the possession couldn't be reversed? He glanced up at one of the tightly wrapped packages he'd purchased in Rome. If Emma was gone, truly gone, if there was no other choice, would he have it in him to slice off her head? A shudder of dread rippled through him. Ever since the call, he'd tried to compartmentalize his fear for his sister, to keep his mind on what he needed to do. He wouldn't have been able to help her; Fra Leoni had assured him of that. She hadn't been sent to Tannourine, so she must be waiting for him at the convent. Because of one thing he was certain: she had been attacked and possessed for one reason—as a weapon to use against him. He couldn't help a second glance at the packages nestled on the rack above his head. *What if she attacks me?* he asked himself. *What if it's her or me? God in heaven, when the confrontation comes what will I do?*

If you're dependent on anyone but yourself, Todao had schooled him over and over, *you will enter the field of battle already defeated.*

The trouble was he didn't think he could defeat this thing, the Guardian of the Testament of Lucifer—whatever it was—on his own. This was the moment he felt Ayla's gaze on him, and he turned from his inner reflections to confront the outside world. His eyes locked with hers. He tried and failed to intuit what she was thinking. But then he'd tried and failed to understand her. She had been steps ahead of him at every turn. What was she playing at? What did she want? There could be no doubt in his mind that her mother had not been fully human. Why else had Tombstone gone to the trouble of decapitating her? According to what Ayla herself had told Bravo, decapitation was the only way to kill the demons, stop them from transpositioning from body to body. But Dilara had not been a demon; she had been decapitated by one. Was decapitation the method of killing immortals as well as demons? If so, if Dilara was an immortal, what did that make Ayla? Too many questions without answers, and he had a strong intimation that he needed those answers before they reached the convent of Saint Angelica Boniface.

He looked back at Ayla and knew where he needed to start. The problem was how to begin. He could smile at her, of course, but that would only startle her. Plus, he doubted he could get himself to manufacture a smile that wasn't false. False was the last thing either of them needed now. The girl who had been sitting across from them with her pal was making her way back to her seat. Noticing him glancing her way, she gave him a shy smile. When she came abreast of him she paused and, leaning over slightly, swaying as the coach swayed, said, "I don't mean to intrude, but your traveling companion seems upset."

"Upset?" Bravo said before he could stop himself.

"Well, maybe not so much upset as sad. Yeah, she's mos def sad." That smile again, brilliant this time and still guileless. "Life's too short." With that she crossed the aisle, slid past her friend's legs, and plopped herself back down in her seat. Soon enough the two of them were texting and laughing softly.

Bravo sighed, pressed his fingertip against his closed eyelids. *Life's too short.* Yes, it was.

Sensing Ayla coming back down the aisle, he opened his eyes, watched her as she approached, settled herself almost primly in her seat opposite him.

"Do you have anything to read?" she asked. "I don't—"

"The girl over there says you're sad."

"How the hell would she—?" Ayla's eyes cut to the girl as she bit her lip. A flush crept up her throat into her cheeks. Then back to Bravo. "Why wouldn't I be sad?"

"Frankly, I can't think of a reason."

"Yeah." She stared out at the blurry landscape, wanting to know what he saw there. "It's a shitty place to be."

"Mos def."

Her eyes cut back to him. "Did you just say . . . ?" She burst out laughing.

Across the aisle, the Pre-Raphaelite girl paused long enough in her texting to give them a thumbs-up.

There was nothing. No time, no space, no light, no dark. So close to the precipice, so close to tumbling over and drowning in her own madness, everything stopped. Emma was held suspended, as if cradled by an immense hand. All the psychic pain and suffering inflicted on her were as nothing, mere echoes, racing away from her, as if terrified. Perhaps she lay in a burn unit, a psych ward, an ICU. Perhaps she was attended to by angels, for whom time and space do not exist. In any event, she was healed. It was a long, arduous process, but as humans count, no more than the blink of an eye passed.

She uncurled, unfurled, returned to the body from which she had been so rudely exiled. The creature that had imprisoned her inside her own mind had vanished along with her seemingly endless suffering. Where had she gone? How had she been banished? Emma had no answers to these questions, just as she had no idea who she was—more accurately, *what* she was.

At the very precipice of madness, when all hope was seemingly lost, something buried deep inside her that she had never before experienced kicked in, like taking a breath, the autonomous nervous system taking control, ensuring survival.

She opened her eyes and looked up into a handsome young male face. He stood over her, peering at her quizzically.

"Malus," she said without quite knowing what she was saying, "she's gone. Emma is gone."

And she found herself smiling someone else's smile.

FIFTY-TWO

"I haven't been forthcoming with you."

"No kidding."

Ayla shifted on her seat. "In my defense—"

"As far as I'm concerned you have no defense," Bravo said.

"In my defense," she resumed doggedly, "I was warned not to tell you anything."

"By your mother, I'm guessing."

"No," Ayla said. "By your father."

"What? You must be joking."

Abruptly aware that they had attracted the Pre-Raphaelite girl's attention and that she might be recording their conversation just for giggles, Bravo gestured. He and Ayla rose and together went to the opposite end of the carriage, where they stood close together, a glass-and-chrome divider between them and the rest of the passengers.

"Now let me get this straight," he said under the clack-clack of the rails. "You're telling me that you were told by my father—"

"'Warned' is more like it," Ayla said. "In no uncertain terms."

"Not to tell me—what?"

Ayla regarded him for what seemed a long time. "Before I begin . . . my mother wanted me to tell you. She was all for it. But your father . . . he wielded great power within the Order, yes?"

"Of course."

"She wouldn't go against him."

"But your mother wasn't in the Order."

Ayla stared at him wordlessly.

Bravo pressed his fingers to his temples, then shook his head as someone will who is trying to rid himself of the tail end of sleep. "So now . . ."

"Now we begin."

The train slowed, pulled into the Orvieto station. They remained silent while passengers departed and others stepped aboard, looked around, stowed their luggage, and settled into seats.

When the train started up again, Bravo said, "First, tell me why my father ordered you to withhold this information from me."

"He was protecting you."

"From what?"

"Conrad."

"My grandfather?"

She nodded. "Everyone in the family hated him, he told my mother and me."

"I don't believe you. I loved my grandfather, though it obviously pained my father. I took care of Conrad after his accident. He fell off a ladder he had no business being on at his age. He was paralyzed from the waist down. We'd go for long walks, me pushing him in his wheelchair."

"And he never said anything to you?"

He brushed aside her question. "Why would my father lie to you and Dilara?"

"I'm hardly the one to ask. I scarcely knew him."

She waited while a passenger approached them, asked where the lav was. She pointed to the other end of the carriage.

When they were alone again, she went on. "I'm sorry to say this, Bravo, but I didn't like your father. My mother even less. He was a secretive man, withdrawn, always, it seemed to me, trying to scratch the envy itch he could never get to."

"Who would he be envious of?"

She took a step closer to him, her voice lowered. "Bravo, I

need to tell you something. Omar was not my father—well, he brought me up, so I feel as if he was. But he wasn't my birth father. Conrad was."

Bravo felt all the air go out of his lungs. His heartbeat seemed to rise into his brain, turning all coherent thought into chaos. "But . . . wait a minute . . . I mean, that's impossible. My grandfather was born in 1900."

"Yes, and when he met my mother in Istanbul he was in his early sixties. She was eighteen."

"And you're telling me what? They fell in love?"

"Conrad was a libertine, a bit of a rake. And my mother . . . well, let's just say that since an early age she was something of an experimenter."

"So that would make us—?"

"I'm not sure there's an official name for what we are, Bravo. The important thing is that you and I—and I believe Emma, as well—carry Conrad's very special genes. It's another reason no one knew. Conrad himself was very specific about that with my mother. He told her that I must remain a secret until the day the rough beast raises its head. When she had that dream about you in Tannourine she believed that day had come."

Bravo absorbed these revelations with difficulty. Then he said, "What about my father?"

She shook her head. "The enmity between Dexter and Conrad sprang from the fact that your father was perfectly ordinary."

"My father didn't approve of Conrad's beliefs."

"He didn't share them because he couldn't. He lacked what you and I and, as I said, probably Emma have." She closed her fingers around his upper arm. "We're special, Bravo."

"How?" He did not refute her; what she was saying was something he had suspected for years but could never articulate to himself, let alone anyone else. "How are we special? Are we immortal like Fra Leoni?"

"No."

"But the demon cut off your mother's head to kill her."

"Well, now you understand why she came to Conrad's attention. There was something special about her, too. He recognized it in her before she did. But she learned from him. She learned everything from him."

"So what are we? Conrad, your mother, you, me, Emma. What are we?"

"I can only tell you what Conrad told my mother when they were together. He said that between immortal and demon lie those who will save mankind."

FIFTY-THREE

The bees around the convent of Saint Angelica Boniface were busy in sunlight and shadow, whirring from flower to flower, happily sucking up the essence from which they would manufacture the delicious honey the sisters processed, packaged, and in season sold at the village's weekly organic farmer's market.

Occasionally, butterflies lit on a flowering bush, but only in sunlight, basking like sybarites, their speckled wings levering drowsily up and down. Other insects, hidden in the tree-dappled shade, droned on, going about their daily chores with blind obedience to instinct.

Beside them, on the heavily foliaged hillside, Bravo and Ayla gazed up at the convent's walls, the arched iron-bound doors to the church where the sisters sang the hours, cleaned the time-darkened paintings of bloody scenes of holy intervention, washed the various gilt-painted wooden icons of the martyred Saints Angelica Boniface and Bella dell'Arca. The doors were girdled by the carved stone figures of the four Apostles, crowned by the Virgin Mary cradling the radiant Christ-child.

"We fit right in there, don't we?" Ayla whispered with a wry smile.

"Right now I'd have to say that as far as this convent goes the Apostles are deaf, dumb, and blind."

"Maybe they've been blinded," Ayla said with a warrior's voice.

★

"They're here." Malus stirred, nostrils flared, nose slightly lifted to the wind stirring the lemon tree in the cloister garden. He turned to Bella dell'Arca and Emma. "I can smell them." He grinned, sharp teeth glinting as he strode from shadow to sunlight. "They already smell like death."

Unwrapping one of the packages, Bravo took out a folding shovel. In a relatively flat area behind the copse of trees where they were hidden from view, he dug a shallow grave, placed the watertight cylinder containing the *Nihilus Inusitatus* manuscript into it, covered it over, tamping down the earth and smearing a double layer of leaves over the cache.

"I don't like this plan," Ayla said when he was done.

"You've made that abundantly clear."

"I don't want anything to happen to you."

Their eyes locked for what seemed a long time, and what passed between them no one could say.

"Nothing will," Bravo said.

"Spoken like a true idiot."

"Ayla, if you have a better idea now's the time."

Only the insects and the birds replied, each in their own inscrutable languages.

"All right then." Bravo cut the twine that held the second package's wrapping in place, unrolled the thick undyed cotton.

Ayla's eyes opened wide as light glimmered along the *wakizashi's* blade. "Good Lord."

Bravo looked at her. The grim smile on his face was worth a thousand words.

Toward what rough beast? Bravo thought as he approached the open doorway to the convent's church. It was filled with deep and abiding shadows on either side of the doorway. Seven thick candles burned along the length of the cloth-draped altar, their flames sending shards of light and shadow dancing along the length of the transept, a golden glow that flickered with every stir of the air. The sisters were singing Vespers, the evening prayer, which was a call-and-response.

"In my distress I called to the Lord, and He answered me," sang the *madre vicaria*.

"Lord, deliver me from lying lip, from treacherous tongue," the other nuns intoned.

"What will He inflict on you, with more besides, O treacherous tongue?"

"Sharp arrows of a warrior with fiery coals of brushwood."

Bravo stood stock-still, bathed in blue twilight. An immense plain wooden cross rose from its plinth in the apse behind the altar. Apart from the sisters, he was the only one in the church. There was something different about this Vespers service. Something wrong.

"When I speak of peace," the *madre vicaria* intoned, "they are ready for war."

"Lord, grant him eternal rest," came the reply.

This was not the normal Vespers, Bravo realized. It was the Office for the dead.

At that very moment the *madre vicaria* turned her gaze upon Bravo and sang, "And let perpetual light shine upon him."

As if the ringing of her words had drawn back a curtain, Emma stepped out of the corner shadows. He turned, saw her standing between him and the doorway.

The *madre vicaria* began to read from the book of Job: "'Man, born of woman, is short-lived and full of trouble. Like a flower he springs up and fades; he flees like a shadow, and never continues in the same state. Upon such a one will you cast your eyes so as to bring him into judgment with you?'"

Stepping closer to Bravo, Emma said, "I see you, Brother."

"'Who can make clean one that is conceived of unclean seed? Who but you alone? Short are the days of man. You know the number of his months; you have fixed the limit which he cannot pass. Look away from him and let him be, while like a hireling he completes his day.'"

"I was blind, but now I can see you, as I see the world around me."

The recitation from the altar stopped. He turned slightly, enough to see out of the corner of his eye the *madre vicaria* shooing her nun ducklings silently out either side of the bema. At almost the same instant Emma advanced toward him.

He took a step back, watching both her hands and her face.

"Where's Ayla?" she said.

"I know what's happened. I know you're not Emma."

His sister took another step toward him, and he retreated down the center aisle of the nave, knowing that he was coming closer to the *madre vicaria,* who had been standing just in front of the great golden cross that rose in the center of the semi-circular apse at the far end of the church.

"My sister is dead," Bravo told her. "I will kill you if you give me no other choice."

Still Emma came on. This time, as she stepped toward him, she mouthed, *Don't let Ayla set foot in here.*

Too late. Behind him, Ayla appeared barefoot, in utter silence, from the left transcript, where she had entered the church, as planned. She headed directly toward the *madre vicaria.*

Bella dell'Arca whirled and, snarling, bared the Nihil sigil on her chest. Her long lethal teeth shone in the flickering candle-light. Without an instant's hesitation Ayla raised Bravo's Beretta, which she had kept out of sight against her leg, and fired shot after shot point-blank into the Black Saint's neck. The first bullet tore through Bella dell'Arca's larynx; the second shattered two cervical vertebrae; the third severed her spinal cord.

Bella dell'Arca's head fell to one side, held in place only by a length of bloody skin. Ayla, in a fit of pure rage, did what Bravo had cautioned her not to do: she emptied the gun's magazine into the Black Saint's head, turning it into a bloody pulp of shattered skull and gobbets of gray and pink brain matter.

"Jesus," Emma moaned. "Jesus Christ."

The church interior fell dark; the candle flames lost their luster; the twilight slunk back through the open doorway as if wanting no part in what was to come. The heavy front doors slammed shut, propelled by an invisible hand. With an almost human groan, the colossal cross fell forward. Ayla, throwing a glance over her shoulder, jumped out of the way just in time. The cross toppled off its plinth, split the altar in two, coming to rest on the stone floor of the bema, upside down. A crack zigzagged along its cross-beam.

A swirling mist seemed to have invaded the apse like a living thing. Bravo recognized it from Ayla's vivid description. It was the shadow from the tent in Tannourine to which Dilara had taken her young daughter. And if the shadow was inside the church, it meant that the thing that had conjured it, the boy-child burned to a crisp inside the red tent of shadows, the Guardian of the Book of Deathly Things, was here, too.

Bravo saw him just in front of the church's doors. At Emma's back, he stepped forward, a young man with a sharp face, eyes black as the void of outer space. On his bare chest was emblazoned the Nihil, the sigil of the Unholy Trinity.

"You've done your job to perfection, holding your brother in place," he told Emma. "Now stand aside."

Bravo, Emma mouthed, *I'm not a monster. I'm your sister.*

"What are you doing?" Malus thundered. "I ordered you to step aside."

Bravo, please!

With a swat of his hand, Malus threw her to one side. Her head hit a corner of a wooden pew, and she fell unconscious.

At the far end of the church, amid the rubble of the altar, the shadow had taken possession of the inverted cross, crawling across its length like a malignant serpent, thickening into what appeared to be a tar-like substance as it advanced. Ayla recognized it as the same ungodly material that had coated the gold crucifix that Bravo carried with him.

The sight of the coalescing shadow threw her back to the horror she had experienced in the red tent of shadows—Dilara's desperate intent, unknown to her as a child, as was her own part in it: the fusion of power between mother and daughter, used to destroy the boy-child, to stop his conversion by unholy fire into what he had now become: a fully realized manifestation of the Fallen, more dangerous for having successfully taken human form.

She felt again the force of her mother's intent, the terrible power that had lain dormant within Ayla until that moment. In the here and now, she had never missed her mother's presence so deeply, so keenly. Thrown back in time, Ayla felt helpless again—helpless, in her pain and high fever, to assist her mother, helpless against the sight of what was being born in the tent's center, helpless to resist the gaze of that dreadful creature, moving its preternatural eyes toward her, its gaze falling on her, at last, with the force of a collapsing building wall.

Her mother's hubris had linked her with Malus, the thing that now confronted Bravo at the other end of the church. And here she was cowering beneath the slithering shadow, coming for her at last, her gun empty, useless, in any event, to halt its progress toward her. Turning, she slipped on the muck of the Black Saint's exploded skull, went to her knees as the black shining serpent neared her.

Her mind, slipped back into its childhood state, seemed paralyzed, her thoughts scattering like a school of fish at a predator's approach. She put a hand out to steady herself, felt the waxy bulk of one of the candles that had been atop the shattered altar. The flame was guttering in the spreading wetness.

The flame.

All at once Ayla's mind snapped into gear. Snatching up the candle, she thrust it past the serpent, toward the sacred cloth that had covered the altar. The serpent reached her wrist.

A terrible chill passed through her, but she knew if she withdrew her hand, if the flame failed to do its job, she would be lost.

The serpent wound around her wrist, climbed up her arm, and now she could see its diamond eyes, cold and cruel as starlight. A black tar tongue flicked out, tasting the sweat on her skin. She all but cried out. Her hand shook with her terror at what was to come, but she did not withdraw it.

The serpent had reached the crook of her elbow when the fabric caught fire. With a desperate lunge she poked it into the crack in the wooden cross. The dried wood ignited almost immediately. Its heat was so intense that the serpent was halted. The flames licked out, consuming the coalesced shadow just as they had so many years ago in the red tent of shadows.

Ayla was aware of a horrific screaming that was no real sound at all, that seemed to echo over and over inside her head. She stared into the diamond eyes of the shadow-serpent. For a moment she was transfixed, hovering between the darkness and the light, aware of both at once, the vision so overwhelming she nearly lost consciousness.

Then a spear of flame shot out of the serpent's mouth and, with the sound of crunching leaves, devoured its forked tongue.

"This time fire won't save her," Malus said. "Or you." He moved fast. "She's mine. She always was mine." Faster than was imaginable. "And she always will be."

He reached out for Bravo. "You're the only one standing between me and her." Malus caught Bravo by the throat. "Do you imagine I would let that happen? We were fated to be together, Ayla and me, from the beginning of time, until the end of time." His fingers began to dig in on either side of Bravo's windpipe.

"We failed with your accursed grandfather." Malus's eyes blazed with malevolent fury. "He outsmarted us somehow. But we have you now, and we'll never let you go."

"I knew your plan was to kill me after I brought Ayla to you," Bravo said in a strangled voice.

"Kill you?" Malus laughed. His breath held the stench of the pits of hell. "You fool! You're not meant to die. Your grandfather eluded us, but you won't. Death isn't your fate, Braverman; becoming one of us—one of the Fallen—is." The fingernails started to extrude, puncturing skin, drawing blood.

Bravo, one hand curled around the tar-black crucifix, brought it up, pressed it as hard as he could against Malus's forehead.

"Whatever you think you're doing, it won't work. Nothing is left to work against us. You're alone now, Braverman. We've destroyed Dilara and Fra Leoni. We've laid waste to the reliquary in the library. The sanctuary of power your grandfather carefully built is no more. Your Order's end of days has arrived, its influence dealt a mortal blow. And now with you among the Fallen, the last remaining—"

Bravo's thumb turned white with the pressure. Slowly but surely the crucifix, coated with the ichor of the Fallen, sank into Malus's skull. Deeper and deeper it went, as more and more of Bravo's blood flowed from the wounds Malus was inflicting. Something dark and squirmy made its presence felt on the periphery of Bravo's senses. Something was trying to insinuate itself into his bloodstream. But now his thumb was buried in Malus's skull past his knuckle. A heat was growing, burning the pad of his thumb as it began to boil everything beyond the crucifix's face.

Malus's face turned into a writhing mask. "What?" he sputtered. "What . . . ?"

Bravo pulled his thumb from the noxious mass, drew the *wakizashi,* the Japanese short sword very like the one he had seen Tombstone use to decapitate Dilara in the stairwell. Bravo had bought it at great cost from a member of the Accademia Italia Kendo, in Rome. Slashing down, Bravo cut off first Malus's right hand at the wrist, then the left hand. Gathering his ki from his lower belly, as Todao had taught him, he initiated

a powerful horizontal slash that severed Malus's neck from
his torso.

The awful thing lay on the floor, grinning up at him. Raising
the *wakizashi* over his head, he brought it down in a powerful
stroke, splitting Malus's face, his skull, in two.

FIFTY-FOUR

A black rain was falling, hard as lead pellets, and above that a sky full of fire. Bravo on his knees, shoulders hunched, head bowed. The rain battered him. Even in death, Malus on the attack.

It was difficult to see clearly, even more difficult to arrange his thoughts in their proper order. The rush of concentrated energy accompanying the Guardian's death was like being on the fringes of a detonated bomb.

Bravo looked up, finally, dimly saw Ayla helping Emma to her feet. He wanted to shout to Ayla to watch out, to remember Emma was not actually Emma. Battered by the hard rain, he grasped the hilt of the *wakizashi*, staggered to his feet. The rear of the church was burning; the ceiling of the apse was curling and sagging. A moment later it crashed into the remnants of the altar and the burning inverted cross. But, owing to the stone structure in the front, the flames were meeting resistance making headway toward him. Until, that is, the first of the wooden pews caught fire. The fire advanced quickly after that.

The black rain was ending, nothing left of Malus's head or torso but puddles of mush. Picking his way through them, Bravo approached the two women. He could see now that they were holding on to each other, so that it was difficult to tell which one was supporting the other. Bravo, recalling Emma being swept aside, hitting her head against the corner of a pew back, felt a confluence of conflicting emotions swirling in the pit of his stomach. Emma, his beloved sister. Emma, possessed by a demon.

"Ayla!" He raised the *wakizashi*. "Step away! This is not my sister! It's another demon!"

"Bravo." Emma stepped in front of Ayla without letting go of her. "Listen to me."

Bravo brought the blade to bear. "If you hurt her in any way . . ."

"Bravo, she's already hurt," Emma said. "I don't know how badly, but it's serious."

"Emma, let go of her."

"If I do, she'll fall."

"I don't believe—"

At that moment Ayla groaned deeply, fell heavily against Emma's shoulder. As Ayla's eyes rolled up in her head, Bravo dropped the sword, rushed forward in time for her to fall unconscious into his arms.

PART FIVE

WHAT ROUGH BEAST

CAPRAOLA / ALEXANDRIA

FIFTY-FIVE

"I promised no harm would come to you," Ayla said in a very small voice as Bravo, Emma at his side, carried her out of the burning church. "I made good on that promise."

"Quiet," Bravo admonished.

He watched Emma take the lead, a human battering ram, parting gathering people. All the sisters had escaped, shaken to their roots but unharmed, and once outside the convent grounds they knelt in a circle to pray for their beloved *madre vicaria* while volunteer emergency crews from the surrounding villages swarmed past them. The villagers themselves were swaddling them in blankets, offering murmured words of pious support. Some of the women got down on their knees and prayed along with the nuns.

Bravo, taking the lead now that they were past the crowd, directed them to the spot behind the copse of trees where he had buried the cylinder containing the *Nihilus Inusitatus*.

Setting Ayla down, he asked Emma to tend to her. Keeping an eagle eye on his sister, or whoever she was, he dug out his mobile and called the pilot of the Order's plane, standing by on an outer runway in Rome.

"Blue One," Bravo said, which was code for the highest-level emergency.

"Local," the pilot said, meaning "location."

When Bravo gave it to him, the pilot said, "Hang on." Bravo could hear him riffling pages. "Okay. There's a local airstrip three kilometers southeast of you. It'll be tight, but I'll be there in twenty." He meant minutes. They rang off.

Taking a risk, Bravo turned his back on the two women, dug up the cylinder, only to find that it was gone. He dropped back onto his haunches, stunned, stared at the empty grave he had dug.

"Bravo!" Emma called from behind him. "I think Ayla might be dying."

Who could have found it in such a short period of time? One thing he was certain of: this was no accidental find. Someone had been following them, watching their every move. But who?

This was the question vexing Bravo as he carried Ayla up the folding stairs into the belly of the Order's plane. They had made it to the airfield without encountering anyone. The air was acrid, distorted with smoke from the fire, even this far from the convent, but by the time they arrived they had passed beyond the fall of ash. The dimming sky behind them was tinged a filthy reddish brown, like coagulated blood. The trek had been relatively short but arduous; Bravo had carried Ayla over his shoulder in a classic fireman's lift. Toward the end, the sky had clamped down on the countryside, sending rain down in phalanxes. They slogged the last half kilometer through muddy terrain. At their backs, the flames died, replaced by a funnel cloud of smoke spiraling higher, spiraling wider.

The pilot was smoking, waiting at the foot of the folding stairs. He and the navigator helped Bravo maneuver Ayla into the plane. Bravo perched on one of the flatbed seats and quickly dried off with towels provided by the crew. Then he bent to examine Ayla's right arm, which, along with her head, was the only part of her not under a blanket Emma had tucked around her. At his feet was the plane's well-stocked first-aid kit.

He had yet to give the pilot a flight plan. Bravo was acutely aware that that was as urgent as seeing to Ayla. Had there been time to mourn the passing of Fra Leoni he would have, but his thoughts were consumed with the disappearance of the *Nihilus Inusitatus*. Having read most, if not all, of it, he knew just how valuable—and potentially dangerous—it was. In the hands of the wrong person or, far, far worse, one of the Fallen, it would constitute a disaster of unimaginable proportions. He now knew, as his grandfather Conrad had, though perhaps no one else, that the manuscript was far more than it was purported to be. Only someone like Bravo—and Conrad before him—who could read Tifinagh would suspect that the *Nihilus Inusitatus* contained within it the secret of the hiding place of the Testament of Lucifer.

Now Bravo strongly suspected that the disappearance of the *Nihilus Inusitatus* was directly related to its elevated status. He was convinced that whoever had stolen it knew precisely what it really was. Despite Ayla's condition, he rose, went quickly up to the cockpit, told the pilot where he wanted to go.

"Take the most direct route possible. We've no time to waste," he told the pilot before returning to where Ayla lay. Emma was trying to feed her ice water through a bendy straw, with no luck.

"Step back," he told Emma sternly. "I need to take a good look at her."

"You don't believe me," Emma said as she complied. "Even now."

Bravo didn't answer her; he had a more urgent issue to deal with now. For the first time, he was able to inspect Ayla's right arm without fire or flight interfering. He didn't like what he saw: an ugly black welt approximately the width of his forefinger wound around her wrist and forearm to just below the inner part of her elbow. The welt was veiny, and the veins were pulsing, as if from a second heartbeat.

"What the hell is that?" Emma asked. "It wasn't doing that before."

Bravo shot her a sideways glance. "You mean you don't know?"

"Why won't you believe me?"

"The evil I'm fighting, the evil Conrad uncovered, that Yeats wrote about, whose imminent coming Dilara foresaw, is monolithic. It wants what it wants."

"And what is that?"

"Everything. It wants to regain the kingdom of heaven, but it also wants God's greatest creation—mankind. It's come for us—all of us. And it's going to do that in every manner it can, which includes seduction. For the people who it has marked as most dangerous to its aims it will try to give them what they want most." His eyes traveled over her face. "In my case, it's getting my beloved sister back."

"Oh, Bravo." Tears sprang out of Emma's eyes. "What do I have to do, kill myself?"

"Fra Leoni is dead," Bravo said shortly, cruelly. "That's enough."

"What?" Emma fell back. "Dead?" She wrapped her arms around her middle. "But how? When?"

Bravo was too busy to answer her and, besides, he had no answers to her questions. Plus, the information had come from Malus. Was he capable of telling the truth about anything? Fra Leoni could very well still be alive.

"Ayla?" Her eyes were half-closed in pain. "Talk to me."

"*Now* you want to talk." She laughed, but that soon turned into a coughing fit, a strangled sob. "Shit." Tears rolled down her cheeks.

Bravo smoothed the damp hair off her forehead. "Deep breaths."

She nodded, grimaced. "The shadow . . . the shadow from the red tent of shadows remanifested itself. Only this time . . . this time it was far stronger, less like smoke, more like that tar-like substance coating the crucifix." She paused to take several gasping breaths, and the veins began to pulse faster.

"Slow," Bravo said gently. "Slow. Try to relax your breathing."

As she did so, the pulsing subsided.

"Anyway, it came after me, coalescing into a serpent-like

creature slithering down the inverted cross. By that time I was trying to set it on fire. It wrapped itself around me in order to prevent me. I could . . . I think I could have escaped it, but the fire had been set." Her eyes turned toward him, the whites visible all around the irises. "I had to light the fire. I had to."

"I know you did, Ayla. I know."

Ayla gave a sharp cry, her body arching up with such force it threw the blanket off her. Her eyes rolled; sweat dripped off her; she was feverish. The skin of her ankles was grayish. Both Bravo and Emma saw the anomaly at the same time and exchanged a knowing glance that only siblings understand.

"The shadow-serpent delivered a potent toxin to her system," Bravo said.

"How d'you know?" Emma had finally recovered enough of her equilibrium to think clearly again.

"I read about it in the ancient manuscript Val took from the Cave of Shadows."

"But how did you get to read it?"

"It's a long story," Bravo said, "and even I don't know the whole of it." He looked at Emma. "The point being, if we don't arrest the toxin soon it will take over her entire system."

"And then?"

"You don't want to know and I don't want to see it happen."

Emma moved in closer. "We need to bleed her, right? I mean, that's what you do with a viper's bite."

"That's just what we *won't* do." Bravo took out a knife from the first-aid kit. "That would only weaken her, and speed the toxin through her system." He ran the flame from a lighter he had borrowed from the pilot up and down the length of the knife blade. "This is the secret of this particular poison, what makes it almost always fatal."

"Then what?"

"I can't do it myself." He raised his eyes, his gaze flat and unforgiving. "You asked what it would take for me to trust that you're really my sister."

"Yes."

"This is it." The blade hovered over the inside of his forearm. "She needs to ingest some of my blood."

Emma reared back. "What?"

"It's too long a story to go into now, but the three of us are special. We are directly descended from Conrad, who was, apparently, very special indeed."

"What are you saying? How could Ayla be—?"

He had drawn blood. "Listen to me, Emma. As you saw, Ayla won't want to swallow. Open her mouth, keep it open, and make sure she does. Clear?"

Emma nodded. Her eyes were clouded with a thousand questions, but she did as Bravo had instructed. Ayla was writhing now, but Emma managed to clamp her hands over the lower part of her face. She pried the jaws open.

"Now," she said.

Holding his arm above Ayla, Bravo allowed his blood to flow into her mouth. As if the welt knew what was about to happen to it, Ayla's writhing increased.

"Hurry, Bravo," Emma said. "I can't hold her much longer."

The blood filled Ayla's mouth.

"All right," Bravo said.

"She . . . Bravo, she won't swallow."

"Hold her," Bravo said. "Tight now. No, tighter."

Reaching out, he pinched Ayla's nostrils. At the same time, he flicked the center of her windpipe with the back of his fingertip. She swallowed in a great convulsion that almost threw Emma head over heels. But she held on like a cowboy on the back of a Brahma bull.

Bravo and Emma looked at each other, and he gave her the smallest of nods. What she returned was the smallest of smiles. Then they returned their attention to Ayla. Her convulsions were at an end; her writhing had subsided. She lay perfectly still, eyes closed.

Emma sat back, sighing. "It's working. The toxin is gone."

"Not gone," Bravo said. "Arrested. According to the *Nihilus Inusitatus* the two are in a kind of stasis."

"Like Sleeping Beauty."

He nodded. "In a manner of speaking."

"So . . . what's the next step? Tell me we can save her."

Bravo ran a hand across his eyes. He was so enormously tired, but there were still miles to run, and almost all of them in pitch blackness.

"We can, according to the manuscript, but we need a third person. An immortal."

"Fra Leoni. But you said he's dead."

"Malus told me he was dead; that's not the same thing."

"Then . . . ?"

"I know where he is." Bravo looked down at Ayla. His hand stroked her brow. "At least I think I do."

"We have time now," Emma said. "Tell me about Grandfather."

FIFTY-SIX

Toward sunset, the pelagic birds that crisscrossed Alexandria's harbor, wheeling on the thermals and calling to one another, fell strangely silent. The sky was clear; not a cloud dotted the horizon, which made the silence that much more eerie. For moments at a time, people stopped their wandering, shopping, sightseeing, arguing, or idle rumormongering to glance anxiously out at the fire-tinged water beyond the semi-circular harbor, dotted with small fishing boats and pleasure craft bobbing at anchor. But there was nothing to see, nothing visible coming inland, nothing that would make the bird population fall silent. The sun, bloated by pollution, as its dying light refracted through the atmosphere, was slowly being swallowed by the southern Mediterranean. Everything else was as it should be, and soon enough the population nearest the harbor returned to their daily pursuits, forgetting the silence of the birds.

They arrived at the library at twilight. Bravo was carrying Ayla in his arms. She had been going in and out of a kind of semi-consciousness since a half hour out from the Egyptian shoreline. Bravo had tried to talk to her, but she seemed not to hear him. She was straddling two worlds—her own and the one defined by the shadow-serpent's toxin.

Emma pushed the door open, and they entered the shadowy interior.

"*Mawlānā!*" the curator cried upon seeing Bravo. "How good it is for these old eyes to behold you again!"

"And you, Aither. This is my sister, Emma." Bravo swung Ayla around for the curator to see. "My friend is very sick, Aither. Is there somewhere she can rest?"

"Of course, of course, *mawlānā*." The curator slipped off his stool and, using his cane, beckoned them to the area behind his high desk. "This way. We shall make your patient as comfortable as is humanly possible."

He led them back down a twisting corridor Bravo had never known existed, for it seemed as if the library was built more like a labyrinth than any normal library.

"My quarters," Aither said, showing them into a series of small rooms. The first one they passed through served as a living space, with chairs and reading lamps. Tapestries lined the walls; stacks of books littered the stone floor. Beyond was a tiny lavatory, and beyond that, at the rear, were Aither's sleeping quarters, as spare and comfortless as a monk's cell.

"Lay her just there," he said, pointing. "My bed will do nicely." When Bravo had done so, Aither advanced toward where Ayla lay. As he closed in, he started and, seeing the black spiral on her forearm, said, "Oh, dear, oh, dear." He turned to Bravo. "How on earth—?"

"It's a long story," Bravo said. "For now, I have urgent need of Fra Leoni. He came here, did he not?"

Aither nodded. "Indeed, yes." His eyes kept straying back to Ayla's arm, his frown ever deepening.

"Tell me he's still here."

"It's true," the curator said, "he is still at his studies."

"Please take me to him," Bravo said.

"With pleasure, but your friend—"

"Her condition is currently in stasis."

"You don't say."

Bravo seemed not to have heard the old man. "Emma will stay with her. She'll be safe enough."

"Of course, of course." Aither was bobbing up and down, anxious as Bravo to get moving. "Safe as houses, *mawlānā*."

He stepped toward the doorway. "This way. Fra Leoni is on the second floor, in the reliquary. I'll need to let you in."

"What can you tell me about Conrad?" Bravo asked as they ascended one of the three spiral staircases to the second floor.

"Who?" Aither said from in front of him.

"Conrad Shaw." Bravo noted the slight hitch in his limping step. "My grandfather."

"Ah, well," the curator said. "He was before my time, so anything I know is secondhand. You understand."

"Completely."

They reached the top of the staircase. Aither turned left, led Bravo down the same dusty corridors he had led Fra Leoni down days ago.

"From all reports, your grandfather was a strange man, dabbling in questionable Gnostic beliefs, veering far away from the central mission of the Order. Your father had the devil of a time with him, let me tell you." The curator shook his head. "Many's the time your father and I would sit at my desk, drinking mint tea, talking about the old man. He had come under the influence of the mystical poet William Butler Yeats. Yeats's crazy ideas about time cycles, about the struggle between God and Lucifer, went entirely against the grain of Catholic dogma. This put Conrad outside the scope of even the most liberal thinkers inside the Order. Your father had no choice but to exile him."

"He never told me that," Bravo said.

"I imagine there are many things about Conrad your father didn't tell you. And why should he have? They just would have upset you."

"I was already upset with the way my family treated him."

Aither paused, turned to face Bravo. "But not you, eh? You loved the old man."

"He was my grandfather. He deserved respect."

"Indeed. Well, in his day he certainly haunted this library; that I can tell you. Once, he brought his friend Yeats with him. They stayed a long time. Thick as lovers, those two, so I'm told." Without another word, he turned back, resuming their journey along corridors that looked as if they hadn't seen much traffic.

And so they came at last to a chamber dominated by a large breakfront that held the imposing basalt statue of jackal-headed Anubis.

"Strange to see the Egyptian god of the dead guarding the reliquary," Bravo observed.

"The better to hide its existence." Bending over, Aither opened the breakfront with his gold key. Soon enough the door to the reliquary stood open. "He's in there, lost in contemplation of life's deepest mysteries, I shouldn't wonder."

Bravo stepped through. The instant he did so the door slammed shut, a locking mechanism echoing like a rifle shot in the enclosed space.

"Where am I?"

Ayla had opened her eyes. They looked glazed, the whites yellowish around the outer edge.

"In Alexandria," Emma said as she bent over her.

"Virginia?"

"No, Egypt."

Ayla licked her lips. "Why?"

"Bravo's finding someone who will heal you completely."

A flicker of horror darkened Ayla's eyes, and she tried to lift her arm to look at the black spiral. Emma stopped her. "It's arrested for the time being," she said. "Rest now. You're almost home."

Ayla licked her lips as she stared up at Emma. "You can see."

"Yes, I . . . That was the Fallen's doing."

Ayla's face was blotchy, as if the blood was having difficulty making its way through her veins and arteries. "The Fallen?"

"Those who were . . . exiled . . . thrown down with Lucifer."

"How many?"

A very good question. "I don't know. My sense is perhaps a hundred or so."

Ayla's lips trembled, and Emma stroked her forehead as she had seen Bravo doing. "Rest now," she said again.

"My brain is too restless. If we don't talk the same awful thoughts keep racing around, chasing their own tails."

Emma could see that she was becoming dehydrated, but Bravo had given her strict orders not to give Ayla any liquids while the toxin was still in her system. *And if her dehydration becomes too acute?* Emma had asked him. *If that happens,* Bravo had replied, *she'll be dead.*

"All right," Emma said. "Tell me how you're related to us. Through Conrad, Bravo said, but I don't see how."

So Ayla told her the story of how Conrad had met Dilara when Dilara was very young, of how she, Ayla, had been born, and all that had transpired afterward.

"My God," Emma said. Her hands closed around one of Ayla's. "A terrible time to say this, I suppose, but, well, there's no time like the present: welcome to the family."

Ayla gave her a wan smile. "Maybe the present is all I have."

FIFTY-SEVEN

Bravo was sitting, back against the circular wall of the reliquary. Tears had been sliding down his face, it seemed to him, for a very long time. Apart from the single vitrine, the room was entirely bare. Several pale splotches on the wooden floor, the acrid smell of carbolic. And, of course, death.

Through his trembling tears, his vision distorted, smeary, he stared straight ahead at the contents of the vitrine: Fra Leoni's head. Just his head, nothing more. It had been decapitated from his trunk in one swift, surgical strike. Whoever had perpetrated this outrage had done it before, possibly many times over.

As the shock wore off, the sorrow had rushed into the pit, nature abhorring a vacuum in human beings as well as everywhere else except outer space. Bravo felt hollowed out, as if whoever had taken Fra Leoni's head off had also taken a chunk of his own flesh. He felt, somehow, less than he had been, cut down to size, as it were. It was a terrible thing to see your mentor—a man you loved unconditionally—taken from you in such unendurable fashion. There could be no relief, no surcease from this abominable sight.

Bravo, head in hands, elbows on drawn-up knees, rocked back and forth, in an effort to find comfort where he knew none to exist. His heart was breaking. His shoulders shook with sobs, and as the wall of his defenses crumbled it all came out, everything he'd been holding on to: Jenny's death, losing Emma, finding out his father wasn't quite what he'd thought, that he had lied to Bravo about Conrad. Bravo remembered a time, one winter—he must have been thirteen or so—on his way to see Todao, his father walking with him, which, at this age, was unusual. *"You and I, Bravo, must be true to each other, no matter what. No lies, no withholding information. Okay?"* *"Sure, Dad,"* he'd said with the warmth of closeness, of being inside an inner circle, not giving a thought to the fact that he and his father withheld information from Bravo's mother every day.

Now Fra Leoni's ghastly murder. And Ayla dying of a toxin no medical doctor would be able to identify, let alone treat. *Ayla!*

All at once, he shook himself like a dog coming in out of a downpour. Disgusted by his bout of self-pity, he rose and began to deal with the situation at hand.

"The world is built on lies; it's a web of lies." Conrad Shaw sitting in his wheelchair as Bravo pushed him. "Everything you think you've learned is false. Everything you want to learn you don't." Pushed him toward the old, gnarled tree he loved so much. Birds sang over their heads, heading for the tree, fellow travelers. "You think this is the philosophy of a bitter old man."

"No, sir, I don't."

"A heretic."

"My father says—"

"Your father," Conrad scoffed. "Must we talk of him?"

"No, sir, we don't have to."

"I am an outsider, Bravo, and an exile. But I am no heretic." A black-striped dragonfly landed on his right knee, its four wings lifting and lowering as if communicating in Morse code. He watched the insect for some time, absorbed, it seemed, in the pattern of movement. At length, the dragonfly lifted off, sunlight making its gossamer wings shimmer like jewels thrown into the air.

"Give me your hand."

Bravo placed his hand in his grandfather's. It was calloused, horny as a rhino's hide. Still, Bravo could feel the complex scar raised and ropy in the center of Conrad's palm.

"You feel that, Bravo?"

"Yes, sir, I do."

"That, my boy, is life." He gave a little chuckle. "Never forget the nature of life. Never forget it. Because there are always alternate endings, if we but recognize them."

Bravo, standing in the reliquary, forced himself not to look into the vitrine. The *Nihilus Inusitatus* had said this about the Book of Deathly Things' hiding place: "It abides in a mouth surrounded by a circle within a labyrinth."

And here he was in a circular room within a labyrinth. He glanced around, looking for the mouth. It was hardly a surprise to him that the Testament of Lucifer would be hidden here. All roads had led back here—from Conrad's frequent trips, to his father taking him repeatedly, to Fra Leoni heading back here when the rise of the Fallen had begun. And then there was the fact that the *Nihilus Inusitatus* had been stolen from him. His subconscious had deduced there could only be one person who would have successfully spied on him, who would have taken it: Aither. And now he knew he had been right.

Inevitably, his gaze lit on Fra Leoni's head. How on earth was he going to save Ayla's life when the *Nihilus Inusitatus* stated that she needed an immortal to neutralize the toxin in her system and restore her to life? The specific Tifinagh phrase was difficult to read, even for him. There was an addendum to the instructions, which, so far as Bravo could make out, meant "or, in extremis, a *msawan*." As he had known it, until now, *msawan* meant "dignity." But, like many other later languages, Tifinagh was notorious for ascribing numerous meanings to a single written word. Often enough, the differences came in the pronunciation of the spoken language, but context was key in the writing. In the sentence from the *Nihilus Inusitatus* "dignity" was clearly the wrong translation. There comes a time in the work of any translator of ancient languages when he recognizes he's in terra incognita. For Bravo, this was such a time. Possibly "dignitary" was the correct translation. And what was meant by "in extremis"?

If he allowed Ayla to die because of his failure to translate correctly . . . But then there was another possibility. *There are always alternate endings,* Conrad had told him, *if we but recognize them.*

A cold chill ran down his spine.

Steeling himself, he stepped toward the vitrine, bent over for a closer look. The monk's eyes were half-closed, as if he were about to lapse into sleep. There was serenity on his face, as if he had foreseen his fate or had already accepted it. That would be typical of him.

As Bravo lifted his head back up, something caught in the corner of his eye, and he turned toward the section of the wall against which he had sat slumped over moments before. Was it a trick of the lamplight or was the room not entirely circular? Turning his head slowly, he saw that the section of the wall behind him was slightly elongated, as was its counterpart across the room. Approaching the wall, he felt along its circumference, using his knuckles to listen for a hollowness. Finding none, he stepped across the room to the other side.

Here the wall sounded as solid as its counterpart. Then he glanced down at the floor. Using the toe of one boot, he pressed down on one board after another that abutted the wall. On the fourth try, he heard the faintest of clicks and jumped back just in time as a section of the floor drew back, revealing a steep circular staircase descending into darkness.

Taking up the lamp, he started down the stairs, the golden glow of lamplight lost to gathering shadows as he headed into the unknown.

Eyes glowing like coals in the darkness, tawny as glass clouded by ages in a sand-swept landscape. Bravo halted his descent in order to regain his bearings. Lifting the lamp on high, he could make out the outlines of a basalt statue, a lion with the head of a man. Yeats's depiction of the Sphinx, the beast that comes to shuddering life at the end of the era of widening gyres. The rough beast that once awakened, when things fall apart and the center can no longer hold, "slouches towards Bethlehem to be born."

Bravo, his head ringing with the prophetic poem, resumed his descent, until at last he stood before the rough beast, who stared straight ahead with depthless eyes, its gaze pitiless. The statue was marvelously rendered, the man's face as beautiful as his gaze was blank. The lips were apart, the mouth open, a pit of blackest night.

Reaching up, Bravo put his hand into the mouth, surrounded by a circle enclosed in a labyrinth. In it went, deeper and deeper until even his wrist was swallowed up. His fingertips brushed against something. Feeling around, he could tell it was rolled up tight, and his heartrate jumped. Slowly and surely, he pulled it out.

He felt another cold chill, this one threatening to turn his blood to ice. If it was the Testament of Lucifer and if he opened it, read it through, surely that was "in extremis." Surely some part of it would help him return Ayla to life.

But, God help him, what else would it do?

The rough beast looked down on him, silent as the sun.

FIFTY-EIGHT

Emma was still holding Ayla's hand when Aither made his limping return.

"Where's Bravo?" she said. "Where's Fra Leoni?"

"There are preparations to be made," he said with an avuncular smile. "They are extremely complicated. Texts must be consulted, decisions to be made, so forth. Nothing to be concerned about." He drew up an old rickety chair beside his bed, settled himself in it. "Has your friend opened her eyes? Has she said anything?"

"No," Emma lied, her body stiffening despite her best efforts. She felt like a cat, hackles raised by a circling danger. Both his voice and his eyes had become avid. "It's like she's in a coma. Can you explain to me what happened?"

"I'm afraid not."

Emma, aware of the relaxing of his expression, as a kind of relief flooded through him, kept her vigil, as she and Bravo had agreed. Clearly, Aither was uneasy with whatever he imagined Ayla might tell her.

"I was rather hoping that you would be able to tell me," the curator said, eyes bird bright. "After all, you were there."

Emma studied him for a moment, focusing her thoughts. She realized that despite all the prep Bravo had put her through during the flight across the Mediterranean, she had only the haziest of ideas who Aither really was. Other than the sure knowledge that he was not who he presented himself to be, and probably never had been, she did not know his nature. Was he, as she had briefly been, one of the Fallen? If so, he might assume that he was speaking to one of his kin. She had to be exceedingly careful in her responses.

"Malus manifested the shadow," she said. "It caught hold of Bravo's friend, coalesced, wrapped her arms, as you see, until fire consumed it."

"And how, pray tell, was the toxin's advance arrested?"

"It was Bravo's doing."

"Why didn't you stop him?"

More parts of the puzzle clicked into place. So he did think she was still possessed by one of the Fallen. "I was leaving him for Malus."

"And where is Malus now?"

Keep it going, she told herself. "Urgent business."

"More urgent than this?"

"Should I have questioned him?" Emma put steel into her voice. "Would you?"

His tongue clucked against the roof of his mouth. "And still I am puzzled. What method could Bravo have used to stymie the toxin's progress? He had nothing at his disposal."

"He opened up a vein."

"He did what?" The question was like an explosion forced out of the curator's mouth.

Good, she thought. *We're getting somewhere.* "He fed his blood to her."

Aither stiffened. An expression of terror flitted so briefly across his face Emma wondered if she had imagined it. "I beg your pardon."

She repeated what she had just told him.

"But that's impossible." Of a sudden he seemed to have trouble breathing. He clutched his cane so hard his knuckles turned white. "No one can do that."

"Look." Emma tried to keep the elation out of her voice. She pointed to the scar the shadow-serpent had left on Ayla's arm. "It's no longer black. It's fading."

And, indeed, it was already a gunmetal gray, lightening even as they watched it.

A profound shudder went through him like a lightning bolt. "His blood. It shouldn't be able to do that."

"What does it mean?" Emma was desperate to know.

"No one should have that kind of blood. No one except—"

Without warning he lunged for Ayla, slamming the handle of his cane into her windpipe. Ayla convulsed, gasped.

"What are you doing?" Emma shouted. "Stop it! You're killing her."

Aither whacked Ayla again. "That's the idea, my dear. Fra Leoni is dead, Bravo was locked away for good, I thought, but if he's what you say he is he'll find a way out soon enough." He drew the cane back for another strike. Ayla's throat was already turning awful shades of purplish red, beginning to swell.

Emma could no longer maintain her ruse. Rising, she slipped the *wakizashi* from its wooden scabbard, tried for the horizontal blow that would at least partially sever his head from his torso. But he was too quick. His arm came up, blocking her. The blade sank into his forearm. He turned to her, grinning like a death's-head.

"Who are you?" he said, drawing the blade out of his cane. "Who are you really?"

Emma withdrew the *wakizashi* from his arm, rammed it point first into his chest above and just to the left of his sternum. *When all else fails,* Bravo had told her on the plane, *use the heart-thrust.*

The blade sank in to the hilt, but Aither just grinned wider. "No, my dear," he said, "that just won't cut it." And then he hit her very hard on the side of her head.

Aither withdrew the *wakizashi* from his chest, raised it up to slash it across Emma, who half-lay across Ayla, stunned, sickened from the force of the blow. But the downstroke was arrested so abruptly, so violently, that he cried out, blinding pain traveling like an electric shock from wrist to shoulder. A moment later he heard a crack like a tree branch snapped off in a heavy snowfall. His right arm hung, nerveless at his side. He tried to move his fingers, but it was as if they were trapped in amber. Paralyzed.

Even turning his head was an agonizing proposition. Bravo, looming behind him, picked him up as if he were a rag doll, forearm like the bar of a prison cell against the bloody place where Emma had stabbed him. Aither tried to squirm away, his eyes wide and staring, but Bravo's grip was iron, shaking him in fury.

"I found the Sphinx, old man." Bravo so close he could smell Aither's breath, fetid as the grave, rotted as death. "And in his mouth what d'you suppose I found?"

Aither, mute, stared at him wide-eyed, as if he'd never seen him before.

"The Book of Deathly Things. Lucifer's first and last Testament."

Aither laughed like a hyena. "The Vault. I built that space. As for that manuscript, have you looked at it? Haven't had the time, have you? Had to get back here lickety-split." His laugh could send a wolf running for cover. "It's blank, boy. Nothing but blank pages."

"It's of no consequence," Bravo said. "I have the *Nihilus Inusitatus*. I found your hiding place between the Sphinx's front paws."

"You found your way out."

"Finding my way in was the difficult part," Bravo said. "The rest was easy."

"For you."

Bravo deflected his words away. *Keep on the offensive,* he thought. "I can read Tifinagh, Aither. I know the central part is an excerpt from the Book of Deathly Things, the section used by King Solomon's alchemists to create the spectral gold."

Aither shook his head, arrogant but, staring into Bravo's steady gaze, blinking rapidly, as if he were looking into the sun. "It's too late. We have reached the end of the widening gyre. We are fully awake. There is no turning back."

Bravo forced himself to ignore Aither's meaning, but the tawny final stare of the Sphinx haunted him. *Steady on,* he told himself. *Squeeze everything you can out of him.* "You followed me to Italy."

"I was there when you arrived. I knew you were headed for the convent."

"How?"

"How do you think? I am the Guardian of the Testament of Lucifer."

"You!" Bravo could not have been more surprised. "I thought Malus—"

"As you were meant to," Aither said. "But Malus was a Fallen with ambition to rise above his station."

"Ambition led to your downfall, literally and figuratively."

The last of a long-nursed fire flared in Aither's eyes. "That's right! Cleave to the lie your religion carved in stone."

Another lie, Bravo thought, but who was lying? "Enlighten me, then."

"'Repent!' God cried, His wrath terrible to behold. But Lucifer would not. We, his brothers, would not. 'Bow down to me!' God cried. But Lucifer would not. We, his brothers, would not."

"And that wasn't ambition?"

"Ambition is a right, the root of the decisive argument."

"God had other ideas."

"Oh, yes. He cast us downward to the earth. For our arrogance, yes, of course. But our real sin, the unforgivable, was Lucifer taking with him the pomegranate of forbidden knowledge, the fruit he seduced Eve to bite into. To keep it safe from God, Lucifer clove it into three pieces, which became the Unholy Trinity."

Bravo felt as if he were on the edge of a vast whirlpool and, despite his best efforts, he was being inexorably pulled into it.

Everything seemed fluid, shifting, unfamiliar. "I was told a different version of the story," he said, trying to regain his equilibrium. But even to him, his voice sounded thin and strained. "That God made it so that Lucifer could not find the Unholy Trinity himself."

Now true contempt curled Aither's upper lip. "By the monk, Leoni, I shouldn't doubt. Tragic you came under his wing, he was such a well-known liar."

"Why would he lie about that?"

"I should think it would be obvious to you, boy. To keep you ignorant of Lucifer's true power, which even now is far greater than you can imagine." He gave a great shudder. "God has turned His back on you—on all of humankind—just as He did with us." A flash of the old contempt returned to Aither's face like a jewel to its setting. "You too are the Fallen. You're ours now."

Again Bravo had to steady his resolve in the face of such an unthinkable future. "You dug up the *Nihilus Inusitatus*. You stole it."

"It was stolen from me!" Aither's teeth bared. "By your accursed grandfather." A dreadful smile crossed his thin, livery lips. "But we took care of that. We got it back. Paralyzed him in the process."

"He fell off a ladder."

Aither laughed. "My dear, you are surrounded by lies."

A sinking in the pit of Bravo's stomach.

"Conrad was no exception." A rueful expression flitted across Aither's craggy face. "In the end, he outsmarted us. We couldn't kill him. He had a gift. At first, we thought he'd passed it on to Dilara Tusik. For the longest time we couldn't get to her. She was being protected."

"By Conrad."

"And then after he died by your father." Aither sneered. "Then we did kill her, only to find that the threat to us still existed. Now we know Conrad passed his gift on to you."

"What? How?" In a flash of insight Bravo knew. He felt again those leathery fingers closing around his, felt the raised weal in the center of Conrad's palm press against his. That was when the transposition was made, from his grandfather to him.

"If we knew that . . ." For a moment Aither's eyes went out of focus. "You're poisoning me, boy. You know that."

Bravo saw that the makeshift bandage he'd fashioned from ripping the sleeve of his shirt was askew. It was dark red now, glimmering wetly, his blood mingling with Aither's in the stab wound.

"Your blood. No help for it now," Aither continued. "But there are others, far more powerful than I, who are stirring out of ages-long slumber. No matter that you are *msawan*. There is only one of you, and many, many of us." The curator's smile turned into the rictus of oncoming death. "More than you imagine, boy." A fatal spasm passed through him. "Far more."

FIFTY-NINE

"Don't be. I would've done the same," Emma said as she and Bravo embraced.

"After what Fra Leoni told me, after seeing your vision restored, what else was I to think?"

"Bravo, Bravo." Emma pulled her head back so their eyes locked. "I told you." A hand gentling his cheek. "Please believe me."

"I do, Sis. It's just I missed you more than words can explain."

She smiled. "We're always in each other's hearts. What more is there to say?"

The three of them were aboard the refueled plane, starting the first leg of their journey back to New York City. Bravo, as he'd promised his sister, had no more use for Istanbul. They both missed their home far too much to stay away any longer.

Twenty thousand feet above the Mediterranean, the three of them had the oddest reunion imaginable. Ayla was completely recovered, no mark remaining on her forearm. It was as if the shadow-serpent's coiling had never happened.

Ayla was sitting back in her seat, an ice pack on her throat. She had tried to talk as Bravo and Emma were taking her out of the library, but all that had come out was a dry croak and an awful clicking sound painful enough to cause her to stop trying.

"You're good," Emma had said to her, over and over, in the private ambulance. "You're not going to die."

Ayla had looked up at her and smiled, but it was Bravo's

391

hand she clutched tightly all the way to the airfield, while a doctor who worked with the Order tended to her neck, injected her with a mild sedative, before checking Emma's head bruise, cleaning and dressing Bravo's wound. When the ambulance arrived at the airfield it had been met by the three-person flight crew. They didn't blink an eye at the physical state of the trio. It seemed they were getting used to helping their passengers board.

The moment after Bravo and Emma had seen to Ayla, made sure she was resting comfortably, they had fallen into each other's arms. For Bravo, it was as if the clock had been reset to a time before the explosion, before his father had died, before his sister had lost her sight. For him, as well as for her, the return of her sight was a miracle. There would come a time for exploring the reasons and mechanisms behind the miracle, but now was not it. They were all spent physically and emotionally. Now all they wanted to do was hug each other, drink the lemonade made with fresh Egyptian lemons that Lida brought them, and slide into a well-earned sleep.

Bravo went out like a light, as had Ayla. As for Emma, her sleep was fitful, shallow, stalked by shadows that moved contrary to the way normal shadows might slowly creep across the floor as afternoon was swallowed by the coming of night.

She awoke with a start, her hair and brow slick with sweat. Her armpits felt swampy. She rose, went to the lav, and, after voiding, threw cold water on her face. Staring at her face in the mirror was so strange. She had aged since the last time she had seen herself. She had to remind herself that everything had shifted while she had been sightless; the world had moved on, rolling from day to day without her. Looking back, she had felt marooned in a land of perpetual night, darker even than the dark side of the moon. And yet here she was now on the other side of it—fantastic luck or something else altogether, she couldn't say. A surge of gratitude flushed her cheeks and neck, but soon enough the strangeness of it all began again to overwhelm her. She didn't look the same—this was to be expected, she supposed—but not to feel the same was a mystery that, deep down, frightened her. Who was she now? Spent, she felt inadequate to the monumental task of finding out.

When she returned down the aisle Lida was refilling her glass. Bravo's mouth was partly open, his features at rest. She felt such love for him. Everything they had been through in the last days had been worth it for them to feel closer to each other than ever.

He had fallen asleep while reading the *Nihilus Inusitatus*. On the seat beside him was the rolled manuscript that was supposed to have been the Book of Deathly Things, the Testament of Lucifer. But Aither had claimed that it was blank. In a way, she was glad that it was blank, that the real Testament remained hidden. The manuscript was terribly dangerous. It was even dangerous for the reader, for, as Fra Leoni had told them, anything to do with Lucifer, with that ultimate evil, was seductive. It could drag you into the abyss before you knew what was happening.

Even if the manuscript was blank, it appeared very old, but who knew if it was? She had read about numerous archeological finds purporting to stand ancient history or the foundations of religion on their head, only to discover that they were fakes, ingeniously doctored by clever scam artists wanting to make a quick buck or be spotlit by their fifteen days of fame.

Idly, she reached over, took it up, settled back in her seat. Following her brother's lead, she'd become an expert in identification of artifacts. Within thirty minutes or so, she'd be able to tell whether its apparent age was real or fake.

The manuscript was covered in what seemed to be calfskin, or something like it, the sickly yellowish hue of an onion's skin. A strip of some unidentifiable black cloth wrapped it tight, held it in a roll. That was enough to set off alarms inside her head. No cloth she knew of would have survived the centuries intact.

Unrolling the manuscript, she studied the first page. The paper was undeniably ancient—just how old she couldn't tell without a laboratory. A conundrum, then. She leafed through page after page. Aither hadn't been lying; not a single letter, character, or rune was to be seen; the pages were blank. She sighed. Now the whole thing seemed worthless. Who cared how old it was?

Her gaze drifted to the window. She watched the clouds, fascinated by their changing shapes, their seeming contradiction, so solid in their weightlessness. She was like a child again, remembering how it had been the first time her parents had taken her and Bravo on a plane. How her face had been plastered to the window, nose mashed nearly to the cartilage, her breath fogging up the Perspex. She could not get enough of the clouds and what wonders lay spread out beneath her, shifting with every breath she took.

The drone of the plane's engines lulled her back to sleep, into a dream where a creature of immense size—not man, not lion, but a combination of both—was speaking to her with its tawny, final gaze. The light was dense, filthy, as if underwater or in a deep cave, the source of it from some other place Emma had never imagined.

The beast crouched on a vast plinth made up of naked humans bent over double—thousands of them, tens of thousands, hundreds of thousands, all bowed down in obeisance. It stirred its heavy thighs, half-rising, launching itself toward her.

At that moment the plane hit an air pocket, and she awoke with a cry lodged in her throat like a bone. As the turbulence accelerated, everything around her trembled and resonated, as if in a wind tunnel. Her ears popped as the plane was momentarily sucked downward. Her shivering glass began to tip over. She reached out, caught it, but some of the lemonade slopped over onto the manuscript.

She cursed wildly, unsure what to do. Bravo would kill her. But then everything changed. The moment she was living in seemed to go on forever. She had come across secret writing before that was invisible until sprayed with lemon juice. Something in the acid reacted with the kind of ink used to hide the text. It was an ancient method of keeping secrets—no one really knew how old. But the fact was before her: a text that had not been visible moments before.

Slowly, with infinite care, she spread more lemon juice on the pages until all of the text had been revealed. She knew she should stop, put this thing aside, wake Bravo and tell him what she had discovered. But there was something pulling on her, a pinprick of envy, dark and heavy, that had caught her, a fishhook dragging her down, to another place.

Why was it Bravo who found everything first? Why was it Bravo who got the special training? Why was it Bravo who received all the credit, all the accolades from the Order? Who had been elected *Magister Regens*? All because of their father, when she had been the one taking care of Dexter ever since their mother had died? It wasn't Emma. Never her. Where was the fairness in that? And now, now, when they were becoming even closer, there was Ayla, insinuating herself into their lives. Emma saw how Ayla had hung on to Bravo all through the hectic, dreamlike drive to the airfield, clutched his hand like the two of them were bonded somehow, like she, Emma, was the outsider.

No, no, no. The fishhook was tugging, tugging, tugging at her. Not this time. This time was different. This time there would be an alternate ending.

Without a second thought she flipped to the first page, where the first words had by fateful accident come alive, and started to read the mixture of High Latin and Old Greek, two languages in which she was fluent:

herein the TESTAMENT of the FIRST ONE to fall,
the Archangel LUCIFER, King of Kings

ACKNOWLEDGMENTS

Thanks are due to the many people whom I met with and consulted during the research portion of this project. In particular, I would like to thank Fr. Louis Melahn for his hospitality and generosity during our time together in Rome. Heartfelt thanks also to my other guides in Rome, my friend Salvatore Barberi and his wonderful family, Marilena and Rosi, who make me feel like a true Roman. Thanks, too, to Lucie Melahn for introducing me to her brother.

AFTERWORD

FACTS, FIGURATIVES, AND FURTHER READING

Facts are of paramount importance to me. In a novel such as this factual underpinnings are essential. Much of what is in *The Fallen* is real. To begin with, Baatara Gorge Waterfall, in Tannourine, Lebanon, does, indeed, exist. Whether or not the cave I have described exists is a matter of conjecture.

It is well known that the Phoenicians, intrepid sailors, explorers, and traders, traveled the known world at a very early time in history. It is also a fact that they built temples for King Solomon, so it's altogether possible that they also located and designed the place, known inaccurately as King Solomon's mine, for storing the gold he and his weak-willed and despotic son ordered created by his infamous alchemists.

Likewise, the language Tifinagh (written)/Tamazight (spoken) is precisely as described, the root language of Phoenician and Old Greek. It is arguably the first known language, though some scholars posit that an ancient version of Ethiopian may have preceded it. But, if so, it can't be by much. A version of it is used by almost all Berber peoples today.

The prayer excerpts I have presented in the library at Alexandria are from the actual rite of canonical exorcism, officially abhorred by the Church hierarchy, nevertheless used by specially trained priests, usually in secret.

The internal night life of the fictional convent of Saint Angelica Boniface I have described was inspired by a factual case meticulously and beautifully laid out by Hubert Wolf in his book, *The Nuns of Sant'Ambrogio: The True Story of a Convent in Scandal* (Knopf, 2015). I highly recommend reading it.

William Butler Yeats, whose powerful poem "The Second Coming" affected me from an early age, and which is given a prominent place in the novel, was not, of course, a member of the Antaeus London men's club, but had it existed he probably would have been, just as he would have become fast friends with Conrad Shaw, if that great man had actually existed.

William Butler Yeats (1865–1939), an Irish poet, a philosopher, a two-time Irish senator, and an explorer of the occult, was one of the leading lights of early-twentieth-century literature. In 1923, he became the first Irishman to be awarded the Nobel Prize in Literature. "The Second Coming" (1919), his best-known and arguably his most chilling poem, was also, it is believed by many, to be a prophecy, to the ire and dismay of the Catholic Church, among whose leaders he was known as a man of "monstrous discourtesy." It is presented here in full:

THE SECOND COMING

Turning and turning in the widening gyre
The falcon cannot hear the falconer;
Things fall apart; the centre cannot hold;
Mere anarchy is loosed upon the world,
The blood-dimmed tide is loosed, and everywhere
The ceremony of innocence is drowned;
The best lack all conviction, while the worst
Are full of passionate intensity.
Surely some revelation is at hand;
Surely the Second Coming is at hand.
The Second Coming! Hardly are those words out

When a vast image out of Spiritus Mundi
Troubles my sight; somewhere in sands of the desert
A shape with a lion body and the head of a man,
A gaze blank and pitiless as the sun,
Is moving its slow thighs, while all about it
Reel shadows of indignant desert birds.
The darkness drops again; but now I know
That twenty centuries of stony sleep
Were vexed to nightmare by a rocking cradle,
And what rough beast, its hour come round at last,
Slouches towards Bethlehem to be born?

Printings: *The Dial* (Chicago), November 1920; *The Nation* (London), 6 November 1920; *Michael Robartes and the Dancer* (Dundrum: Cuala, 1921); *Later Poems* (London: Macmillan, 1922, 1924, 1926, 1931).